Four Days in Panama

A Drug Cartel Armageddon

Lawrence Scofield

Acknowledgments

This book would not have been possible without the efforts of Judy, my wonderful editor. My thanks and love go to my family for everything they do to enrich my life: Jennifer, Elizabeth, Daniel and John. They're the best.

Neither products nor brand names used in this novel represent or imply any relationship with, or endorsement by, the author or publisher.

Copyright Notice and Disclaimers

Dedication

This book is dedicated to Bill Sharp, the person upon whom the character of the same name is based. Bill passed away before the novel could be published. I regret it wasn't finished in time. He would have enjoyed reading about himself. Rest in peace, Bill.

Books by Lawrence Scofield

"The Laura Messier Files"

Three Days in Tripoli

Two Days in Moscow

One Day in Lebanon

Four Days in Panama

Four Days in Panama

A Drug Cartel Armageddon

Table of Contents

Chapter One	1
Chapter Two	8
Chapter Three	10
Chapter Four	17
Chapter Five	22
Chapter Six	26
Chapter Seven	30
Chapter Eight	33
Chapter Nine	35
Chapter Ten	40
Chapter Eleven	45
Chapter Twelve	50
Chapter Thirteen	52
Chapter Fourteen	55
Chapter Fifteen	60
Chapter Sixteen	66
Chapter Seventeen	69
Chapter Eighteen	73
Chapter Nineteen	78
Chapter Twenty	82
Chapter Twenty-One	85
Chapter Twenty-Two	87
Chapter Twenty-Three	96
Chapter Twenty-Four	102
Chapter Twenty-Five	106
Chapter Twenty-Six	110
Chapter Twenty-Seven	114
Chapter Twenty-Eight	121
Chapter Twenty-Nine	124
Chapter Thirty	127
Chapter Thirty-One	131
Chapter Thirty-Two	136
Chapter Thirty-Three	140
Chapter Thirty-Four	144

Chapter Thirty-Five	150
Chapter Thirty-Six	152
Chapter Thirty-Seven	154
Chapter Thirty-Eight	160
Chapter Thirty-Nine	164
Chapter Forty	168
Chapter Forty-One	171
Chapter Forty-Two	174
Chapter Forty-Three	176
Chapter Forty-Four	179
Chapter Forty-Five	184
Chapter Forty-Six	188
Chapter Forty-Seven	192
Chapter Forty-Eight	194
Chapter Forty-Nine	197
Chapter Fifty	201
Chapter Fifty-One	206
Chapter Fifty-Two	210
Chapter Fifty-Three	212
Chapter Fifty-Four	216
Chapter Fifty-Five	220
Chapter Fifty-Six	223
Chapter Fifty-Seven	224
Chapter Fifty-Eight	229
Chapter Fifty-Nine	233
Chapter Sixty	236
Chapter Sixty-One	238
Chapter Sixty-Two	241
Chapter Sixty-Three	246
Chapter Sixty-Four	248
Chapter Sixty-Five	251
Chapter Sixty-Six	258
Chapter Sixty-Seven	261
Chapter Sixty-Eight	265
Chapter Sixty-Nine	267

Chapter Seventy   268
Chapter Seventy-One   270
Chapter Seventy-Two   272
Chapter Seventy-Three   274
Chapter Seventy-Four   275
Chapter Seventy-Five   277
Chapter Seventy-Six   278
Chapter Seventy-Seven   279
Chapter Seventy-Eight   281
Chapter Seventy-Nine   283
Chapter Eighty   284
Chapter Eighty-One   287
Chapter Eighty-Two   289
Chapter Eighty-Three   292
Chapter Eighty-Four   294
Chapter Eighty-Five   296
Chapter Eighty-Six   298
Chapter Eighty-Seven   300
Chapter Eighty-Eight   305
Chapter Eighty-Nine   308
Chapter Ninety   311
Chapter Ninety-One   314
Chapter Ninety-Two   317
Chapter Ninety-Three   319
Chapter Ninety-Four   320
Chapter Ninety-Five   322
Chapter Ninety-Six   324
Chapter Ninety-Seven   325
Chapter Ninety-Eight   328
Chapter Ninety-Nine   334
Chapter One Hundred   339
Chapter One Hundred One   342
Chapter One Hundred Two   344
Chapter One Hundred Three   346
Sneak Peek   1

Chapter One

Freeport, Grand Bahama Island
Thursday, December 8, 1988

THE POSTMAN ROUNDED the corner onto Logwood Avenue, glanced in his bag and pulled the next piece from his pouch. He stopped. I've never delivered to 1701. Didn't know the place was occupied. Oh well. He shrugged, walked across the street and pushed the letter through the slot embedded in the door.

Inside the two-person office, however, the reaction was far different. Jack Mason, a retired Central Intelligence Agency officer, spotted the letter as soon as it hit the floor. "Maria," he said, glancing at the young clerk, "after you've finished the pay …" He didn't complete the sentence. "What's that?"

"I have no idea, Mr. Mason."

"We don't accept mail here. Everything goes to the PO box." Maria looked up from her work.

"Give me a minute and I'll take a look at it."

"It's all right, I'll take care of it." Jack walked to the door, picked up the letter and read the addressee. He froze. "Maria, I need you to leave the office."

"What about payroll?"

"I'll handle it. Let me know when you're ready, I'll walk you out." Jack returned to his office, laid the letter on his desk and took a handgun from the middle office drawer. He checked the clip and slid it underneath his belt behind his back. Maria appeared in the doorway soon afterward, her sweater and purse in hand. This wasn't the first time she'd been asked to leave the office. She knew she worked for an espionage agency and some of their requests were downright odd. The job paid triple what she could get anywhere else on island, so she ignored the irregular aspects of the position, kept her head down and did her job.

"Am I fired?"

"Of course not." Jack smiled. "What gave you that idea?"

"Your tone of voice."

"No, it's nothing like that."

"Okay, I'm ready," she said with a cooperative smile.

"Are you parked out back?"

"Yes."

"Let's go." Jack led Maria to the back door off the kitchen at the rear of the building. He withdrew the handgun from his belt and held it at his side. "Hang on a minute."

"What's wrong," Maria asked, anxious at the sight of a weapon.

"Nothing. Just taking precautions." Jack walked outside, looked around, saw nothing threatening and stuck his head back in the door. "Come on out." Jack walked Maria to her car, his head moving back and forth looking for danger. Once she'd started the car, Jack knocked on the window. "I'll mail your checks. I'll let you know when to come back," he said after Maria opened the window. Jack slapped the roof of the car. "Off with you now."

Security Associates of the Bahamas was a front company for a group of intelligence experts that performed contract work for the Central Intelligence Agency. CIA used the group for operations they deemed illegal under U.S. law. The firm's office in Freeport was the tip of the iceberg, so to speak, as the headquarters was hidden amid the marshes at the east end of Grand Bahama Island. No address or phone could be found for the firm and anyone looking had a difficult task, but that was the point. It was the office that would be discovered, not their base of operations. Jack was fond of saying the office existed to watch spies looking for spies.

Jack returned to his office, sat at his desk and stared at the unopened letter. Am I overreacting? No. A handwritten envelope addressed to a specific covert identity? We've been outed. He picked up the phone and called the Freeport dock. "Miguel, please?" A man with a decidedly Rastafarian accent came on the line.

"Miguel here."

"It's Jack. Where are your people right now?" Jack hired several local men to serve as informants. They roamed about the island and reported to Miguel who relayed the information to Jack as needed.

"They're scattered about the island, man."

"I need round the clock surveillance on the office. Can you ask three men to work eight-hour shifts round the clock for a while?"

"Sure, man, no problem. It's done." Jack hung up and resumed staring at the envelope. Laura Messier, 1701 Logwood, Freeport, Bahamas. Who the hell knows her name? Laura Messier was a cover identity known only to a small community of intelligence professionals. The postmark says Tallahassee, Florida. What the hell's in Tallahassee? Jack hesitated for a moment. I've got to take this out there, she needs to see it. Jack picked up the phone again and dialed the compound.

"Hello," a deep male voice said blandly.

"Rick? It's Jack." Rick Williams was a trusted friend of Laura. They'd met when she worked for CIA out of the Paris embassy. He resigned to work for her after she left CIA.

"What have you got?" Rick asked.

"Something strange came in the mail today. I'm bringing it out to the compound."

"Okay." The line disconnected.

Jack exited the building using the rear door and hopped into his '76 red Triumph Spitfire which he'd parked across two spaces to keep neighbors from using them. His large frame barely fit in the seat and the top of his head protruded slightly above the windshield when the soft top was down. Heading east on Grand Bahama Highway, Jack traveled the thirty miles between Freeport and the east end of the island in less than a half-hour, turning right onto an unmarked gravel drive along a desolate stretch of highway. None of the compound's buildings could be seen from the roadway due to thick foliage that gave the impression the property was undeveloped. A wrought iron security gate a few yards up the drive blocked unwanted visitors.

Mason punched in his personal security code and waited for the gate to automatically retreat. He gave the security camera a middle finger salute, then spread gravel behind him as he gunned the car through the checkpoint and on up the road. He drove past the barracks built for the full-time staff, the garage which doubled as an armory, and on to the main house another quarter mile away. The headquarters was a large, white two-story Colonial with a wrap-around porch. He parked in the circle drive, walked up the stairs and into the house. He promptly ran into Jean Broussard, a short, wiry Frenchman in his mid-60s with gray hair, a goatee and lively eyes. Jean was Laura's partner, a veteran with decades of experience in intelligence.

"Ah, Jack. There you are. I heard you were coming out." Jean turned his head and nodded. "Laura's on the back porch."

Laura, an American in her early 30s, belied the stereotype of an intelligence agent. She was tall, thin, and drop-dead gorgeous. A former runway model, she had a sparkling personality when she wanted to show it. Her enemies often misjudged her. She was a formidable martial arts expert. Jack found her reading the local newspaper with her feet propped on the coffee table. She rose from her seat, pushed her long brown hair behind her shoulder and hugged Jack. "I haven't seen you in a while, stranger," she teased. She motioned to the chairs. "Come, sit. What's going on in town?"

"You received a letter today. I thought you ought to see it."

"Are you doing special delivery now?" she asked with a smile. She grabbed the letter and hesitated, her mood growing serious staring at the envelope. "This could be a problem."

"That's what I thought," Jack replied.

Jean sat alongside Laura while Rick walked up the back stairs onto the porch. He'd heard Jack's car in the driveway. "Hey Jack, what's going on?" Rick asked as an introduction. Rick was also in his 30s and had the look of a soldier. He sat down uninvited, his muscular frame barely squeezing into a deck chair. Laura handed the envelope to Jean. "What do you make of it?"

"This is serious," Jean said after studying the envelope. "Do you want to open it?"

"I think we have to."

Then let's be careful. Give me a moment to retrieve disposable gloves." He laid the letter on the small table between chairs. Laura nodded at the letter. "What do you think, Rick?" Rick leaned over, turned the letter toward him with his index finger and read the address.

"I think it's safe to say it's not a utility bill," Rick replied with a chuckle.

"Jack, have you taken precautions at the office?" Laura asked. Jack nodded.

5

"I sent Maria home and I put round the clock surveillance on the building."

"Don't go back there."

"I think I have to. If we're going to get hit, better there than here. I've got people watching."

Jean returned with a letter opener and after squeezing his hands into the gloves, he gently separated the flap from the envelope. "One always wonders about these things," he said, glancing at Laura while pulling the one-page letter from the envelope. "Remember the poison in our coffee cups at that Paris cafe?" Laura and Jean were nearly poisoned at a popular tourist spot. It ended in a firefight at the café on a busy midday morning.

"That started an ugly episode, didn't it?"

"Most assuredly so," Jean said nodding. He gently unfolded the letter. He stared at it briefly before motioning to Laura. "Take a look." He laid the letter on the table in front of Laura. "Don't touch it," he warned. She leaned over and studied it briefly.

"This is about the drug bust," she said resolutely, glancing at those seated around her. She read the note aloud. "You owe me 30 million dollars. Pay or you will be killed. My men will be in touch." She looked at her colleagues. "It's unsigned."

"I think you're right," Jean said. "It's something to do with the drug incident at the airstrip. The words seem to have been cut from magazines and glued to the page." He looked at his colleagues. "There could be fingerprints on this. Let's refer this to the Constable's Office in Freeport."

"Jack, where's the plane right now?" Laura asked.

"In Nassau. Dmitri's bringing tourists back to the States today." Laura had stolen the Dassault Falcon 50 from the Russians during an escape after a mission in Moscow. Dmitri and Svetlana Polzin escaped along with Laura and had begun a charter service to finance the jet's expense.

6

"Would you ask him to pick me up on his way back?"

"Sure, I'll call him now."

"We need more expertise than the local police, Jean," Laura said. "I'd like Dan Jenkins to have a look at it." Jenkins was her contact at FBI headquarters in D.C. "If this," she said pointing at the letter, "came from the States, Jenkins would have jurisdiction."

"Are we still following the drug runners?" Jean asked.

"One of them. Pierre and Sharp are handling the surveillance. So far, he doesn't suspect we're watching." Pierre Thibault and Bill Sharp were skilled professionals, an integral part of Laura's group. "It's funny. I'd pick up something like that in five minutes."

"He's not a professional."

"He's contract CIA, Jean. They don't train their people anymore."

"Let's pick him up and interrogate him," Rick suggested. "Rough him up a little. Get him to talk." Laura shook her head.

"Once I lay this out to Jenkins," Laura replied, "he's going to tell me to stand down. Obviously, we won't do that, but I don't think we should pick him up, either."

"The CIA's gotten themselves in such a mess with drug sales for arms," Jean said shaking his head in disgust.

"If you go to Jenkins," Rick pointed out, "you'll be asking the government to investigate the government. Jenkins won't find a damn thing."

"Look, Dan's a friend. He'll dust the letter for prints as a favor. Let's start with that. Regardless of what he says, though, let's keep the surveillance going. Eventually, the man will go back to work."

"And when he does, perhaps we'll find the letter's author," Jean said in agreement.

Laura smiled. "You read my mind. We've got two leads, the letter and the drug runner. If we're patient, one of them might come through."

Jack returned and stood in the doorway. "Laura, you better get ready," he said. "Dmitri will be here within the hour."

Chapter Two

THE DASSAULT FALCON touched down an hour later at an airstrip across the highway that Laura and Jean had purchased from the Bahamian government. Although they'd spent a fortune to upgrade the facility, it was still unacceptable by commercial airport standards. The runway had been paved and lengthened to 7,500 feet but lacked runway lighting or a hanger. It was more than enough to accommodate the Falcon that taxied back to the circular apron where Rick and Laura were waiting. Svetlana opened the cabin door and lowered the stairs. Pete Franklin, Dmitri's co-pilot, stepped off the aircraft and met Laura as she walked toward the plane. "Dmitri's staying on board. Is this your only bag, Laura?" he asked.

"Yes, just this travel bag." Laura bounded up the stairs and found the rear seats occupied by four adult passengers who appeared to be returning from vacation. Svetlana, who served as flight attendant, admonished the rear passengers to keep their seatbelts on and drew a curtain between the front and rear seating to give their paying passengers a sense of privacy. "Hi, Laura," Svetlana said with a smile. A pretty Russian woman in her thirties, she had a thick accent which added to an exotic charm she possessed. "Settle in and buckle up. We're taking off immediately." Svetlana turned to Franklin. "We're ready to go, Pete."

"Thanks, Lana," Pete said before climbing back into the cockpit.

A minute later, the plane rolled down the runway and lifted off for St. Petersburg where the passengers would be dropped off. Once in the air, Svetlana walked back and leaned over Laura. "Dmitri wants to know where we're taking you."

"D.C."

"That's what he figured. We'll have a delay in St. Pete while he amends the flight plan. Sit tight and we'll get going as soon as possible."

"I know this makes a long day for you. I'm sorry."

Svetlana smiled, unperturbed. "Are we waiting for you in D.C.?"

"That'd be great. I'm not sure how long I'll be, though. It could be a day or two."

"The layover's not a problem," Svetlana said with a smile. "I don't think we've got another flight for a few days. I'll let Dmitri know. Can I get you something to drink?"

"Maybe once we get to St. Pete."

Svetlana entered the cockpit to relay the message. Forty minutes later, the plane landed at St. Petersburg-Clearwater International Airport, the passengers disembarked, and the plane took to the air again a half-hour later for the 2-hour, 20-minute flight into National Airport in Virginia.

Upon arrival at National, Laura booked rooms for Dmitri, Svetlana, the co-pilot Pete Franklin and herself at an airport hotel. She rented a car for herself and drove to the hotel while the others stayed at the airport for an hour arranging hangar space and a maintenance check to be done on the plane the next day. The following morning, Laura made an appointment at FBI headquarters downtown with Dan Jenkins, an Assistant Director at the agency.

Chapter Three

Friday, December 9, 1988

STANDING IN THE lobby of the J. Edgar Hoover Building, Laura wondered whether Rick had been right. Is meeting Dan a good idea? She'd known Dan for years, having served together at the American Embassy in Paris. He was not only a friend, but an occasional lover. An attractive man, ten years older than herself, he was tall with short gray hair and kind, gentle brown eyes. Their affection for each other had grown through the years, but Laura knew personal feelings wouldn't have any effect on Dan's judgment. He'd surely warn her to stay away from the pilot of the plane that made an emergency landing at the airstrip. If she pursued the pilot and Dan discovered that, she'd lose his friendship. She was deep in thought when he approached.

"Hey there," he said with a smile. "It's been a while." They hugged tightly and Dan gave her a kiss on the cheek.

"I've missed you," she whispered in his ear.

"I've missed you, too. Come on," he motioned, "let's go up to my office."

Dan led her upstairs to the same office where she'd spent considerable time after the Moscow mission. He'd protected her after she'd been indicted by the Justice Department. Dan's clout within government was instrumental in getting Laura's name cleared. He pushed the door shut and they sat down in the chairs in front of his desk. Although the office was a small, bland room, he'd dressed it nicely with photos from his days with the bureau. Dan was a distinguished man, someone rumored to be in line for the Director's job someday. "Aside from the fact that you're gorgeous and I'm madly in love with you, how can I help?" he began. Laura blushed and looked at the carpet, unprepared for the comment.

"You sound like you meant that."

"I did," Dan replied, knowing he'd just cut through the tough exterior she liked to project. She looked up and realized his strategy.

"You certainly know how to break a subject down," she said with a wry smile. He leaned over and squeezed her hand.

"Now that we've gotten that out of the way, what brings you all the way in from the Bahamas?" She took a deep breath.

"I've got something to show you," she began, pulling the letter wrapped in plastic from her purse. Dan stared at the letter.

"Is this evidence?"

"Possibly."

Dan rummaged through his desk drawers until he found a pair of disposable gloves. He used the gloves to withdraw the letter from its protective plastic covering and carefully unfolded the tri-fold creases. "Has anyone touched the lettering?" he asked pointing at the glued letters.

"No. We were careful with it."

He laid the letter on the desk while he searched again, this time for a magnifying glass. "Give me some background," he said, this time sitting behind his desk to study the letter with magnification.

"A cargo plane landed ten days ago at the airstrip we own. It had engine trouble and made an emergency landing." As she spoke, Dan continued to study the letter.

"This is in the Bahamas, correct?" he asked without looking up.

"That's right."

"What was the exact date?"

"Twenty-nine, November."

"Hang on, I want to take some notes." He laid the magnifying glass aside and grabbed a legal pad and pen. "Okay, go ahead."

"We watched the plane fly right over the treetops as it struggled to make the landing. We drove out to help and when we arrived, we found the plane surrounded by men. Some were unloading cargo; others were guarding the plane with automatic weapons." Laura paused to allow Dan to finish his note.

"I'm with you so far. Go on."

"We approached the plane to offer assistance and the pilot walked over and flashed a CIA ID card. He warned us to stay away, claiming the flight was classified. Official U.S. government business, he said."

"What kind of plane was it?"

"A C-123K cargo plane is what I've been told."

"Did you get a tail number?"

"Yes, N34773." Dan wrote down the number, then sat back and thought for a moment.

"That's not a government number, I can tell you that. Maybe it's a commercial aircraft or a private plane."

Laura nodded. "That's what we think."

"I'll run the tail number past the FAA. Who owns it, where it's based, that sort of thing. Did you get the pilot's name?"

"Young. Derek Young. He told us they were carrying bananas to South Florida. He told us a couple of small private planes were flying in to transfer the cargo."

"So, bananas are now official U.S. government business?" Dan laughed. "That's funny. And they were going to transfer the cargo to other planes?"

"That's what they told us." Dan gave her a look of disbelief.

13

"That sounds like amateur hour. And, of course, you told him you'd have to search the cargo."

"That's precisely what I said. I told him if the cargo remained aboard, they'd be okay. But, if they off-loaded anything, the government had a right to conduct a search."

"That's technically correct. Cargo can remain on the plane, but if it's offloaded, it must be searched, and a bill of lading provided to the government. What was his reaction?"

"He told us that was impossible. Three men pointed their weapons at us."

"It must have been some pretty valuable bananas," Dan said with a chuckle.

Laura smiled. "Apparently so."

"Did the local police get involved?"

Laura nodded. "We asked them to call the Customs Office in Freeport. After they refused, we alerted the Constable's office. They sent out a couple of squad cars."

"So, the police searched the cargo?"

"Yes," Laura said nodding her head. "The armed men stood down when the police arrived."

"So, at that point, you became a bystander?"

"Not exactly. We blocked the runway with our vehicles so the incoming planes couldn't land."

Dan leaned back in his chair, thinking. "Well, that's an all too familiar story these days. Pilots flying drugs into South Florida. I presume that's what they found, isn't it?"

Laura nodded. "Hundreds of pounds of cocaine hidden underneath bananas. The police brought out a tactical unit and a couple of vans. The drugs were confiscated, and all seven men were arrested, including the pilot and co-pilot."

"You mentioned the pilot identified himself as CIA?"

"Mr. Young's ID appeared to be legitimate."

Dan thought about the situation for a moment before responding. "Have the men been held over for trial in Freeport?"

"They've been transferred to Nassau, but yes, they're still in custody, all except Young and his co-pilot. The U.S. requested extradition and they're back in the States."

"What happened to the plane?"

"Mechanics arrived the next morning to repair it. It was flown out later in the day. We have no idea where it went."

"I'll check and see if they filed a flight plan. Were you able to interview the men in custody?"

"No. The Constable's Office wouldn't permit it."

"Where are the drugs?"

"I assume the authorities secured the cocaine as evidence, but I don't really know."

Dan considered the information, then glanced at Laura. "And now, someone's sent this letter threatening to kill you," he said pointing to the letter. "Presumably over the bust."

"That's right."

"What do you know about the pilot?"

"Derek Young? We checked the CIA database. He's a contract employee."

"You mean a part-timer?"

"Yes, and that's unusual. As far as I know, CIA's never had pilots on staff."

"I'll find out if he's been charged. This didn't happen inside the U.S., so he'll probably walk away from it. However, I can investigate the letter." He paused to think about how to phrase his next statement.

This is where he tells me to avoid contact with Derek Young, she thought.

"I want you to stand down and let our guys do the investigation."

"I understand."

Dan stared at her for a moment, wondering whether she was sincere. "Who do you know in Tallahassee?" Dan asked pointing at the envelope.

"No one."

Dan gave Laura a serious look. "Well, under the circumstances, I want you to take the threat seriously. Are you sticking around D.C. for a few days?"

"Yes."

Dan frowned. "If I were you, I'd go back home. Walking around D.C. by yourself could be dangerous. Tell you what, I'll assign a couple of men to shadow you." Laura didn't like where the conversation was headed.

"Thank you, but no. I'm perfectly capable of defending myself."

"I understand that," Dan said with a sigh, "but if you're attacked while you're in town, I'd rather our guys do the shooting. Your actions cannot be misconstrued to mean you're doing an op here in the States. Where are you staying?"

"Out near National."

"Check into another hotel. Do you have a rental car?"

"Yes," she said.

"Get rid of it and rent another. How about alternate ID?"

"Of course."

"Use it. Leave no trail. And stay away from Derek Young. Don't go anywhere near him."

"Okay."

Dan laid down the pen and paper. He considered her answer to be a bit too flippant. He looked her straight in the eyes. "I mean it. You have no authority to run down these leads." Dan watched Laura get uncomfortable.

"I know that, Dan," she said, tension rising in her voice.

Dan smiled to avoid a confrontation. "Our people are effective, Laura, and we've got the authority to get answers. Let us do the heavy lifting."

"I get it. I won't do anything on U.S. soil. I'll let you handle it."

"Good." Dan gave the impression the meeting was wrapping up. "Keep me informed about your whereabouts and I'll be in touch when I have more information. Anything else I ought to know?"

"Where are we going to dinner this evening?"

"I'd love to, Laura, but I'm in Congressional hearings on Monday. I've got to prepare testimony."

"Some other time then." He rose and the two embraced.

"We'll talk soon. Be safe out there."

"I will."

Chapter Four

ON HER WAY out of the building, Laura stopped at a bank of pay phones. She dialed the number Jean had given her before she'd left. "Here's the contact number for the surveillance team we have on Young," he'd told her.

"Yes?" the male voice answered.

"No names," she replied. "You recognize the voice?"

"Yes."

"I want to meet."

"You have the address?" the voice asked.

"I do."

"Meet me in the parking garage next door. Level two, by the elevator."

"Thirty minutes." She hung up.

Laura glanced up and down the sidewalk exiting the building and seeing nothing she determined to be a tail, she retrieved her car and headed to the northwest part of the city. Checking her rear-view mirror frequently, she found no car following her. She'd gotten in and out of FBI headquarters unnoticed.

This has got to be it, she thought, passing a newer looking high-rise building with no number. She drove around the block, passing it a second time and pulled into the attached parking garage. She parked on the second level within view of the elevator. A panel work truck passed the elevator twice, briefly slowing each time. It must be them, she thought. She climbed out and walked to the elevator, pretending to push the down button. A moment later, the truck appeared again and stopped. The driver leaned over and opened the passenger door. He motioned her forward. "Hold on a second," he said before she climbed in. "Let me get rid of the trash." He threw the empty fast food bags on the floorboard. Laura climbed in, stepping on the trash with her feet.

"You guys are disgusting. Do you know that?"

Bill Sharp laughed at her comment. "It's part of our disguise. Workmen eat fast food, so we do, too."

"Don't you think you're going overboard a bit?"

"Hey, we're spies. You can't be too careful." Laura rolled her eyes in disbelief.

Sharp drove to the top level where he parked near the down ramp in case a quick exit was needed. He left the van running, looked over and grinned. "Hello, boss."

"Hello, Sharp," Laura replied. He insisted on calling her "boss," which she detested, so she countered by calling him by his last name. Bill Sharp had come to work for the firm after his rescue in Lebanon a few weeks earlier. He'd been a Foreign Service officer working out of the American Embassy in Damascus when he was kidnapped by a militant Lebanese faction. The kidnappers thought they were kidnapping the Ambassador and ended up with Sharp, a hardheaded individual they found impossible to break. He was a former Army Delta Force officer, short, stocky and as tough as they come. During the rescue, he helped Laura and her team fight their way to the extraction point where they were picked up by Israeli helicopters. After his return to the States, he resigned from government work and Laura found his skills useful. "Those work overalls are part of your disguise, too?" she asked, pointing to his clothing. This time, both laughed.

"We wanted to look like maintenance workers in case we were stopped. We've even got tools in the back."

"Pierre has overalls, too?"

"Yeah, but I had to teach him how to put them on. He's a Frenchie." Sharp laughed at his own joke.

Pierre Thibault came to the firm through Jean. He was a former French paratrooper who served in the Middle East and survived the Beirut Embassy bombing in 1983. When his enlistment was complete, he began advising French Intelligence on matters concerning Lebanon. When Jean partnered with Laura, he came along. He was a short, muscular man in his late 30s with a tanned, weathered face. Pierre was an expert with weapons, especially knives.

"Talk to me about Derek Young," Laura said.

Sharp shrugged. "We watched the address CIA had on file, but it was a dead end. He never showed. So, we hung around the entrance to Langley and finally saw him."

"And followed him here?"

Sharp shrugged. "That's right."

"So, you've seen him?"

"Young? Oh yeah, plenty. By the way, your man Postl's a fucking genius. We rented an apartment in the building and ..."

Laura interrupted. "You rented an apartment?" she asked, astonished they'd take the risk.

"Yeah, it was the easiest way to get Postl in the building. So, he comes in like he's a telephone installer and tells the maintenance super he's got an order to install a second line into our apartment. Get this," Sharp said for emphasis. "They believe him and give him a pass key."

Benjamin Postl was an electronics wizard who defected from the Soviet Union along with Dmitri and Svetlana during Laura's Moscow mission. Previously called Jack, he'd decided to change his first name to Ben to make it more difficult for authorities who searched for hackers and codebreakers. When asked why he chose the name Benjamin, he'd reply, "Benjamin Franklin, of course."

Laura had responded, "It's your last name that needs changing."

"Nope, it's going to be Ben Postl. Get used to it." Laura had given up trying to convince him otherwise. Laura and Jean had rented office space for Postl in D.C.

"So Postl tapped Young's phone line?" Laura asked Sharp.

"He did way more than that," Sharp replied. "He tied us into the building video feed. Everything security sees, we see. The hallways, the lobby, even the parking lot. Every time Young leaves, we pick him up."

"Where does he go?"

"Well, that's the thing. He hasn't done much. He's been to the supermarket, the barber, stopped for fuel. He drove out to Langley twice."

"And you don't think he's noticed you?"

"Not that we can tell. We've got two vehicles we use. We hired an additional man, a local PI so Young never sees the same face. The local guy takes one shift, Pierre and I take the other two."

"What about Young's phone?"

"We hear everything going in and coming out."

"Who's he been talking to?"

"This is where it gets interesting. Postl's been tracing the calls. Young received a call from Tallahassee, and he gave the woman your name. We figure that ties into the letter you received."

"A woman?"

"Yeah. She didn't give her name and we don't know where in Tallahassee the call came from, but it's a link."

"It's certainly suspicious. Anything else?"

"A man who identified himself as Pritchard called asking if Young was available for work next week. That call came from the Pentagon."

"It could be some sort of off-book op the Pentagon's running with CIA. That's it?" Laura asked.

"One more call of interest, an unidentified person telling Young a shipment would be ready next week. That call came from the Pentagon, too."

"All right, sit tight and continue the surveillance. Once we know his travel plans, we'll decide what to do next."

"Okay, boss. Whatever you say." Laura laughed again.

"Stop calling me boss."

"You got it, boss."

Laura shook her head. "You're impossible, you know that? Drive me back to my car before we're seen."

Sharp saluted her. "Yes, boss."

Chapter Five

Sunday, December 11, 1988

JACK MASON SPENT Sunday afternoon alone at the office processing company paperwork. He paid a few bills, finished the next payroll and called Laura regarding her change of hotels. His office time was uneventful until a call came from Miguel. He let Jack know the building was staked out by three individuals who, in the opinion of Miguel, were the same men who'd arrived on a large yacht the previous day. They'd pulled the vessel into the Freeport dock and cleared themselves through the Customs facility.

Jack swung into action immediately, taking his protective vest and shoulder holster from the closet. He checked the pistol's clip; it was full. After strapping on the vest and donning the holster, he ran into the kitchen where a trap door in the floor led to the crawl space beneath the building. Once in the crawl space, it was only a few feet to the rear foundation wall where a small metal door provided outside access. It was hidden from view by a trash dumpster pushed against the building.

He opened the metal door and managed to exit the building by squeezing through the opening and pushing the dumpster aside. Jack withdrew his pistol and poked his head above the dumpster. He saw nothing threatening so he stood and walked left to the corner of the building and looked down the alley where a man was peeking in one of the building's windows. He pointed his weapon, stepped into view and yelled, "Freeze!" The man looked up, surprised to see Jack, and ran toward the street. Jack followed, but by the time he'd reached the street, the man was gone. However, a second man was setting a brown cardboard box at the front door.

"Hey! What are you doing?" Jack shouted walking toward the man.

The man quickly looked at Jack and ran. What the hell, Jack thought. I can't run him down. Check the box. He approached the box and studied it without touching it. He'd heard of people delivering piles of animal excrement to unpopular business establishments. Let's peek inside. The top flaps weren't taped shut, but rather folded together to keep the box closed. He gently tugged at the flaps until they came loose.

"Holy shit!" He shouted. "It's a fucking bomb!" The box contained three blocks of C-4 explosive attached to a timer with an LED readout counting down from 2 minutes. "Fuck! This thing will blow up a square block." Calm down. Slow your breathing. You've got to disable it. Think, Jack. Think! You've taken classes in this stuff. Look at it. What do you see?

His hands began to sweat profusely as he leaned over and gently lifted the timer. It was sitting on top of a construction blasting cap wired to a nine-volt battery. It's all wired together. The battery, the LED timer, the blasting cap and the C4. Jack trembled involuntarily. The battery's the power source. It connects to the timer and then on to the blasting cap. The wires protruding from the blasting cap are stuck into the blocks of C-4. Fuck, the wires run through a spring. It's like a mousetrap. There's a lever there. If I move those wires before I disconnect the power, this thing blows. Okay, I understand it. I can do this. How much time? He glanced at the timer. 55 seconds left, 54, 53, 52. Stop watching the timer. Do something! Jack lifted the LED timer and tugged at the battery wires. Come on! Come loose. 40,

39, 38, 37. The wires finally disconnected from the battery. The LED readout went dark. Okay, the power source is disconnected. The blasting cap can still go off. Put your thumb over the lever and pull the wires from the C4. Okay, that's done. Now, take the C-4 out of the box. Jack gently lifted the C-4 bricks out of the box and set them on the sidewalk a few yards away. It's done. Over. Jack collapsed on the sidewalk and leaned back against the building. Heart pounding, sweat dripping off his face, he took a deep breath and wiped his face with his arm. Shit! I'm too old for this.

Jack called the Constable's office from the lobby. He walked back outside to wait. Jack took a handkerchief from his pocket and wiped his face. Calm down. It's over.

The police pulled up within five minutes, introduced themselves and peeked inside the box. The bomb needed no explanation. "Stand back," one officer said, pushing Jack away. "Call a bomb unit," the Sergeant yelled to his colleague. The entire block was cordoned off during the wait. When the explosives experts arrived shortly afterward, two technicians dressed in protective clothing gently lifted the box and the C-4 into a steel reinforced container. The police took Jack's statement and a brief description of the men who'd left it. Jack was advised to leave the premises in case the men returned and then the steel container was loaded into the back of a van. Jack was left alone standing on the street. As quickly as the event began, it was over. Jack looked up and down the sidewalk. I better get the hell out of here. He went back into the office to grab his jacket and briefcase and drove to his condo where he was careful about entering the flat. He found it safe; the attackers hadn't targeted him so much as they had the firm. Later in the day, after doing a bit of research, Jack finally called Jean at the compound to advise him of the incident.

"It's Jack. We had an incident at the office."

"Go ahead," Jean replied.

Jack described the details of the bomb attempt from beginning to end, from Miguel's phone call to disarming of the device.

"Thank God you weren't killed, Jack."

"My thought exactly. The timing of that call saved my life."

"Three blocks of C-4 would have leveled an entire block."

"Somebody up there must like me," Jack said with relief.

"If this incident is connected with the letter, we're a target. You mentioned the men came off a yacht in the harbor?"

"That's what Miguel told me."

"Will the police search the yacht?"

"They said they would, but I doubt it. You know these guys. They'll not lift a finger down at the docks to frighten tourists."

"Can Miguel take a look at the vessel?"

"He already did. It's a sixty-footer named 'Manatee.' He checked the dock registry, too. Apparently, it came in from Miami."

"Any way to know who owns it?"

"Miguel says it's registered in Panama to a Francisco Valera."

"I don't know the name," Jean replied.

"There's no reason you'd have heard of him. I did some checking. He's the Panamanian Minister of Trade."

"You mean Panama the country?"

"Yes."

"So, he's connected with the Panamanian government."

"Right to the top," Jack replied.

Jean sighed. "Well, as long as the yacht's in Freeport, we're in danger. I don't expect an attack on the compound, but they might make an attempt on you. Don't go back to the office. I'm sending three guards to provide security at your condo. I'll contact Laura to let her know what's going on. In the meantime, get some rest and I'll contact you tomorrow."

"Will do."

Chapter Six

Tuesday, December 13, 1988

DAN JENKINS PICKED up the phone when Laura called his direct line from her hotel room Tuesday morning.

"Hi, Dan, it's Laura. I'm checking in."

"Good morning. I'm glad you called."

"How'd your testimony go?"

Dan chuckled. "The opening statement went well. That's about all I can say about it."

"They give you a hard time?" Laura could hear Dan chuckle.

"No, not really. I hate to be cynical, but those hearings are a show. Congressmen like to get themselves on TV." Laura heard Dan riffling through paperwork. "Can you hang on a minute? I need to find a file." A moment later, Dan was back on the line. "I had some of our people research the plane and we couldn't find much. We know it was sold by the Air Force to a company named Paradigm Import-Export. However, their business filings have been classified by the DOD."

"It must be a front for CIA."

"Possibly."

"What about the FAA?"

"They refused the RFI, too," Dan replied. "That suggests the government's still using the plane, perhaps through Paradigm."

"I thought Iran-Contra shut down those off-book ops."

"Supposedly. Your friend, Clair George, certainly got into trouble over that, didn't he?"

"Yes, he did. Clair's a dear friend. He was my boss at CIA."

CIA Director of Operations Clair George was indicted in the aftermath of the Iran-Contra scandal, a clandestine operation run by the Pentagon and CIA to ship arms to Iran in exchange for cash payments to support the Nicaraguan rebels.

"This is only speculation, but what if the Pentagon and CIA are now doing drug ops?"

"Drugs for arms?" Laura asked.

"Drugs, weapons, cash, who knows. But, if that's what you've stumbled into, it could get nasty. They wouldn't necessarily move to silence me, but you're fair game, considering your relationship with Bates." Bill Bates was the current Director of the Central Intelligence Agency and a dispute with Bates led to Laura's resignation after her Moscow mission. "All the more reason to let me take the lead on this."

"Dan, we've done nothing."

"I believe you. Derek Young is a solid lead, but I'd have to open an official investigation to pursue him. I can't do that; it's political dynamite. He's CIA."

"So, you're not going to investigate Derek Young?"

"Well, I wouldn't phrase it like that. Let's just say he's on hold right now pending more evidence."

I don't know how much more evidence you need, she thought. CIA employees caught red-handed bringing drugs into the country.

"And the plane's a dead end?" she asked.

Laura could hear Dan sigh. "I think it is. If DOD finds out I'm asking questions, I could get fired. I'm not going to do that."

This is the part of Dan I can't stand, she thought. He's become a politician, not a law enforcement officer. There was silence on the line for a moment while Laura wondered whether to voice her frustration.

"Laura, are you still there?" Dan asked.

"I'm just frustrated at how political you've become. What happened to the Dan I knew in Paris?"

This time, the silence on the line was Dan's. She doesn't get it. She never has.

"Laura, we've been over this before," he said, his impatience beginning to show. "Remember our conversation walking out of Langley the day you resigned. You have to pick fights you can win. You can't go up against the CIA and DOD. They're too powerful."

Laura was getting angry. "To hell with them. I'll go above their heads. I'll take this straight to the President."

Again, there was silence on the line. This woman will do anything to win, Dan thought. "Step back for a minute and listen to yourself. I know the President is a friend of yours, but do you think you can get past his Chief of Staff? Suppose the White House is in the loop? Think about it. You can't win this."

There was a brief silence on the line as she concluded Dan was right. "Okay, I hear you," she said with a sigh.

"It doesn't mean we're giving up, though," Dan continued. "We have to go about it another way. The letter you gave me is important. It's a felony threat using the Postal Service. That's a winnable case. I had the letter run through the lab and we found prints on the cut-out letters. Those prints match a person in federal custody."

"What?" She said, surprised.

"It's hard to believe someone could be that stupid, isn't it?" Laura didn't quite believe what she was hearing.

"You're saying the letter came from a federal prison?"

"That's exactly what I'm saying. It came from the minimum-security institution in Tallahassee. The prints belong to a woman named Renata Sanchez."

"You mean the Renata Sanchez who heads the South American drug cartels?" Laura asked, astonished by the information.

"The same," Dan said. "The most powerful cartel boss in the world. As you may remember, we picked her up in Miami a few years ago. She was indicted, convicted and sent to FCI Tallahassee. Word has it that she runs her entire drug operation from prison. She probably bribed guards to smuggle the letter out."

"That's incredible."

"She's up for parole in a few months and I can use the letter to deny it. But I might be able to make a deal. She gives me information and I don't show the letter to the parole board. I'm going down there tomorrow to interview her."

"I'd like to come with you."

"I suggest you don't. She's got billions of dollars and hundreds of men at her disposal. She's not going to attack me, but she might make an attempt on you while you're in town."

"How would she know I'm coming?"

"I'd have to put you on the visitor's list. Believe me, she'll find out."

Laura decided to tell Dan about the attempted bombing of her office in Freeport. Jean had called her the previous evening with the news. "I'd like to bring up the bomb face to face."

Dan took his time thinking about the risk. When he spoke, he'd made his decision.

"Can you meet me at Dulles tomorrow at 7:00 a.m.?"

"There's no need, my plane's out at National. I'll fly into Tallahassee tonight. Can you pick me up in the morning at the airport Marriott?"

"Sure," Dan replied. "The appointment's at 11:00 a.m. I'll pick you up at 10:30 a.m. We'll compare notes on the way over."

"I'll see you tomorrow."

Chapter Seven

AFTER THE CALL, Laura tried to remember what she knew about the circumstances surrounding Renata Sanchez's capture. Sanchez was a native Colombian who murdered her way to the top of the drug cartels. Known for a vicious temper, stories of her killing sprees had become legend. Anyone who disagreed with her ended up dead, including two husbands. Apprehended at the Miami airport a few years ago after an anonymous tip from one of her enemies, she was convicted of drug trafficking in a federal trial that splashed across every newspaper in America. Laura remembered watching the press conference on television announcing the capture. It was a coup for the FBI who'd been largely ineffective prosecuting the cartels. After her incarceration, Sanchez vanished from public view, however it would be naïve to assume she couldn't run her operation from a minimum-security prison.

Would it be so hard to imagine her knowing about the visit in advance? Sanchez probably paid off every employee at the facility. However, the opportunity to get direct testimony without it being sanitized by Dan was too much to resist. Besides which, Laura was genuinely interested in meeting one of the great villains of all time.

She picked up the phone and dialed her compound in the Bahamas. "Rick, how are things going down there?" Laura asked.

"We're secure. We've abandoned the office and Jack's here at the compound. What's going on with you?"

"I've got a job for you."

"Sure. What do you need?"

"Who's the best marksman we've got besides yourself?"

"That'd be Sharp."

"After him?"

"Oh, probably Pierre."

"Okay. I need the three of you in Tallahassee, Florida, ASAP. I'm coming down to pick you up. Bring weapons and ammo. Oh, and a couple of sniper rifles, too."

"I'll have to pull 'em off Derek Young."

"Sharp has an extra man on the op who can cover it. I'll call Sharp and Pierre from here."

"All right. See you later today."

The next call was placed to Bill Sharp. "You recognize the voice," she said.

"Yep," Sharp replied.

"I need to pull you and Pierre off surveillance for a day."

"What's going on?"

"I'll explain later tonight. Can you and Pierre meet me in the private terminal at National?"

"Sure. When?"

"Right now."

"You got it, boss."

Another call was placed to Ben Postl at his small computer repair shop in downtown D.C. "Ben, its Laura."

"I didn't know you were in town."

"It's a quick one-day trip. Do you have passport pictures of everyone in the firm?"

"I think I've got them in a file somewhere. What do you need?"

"I need authentic CIA identification cards for Rick, Sharp, Pierre and myself."

"That shouldn't be a problem. I've got a laminating machine here in the office. When do you want them?"

"Right now, Ben."

"Give me an hour. You want me to bring them to you?"

"No, I'll stop by."

"Okay."

One more call was placed to inform Dmitri of her plan. He and his crew left immediately for the airport to prep the plane for departure. After the flurry of phone calls, Laura packed her bag, checked out of the hotel and headed for Postl's computer shop.

Chapter Eight

BEN POSTL WAS quickly becoming a master forger and Laura marveled at the quality of the CIA identification cards he produced. The expensive machines in his office allowed him to fulfill most, if not all, of the requests Laura made.

"This is outstanding work, Ben," she said with a smile, thumbing through the stack of cards. "I can't tell them from the real thing."

"You ought to know since you worked there. It was fun. I even made one for myself," he said with a chuckle, holding up one with his name and photo on it."

"We pay you a lot of money, but damn, it's worth it."

"Good ID is a valuable commodity," Ben said, shrugging.

"Well, you've saved our butts many times and I thank you for it."

"No problem, Laura. Where are you off to?"

"We've got a job in Florida tomorrow. Oh, I forgot something. Do you have stickers?"

What kind?"

"CIA classified material stickers for luggage."

"Sure, I've got them in a drawer somewhere." He rummaged around a drawer in his desk before finding them. "Here. Will these work?"

Laura took the stickers. "I'm sure they will." She paused, looking around the shop at all of Ben's expensive hardware. "You've got quite an operation going, Ben. My compliments. Listen, I've got to run. I'll keep in touch." With that, she turned and left, heading for the airport.

Chapter Nine

LAURA MET PIERRE and Sharp in the private terminal where they boarded the Dassault Falcon idling on the tarmac. Dmitri and Pete Franklin were already on board, completing their pre-flight checklist while Svetlana prepared the cabin. The engines whined after Svetlana closed the door and the group strapped themselves in for takeoff. The jet took off moments later bound for Grand Bahama Island.

The two-hour fifteen-minute flight to the air strip on the east end of the island was uneventful. Pierre and Sharp inquired about Laura's plans, but were politely rebuffed when she asked them to wait. In truth, she hadn't quite figured out how to proceed. After Svetlana served sandwiches and soft drinks, the casual conversation turned to silence as Laura worked out a plan in her mind.

The Falcon 50 arrived at the airstrip late in the afternoon where Rick Williams waited to board with containers of weapons and ammunition. Laura walked down the stairs and affixed the U.S. Classified Material stickers on the containers to prevent a customs inspection. "Customs will leave you alone, Rick," she said handing him the fake CIA identification card, "as long as you flash this." Rick looked closely at the ID before sliding it in his billfold.

"Postl does great work, doesn't he?"

"I've rarely seen anyone better. That," she said, pointing at the card as he slipped into its place, "will get you inside any embassy in the world."

Dmitri kept the plane's engines at idle while Pete walked down the stairs to help Rick lift the containers into storage underneath the cabin. Once the material was stowed below and the passengers belted into their seats, Dmitri wheeled the plane around and took off for Tallahassee International Airport.

Once the plane reached its flight altitude, Dmitri leveled the ascent and Svetlana served drinks in the cabin. She drew a curtain to give them privacy while she sat near the cockpit to chat with Pete and Dmitri who'd left the cockpit door open. Laura gathered her group in the back of the plane where a sofa and padded chairs accommodated them.

"Thanks, everyone, for responding so quickly," Laura began. "Sorry I haven't explained what's going on. Here's what you're walking into."

"It's about the drug bust, right?" Rick asked. Laura nodded.

"Yeah, the problem that won't go away. Dan Jenkins, over at FBI, identified the author of the letter."

"And?" Rick replied.

"It came from Renata Sanchez," knowing the name would elicit a response.

"Holy shit!" Sharp exclaimed excitedly. "You mean the Brown Recluse? The drug kingpin?"

"The same," Laura said with a nod. She looked at Pierre. "In case you don't know, Sanchez runs all the drug cartels in Central and South America. All the drug producers report to her."

"I wasn't familiar with the name," Pierre said.

"She's a big fish."

"The biggest," Sharp added.

"The letter came from a federal prison in Tallahassee where she's incarcerated. Apparently, she operates her drug operation from prison."

"How in hell does someone like that manage to get caught in the first place?" Sharp asked. "She has all the resources she needs to protect herself."

Laura laughed. "I'd imagine she does. When she slipped into Miami to visit her ailing sister, the DEA found out and picked her up at the airport."

"It was kind of stupid of her to come to the U.S., wasn't it?"

"Even drug kingpins have relatives, Sharp," she replied with a smile.

"Well, she's probably got every guard in the joint on her payroll."

"I'm sure you're right. Jenkins suspects one of the guards slipped the letter out of prison for her."

"Was Sanchez behind the attack on the office?"

"I'm sure she was," Laura responded with a nod, "but I can't prove it."

"We can't fight her entire organization," Rick said. "So, what the hell are we going to do?"

He saw a hint of a smile from her. "Jenkins and I are going to interview Sanchez tomorrow morning at the prison. Dan plans to use the letter to threaten her with more prison time. Maybe we can make a deal. She stops pursuing us and Dan forgets about the letter. We'll see."

"I'm not sure she's the type who negotiates," Rick said.

"Maybe not, but it's worth a shot, don't you think?"

"Maybe. Did it occur to you she may know you're coming?"

"I'm sure she does."

"I think her way of negotiating is killing you," Rick said bluntly.

"Which is why I've called everyone together," she said gesturing toward Pierre and Sharp. "She might attempt an assassination in Tallahassee."

Rick thought about the possibility. "She'd certainly have advance knowledge of where you'll be and when."

"Would you mind if I said something?" Pierre asked.

"Speak freely, Pierre. We need everyone to weigh in on this."

"Sanchez has enough manpower, expertise and money to mount an attack anywhere. Why would she choose Tallahassee?"

"Well, it's convenient," Laura replied. "My intuition tells me to be ready."

"How do we be ready for anything?" Pierre asked.

"Well, that's the challenge, isn't it? An attack could come anywhere. The airport, the hotel; even an ambush on the road."

"Outside the prison is the best place," Sharp said. "It's like Rick said, she'll know exactly where you'll be and when."

"Go on," Laura replied, glancing at him.

"I don't think she'll plan anything at the airport," Sharp followed, "because there are too many people around."

"And since we fly private," Rick added, "she wouldn't necessarily know which airport we'd use."

"On the road would be a good choice. Plenty of escape routes," Pierre said.

"I thought of that," Laura replied. "For instance, they could park vehicles near the prison and attack as I drove away."

"That'd be tough to stop," Pierre observed. "We wouldn't know who's involved until it happens."

"We could convoy our vehicles like politicians do," Rick mentioned. "That would give us a fighting chance."

"True," Laura said. "It would mean a shootout on city streets, though. That's messy, hard to coordinate."

"I saw that in a movie once," Sharp said. "Motorcycles pull up beside a car and fire through the windows. Boom! Everyone dies." Laura grimaced.

"But I'll be riding with an FBI agent. She's too smart to kill him."

"Okay, what about inside the prison?" Sharp asked.

"Inmates on her payroll," Pierre offered. "They create a disturbance, and in the confusion, you get shot or stabbed."

"Prisons have video surveillance," Rick countered. "They'd find the killer," Rick said.

Laura turned to Sharp. "You mentioned outside the prison. Describe that scenario."

"A sniper hits you on the sidewalk outside the prison. Prison grounds are set off the street with plenty of sightlines for shooters."

Laura hesitated a moment, thinking. "That sounds right to me." She looked around. "What do the rest of you think?"

"A sniper could certainly get away quickly," Rick said.

"And you'd never see it coming," Pierre added. "It'd be practically impossible to stop."

"That's what I would do," Laura said. "It's professional and it's clean. Let's go with that."

"As you go in the prison or come out?" Rick asked.

"Definitely on the way out," Sharp said.

"Why on the way out?" Pierre asked.

Sharp shrugged. "She'll want to meet Laura first before killing her. It's an ego thing."

"Here's what I'd like to do," Laura said. "Let's ask Dmitri to hanger the plane and once the plane is inside, we exit the plane and walk into the terminal separately. Rick," she said looking at him, "you rent a car. Drive to the hotel and everybody else," she said looking at the others, "take the airport shuttle. We'll use the airport Marriott. Everyone check in as a single and we'll meet behind the hotel at dawn to scout the location. Any questions?"

"I think that covers it for now," Rick replied.

Laura looked around the cabin. "We'll know more once we scout the prison. For now, let's get through the airport and into the city."

"Okay!" Sharp said. "Can I buy everyone a drink now?"

Laura rolled her eyes and smiled. "The drinks are free, Sharp."

"That's why I'm buying!"

That put the group at ease for the remainder of the flight, putting tomorrow's difficulties aside.

Chapter Ten

MIAMI'S BIGGEST DRUG importer and distributor was Diego Marty, a ruthless thug who'd managed to gain control of the drug trade in Greater Miami by the time he was in his late twenties. His rise to prominence was spectacular, forging alliances with international crime syndicates, murdering his competition and flooding the streets with drugs. Due to his large purchases of drugs from Central and South American cartels, he'd come to the attention of Renata Sanchez who served as a mentor to Diego. Although he had little formal education, Diego was smart. He mastered the complex aspects of personnel management, shipping, inventory and accounting as well as any corporate CEO, all under the watchful eye of Sanchez who, over time, gained confidence in Diego. By the time he'd reached his late thirties, Diego was a key ally of Sanchez.

Diego relied heavily on four lieutenants to run his operation, men who were childhood friends and trusted allies. Each of the men ran a different part of South Florida. Together, the five were among the worst criminals in the country, yet they were untouchable. They controlled the local police on the street through large payoffs; they retained the best lawyers in the city and whatever prosecutions came about as the result of their operations languished in the courts from lack of witnesses and missing evidence. Diego Marty had built a safety net around his organization which allowed him to operate openly on the streets of Miami without fear.

Diego conducted business from an office inside his Miami nightclub, The Hacienda, known in the Little Havana community as a haven for people in the drug trade. Diego's appearance each evening was an event, walking through the club wearing his signature sunglasses and silk shirts, stopping to glad hand patrons and business partners.

On this particular evening, Diego had requested a meeting with his lieutenants to discuss pending business. His trusted confidants dutifully arrived early that evening, all nearly carbon copies of Diego; thirties, black hair combed back over their foreheads, long sleeve silk shirts, dress slacks and shoes.

Although Diego hadn't told them the purpose of the meeting, as they sat around his office waiting for him to arrive, they speculated as to its purpose. Someone wasn't producing enough income, someone had a police problem, an accounting discrepancy. The list went on and on. Whatever problems Diego identified, these men were ready to satisfy his demands, whatever they might be. The drug trade on this level was big business and all of them made too much money to do otherwise.

Diego entered his office, as he usually did, with a bodyguard to make sure he wasn't the target of an enterprising associate bent on taking over his business. He had no worries, though. Each man had previously been searched by a guard standing outside Diego's office.

"Good evening, gentlemen," Diego said, nodding toward his men. He sat in his captain's chair as any corporate executive might when addressing subordinates. "Let's do a quick check on business before we begin." Diego turned to the man sitting on his left. "Luis, what's the status of the shipment coming in tonight?"

"We've got men on the dock in Biscayne as we speak, waiting for the yacht to arrive."

"Do you anticipate any police problems?"

"No. I've taken care of the authorities. They'll leave us alone."

"How do you plan to get it to the warehouse?"

"It's hidden in crates of pineapples. We'll deliver it to the warehouse using a refrigerated truck." Luis ran his part of the business through a legitimate business as a supplier of fruits to local markets. "We'll separate the shipment at the warehouse and the fruit will be moved to west Miami for delivery to groceries."

"Perfect." Diego turned to another lieutenant. "Santiago, where are we on that incident in the neighborhood the other night?"

"The police showed up immediately after the shooting. The thieves were charged with armed robbery and our people were released with no charges."

"That's what I like to hear," he said with a nod and a smile. He looked around the room and addressed them as a group. "I want to remind you to stay on top of your responsibilities. Don't allow your problems to become my problems. Now, on to the next subject." Diego paused and took a deep breath.

"The big boss was angry over what happened in the Bahamas. You were sent down there to blow up a building. How could you screw that up?"

"Some guy came out of the alley with a gun, Diego," Santiago opined. "What were we supposed to do? The building looked vacant."

"You blow up the fucking building in the middle of the night, Santiago! Nobody blows a building during the daytime. What's even worse is you used the yacht to go down there."

"No one can connect the yacht to us, Diego."

"If someone looks hard enough, the registration on that yacht can be traced to our Panamanian friends. Gentlemen, if we lose that Panama pipeline, we've got a serious problem." Diego waited for a response, but his colleagues remained silent. "The woman who owns that building stole a shipment from Sanchez and she wanted to send a message. We fucked that up so now Sanchez wants us to kill the woman. I've promised her we'll do it." Diego leaned forward, looked at his men and raised his voice. "This is your problem! You fix it!" Each man in the room nodded and said, "Yes, Sir," one by one.

Diego slapped his desk and leaned back. "That's what I wanted to hear." He opened the center drawer and withdrew copies of a photo. "This is what the woman looks like," he said distributing the pictures. "Her name is Laura Messier." He allowed the men to study the photo for a moment. "She'll be at the Tallahassee prison tomorrow morning to interview Sanchez at 11:00 a.m. Do not hit her before the interview. The boss wants to find out what she knows. But after the interview, the boss wants her eliminated immediately."

"I don't mean to question you, Diego," Santiago said, "but, why do it on the prison grounds?"

"Because Sanchez has the entire prison on her payroll. It's the safest place to do it." Diego looked at his watch. "It takes seven hours to drive up there and it's what, eight-thirty now? You'll have plenty of time. Take a couple of shooters with you. Julian, you and David take the lead. Luis, you and Santiago stay here and handle business." Julian spoke next.

"What do we know about this woman?"

"You don't need to know a fucking thing about her, Julian. Just kill her as she walks out of the prison. You think you can do that?"

"Sure, Diego, no problem. We'll take care of it."

Diego pulled copies of another photo from his desk. "Here's a picture of the front of the prison. See that row of trees by the road? They're supposed to hide the prison from the street. Your shooters can shoot from cover in those trees." Diego laid the photo aside and unfolded a map. "Now look at the map. I've circled the prison." Diego pointed to the circle. "After you make the hit, drive north on Capital to Route 90. Go east to I-10 and then south on I-75. You'll be out of town in fifteen minutes."

"Will she be alone?" Julian asked.

"No. She'll be with an FBI agent, but don't worry. He won't do a fucking thing. This is a local police matter. Just make sure you don't shoot him. Messier's the target."

"I don't mean to argue, but wouldn't the airport be a better place?" Julian asked. Diego shook his head.

"No. The airport has a lot of problems. Lots of people around, it's hard to get out of there, too many police. The area outside the prison is open ground. No one is around. Do it there, Julian, just like Sanchez wants."

"It's as good as done." Julian looked at his colleagues. "Come on compadres, we've got a job to do."

The men filed out of the room and met in the parking lot. "I've got a couple of rifles at the house. I'll go get 'em," Julian said. "David, you go pick up Andres and Mateo. They're the best shooters we've got. Let's meet back here in an hour."

One hour later, Julian and David, plus the two shooters, Mateo and Andres, met in an alley behind the club, put the weapons in the trunk of a rented sedan and left for Tallahassee.

Chapter Eleven

Friday, December 16, 1988

AFTER RICK, PIERRE and Sharp scouted the prison grounds shortly after dawn, they returned to the hotel to attack the breakfast bar before checking out.

"Two helpings of potatoes, Sharp? Really?" Rick asked.

"I never go to work on empty, big guy," Sharp replied.

"As soon as you're finished stuffing your face, let's check out. Did everyone wipe their room of fingerprints?"

"I did," Pierre replied.

"Fuck, I forgot," Sharp said. Rick and Pierre looked at each other and laughed.

"Sharp's still in training," Rick said to Pierre.

"You guys can fuck off," Sharp said in response to the laughter.

"I'm sure it'll be fine," Pierre said. "If you're caught, we don't know you."

"Ya think?"

"Is everyone ready?" Rick asked, after the trio climbed in the car. He answered his own question. "Let's go do this."

After the fifteen-minute trip, Rick pulled in the fuel station across the street from the prison. Pierre waited in the car while Rick and Sharp entered the storefront and walked to the attendant behind the counter. "Could I see the manager please?" Rick asked.

"I'm the only one here so I guess I'm the manager," the young gentleman said behind the counter. The man became nervous and looked back and forth between Rick and Sharp. "How can I help you?"

Rick sensed the alarm. "Relax, we're government agents. He and Sharp flashed their CIA identification cards. The man immediately calmed himself. "We're providing security for a high value prisoner transfer this morning across the street. We need access to the roof above your gas pumps." The manager looked puzzled. Rick explained. "We're putting a man on your roof until the prison van leaves the facility."

"I guess it'll be okay," the manager said weakly. "We've never done that before."

"It's just a precaution. We'll be up there for about an hour and then we'll be gone. You'll never know we were there. How do we get on the roof?"

The man looked indecisive. "We have a ladder out back we use for maintenance. Would that work?"

"That'll be fine," Rick said.

"I can't leave the counter, but you'll find it if you walk around the building. Once you're on the roof, though, you'll have to take the ladder down. It blocks the pumps."

Rick gave the man a confident, friendly smile. "No problem. And don't worry. We'll have things wrapped up in an hour or so," he said. "Thanks for your cooperation." Rick and Sharp began to walk away.

"Am I in danger here?" The young man asked.

Rick turned back to reassure him. "You? Not at all. As I said, it's just a precaution. I'm sure things will be fine." Rick flashed him a smile. "You have a great day."

"Uh … okay," the manager replied. "You, too."

Rick and Sharp carried the ladder they found behind the station and propped it against the roof. "Get your ass up there, Sharp," Rick said.

"Fuck you, Rick." Sharp climbed the ladder carrying a large case that contained his rifle. Once he'd accessed the roof, Rick looked up and shouted, "You okay up there?" Sharp peeked over the edge.

"There's bird shit all over the place up here."

"Well, since you're full of shit anyway, you'll feel right at home."

"Fuck off," Sharp replied.

Rick chuckled as he carried the ladder to the side of the building and threw it on the ground. He got back in the car.

"Sharp okay up there?" Pierre asked.

Rick looked amused. "Sharp's gonna fit right in with the rest of us."

Rick turned left out of the station and immediately pulled off the roadway next to a bus stop in front of the prison. "We'll check coms as soon as I get in position," Rick said before Pierre exited the vehicle.

"Talk to you soon," Pierre replied. He sat down on the bench at the empty bus stop looking as bored as any passenger might while waiting for a bus. Rick pulled away and turned in the visitor's parking lot at the prison. He found the lot nearly empty as visitor hours weren't scheduled until later in the morning. He backed into a space at the rear of the lot where the entire parking area could be viewed. There were only two cars parked in the lot, both at the front near the sidewalk that led to the prison doors. From the dew on the windows, Rick figured the cars had been left there overnight.

From Sharp's vantage point across the street, he had a clear view of the trees that partially obscured the grounds from the street. He unpacked the M24 sniper rifle, screwed the suppressor onto the barrel, attached the telescopic sight and loaded the internal five round magazine. He lay down and peered through the sight gauging the distance to each landmark, and like any accomplished sniper, considered wind speed and position of the sun. Hoping none of this was necessary, Sharp unpacked the rifle tripod and then sat up with his legs crossed Indian style and poured himself a cup of coffee from a thermos he'd brought. He looked at his watch. 8:35 am. This is a fucking boring job, he thought. Well, it's better than being held hostage in some shithole in Lebanon. I'm gonna need some hazard pay, though, if I get sick from this bird shit.

Pierre wore his travel clothes from the previous day, jeans, sweatshirt and sneakers. He ruffled his hair, trying to look disheveled as though he'd just arose. This must be where newly released inmates catch a bus, he thought, looking around. He screwed the suppressor onto the barrel of his Sig Sauer P226 and checked the magazine. Full. He stuck the pistol inside his pants and looked at his watch. 8:38 am. Will anyone notice I don't board a bus?

After a few minutes, Sharp and Pierre heard Rick's voice through their earpieces. "Can everyone hear me?"

"I read you," Sharp said into the microphone pinned to his collar.

"Pierre?"

"I've got you."

Rick looked at his watch. "08:45 here. Any problems?"

"I've got no way to get off the roof," Sharp said.

"No worries. I'll drive by the gas pumps and pick you up. Jump on the roof of the car."

"Okay. I guess that works. Won't that dent the roof?"

"I'll give 'em your name when I turn the car in. I'm sure your insurance will take care of it."

"Fuck you, Rick." Sharp could hear Rick laughing in his earpiece.

"Pierre, walk across the street to the service station after this is over. I'll pick you up there."

"Got it."

"Let's hope nothing happens, fellas," Rick advised. "But if it does, remember, we're not sticking around for police interviews. Sharp, wipe down the rifle and the case. Leave them on the roof."

"I hear you," Sharp replied.

"Rick out."

Chapter Twelve

DIEGO'S SHOOTERS, JULIAN, David, Andres and Mateo cruised around the prison at 10:15 am, slowing each time to view the prison. "What time will this chick show up?" David asked.

"The interview's supposed to be at eleven," Julian answered.

"Aren't we here early?"

"So what?"

"Won't people notice Andres and Mateo in the trees with rifles?" David asked, pointing toward the trees as they drove by.

"Nobody's gonna notice anything, David," Julian replied. "If anyone looks over, they'll think they're guards. Relax."

Julian pulled onto the shoulder the third time around and nodded toward the trees. "Guys, you're going to set up in those trees. You've got a clear view of the sidewalk in front of the prison."

"Go around one more time, Julian," Andres said. "What about that asshole at the bus stop back there?"

"Leave him alone," Julian said as he pulled back onto the road. "He'll probably run when he hears gunfire. If he bothers you, shoot him."

"What about the prison guards?" Mateo asked.

"Mateo," Julian sighed, "do you see any prison guards walking around outside?"

"No."

"That's because they're all inside guarding prisoners. Besides, the big boss has 'em all on the payroll. Don't worry about the guards. Remember, we're doing the hit when the woman leaves, not when she arrives. Let her walk in the prison and line up your target as she walks in. Wait until she comes out and kill her right as she enters the parking lot. That's your shortest shot. If you happen to miss, we want her running to her car."

"We're not going to miss, Julian."

"Good." Julian looked over at David. "After I drop off the shooters, I'll pull in the parking lot. You're the back-up, David. If she makes it into the lot, take her down."

"Julian, we're not going to miss," Mateo insisted.

"Shut the fuck up, Mateo," David said. "Nothing against you. It's smart to have a back-up. We don't want to drive home and tell Diego we screwed this up."

"That's right," Julian said looking in the rear-view mirror. "After it's over, Andres, you and Mateo run back to the road. We'll pick you up there. Wipe the prints off the rifles and leave them on the ground."

Chapter Thirteen

THE THIRD TIME the black sedan slowed in front of the prison, Pierre spoke into the coms. "Rick, I think we've got some action here."

"What's going on?"

"Four men in a black sedan just made their third pass around the prison. They pulled onto the shoulder the last time, about thirty yards from where I'm sitting."

"They're gone now?"

"They pulled away, but I think they'll be back in three or four minutes."

"Sharp, are you hearing this?"

"Copy that, Rick."

"They may be who we're looking for," Rick said. He looked in the rear-view mirror. "Make sure you're lying down if they roll by again, Sharp. I can see your head."

"Roger that, Rick."

A couple of minutes later, the black sedan came by again, slowed and pulled off the road. Two men emerged from the back seat wearing black leather jackets and black pants. They were each carrying long leather bags. Pierre spoke into the coms. "Sharp, are you seeing this?"

"I'm looking right at them through the scope."

"Are those soft rifle cases?"

"That's what it looks like."

The two men walked into the trees as the sedan pulled away and turned into the driveway leading to the parking lot. "Rick, you've got company coming your way," Sharp warned. "Two men in a black sedan."

Rick slumped down behind the steering wheel. "I see them."

The black sedan parked in the second row of the parking area next to the prison. The man in the passenger seat got out and looked around before getting back in the car. Rick spoke into the coms.

"Pierre, you're going to have to get on a bus. A man in the black sedan got out and stared at you. Flash your ID when you board and have the driver let you off at the stoplight down the road. You'll have to walk back to the prison. Sharp, can you see the sedan?"

"The trees block some of the lot, Rick. I can see your car, but the sedan is hidden."

"What about the men in the trees?"

"I can see them well enough. They've laid on the ground using the trees as cover. They're definitely unpacking rifles. I've got a clean shot at the one on the left. The one to the right is partially hidden by a tree."

"When this begins, if you've got any kind of shot, take it."

"Once I nail the shooter on the left, the second man will probably move a bit. It might not be a kill, but I'll get a shot off. Just know that if I can't bring him down, you may have a shooter up your ass."

"Understood. Pierre, can you hear me?"

"Loud and clear, Rick. There's a bus coming. I'll get on it."

"When you get back, stop at the head of the drive. If they manage to escape the parking lot, you'll have to stop them. I'll pick you up at the head of the drive."

"Roger that, Rick."

"Sharp, if they try to take our girl on the way into the prison, take them down. Don't let them get a shot off."

"I read you."

"I'll take the men in the car. Remember, when this thing goes down, it'll be fast. Be ready for anything. Rick out."

The bus pulled over in front of the bus stop and Pierre got on flashing his CIA card. After a minute of hesitation, the bus pulled out and Rick picked up binoculars to watch Pierre get off at the stoplight a couple of hundred yards away and begin walking back up the road.

Chapter Fourteen

DAN JENKINS PULLED up to the hotel front door at 10:30 a.m. and found Laura waiting outside. He rolled down the passenger window. "Ready?" Laura hopped in the passenger seat.

"Hi, Dan. Thanks for picking me up." Dan pulled out into traffic and headed east toward the prison.

"We're pretty close to the prison. It should be about fifteen minutes."

"Have you talked with Sanchez before?"

"Yes, I've interviewed her twice," Dan replied with a nod.

"Your impression?"

"She's abrasive, threatening. And she rarely speaks English, although I'm sure she can."

Laura chuckled. "Just my type."

Dan glanced at his watch. "We're right on time. We should pull in about 10:45 a.m. Anything else you want to know about her?"

"Nope. I'm fine with what I've got."

"I'll press her hard on the letter. She committed a federal crime by sending it and we could add to her sentence if she doesn't answer questions."

"Will she have an attorney present?"

"On short notice like this? Probably not. It'd be easier if she had one to explain the consequences of the letter. She's looking at ten more years if we choose to prosecute."

"Will she understand that?"

"I'm sure she will. Whether it's enough to get her to cooperate, I'm not sure."

Dan turned into the visitors' lot and parked in the spot nearest to the sidewalk. Visiting hours began at 10:00 am and by the time they'd arrived, a half-dozen cars had already pulled into the lot. Laura looked around her surroundings after she exited the car. She saw Rick's rental car parked at the back of the lot but couldn't see Rick inside. The trees blocked her view of the service station across the street so she couldn't see Sharp, either. Pierre was nowhere to be found. *If they're out there, I certainly can't see them.*

"This way, Laura," Dan said, holding his hand out.

"Sure."

Julian pulled out the photo of Messier and showed it to David as Messier passed in front of their parked car. "That's the target, David," Julian said. "Pretty little thing, isn't she?"

"Let's kidnap her," David suggested. "Fuck the shit out of her before we kill her."

"Would you shut up?" David pulled his weapon from the glovebox.

"Or we could just shoot her right now? She's fucking walking right in front of us, Julian."

"You heard Diego," Julian replied. "She's not to be touched until after the meeting."

"You want to kill someone, you do it the first chance you get. You wait and things get fucked up."

Julian shook his head no. "My experience is do what Diego tells you or he fucks you up."

"Yeah, I know, but he's not the trigger man in this organization."

"Diego's killed plenty. Don't underestimate him."

David acknowledged the obvious. "I know. I'm just saying if a contract is placed on someone, you hit 'em quickly. You wait around, you lose your advantage."

"Shut the fuck up!" Julian demanded.

"All right! Sorry I mentioned it."

As Dan escorted Laura toward the sidewalk, Laura noticed the two men sitting in the black sedan. She knew Rick was at the back of the lot somewhere, so she looked straight ahead. Dan sensed the tension in her.

"Something wrong?"

"No, nothing," Laura replied giving him a weak smile.

"Nervous about Sanchez?" Ever quick to form a response, Laura instantly created an excuse.

"No, nothing like that. I get a bit nervous anytime I'm around a prison."

Dan understood the feeling as he felt that way himself. "Understandable. I'm always a bit tense when I enter one of these institutions. Look at it this way, as long as we've got a visitor's badge, we can leave."

"Just don't lose the badge, right?" Laura said.

"Right," Dan said with a smile.

Laura and Dan entered the building to find a line at the counter where a guard checked identification, signed visitors in and passed out badges. Laura looked around the lobby, first at the metal detectors, then at the guards who monitored them. They could be on Sanchez' payroll, she thought. "Will there be any danger inside?" Laura asked Dan.

"No, it would be impossible to mount an attack on a visitor. You're more in danger walking through the parking lot than you are inside the prison."

Prescient words, no doubt, she thought. If he only knew what was about to go down. "I'm sure you're right."

The guard at the check-in desk took their photo IDs, compared it to the morning's schedule and pointed to a sign-in clipboard. "Please sign and print your name." They proceeded to the metal detector where visitors lined up to be searched.

Dan put his briefcase on the conveyor belt after Laura watched her purse be swallowed by the machine. She stepped through the detector only to find a man on the other side who asked her to spread her legs and arms. He waved a wand around her body, capable of detecting small amounts of metal. He must have done this a thousand times.

"Ma'am, we have to search your purse," a guard at the end of the conveyor belt said. He picked up her purse and riffled through the contents and pulled out a small handheld tape recorder. "What's this?"

"It's a tape recorder. I use them in interviews."

The man studied it for a moment before returning it to her. "It's fine. You can take it inside."

Dan received the same treatment. Guards opened his briefcase and shuffled through the paperwork, looked inside the various compartments and even took apart his ink pens. Once they were satisfied, the briefcase was returned with the same warning. "Please step over to the window and give the clerk the name of the inmate you wish to visit," the guard told Dan.

"Actually, we're going to the Warden's office."

"One moment." The guard yelled at a colleague walking down the hall. "Hey, Frank, these two need to go to the Warden's office."

The guard walked over. "Does Warden Beck know you're coming?"

"Yes," Dan replied.

"Follow me please."

Warden John Beck happened to be standing in his outer office on the second floor when Laura and Dan walked in. Beck's face flashed a broad smile. "Hello Dan," he said, grabbing Dan's hand. "You're here for Sanchez?"

"That's right, John."

"I think they've got her ready for you downstairs." He turned to an assistant standing nearby. "Frank, would you run down the hall and see if they've got Inmate ..." he glanced at his paperwork, "46365-104 ready?" He turned back to Dan.

"How the hell have you been?"

"Doing well, John. They keep us pretty busy up in D.C. Let me introduce my colleague, Laura Messier from the CIA." Beck reached to shake hands.

"Ms. Messier."

"The pleasure's mine, Sir."

Frank returned from a short phone call. "Warden, they have her in Room Two."

"Frank will take you down there," Beck said looking at Dan.

Chapter Fifteen

LAURA AND DAN arrived at three interview rooms on the main floor, each with a large window built into the entry door. An attendant outside the rooms looked at a clipboard. "You're Jenkins?"

"Yes, and this is Messier."

"She's in Room 2 waiting for you. Do you want me to remove the cuffs?"

"Yes, please, if you would."

"Follow me."

The attendant unlocked Room Two and Laura and Dan entered to find the infamous Renata Sanchez sitting quietly at an interview table wearing a green short sleeve prison smock and matching loose fitting pants. Her hands were cuffed behind her back. She wore sandals with no socks. The attendant unlocked the handcuffs from behind and Sanchez put her hands on the table, rubbing her wrists. Laura saw marks about her wrists where the cuffs had been applied too tightly.

"Someone will be outside if you need help."

"Thank you," Dan replied with a nod.

The attendant closed the door behind him and stood outside the door. Laura looked around the stark room, light brown painted concrete block walls and a polished concrete floor. She glanced at the white ceiling tiles high above them. Florescent lights were recessed into the false ceiling. There must be listening devices above those tiles, she thought. She heard a faint hum coming from the overhead lights. They sat down at a small metal table opposite Sanchez and Dan stared at her for an uncomfortably long time. Sanchez stared right back with hate in her eyes. She ignored Laura. The lack of outside noise created additional tension. The room must be soundproof, she thought. Laura looked out the window in the door and saw the back of a guard.

Renata Sanchez wasn't an attractive woman. In her early 50s, short and overweight, she had blemishes on her face, bags underneath her eyes, and wore an angry expression. Her forearms had plenty of marks and her hands had a worn look to them. She must have a menial labor position at the prison. "Well, what do you want?" Sanchez finally said in Spanish. Laura interpreted the comment for Dan. He continued to stare at Sanchez without speaking. He lifted his briefcase onto the table and withdrew a thick stack of documents. After laying the documents on the table in front of him, he closed the briefcase and set it on the floor beside him.

"I've got better things to do than sit here," Sanchez said bitterly. "I want to go back to the cell. Guard!" she yelled. Again, Laura repeated the comment in English for Dan.

"Ms. Sanchez, you will sit here as long as I wish," Dan said unperturbed, in the calm, controlling tone of voice of a captor. Laura began to translate it to Spanish, but Sanchez put her hand up and Laura stopped, mid-sentence. Dan continued to stare.

Laura saw an opportunity to study the belligerent woman sitting across the table. She looked mentally unstable and dangerous. It's amazing to see a famous criminal in person, she thought. They looked like caged animals. Confined, yet still dangerous. She'd kill me if she had the chance.

Dan shifted his eyes to the documents and skimmed the pages while Sanchez continued to glare at him. Her anger appeared to increase as she squirmed in her chair and exhaled loudly. Dan finally withdrew a pen from his briefcase and scribbled notes in the margins of several pages.

After he laid the pen on the table beside the documents, he raised his eyes, pointed at the documents and said, "This is a federal criminal complaint against you." Sanchez chuckled as though the documents were unimportant.

"I don't know what you're talking about," Sanchez replied, this time in English. Dan slid one piece of paper across the table.

"The complaint arises from a letter you wrote and mailed from this prison. This is a copy. Your prints were found on the original."

Sanchez laughed in a cynical tone. "No, they're not. I didn't send no letter."

"Those prints are evidence of guilt. They are admissible in court."

"You're setting me up, just like last time. The American government is a criminal enterprise."

"You've committed a serious crime by threatening to kill someone. That's not to mention extortion and using the U.S. Postal Service to issue a capital threat."

"I told you," Sanchez said raising her voice, "I wrote no letter."

"Would you like to speak with an attorney?"

"I don't need an attorney for something I don't know about."

"Are you waiving your right to an attorney?"

"No."

"Are you willing to talk with us today without an attorney present?"

"Why would I talk to you?"

"Because I have the authority to make the complaint disappear. The recipient of the letter is sitting beside me," Dan said, gesturing toward Laura. "She might be willing to drop the charge. However, to do that, we need information from you. And we need it today. If you refuse to cooperate, you'll be convicted of another crime and likely remain in prison until you're in your 70s."

Dan's turning up the pressure, Laura thought. It's a credible threat.

Apparently, Sanchez thought so, too, staring at Dan. "What do you want?" she asked.

"Who's Derek Young?" Dan asked pointedly.

"Never heard of him."

"Ms. Sanchez, have you ever heard of a Supermax prison?"

Sanchez shrugged as though it was unimportant. "No."

"It's a new style of prison here in the United States. I'll make sure you're sent to one. Let me show you what the cells look like." Dan opened his briefcase again and withdrew a photo showing an empty cell, ten feet by eight feet, with just a sink, toilet and metal slab for a bed. "This would be your home, 23 hours per day, for the next ten years. It's total solitary confinement." He allowed her time to study the photo. "Is that what you want for yourself?"

Sanchez considered, for a moment, the risk of giving up a name. "Some people say Derek Young is a pilot. That's a rumor I heard."

"The flight that landed in the Bahamas with engine trouble. Where did it originate?"

"Where they all originate."

"Where is that?"

Sanchez rolled her eyes suggesting the absurdity of the question. "Do you always ask stupid questions?"

"The Dominican?"

"Aren't you supposed to be the FBI? You figure it out."

"Where?"

"Panama!" she said as though it were obvious. "Where else would it come from?"

"Out of Panama City?"

"There or maybe Colon."

"Who did the shipment belong to?"

"You think I know that?"

"Yes, I do."

"He's a dog," Sanchez said with disgust.

"Who are you referring to?"

"You accuse me of being a criminal and you make alliances with a dog? Your government's corrupt, not me."

"Give me a name."

Sanchez laughed. "The man you're in bed with. The man you call a friend. That's who. He preys on women and children; his thugs roam the streets killing and torturing people. You give him millions of dollars so you can sit safely in your homes and watch television while he starves his people."

Dan calmly waited for the diatribe to end. "A name please."

"Noriega!" she shouted as though it were common knowledge. "The blood he sheds drips invisibly from your hands." Dan's calmness was a stark disconnect from Sanchez's emotion. He waited for her outburst to pass.

"Noriega takes a cut, but the shipments belong to others. Who owned the shipment that arrived in the Bahamas?"

Sanchez shrugged. "I would be guessing to tell you."

"Then guess."

"In exchange for dropping the criminal complaint?"

"If the information is accurate, yes."

Sanchez pointed at Dan. "You cannot be trusted to keep your word. The worst criminal in the world has more integrity than the American government."

"I will put my promise in writing before we leave today."

Sanchez thought for a moment. "Malagua owned it."

"And it went through Noriega?"

"Yes."

"I need two names. The man who sent it from Panama and the man who would have received it here in the States."

A slight smile crept to Sanchez' face. "For that, I need a reduction in my sentence."

"I can't promise that, but I can ask."

Sanchez laughed out loud. "I want it in writing." Dan thought for a moment, scooted his chair back and slapped his hand on his knee.

"All right, let me see what I can do." Dan called to the guard who stuck his head in the door.

"Can I help you, Sir?"

"I need to return to the Warden's office for a few minutes. Can you keep her here until I return?" He asked, nodding at Sanchez.

"Of course, Sir." Dan turned to Laura. "If you have questions for her, now's the time."

Laura recognized the only one-on-one opportunity she'd ever get. "Are we audio recording the conversation today?"

"No," Dan replied.

"Then leave us."

Dan left the room, the guard closed the door behind him and two of the most dangerous women in the world faced each other across a table, mere inches from each other. On one side sat Renata Sanchez, the unquestioned head of all the Central and South American drug cartels. She had ordered thousands of innocent people murdered without remorse; so many that she'd been given the nickname the Brown Recluse. Her organization infiltrated the dark corners of cities around the world, weakening the fabric of societies and ruining the lives of millions of young people. Authorities were helpless to stop her. Renata Sanchez' infamy rivaled that of Al Capone.

On the other side sat Laura Messier, perhaps the world's greatest intelligence agent, someone on a first name basis with the President of the United States and Palestine Liberation Organization Chairman Yasser Arafat. Her specialty was killing face to face, often hand to hand, and even Muammar Gaddafi was afraid of her. She was, in fact, a living legend whose successes in intelligence operations were taught at the CIA's spy training facility outside Williamsburg, Virginia.

Chapter Sixteen

LAURA REACHED FOR her oversize purse and withdrew a pen, a small pad of paper and a checkbook laying them on the table. At the same time, unbeknown to Sanchez, she turned on a handheld tape recorder hidden in her bag. "So," she said to begin the conversation between the two of them, "I guess the government isn't recording this. Let's have a private chat, shall we?"

"You owe me 30 million dollars," Sanchez said bluntly.

"Would you take a check?"

"How you pay me is your problem. I want the money today or you're dead."

Laura opened her checkbook. "How do you spell your name?"

"Is this a joke?"

"No," Laura said. "I'll write you a check. How do you spell your first name?" She held the flap over the checkbook to hide the check.

"A check?"

"Well, I'd rather give you a check than be killed," Laura said nonchalantly. Sanchez didn't know whether to believe her. At that point, Laura wasn't sure her ploy would work. She gave it another try.

"Of course, if you don't want it, I'll put the checkbook away." She closed the book and started to return it to her purse.

"You don't have 30 million," Sanchez blurted out angrily.

"If you didn't think I could get it, you'd have killed me by now."

It was Sanchez' turn to smile. "In my world, people pay their debts. You pay or you're dead."

Laura began writing on the check. "In my world, bad people end up dead. Is Sanchez spelled the usual way?" Sanchez nodded. "I need you to tell me verbally. Please spell your name for me. Thirty million is a lot of money."

"R-E-N-A-T-A S-A-N-C-H-E-Z!" Sanchez was becoming visibly agitated not knowing whether to believe Laura.

"Thank you. What's the date today?"

"How the hell would I know? Every day's the same in this shithole." Laura called for the guard standing outside the door.

When he opened the door, before he could speak, Laura asked for the date.

"Friday, December 16th," he replied.

"Thank you. That's all I need."

"Yes, Ma'am."

When Laura had finished writing, she tore it from her checkbook and held it up for Sanchez to see. She'd written on the check in large letters, "FUCK YOU. YOU GET NOTHING."

"You need me to spell that out for you?" Laura asked.

Laura watched Sanchez' face turn beet red and her body tense. Its lucky Dan's left the room, she thought. This wouldn't have been possible in his presence. Here comes the explosion.

Sanchez screamed and lunged over the table trying to grab Laura by the throat. With cat like reflexes developed from years of martial arts training, Laura deftly grabbed Sanchez by one arm, stood and pulled her across the table. The table toppled and Sanchez fell forward as Laura gave ground and kept pulling. Sanchez ended up face down on the floor, arms flailing in an attempt to land a blow. Laura quickly put her boot on Sanchez' neck, pinned her head to the floor and twisted her arm to the breaking point. "Don't move," she said sharply.

The guard burst in, blew a whistle and two more guards came through the door instantaneously, surrounding Sanchez. "Let her go," the guard commanded Laura.

"With pleasure."

Two guards picked Sanchez up and forced her against the wall while the third guard set the table upright and straightened the chairs. "What happened," he asked.

"Ms. Sanchez decided she needed a little exercise," Laura said, shrugging off the incident. "That's all. No harm done." The guard spoke to his colleagues holding Sanchez. "Take her back to her cell."

"No, please. Director Jenkins hasn't returned yet. Can't you just cuff her to the chair?"

The guard mulled the request over. He nodded his head. "Okay," he said, reluctant to take the risk of leaving Sanchez in the room. Two guards forced Sanchez back into the chair, firmly cuffing her hands behind her, and her legs to the front chair legs.

"I'll have to write an incident report to the warden," the head guard said sharply to Sanchez.

"Fuck you!" Sanchez shouted at the guards. "I don't care."

"Calm down. You want a week in isolation?"

Laura interceded. "This is my fault. Ms. Sanchez became overly excited by the conversation. I'm sure things are fine."

The guard glared at Laura. "It's not your decision," he said sharply.

Laura recognized she'd overstepped her authority. "You're right. I'm sorry."

The guard turned again to Sanchez. "Three of us will be outside. No more nonsense out of you." All three guards filed out, slammed the door and the two women were alone again.

Chapter Seventeen

"YOU'LL BE DEAD within the hour," Sanchez hissed.

Laura laughed off the threat. "You think so?"

"You and your friend," she said louder, still in a rage.

"What about my friend?"

"You heard me. Both of you are dead."

The last statement was exactly what Laura needed to leverage Sanchez' cooperation. She picked her purse off the floor and removed the tape recorder. "I can turn this off now. I've gotten what I need."

Sanchez was stunned, realizing she'd been tricked into making threats. She sat staring at the recorder, assessing the damage she'd done to herself.

Laura continued. "You just committed two felonies. Attacking me and threatening the life of a government official. If I give this to my FBI friend," she said nodding at the recorder, "you'll never get out of prison. You'll be a lifer in that Supermax." Laura paused to allow the full impact of her words to take effect. Laura grew serious. "This is really simple. I need information," she demanded. "If you lie, my friend gets the recording. Now, who was the shipment for?" Sanchez shook her head violently.

"You get nothing unless I get the tape." She motioned with her hand. "Give it to me." Laura slid the tape recorder across the table but didn't release it.

"Answer my questions and you can have it." Sanchez' demeanor changed instantly.

"Since you'll be dead within the hour, what's the harm," Sanchez said with a sardonic smile. "Diego Marty." Laura released the recorder and Sanchez grabbed it. She pushed inside her sleeve and folded her fingers over top to secure it.

"Where can I find him?" Sanchez smiled and waved her other hand with a sweeping motion.

"He's around. You never know, he might find you."

"You told my friend the shipment came from Colon or Panama City. Where did it really come from?"

Sanchez hesitated, then shrugged. "Dead people can't use information, so I'll tell you. Yavisa." Laura watched Sanchez break out into a grin, as though she'd just shared a secret that would never be known. "Are you happy now?" she asked cynically.

"See how easy that was," Laura replied with a smile. "We're done."

"Except you haven't made your funeral arrangements," Sanchez said to save face.

Laura looked annoyed. "Pardon me if I'm not frightened by an overweight, old woman in prison."

"You should be," Sanchez hissed.

Laura leaned over the table and smiled in the sardonic fashion she used when facing killers. "I want you to know something. When you're released, I'll be waiting."

Sanchez' face turned red and she began cursing in Spanish. Laura cursed her back in South American accented Spanish. That surprised Sanchez. She stopped to listen to the perfect pronunciation. Laura recognized the impression the dialect made.

"That's right," Laura continued. "You'll never see me coming." Sanchez gave her a malevolent smile.

"I'll tell my men to piss on your grave, bitch."

Dan opened the door without knocking, interrupting the conversation. He stood in the doorway and looked at Laura. "I heard what happened. Are you okay?" He walked into the room and sat down.

Laura laughed. "I'm fine, Dan. Really, I am." She gestured toward Sanchez, "Renata and I were just getting to know each other."

Dan turned to Sanchez. "I have a document to show you. It's a promise by the federal prosecutor in South Florida to put a reduction of your sentence before the court. It's the best I can do on short notice." He pushed the document across the table. "Now, I'd like you to provide names."

While Sanchez read the document, Laura leaned toward Dan. "There's no need. We had a nice chat, and she gave me what we needed."

"She did?" He asked, not quite believing Laura.

"Everything," Laura said flatly.

Sanchez slid the document back toward Dan. "I accept." She glanced at Laura. "You remember what I told you."

"You remember what I told you, too," Laura replied. "The promise I made will be kept," Laura paused to add that sardonic smile again, "for as long as I live."

Sanchez smiled at that. "Which won't be very long."

Dan reacted immediately. "Is that a threat, Ms. Sanchez?"

Laura interceded on Sanchez' behalf. "No, Dan. There's no threat. Renata and I have come to an understanding."

Dan looked at Sanchez. "Threats against the life of anyone will be met with the harshest of penalties. Do you understand?"

Laura answered again, for Sanchez. "I think she understands that."

"I want her to say it."

"Let it go, Dan." She slid the document back toward Sanchez. "You keep that."

Dan looked confused.

"I have a high degree of confidence," Laura continued, "that the information Renata shared is accurate. Why don't we let Ms. Sanchez return to her cell. She's had enough excitement for one day."

Dan still looked confused. "All right," he said. "I'm trusting you."

"Thank you," Laura replied. "Go ahead and call the guard."

Chapter Eighteen

THE COM SYSTEM erupted with a flurry of commentary as soon as Laura and Dan were visible outside the prison.

"Laura's outside, people," Rick said. "I've got her walking toward the parking lot. Sharp?"

"I've got movement in the trees. The shooters look like they're getting ready to fire."

"Don't let them get a shot off. I repeat, don't allow them to shoot."

"As soon as they lift their weapons, they're dead meat."

"Pierre? What's your position?"

"I'm at the head of the driveway behind a bush."

"Can you see the black sedan?"

"I've got it."

"The two men sitting in the car are my targets if they exit the vehicle," Rick said. "If they drive away, they're yours."

"Roger that."

From the tree line, Andres and Mateo watched Laura exit the building. Andres turned his head toward Mateo. "There she is."

"Wait until she gets a little closer. We've only got one chance."

"Okay," Andres replied. Both men lifted their rifles to peer through the scopes.

Inside the black sedan, Julian and David had come to full alert. "You see what I see?" Julian asked. David picked up the photo.

"That's her, all right." He laid the photo aside. "We gotta wait and see if Andres and Mateo take her down."

"If they can't, be ready to jump out and nail that bitch."

Laura swung her head back and forth, looking for danger as she began walking down the sidewalk. "You're awfully quiet," Dan said. "Something on your mind?"

"No, not really."

"What are you looking around for?" Dan chuckled. "An inmate escape?"

"Just concerned about the guards on her payroll. You never know."

"It'd be suicide to try something at the prison."

Laura gave him a hard, cold look. "As I said, you never know."

"Rick, these assholes have raised their guns," Sharp said. "I have to fire."

"Fire at will."

Even with a suppressor, the sharp crack of Sharp's rifle could be heard by Rick in the parking lot across the street. Andres' head exploded as he slumped over, the victim of a sharpshooter who could hit a target within an inch at 600 yards. Mateo heard the shot and raised up to look behind him. That gave Sharp the shot he was looking for. He was ready, squeezing off another round that caught Mateo in the face. He slumped over, dead instantly.

"Shooters down," Sharp said into the coms.

Dan heard the shots and froze for a brief second. "Shots fired, Laura. Come on!" He took Laura by the arm and they made a dash toward their car.

"Shit, they missed," Julian said. "Kill them, David. Both of them. No witnesses." David climbed out of the car and cupped his pistol with his other hand to get better aim.

Rick reacted immediately. He jumped out, aimed at the man and didn't hesitate. He fired. David was struck in the back and slumped over against his car. Rick fired twice more to make sure the man was incapacitated. David collapsed on the pavement, still alive, but barely.

Julian watched his friend fall and made an instant decision to flee. He started the car and pulled out toward the exit, tires burning rubber on the pavement. Rick emptied his clip, one shot after another, as it pulled away. Julian put his head down and headed straight across the lawn.

"He's coming right at you," Rick said to Pierre in the com. Rick took another clip from his belt, reloaded, and hopped back into the car to follow the fleeing sedan.

"I got him," Pierre replied. The sedan came straight toward Pierre as he began firing, first through the windshield, then through the grill. When his clip was empty, the former French soldier reloaded with lightning speed and began firing again. The car careened one way, then the other, as Julian drove blindly trying to avoid the fire and make his way to the road. He peeked above the dashboard and saw the man firing at him. Shots whistled past Julian's head as shards of glass fell around him. Smoke began wafting up from the engine compartment. Julian floored the accelerator pedal, spinning the back wheels, churning up grass and dirt as he increased his speed across the lawn. Rick followed a couple of hundred yards behind.

Dan forced Laura to the ground where they lay in a prone position, lifting their heads to watch the firefight. "They're not shooting at us," Laura said. "Let me up." Dan released her and they climbed to their knees to watch Julian, who by some miracle remained unhurt, pull his sedan out onto the roadway and drive away.

Guards poured out of the prison with guns drawn, too late to fire at Julian, but in plenty of time to shoot at Rick's trailing car. Rick pulled up to Pierre, who hunched over and dove in the back seat as shots flicked off the exterior of the car. "Hold on," Rick shouted as he pulled into traffic straight across the road as soon as Pierre slammed the door shut. Cars traveling in both directions steered away from a collision, spinning out and stopping in the roadway. Traffic blocked the guard's view of Rick's car. They stopped firing to avoid hitting innocent parties and watched Rick pull into the service station where Sharp jumped off the overhead roof at the gas pumps onto Rick's car, then onto the ground and entered the front passenger seat.

"Let's get the fuck out of here," Rick said with the hint of a smile.

"Is she okay?" Sharp asked.

"Completely unhurt. They didn't even get a shot off."

"Good. We're gone," Sharp replied.

Rick pulled out of the station and headed in the same direction as Julian, swerving around cars that had stopped in the roadway. A few blocks away, they approached a second service station where Julian had pulled in to steal a car at the gas pumps. He was fighting with a patron pumping gas.

"There's that bastard," Pierre said. "Stop, Rick."

Rick pulled into the service station near Julian's car. Rick handed Sharp his pistol. "Take this!"

Sharp got out and calmly walked up behind Julian, hiding the pistol behind his back. He shot Julian point blank in the back of the head. Looking at the frightened customer, he smiled and said, "Drive safely and have a nice day."

"But, but …," the shocked customer said.

"Him?" Sharp interrupted, looking down at Julian's corpse. "He was an asshole. He deserved it."

He walked back to Rick's car and they pulled back into traffic as the first sirens began to sound behind them.

Rick slowed down to flow with traffic. "What the fuck are you doing?" Sharp demanded. "Get your ass going."

"We're much harder to find if we act normal." He stole a peek at his watch. "We'll be at the airport in fifteen minutes. Dmitri has the plane on standby. We'll be in the air in less than thirty. Once we're out over the ocean, we're home free."

Back at the prison, guards ran down the sidewalk to help Laura and Dan to their feet. "Are you all right, Ma'am?" one guard asked Laura.

"We're fine," she replied, moving his head back and forth looking for shooters. "Just a few scrapes from the sidewalk." Laura and Dan brushed the dirt from their clothing.

Chapter Nineteen

BY THE TIME Laura had finished a round of police interviews at the prison, Dmitri's Falcon 50 was well out over the Gulf of Mexico. Rick walked back to the small fridge in the galley and pulled out a bottle of champagne. He grabbed plastic cups and poured each man a cup. "A toast to the mission, boys. You were fantastic today!" The men lifted their glasses and the mood changed from one of concern to one of celebration. "Our first mission inside the U.S.," Rick observed.

"We got out clean, too" Pierre said, "except for the bullet holes in the rental car."

"Can you imagine what the rental car company will think seeing those bullet holes?" Rick said, laughing. They'd left the rental in the airport lot and called the agency to tell them where they'd parked. "They'll try to find the renter, a man named Herman Smith from Virginia Beach. We gotta get Postl to give us better names. Herman Smith? Come on, what kind of name is that?"

"You forgot about the dent in the roof where fatty landed," Pierre said with a laugh. "You really should lose some weight, Sharp."

"Damn, and I was just about to ask Svetlana for a sandwich."

"Just kidding, Sharp. Those were two great shots you made."

"Under pressure, too," Rick added. "Really nice job, Sharp."

"Thanks. Now, where's Lana? She makes a great turkey club."

Dan drove Laura back to the airport where he insisted she accompany him back to D.C. "There's no way I'm letting you out of my sight until we're on the ground in D.C." Laura knew she'd lose the argument.

"I'm fine, Dan, really I am. Besides, I've got my plane here."

"Don't argue. You're coming with me. It's not safe here."

Laura laughed. "Okay. I give up."

Dan re-booked a return flight for both of them and waiting at the gate, they watched a local television special report.

"This is Maria Gomez reporting outside FCI Tallahassee on Capitol Boulevard where a shooting has occurred this morning that left four men dead. A press conference is underway. Let's go to the conference now." (The camera focuses on two men speaking from a podium on the steps outside the prison.)

"Good afternoon. I'm Assistant Tallahassee Police Commissioner Randall Jackson and with me is Warden John Beck of FCI Tallahassee who will brief the press on the events of today. Warden Beck?"

"This morning, an attempted escape was made here at the prison. I want to stress that no inmate escaped the prison and the public was never in danger. However, during the attempt, four suspects assisting in the escape attempt were killed outside the prison. Three were killed by our prison security staff and a fourth man was killed by the Tallahassee Police Department a few blocks away. The suspects have not been identified yet, but I want to stress, again, that no inmate escaped the prison and the public is completely safe. At this time, I'd be happy to take questions."

"That doesn't sound like the incident we witnessed," Laura said, standing with Dan in line to board the plane.

"The guards didn't kill anyone," Dan responded. "And it didn't look like an escape, either. It looked more like an ambush."

"An ambush?" Laura asked. "Who was the target?"

Dan scratched his head and shrugged his shoulders. "I suspect it was us."

"No one shot at us, though."

"That's because there were two groups of shooters. The second group was there to eliminate the first group. Did you have a team there today?"

"Me?" Laura asked, surprised.

Dan gave her a suspicious look and then asked the question Laura knew was coming. "Did you have advance intel about an attack?"

Laura sounded surprised. "You're kidding, right? How could I know about an ambush in advance?"

"It's not like you to travel without some kind of back-up."

"Dan, who would mount an attack at a prison? You said it yourself. It'd be suicide."

"Apparently, the second team had a sharpshooter on the roof of the gas station across the street. He had to be ex-military. Those shots were too precise."

Laura smiled. "I'm going to leave the investigating to you, Dan."

Dan chuckled and shook his head. "That's the first time I've ever heard you say that."

Laura shrugged. "First time for everything."

"Walk with me a minute." Dan took her to the far end of the gate where the seats were vacant. "What did Sanchez tell you?"

"She gave me a name. Diego Marty. Ever heard of him?" Dan nodded.

"He's Miami's biggest drug dealer. He's been on our watch list for some time."

"What do you know about him?"

"He runs a nightclub called the Hacienda in the Little Havana district. We believe he runs his entire operation out of the club."

"Why don't you raid it?" Dan sighed.

"The South Florida office did, and they embarrassed the hell out of themselves. We suspect Marty was tipped off by the Miami police. They found nothing but bar receipts. The place was clean. Marty ended up filing a suit against the FBI for harassment."

"Do you have him under surveillance?"

"No. We were forced to back off after the raid."

"But you have a file on him." Dan spread his thumb and index finger apart.

"About this thick."

"Can I take a look at it?" Dan laughed and gave her an amused look.

"You know better than to ask that." The boarding announcement blared over the speaker system. Dan handed Laura her ticket. "Come on, we're in the first boarding group."

Chapter Twenty

Saturday, December 17, 1988

DIEGO MARTY FIRST learned the fate of his four men from television. He thought they might have taken their time getting back, perhaps stopping overnight somewhere; however, when they weren't back by the afternoon, he knew something had gone awry. He reacted with shock watching the newscaster describe the four victims, two were friends from childhood. Shock turned to fear as he wondered where Sanchez would put the blame. What could he do? He had sent his best men. Someone knew they'd be there. That's the only explanation. He brought the two remaining lieutenants to his office the following evening.

"Who knew they'd be there?" Diego demanded to know. Neither Luis nor Santiago had any idea.

"Diego, nobody knew," Luis replied, "except us."

"Did somebody say something inside the club?"

"We don't talk business in the club," Santiago replied. "You know that. David called Andres and Mateo after our meeting; they met Julian out back and the four of them left the same night. Nobody said anything to anyone."

"Is the office bugged?"

"I don't know how it could be. Nobody comes in here except you. The office is the same as it's always been. Maybe the leak didn't come from here. Maybe it came from the prison."

Diego thought for a moment. "Possibly. The warden knew of the meeting. I need to find out how this happened. In the meantime, I need you to cover for Julian and David. Can you split up their territory?"

Santiago and Luis looked at each other. "Sure. I don't see why not," Luis replied. "We'll work it out between us. It'll get done."

"That's what I wanted to hear. Give some thought about who we can promote. Look around. Find men we can trust. And we need more security. More guards at the club, more guarding the shipments; hell, even when we're traveling around the city. We have to protect ourselves."

"We'll get on it right away," Santiago said.

"Let's get to work." After his men left, Diego picked up the phone and dialed a private number.

Renata Sanchez's cell at FCI Tallahassee was out of the ordinary. It was more like a small hotel room, with carpeting, a desk with a lamp, a recliner which rested in front of a large television and a comfortable single bed. There were no bars, just a large window into the room and beside it a door which was kept unlocked. Sanchez had a phone, a private outside line. It was the only cell to have one. She'd sent a bribe of one million dollars to have it installed and guards were paid to overlook it. Every few months, the prison would sweep the rooms for contraband and the phone would be removed. It would be back the next day after another million dollars in unmarked bills was delivered to the appropriate party. It was this phone that rang.

"Yes?" Sanchez asked.

"Who did this?" Diego asked without revealing his name.

"I read the police report today. It says, 'unknown assailants.'"

"Who knew it was going down?"

"No one. The woman brought protection with her. I made a call today and found out about her. She's a spy."

"A spy?"

"She used to work for the CIA. She has a reputation."

"Why would the CIA be involved?" Diego asked.

"I don't think they were. The woman did this on her own."

"How can she take down an entire team of shooters and get away clean?"

"She's a pro."

"A pro what?"

"A professional assassin. I wondered why she didn't seem scared in our meeting. Now, I know.

"What do you want us to do?"

"You need to hire more people. Ex-military if you can find them. They need to be good. This thing isn't over."

"Okay."

Chapter Twenty-One

Thursday, December 29th, 1988

THE MAN IN dark clothing walked out onto the pier and checked yacht after yacht until he found the one he searched for, a large 60-footer named 'Manatee.' It took a while, at 3:00 am the slips were full. It was, after all, Christmas week. The pier was mostly vacant, save for a few people sleeping on their yachts, but their cabin lights had long been extinguished. At the far end of the pier where the man stood, there was little light and the slow lapping of waves against the hulls was the only sound he heard. The man looked around, saw no one, and climbed aboard. The cabin was locked, but it opened easily with a screwdriver and a small amount of force. Once inside, he found the engine compartment and placed a small amount of C-4 explosive on a timer near the engine. He set the timer to count down from 20 minutes, watched it count down for a few seconds and once he was sure the bomb would explode, left the yacht and sauntered back up the dock without a care in the world. His job was finished. He climbed in his rental car and stopped a few blocks away to watch the explosion. The mix of C-4 and combustible elements in the engine produced a vicious explosion which could be seen for miles against the dark background of the ocean. Pleased with his success, he calmly pulled back on the roadway and headed toward Miami Beach to meet his colleagues.

Chapter Twenty-Two

LAURA AND JEAN sat in the living room of a swanky Miami Beach suite Jean had booked for the night. "This is a terrible idea," he said.

"Nonsense," Laura replied. "We've got them on the defensive. They're not accustomed to people fighting back. If we attack now, we can cripple them."

"Kill the man at his headquarters? Right where he's strongest?"

"They won't expect it. It's what the Russians would do."

Jean cocked his head and thought about the KGB. "Mademoiselle, the Russians plan their operations well. With all respect, you don't have a plan, you have an idea. We must be careful doing operations in the States. You know that."

"I can't take the chance they're going to hit us again, Jean. Everyone's at risk."

Jean Broussard was the elder statesman of Laura's team with decades of experience in undercover operations. It wasn't often these days he found himself doing field work, but Laura thought he'd be perfect for this. An older man on holiday with a younger wife, visiting Miami from Europe.

"Let's go over your idea one more time."

"Your job is to get me inside the club," Laura began. "Once I make contact with the target, excuse yourself to use the restroom and you're done. Make your way back to the hotel, check out and take a taxi to the airport where you'll meet Dmitri. Rick and I will handle the rest."

"I've never seen you in such a rush, Mademoiselle."

"If we wait, these people will reorganize."

"Let's assume your ruse at the club works and you gain access to the man. What then? You could find yourself alone and outnumbered. It takes months for someone on the inside to gain the trust of an organization. Rick has been there a matter of days."

"Diego Marty, no matter how intelligent he may be, is still a street thug. His focus is day-to-day drug sales. He fills his vacancies quickly and most of the men he hires are incompetent. That's how Rick has established himself quickly."

"I do hope you're correct about that because our lives depend on it." Jean gave up trying to persuade her. He knew her to be like many women he'd met in life. Once they've made up their mind, trying to convince them otherwise was a waste of time. "If you insist, I'll go back to my room and prepare."

"Let's meet downstairs in two hours."

Jean watched Laura walk through in the hotel lobby two hours later having completely transformed herself. She's a chameleon, he thought, an artist of disguise. From the way her dress sways as she walks, she's reminiscent of a flamenco dancer. Dressed in a long flowered skirt, matching tight top and heels, she appeared as a blond and wore heavy dramatic make-up to hide her identity. Jean, on the other hand, having been behind the scenes so far, wore his usual evening attire, a turtle-neck pullover and a sports jacket.

"Need a date, Mister?" she asked mischievously.

"Very nice disguise, Mademoiselle," Jean replied. "You're wearing enough perfume to choke a horse, but I suppose that's part of your strategy." Laura laughed.

"It's a bit flamboyant, Jean, I know, but none of this works unless I attract Marty's eye. I'm putting on a show this evening."

"Oh dear," Jean replied, wondering what she'd not told him.

Together, they walked outside and hailed a taxi. The driver knew of The Hacienda and after a lengthy drive in Miami traffic, he dropped them at its entrance on a busy block in the Little Havana section of the city. A line for entry stretched outside the club for half a block. Diego Marty had instructed his men to view the line and admit the most beautiful women first. It only took a few moments before a burly, rough looking thug walked up and tapped Jean on the shoulder. "Follow me, please." He led them to the front door where Jean offered to pay the entry fee. The guard shook his head. "No, Sir. It's on the house."

The Hacienda was an old-style club, reminiscent of the forties, with a nightly floor show and tables placed on the main floor around the performance area. The open space served as a dance floor later in the evening. A railing separated the main floor from a raised section with cocktail tables ringing the upper section along the railing. Waiters scurried back and forth between tables serving patrons from bars placed along the walls. The office and kitchen areas were at the rear, separated from the club by a swinging double door. Beyond the doors, at the end of the hallway, next to the rear exit, Diego kept an office. Diego often used the rear exit in the evening when the club was crowded.

Rick Williams had applied for a position on Diego's security staff a few days ago and Rick's muscular 6'5" frame hastened his hire. He interviewed with Luis who liked Rick's military background and thought he'd be a perfect hire. His first evening on the job, Rick endeared himself to the staff by breaking up a fight between two drunk young men. Rick lifted both men by the scruff of their collars and threw them over the sidewalk and into the street.

"Shit, man, that guy's got some chops," Luis said to Diego as both watched Rick in action. "He's one tough dude."

"I like him," Diego said. "Let him get his feet wet for a few weeks before we move him up."

Laura and Jean were taken to a table down front where the maître d' moved tables around to accommodate them. It was a tight fit, but Diego liked beautiful women to be visible. The floor show ended for the evening and the dance floor was quickly filling.

"Rick, you read me?" Laura said into the com.

"Roger."

"I'm attempting contact with the target." Laura leaned over and whispered to Jean. "Ready?"

"Of course, Mademoiselle. Remember, if contact isn't possible, don't push it. We'll try another evening."

Jean led Laura to the dance floor where they began dancing in a flamenco style. Laura, an accomplished dancer from her time working undercover in Jean's Paris nightclub, began a series of spins and kicks while swashing her skirt in all directions. Jean was the perfect partner and as he showcased the gorgeous Laura, the crowd moved into a ring about them while the orchestra slipped into a traditional flamenco tune. Diego, sitting in the front row, couldn't help but notice. He stood smiling, applauding every move. He walked over to one of the bars where he retrieved a pair of finger cymbals, interrupted them on the dance floor and gave them to Laura. "You're missing these, my lady," he said with a bow.

"Thank you, kind Sir," she replied as the slipped them on her fingers.

Laura and Jean danced like professionals, except Jean had a bit of trouble lifting Laura at the appropriate moments. Diego, seeing Jean struggle with a lift, interceded. "Do you mind?" he asked.

Jean laughed. "Please," he said bowing and extending his hand. "Sometimes, she needs a younger partner."

Diego took Laura's hand and wheeled her around the dance floor. He knew all the traditional moves the male used to showcase a female partner. When he lifted Laura completely above his head, she balanced herself perfectly and extended her arms, smiling at the crowd which roared its approval. After the music finished, Diego led her back to Jean's table where he stood over them and introduced himself.

"Allow me to introduce myself. I'm Diego Marty, owner of this establishment. It's nice to have you with us this evening. I've not had the pleasure of your acquaintance." Jean stood and bowed slightly.

"I am Renaldo Christano and this," he said motioning to Laura, "is my lovely wife, Valencia. We are on holiday from Lisbon." Diego recognized the Portuguese language immediately and switched.

"Ah, the language of my youth," he said smiling. "My ancestors were from Portugal."

That much Jean had learned from an investigation of Diego before the mission. Jean relied on the notion that the art of establishing trust depended on a connection to the past and innocent coincidences were persuasive. Diego pulled a chair close and sat down.

"We are visiting America for the first time," Jean explained. He'd previously contacted French Intelligence in Paris, who'd sent him the appropriate documentation, including passports for both of them.

"What are your business interests in Lisbon?"

Jean shrugged as though it was unimportant. "I am an exporter of exquisite wines from our great wine growing regions. I ship them all over the world." Jean withdrew a business card from his billfold and handed it to Diego, who studied it with interest. "I specialize in fine ports and sherries."

"That's something we have little of here at the club." He gestured toward Jean with the card in his hand. "I'll give this to my manager and have him contact you. Our customers might enjoy a fine Portuguese port after dinner." Jean beamed as though he'd just engaged a new client.

"When we return home, I'll ship you a case of my finest product for your inspection, my own private label. All complimentary, of course."

Diego nodded, pleased at the special treatment. "I'd be most grateful. Now, if you'd allow me, I'd like to take your lovely wife back to the dance floor."

"Of course," Jean said, smiling.

"My lady," Diego said extending a hand.

Laura, who'd played the part of a demure wife perfectly, looked in Diego's eyes. "I'd be happy to dance with you, Sir."

"Please call me Diego."

"And I am Valencia."

He led her back to the dance floor where Laura showed off the artistry she'd learned in Paris to the obvious enjoyment of Diego, who couldn't take his eyes off her. Meanwhile, Jean, whose job was finished for the evening, headed toward the restroom and after that, a discreet exit.

After an extended dance number, Laura feigned tiredness and begged Diego for a rest. "Where did your husband go?" Diego asked walking back to their table.

"He's either in the restroom or he's retreated to the hotel." Jean left a note on a paper napkin explaining that he'd gone back to the hotel and inside the napkin was a hundred-dollar bill for a taxi ride.

"It seems he's left you," Diego said, reading the note.

Laura laughed the comment off. "He often wishes to leave before I'm ready, so we have a small arrangement. I stay and enjoy myself while he goes home. This is one of the risks of marrying an older man."

"Perhaps you need a younger man in your life."

"Younger men have yet to acquire the assets necessary to be comfortable," she said with a wry smile. "So, Renaldo and I keep this small compromise."

Diego relished the prospect of a closer look at Laura. "Would the lady be comfortable resting somewhere more private," Diego hesitated, "while I arrange for a car to take you back to the hotel?"

Laura rested her hand on Diego's arm and smiled. "You're most kind, Diego."

Diego led her across the dance floor, through the double doors to the back of the building. He let Laura into his office and motioned toward a leather sofa. "A place to relax." He picked up his desk phone and made a brief call. Laura heard Rick's voice in the com. "I've followed you to the office. I'm standing in the hallway."

Luis came through the double doors walking briskly down the hall. "Rick?"

"Yes, Sir."

"What are you doing? You're supposed to be out in the club."

"I saw the boss bring someone to his office. I followed to make sure he's safe."

Luis nodded. "You want to prove yourself? The boss has a job for you."

"Anything. Name it."

Luis knocked on Diego's door and stuck his head in. "I've got someone to help you, Diego."

"Send him in."

Luis looked at Rick. "Go on in."

Rick entered to find Laura on the sofa and Diego sitting behind his desk.

"Ah, yes, Rick."

"Yes, Sir."

"I've got a job for you." Diego pulled a pistol from a drawer and pointed it at Laura. "This woman is a problem. I need you to get rid of her."

Rick looked at Laura. "Sorry, Ma'am. If you'd follow me, please." He reached for her arm.

"That's not what I had in mind, Rick. I don't want you to remove her from the club."

"I don't understand."

"I want you to kill her." He turned the gun around, so the grip faced Rick. "Use this. Do it out back in the alley. Throw her body in the dumpster." Diego saw indecision in Rick's face. "Is there a problem?"

"No, Sir."

"This is how my men prove themselves."

Rick took the gun and pointed it at Laura. "I'm sorry, Ma'am. You'll have to come with me," he said.

Laura stood while Diego leaned back in his chair with a satisfying smile. "This is what happens when you fuck with me, Laura Messier. I never forget a face."

Rick handed the gun to Laura who pointed it straight at Diego. "No sudden movements, no screams. Put your hands on top of the desk." Diego was shocked. "Now!" she said tensely. Laura and Rick saw panic in his face. He glanced at his phone. "No, no," she admonished. "Don't get clever. Clever gets you killed. Be calm and you just might live through the night. Now, do exactly as I say. Hands on the desktop." Diego reluctantly cooperated. He didn't see how he could reach his phone before she pulled the trigger.

"Rick, dig into my purse. I've got a role of duct tape inside." She saw Diego's eyes shift to Rick. "Diego, look at me." She moved to the edge of his desk opposite him and pointed the gun at his face, just out of Diego's reach. "Look at me," she said louder. Diego looked back at her. "Don't look at Rick. Do exactly as I tell you. Anything else and your life is over right here, right now."

Rick found the duct tape and taped Diego's wrists together. "Diego!" she said emphatically. "Look at me. Don't get ideas in that head of yours." Rick raised Diego up and taped his mouth shut.

"Sharp," Rick said into the com, "are you there?"

"Yep."

"Bring the car into the alley behind the club."

"Roger that."

Rick took Diego by the arm and walked him toward the door with Laura following. She had the barrel of the pistol resting on the back of Diego's neck where he could feel it. Rick looked back at Laura. "Hang on a minute." Rick stepped into the hallway where Luis stood at the opposite end near the double doors.

"Luis?" He asked walking toward him.

"Everything okay in there?"

"Diego's got a woman back there he wants me to get rid of. Can you stand outside the double doors to make sure no one gets back here?"

"Sure." He turned to walk through the doors, then turned back. "Don't do it in the building, Rick. Take her outside in the alley." Rick waited until Luis had gone through the doors. He stepped back into the room.

"We're clear."

"Let's get going, Diego," Laura whispered in his ear. "Stay real quiet. We don't want a shoot-out in your club. You'll be the first to die. Follow Rick." Outside in the alley, Sharp was waiting. He got out and opened the trunk. Sharp looked at Diego.

"In you go, asshole." Sharp pushed Diego into the trunk.

"Duct tape his feet, Rick," Laura said. After Diego's feet were firmly taped together, Laura leaned into the trunk.

"If I hear you moving around, I'll stop and shoot your ass. I'll throw you in the swamp and let you bleed out." Diego looked at her with fear in his eyes. Laura smiled the hard, cold smile of an assassin who'd captured her prey. Sharp slammed the trunk lid closed and the three of them hopped in and drove away.

Chapter Twenty-Three

"DID YOU RENT the storage locker?" She asked Sharp. "It's near the airport."

"How about the equipment I asked for?"

Sharp nodded toward the back. "Already in the locker."

"Good work. Let's head there now."

Forty minutes later, Sharp pulled into a storage facility which had closed for the evening. Sharp used a key card to gain entrance and they drove past rows of garage doors until Sharp found the row he looked for. It was difficult to see in the low light, but Sharp finally pulled up to the locker and stopped. "This is it." He got out, looked around for anyone who might be watching, then opened the padlock.

Rick glanced around at the awnings, the roof, up and down the aisle. "What about security cameras?"

Sharp pointed down the aisle. "One at each end. They're disabled."

"Okay, let's get this prick out."

Rick and Sharp lifted Diego from the trunk. "Heavy fucker, isn't he?" Sharp said.

"Yep. A dead weight. Uh ... figuratively that is."

"Soon to be real dead," Sharp said. Diego looked at him. "You hear that, fuckhead? I hope she burns your ass."

Laura walked inside to find Sharp had set up an impromptu interrogation room, complete with a table, two chairs and a flood light affixed to a boom. "Set him in the chair, Rick" she said pointing to one of the chairs, "and tape his hands to the table, palms down." Laura moved the light behind her and turned it onto Diego's face. The light blinded him, and he turned his head away. "You'll get used to it, Diego," Laura said. "We're going to remove the tape from your mouth. I'm warning you; screams annoy me." Rick ripped the tape from Diego's mouth.

"Fuck!" Diego said, feeling the pain of the adhesive pulling at his facial stubble.

"That hurt?" Laura said with a smirk. "We haven't even begun yet." Diego didn't answer. He stared at her with a mixture of defiance and hate. Laura smiled, seeing Diego's expression. "You'll lose that look."

"Fuck you!"

Laura rolled her eyes in an expression of sarcasm. "Oh, you're a tough guy, huh. Sharp, hand me the hammer out of the bag." She held the claw hammer up for Diego to see. "Would you like the hammer?" she asked before spinning the hammer in her hand, "or the claw? Your choice." Diego said nothing. Laura slammed the hammer down on Diego's right hand. He screamed in agony. She waited until the screams became a whimper. "You're weak, Diego, very, very weak. Do you want me to do the other hand, so they match?" Diego said nothing.

Laura turned to Sharp. "Give Diego some water, would you?" Sharp removed a small plastic bottle of water, jerked Diego's head back by the hair and poured water into his mouth.

"I'm going to ask you a series of questions, Diego. You lie; I give you this." She held up the hammer. "I can make you a cripple, so be smart. Are you ready?" Diego remained silent.

"Perhaps you need more persuasion." She lifted the hammer to strike Diego's other hand.

"Wait!" he shouted.

"I asked you if you're ready." Laura looked impatient. "I don't have a lot of time. If you want to die protecting your sources, let's do it now. Sharp, hand me the P226." Sharp dug the pistol out of the bag, screwed the suppressor onto the barrel and handed it to her. She pointed the weapon at Diego. "One more time, are you ready?" Sharp and Rick knew she was serious and Diego, watching her handle the pistol, was convinced of it.

"Yes," he replied.

"Sanchez has turned on you. She's given up your entire organization."

"That fucking bitch," Diego said under his breath.

"Confirm your home address, please."

"14412 Formosa."

"Correct. Your wife and two children are there now?"

"If you touch my family, we will never rest until you're dead."

"That's not what I asked you." Laura raised the hammer and brought it down hard on his left hand. Diego screamed, grimacing from the pain.

"Is you family at home right now? Answer!"

Diego struggled to free himself of the restraints. "Yes," he managed to say under extreme stress.

"I know. I've got two men sitting outside your house. One call from me and they're dead." That was a lie, but a believable one.

"Please! Leave them alone," Diego said as the pain subsided. "They're innocent."

"I'm surprised no one's threatened your family before."

"Please," Diego begged.

"Can we make an agreement then? I don't touch your family and you stop trying to kill me?"

"Yes."

"If you break the agreement, I'll come back, and I'll kill everyone. You, your family, your friends. Everyone."

"You have my word."

"The word of a drug dealer? Why should I believe you?"

"It wasn't my choice to attack you. Sanchez forced me to do it."

"I want to tell you something. Look at me so you know it's the truth." She leaned forward across the table, so their faces were only inches apart. She slapped him with an open hand and screamed, "Look at me!" He brought his eyes up to face her. "You attacked a professional killer." She waited a moment to heighten the effect of her words. "That's right. I kill people for a living. And I've got an organization just like you do. Believe me, you can't stop us."

Diego looked at her expression and knew she spoke the truth.

"The lives of your family depend on your next answers." She let that comment resonate before continuing. "Sanchez has already given me the information. I'm only looking for confirmation. I'd like you to recall the plane that landed in the Bahamas. Do you remember it?"

"Yes."

"Where was the flight bound for?"

This time he answered quickly. "Destin Executive Airport."

"Why Destin?"

"Sanchez has an agreement with the military to use Destin. The shipments are protected there."

"Protected by who?"

"The military."

"Sanchez runs the operation?"

"Her and one man from the military"

"His name?"

"I've heard Sanchez mention the name Pritchard. That's all I know."

"Do you pay for the shipments with weapons?"

"No. Mena pays with weapons. We pay in cash."

"Mena?" Laura asked.

"Mena, Arkansas. There's an army base there."

"Why do you pay in cash?"

"Sometimes, they need more money."

"Who needs more cash?"

"Sanchez and her contact," Diego said.

Laura stopped and asked Sharp to give Diego more water. "You're doing enough to keep you alive, Diego." Diego looked at her and saw Laura's expression. "One false answer and I'll kill you." Laura waited for a response, but Diego remained silent. "How do you transport your shipment from Destin to Miami?"

"By boat."

"A yacht?" Diego grimaced. It was a mistake to take the boat to the Bahamas, he thought.

"How did you know about the yacht?" Diego asked.

"I ask the questions, Diego. The flight that landed in the Bahamas. Where did the flight originate? The one that had engine trouble."

"Panama."

"Where in Panama?"

"Yavisa," he said after a hesitation.

"Which cartel?" Diego hesitated which resulted in Laura pointing the gun. "Is this information worth losing your life over?"

"Malagua," Diego replied. Laura smiled again.

"See how easy that was?" Diego was silent. "Who was the pilot of the plane?"

"Derek Young."

"Malagua is based out of where?"

"Apartado."

"Apartado, Colombia?"

"Yes," Diego replied.

"Where are the drugs processed?"

"Malagua processes in the jungle."

"How are the drugs transported out of the jungle?"

"By boat."

"To where?"

"Yavisa."

"Where the Pan-American Highway ends?"

"Yes."

"Who guards the shipments?"

"Malagua's men until they get to Yavisa. Noriega's men take over at that point."

"What do you mean at that point?"

"Some shipments are sent by truck to Colon where they're loaded onto fast boats for delivery into Mexico."

"But yours are always flown?"

"Yes."

"What planes do they use?"

"A military transport of some kind. I don't know what it is."

Laura smiled again, with satisfaction. "I think we're done here. Before I release you, let's go over the rules. You will tell no one of our conversation, not even Sanchez. Understand?"

"Yes."

"Because if you do, we'll learn of it. Understand?"

"Yes," Diego said.

"I'm leaving you alive to send a message to your organization. The message is 'Stop!' It's over. Do you understand?"

"Yes."

"Oh, and by the way, don't come around my property in the Bahamas again. Understand?"

"Yes."

"Just to make sure you don't, I destroyed your yacht this evening." Diego groaned. "There will be no more boat trips to the Bahamas. Got it?"

"Yes."

Laura turned to Sharp. "Wipe down everything we touched. Rick, drag Mr. Marty outside and duct tape him to the chair."

After the locker had been scrubbed of prints and Diego set outside, Laura and her crew headed to the Miami airport to meet up with Pierre, Jean and the flight crew to travel home.

Chapter Twenty-Four

Tuesday, January 3rd, 1989

AFTER THE NEW Year's holiday, Laura called a meeting of the principals at the compound to consider further action against Sanchez and the Malagua cartel. The group gathered on the veranda of the main house for a working lunch.

"Sofia," Laura said to her housekeeper and cook, "the food looks beautiful. You didn't have to go to all this trouble." Sofia laughed heartily.

"I didn't, Ma'am. I used leftovers. The only thing fresh is the salad."

"That's good enough for me," Sharp said, loading three meat slices onto homemade bread loaded up with mayonnaise. "Would someone pass the salad, please?"

"I'll pass the salad," Rick said, "if you pass the meat."

"Seems fair," Sharp said handing the tray to Rick.

Laura watched the men around her devour the food. "I've always said you're the most popular person at the compound, Sofia. Thank you."

"You're welcome, Miss Laura."

Jean invited everyone to grab a drink at the bar while Sofia cleared the table. Once they'd reconvened, Jean folded his hands on the table and leaned forward. "Have we done enough to stop these attacks?"

"Are you kidding?" Jack asked. "The answer is no. They'll keep coming at us until we're dead."

"Keep in mind we've hurt their organization severely," Jean countered, arguing his point. "Rational people would end this."

"If the decision was left to the Miami people, you might be right," Jack responded. "I don't think Sanchez is rational."

"In regard to Sanchez, Jack, I agree," Laura responded. "I talked to her face to face and I didn't get the impression she was willing to end it."

"And we've got Derek Young to think about," Sharp added. "I got a note yesterday that he's on the move."

"Hold that thought a moment," Jean said to Sharp. He returned to Laura's point. "You believe she'll keep pursuing us?"

"Unless we pay her, yes, I do."

Jean thought for a moment. "That's insane," he said shaking his head.

"She's filled with rage, Jean. She killed both her spouses just for disagreeing with her."

"Then how do we end the hostilities?"

"We track her supply chain all the way into Central America," Rick said, as though it was obvious, "and eliminate it."

Jean looked astonished. "All of it?"

"Only the Malagua cartel," Rick replied. "If we take them down, everyone else will leave us alone."

"But that would mean ..." Jean thought for a second, "I wouldn't even know where to begin. It would take more money and men than we can muster, Rick."

Rick turned to Laura. "Do we have a way to contact the Special Ops troops we used in Lebanon?"

"Sure. Major Jordan's unit could be in Panama as we speak. The White House is sending additional troops to the Canal Zone."

"Why?" Jean asked.

"In case Noriega needs to be removed from power," Laura replied.

"You mean an invasion?" Jean asked.

"That's what it looks like."

"Military action would disrupt the drug pipeline for us," Jean said.

"Sure it would," Rick admitted, "but an invasion could be a year or more away."

"And Sanchez could order another attack tomorrow," Laura added.

"That's what I'm getting at," Rick affirmed.

"Then how do you propose we pursue it?" Jean asked. Rick leaned back and thought for a minute before answering.

"American troops already come out of the Canal Zone on occasion to guard American assets, like the Embassy, for instance. If we were to use our Special Ops friends to help us, we might find the cover to operate inside Panama."

"I'm not sure I agree, but for the sake of argument, let's say you're right," Jean said. "What's the first step?"

"We follow Derek Young. He'll lead us there."

"We were warned to stay away from him. He's CIA, Rick."

Jack chuckled. "So are we, Jean. Almost everyone at this table has worked for the agency at some point."

"You're suggesting we use our contacts at the agency to gather intelligence?" Jean asked.

"That's exactly what I'm saying," Jack said. "Let's find out how deep this rabbit hole goes."

"You're asking me to talk to Steve?" Laura asked. Steve Tilton, Laura's former husband, was Associate Director of the Intelligence Division at CIA. If anyone at Langley was likely to tell the truth about CIA involvement in the drug trade, it would be Tilton.

"I am."

Jean liked the idea. "I trust Monsieur Tilton. I agree."

"That's a tough ask," Laura replied.

"I realize that," Jack said. "He put his feelings aside to come down here a couple of months ago. Couldn't you do the same?"

Laura stared at Jack. "That's not for you to ask."

Jack became embarrassed. "I'm sorry. You're right."

Jean stepped in to smooth over an awkward moment. "Let's leave that aside for the moment. We're considering taking on a major drug cartel and the U.S. government simultaneously."

"You neglected to mention the Panamanians," Jack said. "If Noriega's involved, add them to the list."

"You're right." Jean shook his head. "This sounds impossible. We're talking about an operation far beyond our means. It's something we've never done. I suggest we take a break, do some serious thinking, and reconvene at the dinner hour to discuss it further."

Chapter Twenty-Five

JEAN KNEW LAURA needed time to consider approaching Steve Tilton. She'd been hurt badly by their divorce and although the monetary settlement was fair, it was the idea that Steve put his job ahead of their marriage that caused Laura the most pain. Nearly a year later, Steve traveled to the Bahamas to ask for Laura's help finding American hostages in Lebanon. It was only on CIA Director Bill Bates' order that he made the trip at all. Neither Laura nor Steve could completely lay aside their personal feelings, but they managed to work together efficiently on the Lebanon mission, and it was a huge success. Laura and her team safely brought home two American hostages from Lebanon. Now, though, it would be Laura's turn to do the asking. And Jean suspected Laura would balk at the prospect.

The meeting continued after dinner as though they'd never stopped. "Getting back to our discussion this afternoon," Jean said, "I'd like to address a few additional points. One, we've not discussed how to pay for this," Jean said. Laura was astonished Jean would mention money.

"In all the years we've worked together, Jean, I've never heard you mention money in connection with a mission."

"In every other mission we've done, Mademoiselle, we've been paid."

"Excuse me," Sharp interrupted, "could I make a suggestion?" Rick immediately gave Sharp a warning look. Rick tried to avoid interrupting discussions between Laura and Jean.

Jean nodded. "You have something to add, Mr. Sharp?"

"We could confiscate some of the drug money."

Shit, that's not a bad idea, Rick thought. Sharp and Rick looked at each other in agreement. "That's a great idea," Rick exclaimed.

"They'll come at us hard, Rick, if we steal money," Jean replied.

"Who? Sanchez?" Jack asked. "She says we already owe her millions. What's a few million more?"

"I was referring to CIA," Jean replied.

"What are they going to say? Don't take our illegal drug profits?" The entire group chuckled at the suggestion.

"Let's say that's possible and we use the money to fund the mission," Jean continued. What's our fighting capability? We've discussed using the special ops troops, but what about air support? In Lebanon, we had the Israelis providing evac helicopters for us. Here, we'll need one for recon, insertion and evac. I mean no disrespect, but have we put enough thought into this?" He looked at Laura.

"We should steal a helicopter," Laura said with a grin. The entire table erupted in laughter, Jean included.

Jean shrugged his shoulders and spread his arms. "Do you know something I'm not aware of?"

"Dimitri knows where the Russians keep their helicopters in Central America," Laura continued.

"Can Dmitri fly one?"

Laura nodded her head, still grinning. "Yep."

"Shit, those Russkies can fly anything," Sharp added.

Jean thought for a moment, still skeptical. "You've spoken to Dmitri about it?"

Laura nodded her head. "Uh-huh."

"What about weapons? Missiles, for instance?" Jean asked with a skeptical look.

"He says to steal one with weapons." The table laughed again. This time, Jean waited for the laughter to completely subside to avoid the rolling laughter phenomenon.

"Just how does one steal a helicopter loaded with weapons?"

"Dmitri says the Russians supply arms with the battle copters they give to Central America. He knows where they're located."

"Are you saying it's as simple as Dmitri walking up to a local commander wearing a Russian uniform, hand him fake orders and fly off with a helicopter loaded with weapons?"

Laura shrugged and smiled again. "Yes, it's just that simple." Jean could not avoid his colleague's laughter.

"Okay!" Sharp exclaimed loudly. "We got us a fucking helo."

Jean waited for the laughter to subside again. "All right. I grant you that might work. Sharp, you mentioned Derek Young earlier. What's going on?" Sharp nodded.

"Our local PI taped a conversation he had with an unidentified person. Young was told to travel to the Executive Airport in Destin, Florida."

"When?" asked Jean.

"Thursday" Sharp looked at the ceiling. "Two days from now."

"The only thing you can count, Sharp, is the number of dessert helpings you take," Rick said sarcastically.

Sharp rolled his eyes. "Then I can easily count to three, Rick. Let me ask you a question. Who's the best sharpshooter in this outfit?"

"You are."

"That's right and I need the extra weight to steady my rifle!"

"Excuse me. Could we get back on point, please?" Laura asked. Both men looked at each other and began laughing. "This is like pre-school," Laura said shaking her head.

Jean waited for silence. "Do we know what Young will be doing in Destin?" Jean asked.

"No," Sharp replied, "only that Young is to be there on Thursday."

"Is he flying a plane down there or going commercial?" Laura asked.

"Unknown at this point."

"We should follow him," Laura suggested. "And by the way, when Young leaves his apartment, tell your local PI to roll up his operation. Remind him to wipe down the apartment you've been using and clear everything out."

"You suspect something?" Rick asked.

Laura gave him a slight smile. "Of course. Young is CIA's boy."

"What about the bugs in Young's apartment?" Sharp asked.

"Leave them. There won't be enough time to remove them. CIA will do a sweep as soon as he leaves."

"Okay."

"We're following him on to Panama?" Rick asked.

Laura nodded. "If that's where he's going, yes. That means we've got a lot of work to do."

Chapter Twenty-Six

Wednesday, January 4, 1989

IT WAS CALLED puddle jumping, an airplane making several short legs before arriving at a final destination. Dmitri dropped Pierre and Sharp off at Destin Executive Airport to wait for Young's arrival. Surveillance required a minimum of two men so Young wouldn't recognize a tail. One would follow him to a shuttle or car rental, then the other would follow him to his hotel.

Dmitri dropped off Laura at Fayetteville, North Carolina, the closest airport to Fort Bragg, and then flew on to D.C. to await further instructions. Laura rented a car at the Fayetteville airport for the short drive to Bragg where she'd made an appointment. The duty sergeant at the front gate checked his clipboard and found Laura's name on the visitor's list, handed her a pass and directed her to the administration building. She entered the office of General Frank Hitchens, head of the U.S. Army Special Forces Command. Hitchen's attaché, Lieutenant Roper, looked up at Laura from his desk and asked simply, "Laura Messier?"

"Yes, Sir."

"The General is ready for you, Ma'am. Please follow me." He led her down a long hallway and opened the door to a surprisingly sparse office where Hitchens rose to meet her.

"Welcome to SOC, Ms. Messier. Your reputation precedes you."

"Thank you, General. I appreciate you giving me a few minutes of your time."

The General smiled. "I assure you, Ms. Messier, the pleasure's mine. Anytime a winner of an Intelligence Star and a Distinguished Service Cross requests a meeting, I lay aside my duties. It's an honor to meet you."

The General motioned toward the two chairs in front of his desk. "I read the report Major Jordan wrote following your Lebanon mission. Both he and General Carey offered high praise of your work. We've not had a great deal of success in that part of the world, as you know, and your rescue mission is a primer on how to conduct special ops.

"It's most kind of you to say. Thank you, Sir."

"Our students at the War College have benefited greatly from studying your missions. When you have the time, you have an open invitation to speak here at the college."

"I'd be honored, Sir."

"What brings you to the fort today?"

"I'm seeking your permission to speak with Major Jordan about another mission."

The general hesitated. "You're correct in assuming that missions involving elements of our Command would have to be approved by me. However, as it happens, Major Jordan is out of the country right now. Could you brief me on the mission?"

"I'm seeking to disrupt the flow of drugs from Panama to the United States." The general studied her for a brief second. Laura couldn't read his thoughts.

"I see," he said. He leaned back in his chair and Laura had no idea what his reaction would be. "That's a broad mission, Ms. Messier. Can you talk about it with more specificity?"

"Yes, Sir, I can. Would you like a full briefing now?"

The General glanced at his watch. "I'm afraid I don't have the time right now. Submit your documents to Lieutenant Roper and I'll review them. Just make sure the documents are in a form I can approve." Hitchens smiled. "This is the Army, Ms. Messier. We need four inches of paperwork to move a car from one end of the parking lot to the other."

"I understand."

"Let me ask a couple of brief questions. Is the mission time sensitive?"

"Yes, Sir."

"And the mission op will be conducted in Panama?"

"Yes, Sir."

"I assume in support of clandestine efforts by the CIA?"

"Yes, Sir." That wasn't the truth, but Laura realized the approval process was by-the-book. She was determined to tell him what he wanted to hear.

"I'll also need an authorization from them."

"I'll include it, Sir. Can I assume that Major Jordan is in Panama at the present time?"

"You may." Hitchens hesitated again. "You'll need to meet with Major General Carson at Fort Clayton inside the Canal Zone. Give him a briefing on the mission and turn in duplicates of your paperwork to him. The General must approve the use of U.S. forces in Panama. If he approves it, he'll get in touch with me and the two of us will discuss it."

"Yes, Sir."

"I want to stress there's no guarantee General Carson will approve your mission."

"I understand, Sir."

"And if he does, he may assign it to someone other than Major Jordan."

"I'd be disappointed, Sir."

"All you can do is make the request."

"Yes, Sir."

"I'm going to ask that you wait a few minutes in the outer office while I dictate a letter of introduction for you to the General. When will you travel to the Canal Zone?"

"Friday."

"Are you flying private?"

"Yes."

"Give the flight information to Lieutenant Roper and he'll notify Albrook to give you landing privileges." The general stood. "Anything else?

"No, Sir. Thank you for making this easy."

"When you return, give me a call about a lecture here at the college."

"I will, Sir. It was a pleasure to meet you."

"Likewise."

Chapter Twenty-Seven

LAURA LEFT FORT Bragg and drove the 300 miles to D.C., arriving early that evening. She called Steve Tilton's home and not receiving an answer, decided to stop by the attractive brownstone in Georgetown. She used her old house keys to let herself in and prepared a meal for herself while waiting for Steve to return. During the wait, she completed the forms given her by General Hitchens. Steve walked in later to find her asleep on the sofa. "Laura! What are you doing here?" She opened her eyes and smiled.

"Sorry to barge in on you like this. Do you mind me letting myself in?"

"No, but I wish you'd called."

"I did earlier this evening."

"Yeah, I wasn't home."

"As I found out. Can we talk for a few minutes?"

"Sure," he replied with a smile. "You want a glass of wine?"

"Why not?"

Steve Tilton was an attractive man, in his late 40s, tall, with steely blue eyes and short gray hair that fell over his forehead. He had one of the sharpest minds at CIA, a near photographic memory and had a knack for manipulating the political environment. Before their divorce, many at the agency considered Laura and Steve to be the perfect couple.

Laura sat up and straightened out her clothing while Steve found a half empty bottle of merlot in the kitchen. He came back to the living room, handed her a goblet and sat down. "Remember the round that came through the kitchen window. It's lucky you had the fridge door open. That round had your name on it."

"I was surprised a metal fridge door and a jug of milk stopped it."

"Ilitch was his name, wasn't it?"

Laura nodded. "I showed him no mercy when I found him."

"I read the French report. Walking in on a four-man assassination team like you did, killing all of them. Remarkable." Laura had performed the mission under the auspices of the DST, the French Intelligence Service.

"I was angry," she said more as an admission than an explanation.

"Remind me to never get you angry." Laura hesitated, wondering whether Steve was referring to the incident or their divorce. The pain of the divorce came upon her immediately and she looked at him with hurt in her eyes.

"I'm not angry, Steve. At least, not at you." Steve reached over to put his hand atop hers.

"Maybe one day we can put it behind us." Laura withdrew her hand and took a moment to control her emotions.

"Perhaps." Steve wisely decided to change the subject.

"Well, you're not here to talk about that. What's on your mind?"

"I need information."

"Of course. How can I help?"

"What can you tell me about CIA/Pentagon drug ops?" she asked, wondering if he'd speak of one of the worst kept secrets in the agency.

Steve grimaced. "You mean the fiasco in the Bahamas a few weeks ago?"

"Yes."

Steve took a sip of wine and shook his head. "That's a tough one."

"You weren't involved, were you?"

"Oh no," Steve replied, setting his wine goblet on the coffee table. He shook his head and sighed. "That's not something I'd do. However, it is a black eye for the seventh floor." The seventh floor at Langley contained the administrative offices.

"I've accidently found myself in the middle of it."

"I expected you to contact me sooner or later."

"And here I am," she said with a smile. She picked up her wine glass. I hope he doesn't think I'm flirting.

"It's the Pentagon's op," Steve said flatly. "We're just babysitters."

"Who runs it over there?"

"A Marine Colonel named Kevin Pritchard."

"Never heard of him."

"There's no reason why you would have. He runs an office, just him and a secretary. It's called Asymmetrical Special Projects."

Laura laughed. "Seriously? That's what they call it?"

"Yeah. They should just call it illegal shit we're not supposed to be doing."

"Who runs CIA's end of it?"

"Pratt. Bates hasn't appointed a new Op Director yet." Mike Pratt, an Assistant Director of Operations, was temporarily serving as Acting Director until a replacement could be found.

"I'm surprised Bates would authorize something like that." Steve shook his head in disgust.

"I argued against it, but Bates went ahead anyway. Believe me, Pritchard's nothing but trouble."

"So, Pratt doesn't actively manage it?"

"No. He just provides support. Pritchard runs his own ops. He's sort of out there on his own."

"Pritchard doesn't run his operations through the DOD?"

"Nope," Steve said with disgust. "Believe me, this stuff is political dynamite. DOD ignored the Boland Amendment and provided aid to the Contras in a different form. They keep Pritchard at arm's length to protect themselves."

"Surely it's in the DOD budget. I mean, Senate and House committees review it."

"Congress doesn't know about it because Pritchard's operations are off-book. He runs them on drug profits."

"That's Iran-Contra all over again," Laura said. Steve grimaced.

"Yeah, it is. I stay away from it because I don't want my ass hauled off to jail.

"The Boland Amendment applies to the CIA, doesn't it?" Laura asked.

"It does, but here's where Bates relies on a technicality. Pritchard requests CIA support for his office, not for any particular mission. Bates believes the responsibility lies with Pritchard."

"Wow. That's a fine line."

"No shit," Steve said pointedly. "What Pritchard does is clearly illegal." The wine bottle was empty. "Give me a minute to grab another bottle of wine." Steve returned with a bottle of Cabernet Sauvignon. "Is this all right?" He asked showing her the label.

"You always did love fine wines." That brought a reaction from Steve. He wasn't immune from the pain of divorce, either.

"Ouch. That hurt."

"I'm sorry," Laura replied, realizing the comment was a mistake.

"That's okay." He poised the bottle above her glass. "Yes or no on the wine?"

"Definitely yes, but aren't you going to decant it?"

"Already did. I figured half a bottle wouldn't be enough." Laura waited while Steve filled their wines glasses. "Would you like some cheese or bread?"

"No, I'm fine. I made a bit of dinner waiting for you." Steve sat down and kicked his shoes off. He leaned back into the stuffed chair, propped his feet on the coffee table and put his hands behind his head.

"Okay, where were we?"

"Derek Young. What can you tell me about him?"

Steve thought for a minute. "I believe Young is a contract employee. I'd have to check with Roger on that to be sure." Roger Wilson was CIA's Chief of Staff.

"Derek Young is Pritchard's pilot, or one of them anyway."

"Roger would know about him. He could be some unemployed pilot Pratt dug up somewhere. He didn't do the training school. I know that much." The CIA training school, outside Williamsburg, VA, was required of all full-time agents.

"It was Young who made the emergency landing that night in the Bahamas. He tried to intimidate me with a badge and an automatic rifle."

"I don't believe Young has any background in clandestine operations. Pratt should have dismissed him afterwards."

"Plausible deniability?" Laura asked.

"Well, that's how Bates would describe it. Bates could have accused Young of drug running, fired him and that would have been the end of it. That didn't happen, obviously. I told Bill he can't continue to pay Young and stay at arms-length from his activities. If this becomes public, all hell's going to break loose. It's a potential scandal."

"There were other people on the plane that night. Any idea who they were?"

"Pratt assigned a number of people to Pritchard, field agents who were on the bench at the time. If you run into them, be careful. They're pretty good."

"How many?"

"Honestly, I don't know."

"Well, I've got to bring down the op."

"As soon as I heard the plane landed on your property, I knew the op was doomed. I told Pratt to shut it down."

"Derek Young's on his way to Florida right now to do another mission."

Steve's face turned red. "Dammit to hell." He took his feet off the table and sat up. "Doesn't Pratt have any sense? Putting Young back in the field is insane."

"That's what I thought. I could use your help."

"What do you need?"

"I need a back door into the op."

"I'll help you. I'd like to shut it down as much as you."

"We think Young's going to southern Panama to pick up a drug shipment at an airstrip in Yavisa."

Steve thought for a moment. "Yavisa, Yavisa," he repeated aloud, trying to recall it. "Yes, I know the place. It's where the Pan-American Highway ends."

"I'm impressed."

"Okay, here's what you need to know. Yavisa is the beginning of the Darien Gap, the dense jungle that runs a couple of hundred miles from southern Panama into Colombia. The rivers are the only way to get in there." Steve hesitated a moment, his face turning deadly serious. "If you intend on shutting down a drug op there, Young's guards will be the least of your problems."

"How so?" Laura asked.

"You're going to run into FARC rebels. They'll smuggle the drugs into Yavisa."

"FARC works for the cartels?"

"Yeah, and it's easy to understand why. They know every inch of the jungle; they number in the thousands and they're vicious fighters."

"They'll come as far north as Yavisa?"

"To do large drug deals like Pritchard does? Sure, and they'll bring plenty of men."

"Can you get me sat photos of the area?"

"We run satellites over the Canal daily. I'll see what I can find."

"Thanks. What can you tell me about Apartado, Colombia?"

Steve nodded. "I know the place. There's a small bay near there and you'll find a number of small towns up and down the coast, Apartado among them."

"Wow, you could teach geography. The head of the Malagua cartel lives there. Can you get sat photos of that area, too?"

"Sure, when do you need them?"

"By tomorrow."

"Well, some might not be recent, but I'll see what's in the files. You want to pick them up?"

"Send them to the general aviation terminal at Dulles to the attention of Island Airlines."

"I'll do it first thing in the morning. How can I contact you by phone?"

"Jean's still got his phone drop at DST. Leave a message there. You have the number?"

Steve nodded. "I think I have it somewhere."

"You're a big help, Steve. That's all I've got."

"You want to stay the night? You can use the second bedroom if you like."

"That'd be great. I'll be out of here early tomorrow."

"Just like old times, huh?"

"You still leave in the morning at the same time?" Laura asked.

"Yep. Some things never change."

"I'll make you breakfast."

"You got a deal."

Chapter Twenty-Eight

Thursday, January 5ᵗʰ, 1989

LAURA PLACED FIVE calls the following morning from Steve's residence after he left for work. The first, to Jean, informed him that Steve would use the DST phone drop to leave messages.

The second call was placed to Rick Williams at the compound in the Bahamas. Laura asked him to prepare weapons and supplies for a four-day mission to Panama.

The third call was to Dmitri, letting him know she'd be flying out later in the day.

The fourth was to Pierre telling him to hold in place and she'd join both him and Sharp at Destin late that afternoon.

The last call, interestingly enough, was to a number in East Berlin that belonged to an old man. Not any old man, but a powerful one. Markus Wolf was the head of the East German Intelligence Foreign Division, called Stazi. Wolf was so secretive that in over thirty years of service, no intelligence agency in the West had information about his background. No photo of him existed anywhere. Yet, he and Laura had a back-channel relationship, something more than professionals on opposite sides. Wolf looked upon Laura as the granddaughter he never had. To put it simply, they ignored the antipathy of their respective governments and established a relationship of mutual respect.

"Hello Markus."

"My dear girl, how nice to hear from you."

"How are you doing?"

"I'm cold, dear. The superintendent turns the heat off from time to time on cold winter days and these old bones ache."

"I keep telling you to defect, my friend. The American government will set you up in a house on the beach with young girls in bikinis."

"A tempting thought."

"I think of you from time to time. I've heard rumors East and West Germany are going to merge. If that happens, there'll be a purge. It would be better to negotiate a departure beforehand."

"You're such a sweet girl to worry about an old man. I have contingency plans, my dear. There's no need to worry. How are you and that charming fellow, Jean Broussard, doing with your little enterprise in the Bahamas?"

"Jean and I get along well."

"That's Jean's talent. He's everyone's friend. You know I met him once?"

"I had no idea. Where?" Laura could hear Markus laugh over the phone.

"Years ago, in Paris. I liked him immediately."

"He's a gifted man. I'm still learning from him."

"I read a report of your exploits in Lebanon. My compliments on a stunning success."

"I got lucky."

"Luck had nothing to do with it. I'm amused that you embarrassed my Russian colleagues again."

"I sent Petrovsky a message after the op." Viktor Petrovsky was the head of Russian Intelligence, the KGB.

"I heard. He was quite upset about it."

"I can't blame him for sending men to interrogate the hostages but sending men to my home was out of line. They deserved what they got."

"Quite right."

"Hopefully, the entire episode's over. I'm sure he's got more important things to do than think about me." Laura heard a chuckle on the phone.

"I wouldn't count on that. The man holds a grudge forever."

"Then our paths may cross again."

"Most assuredly so."

"Markus, I need a favor."

"Of course, dear, what can I do for you?"

"Do you have anyone in Panama?"

"I'm afraid not. My closest man is in Mexico City."

"How would you feel about sending him to watch my back?"

"I think he'd enjoy the prospect. What are the circumstances?"

"The CIA is running drugs into the United States from Panama. I've accidently become involved. For my own safety, I must shut the op down. I'm quite sure CIA will send agents to stop me."

"Drugs are such a nasty business. Your CIA does some very bad things."

"I'm sometimes ashamed of my own country."

"I'll contact my man immediately. Don't worry, dear, Franz will take care of you."

"Do you need anything from me?" Laura heard Markus chuckle again.

"No, no, dear. He can find you. He'll be in the background somewhere watching."

"I owe you for this, Markus."

"You owe me nothing. It's my pleasure to help."

"Thank you, my dear friend."

Chapter Twenty-Nine

MIKE PRATT WAS in his late 30s, a little young to have an executive position at the agency. He came to the agency after graduating from the University of Virginia with a degree in computer science. He was short with black hair and wore black plastic rimmed glasses which gave him the look of an academic. Aggressive and arrogant, something that offended his colleagues, he bounced around the agency for several years before landing on Claire George's staff in operations. Steve thought Mike was a poor fit for Director of Operations. He'd say so at the proper time.

Pratt's office was hardly bigger than a closet, adjacent to the Operations Center at Langley. He spent most of his time on the floor in the Op Center and that's where Steve Tilton found him the next afternoon. "Mike, I need a word."

Pratt responded in his usual arrogant fashion. "I'm a little busy right now, Steve. Can it wait?"

Steve, who outranked Pratt, smiled patiently. "Let's go back to your office."

Mike, a candidate for the Ops Director position, couldn't afford to alienate someone who had influence over hiring. He leaned over a young man sitting at a computer monitor. "I'll be back in a minute." He turned back to Steve. "I hope this won't take long."

As they passed Pratt's secretary, he said, "Lisa, make sure Mr. Tilton and I aren't interrupted."

Mike pushed his door shut, folded his arms and asked, "Okay, what can I do for you?"

"The Pritchard op. What's going on?"

"Who's asking, you or your ex-wife?"

"Don't be a smart ass. Is the op still active?"

"No. Young's on the shelf."

"How many men did you assign to Pritchard?"

Pratt began to get nervous. He shifted his weight from one foot to the other. "Read the report, Steve. Young had six men with him when the op went down in the Bahamas."

"Where are those men now?"

"How the fuck would I know?" Pratt raised his voice. "Did you check the cafeteria? When Young went on the shelf, they did, too. What's with all the questions?"

"I'm saving your ass, Mike. We're testifying before the Senate Intelligence Committee next week. If they ask, I've got to be prepared to talk about it." That much was true, Pratt thought, although the hearing was routine.

"That's a regularly scheduled hearing. Besides, it's in open session," Pratt said as though it was unimportant.

Time to put some pressure on him, Steve thought. He raised his voice slightly. "Get your head out of your ass, Mike. Young was extradited out of the Bahamas. Extraditions are public information. The press hasn't put it together yet, but they will. And when they do, it's going to cause a shit storm. Do you honestly think Bates will protect you?"

Pratt used the excuse he figured would protect him. "It was Pritchard's op, Steve."

"It was your men!" Steve raised his voice even louder. "You assigned them. Listen, this op is radioactive. It's Iran-Contra all over again and your fingerprints are on it. What do you think The Post will do with that information?"

Pratt glared at Steve. "What the fuck do you want?"

"I want complete disclosure," Steve said firmly. "And I want it now. Start by giving me your file."

"Why the fuck would I do that?"

"I'm going to cut you some slack, Mike. I'm the one Bates sends up on the Hill. I routinely ask the Ops Director for information on all CIA activities prior to the hearing. I'll need access to all your files, but this one's problematic because there's a chance it'll be exposed. I'll take that one now."

"You don't mind if I check your story, do you? Hang on a minute."

Steve shook his head. "Dear Lord, I'm dealing with idiots here," he said under his breath.

Pratt picked up his desk phone and called Director Bates' direct line.

"Yes," Bates said.

"It's Pratt. Tilton's in my office wanting files. He says he's going up on the Hill to testify. Can you confirm that?"

"Steve's our liaison to Congress, Mike. He's getting ready for the next hearing. Give him whatever he wants."

"What about the Pritchard op?"

"Give him access to everything."

"Okay. Thanks." Pratt slammed the phone down and walked to the file cabinet in the corner. He fished a key out of his pocket, thumbed through the first drawer and handed the file over. "Here's your fucking file! Now, if you don't mind, I've got work to do."

Steve began to walk out, but as an afterthought, he turned around in the doorway. "Have Lisa bring the rest of active files to my office tomorrow."

Chapter Thirty

IMMEDIATELY AFTER TILTON left, Mike's secretary flagged him down as he was leaving. "Mike, I've got Colonel Pritchard on the line. Do you want to take the call?"

Fucking great, Pratt thought to himself in disgust. "Go ahead and put him through, Lisa." Pratt turned around and walked back in his office.

"Yes?"

"I told you to tell that bitch to stay away from Young," Pritchard yelled.

"What are you talking about?"

"Messier! Who the fuck do you think I'm talking about?"

"I did. The FBI told her Young was off limits."

"Yeah, well, we just finished sweeping Young's apartment after he left for Florida and guess what we found?"

"Wait a minute. You sent Young on another trip?"

"Hell yes, I did, and my electronics team found Young's apartment full of eavesdropping equipment. Audio, video, hell, they were even patched into the building's security system."

"What makes you think it was Messier?" Pratt asked.

"Good God, man, who else could it be?"

"Did you trace the equipment back to its source?"

"As a matter fact, we did. This wasn't your garden variety electronics store stuff. It was CIA issue surveillance gear. My men talked to the building manager and he gave them the installer's contact information. Guess what? The phone number is disconnected, and the address is a vacant office. This was a surveillance op, Mike. Back that fucking bitch off!"

"I told you before, Laura Messier doesn't work for us. I don't have any control over her. Report the incident to the FBI. Give them the gear and let them investigate it."

"Get this through that thick head of yours, I've given orders to shoot her on sight."

By this time, Pratt was shouting again. "You told our agents to kill an Intelligence Star winner who is personal friends with the President? Are you out of your fucking mind?"

"Damn straight I did. She's the only one who can hurt us. If she comes anywhere near this op, she's dead."

"What the hell are you doing starting the op again? We agreed to suspend it."

"We agreed to continue the operation with a different pilot. However, our friends in Central America told me they only trust Derek. So, he's back in the game."

"Goddammit," Pratt yelled. "I'm pulling my guys back."

"You can't. They've already left."

"Then you're using CIA assets without permission. If this thing gets out of hand, you're responsible."

"It's your goddam plane, Mike. Don't come at me with this horseshit. You're up to your eyeballs in this." There was silence on the line. Pritchard finally said, "Look, if I take care of Messier, our problems go away."

"You better fucking hope so." He slammed the phone down hard wondering whether Lisa might have heard the conversation.

Get yourself together, he said to himself. He wiped his brow and used a minute to compose himself before walking out of the office. "Lisa, I'm taking the rest of the day off. Take messages and tell everyone I'll return calls in the morning."

Before Pratt left the building, he had an idea. He stopped by the Communications Center. "Hi, Kenny," he said to Kenneth Ragsdale, the Director of Communications.

Ragsdale looked up from a computer monitor. "What's up, Mike?"

"I need a phone tap."

"For whom?"

"Someone in the building."

"Got a warrant?"

Pratt grimaced. "That's the thing, I don't."

"Whose phone?"

"Steven Tilton."

"Tilton? Get the fuck out of my office."

"It's just for a day or two, Ken."

Ragsdale swung his chair around to face Pratt. "I'm gonna do you a favor, Mike. I'm going to forget this conversation ever took place. Now get the fuck out of here!"

Dammit, Pratt said to himself. Ragsdale watched Pratt walk away. Jesus, he knows better than to ask that.

As soon as Pratt was out of sight, Ragsdale kicked his door shut and dialed Steve Tilton's office.

"Steve, Ken here. Pratt was in my office wanting me to tap your phone."

"He's nervous, Ken."

"Is he in trouble?"

"Well, he's in over his head if that's what you mean."

"I gotcha. I just thought you'd like to know."

"Thanks, Ken."

Steve hung up and walked down the hall to Director Bates' office. "Is the boss in?" He asked the secretary.

"Sure. Go on in."

Bates' door was open so Steve stuck his head inside. "Got a minute, Bill?"

Bates motioned Steve forward with his hand. "What's on your mind?"

"The Pritchard op is in play again."

"Have a seat, Steve," Bates said, motioning to the chairs in front of his desk. Bates leaned back in his chair. "I figured as much from Pratt's call."

"He's panicking, Bill."

"I know. Pratt doesn't know this yet, but to protect us, I assigned Derek Young, Bret Wexler and all the rest of them to the Pentagon. Technically, they work for Pritchard."

"Does that even matter?"

"Technically, yes. If the operation goes sideways, we don't bear any responsibility."

"With all due respect, Bill, I don't think you should have authorized it in the first place."

"Steve, according to the President's policy, we're required to provide support for Pritchard."

"Are you saying the President knows what's going on?"

"No, I'm not. I'm saying the President has enunciated a strategy for Central America that we're obliged to follow. He's unaware of the operational details, but our support falls within that strategy."

I've got to get the hell out of here before I hear something that will incriminate me, Steve thought. He stood as if to leave. "If that's enough for you, Bill, it's enough for me." Steve put on his best administrative smile. "Thanks for letting me know."

Steve walked back to his office and closed the door. This thing is going to blow sky high.

Chapter Thirty-One

LAURA RETURNED HER rental car at Dulles, then hopped a shuttle to the general aviation terminal where she found Dmitri, Svetlana and Pete Franklin waiting.

"Are we ready to go?" Dmitri asked.

"Almost. I need to make a couple of calls first. Do you know where I can go?"

"Follow me, there's a private office we can use when we're here." He led her to an empty office containing only desk furniture, a phone and fax machine. "By the way, this was delivered here for you." It was marked 'Do Not Bend.' Laura opened the envelope and began studying the sat photos.

"Hang on, do you mind waiting a minute?" Laura asked Dmitri. "I'd like you to take a look at something."

"Sure."

While thumbing through the photos, she called Ben Postl at his office in downtown D.C. "Ben, I've got a question for you? Can you hack into a foreign bank?"

"Well, yes, but I'd have to be on a terminal inside the bank."

"Another question. Can you print business cards for Jean?"

"Hold on a minute, you lost me."

"I need to get you inside a bank, Ben. The National Bank of Panama. If you print business cards making Jean a bank examiner and then print an order from President Noriega ordering Jean to examine the bank's records, I think we can get the two of you inside. Jean will get you access to a terminal and you can do your magic."

"Okay, when do you want this?"

"Right now. I need a few other things as well. One is a signed CIA authorization giving us permission to operate in Panama."

"Sure, I can do that."

"How about a Russian Defense Ministry requisition?"

"Actually, I can do that. I have a Russian typewriter. What would you like to requisition?"

"A helicopter."

"You're kidding, right?"

"No, I'm not."

"What kind of helicopter?"

"Hang on a minute." She turned to Dmitri, "What kind of Russian helicopter are we getting?"

"An Mi8-T. Here, I'll write it down for you." Dmitri scribbled it on a notepad.

"Okay, Ben, we're requesting an Mi8-T. Got it?"

"Yep."

"One more thing, Ben. I need you to come with us. Can you meet us at the general aviation terminal out at Dulles and bring that stuff with you?"

"What?"

"I need you to come on a mission with us."

"When?"

"Right now, Ben."

"Now?" Postl hesitated. "Laura, it's going to take a couple of hours to get these documents together. Besides that, I don't have a change of clothes with me."

"We'll wait for you."

Postl hesitated a moment before deciding. "Okay, give me a couple of hours."

"Thanks." She turned to Dmitri. "I need to fax these forms to this number at Fort Bragg, North Carolina. Do you know how to use this thing?" she asked nodding at the fax machine. Dmitri chuckled.

"I use it every time I'm here. Hand me the forms."

Laura took a first pass through the photos while Dmitri sent the fax. Once the fax was completed, she called Steve Tilton's direct line at Langley.

"I have the photos, Steve. Can you interpret them for me?"

"Give me a minute to find my copies." Steve located the photos buried on his desk. "Got 'em. Take a look at the airstrip photo first." Laura found it. "That's the dirt strip in Yavisa. It should be long enough to land a cargo plane. Check with Dmitri on that. See the two large tanks by the building at the end of the strip?"

"Yes."

"Those would be fuel tanks, probably two kinds of fuel. I'm guessing one tank would be avgas and the other would be jet fuel. There must be someone in town who fuels planes."

"Hang on a moment." She put her hand over the receiver and turned to Dmitri. "Can you look at this photo? Do you think a cargo plane could land there?"

"I'd say yes, judging from the size of the buildings."

"What kind of fuel does your helicopter use?"

"Jet fuel."

"Thanks." She returned her attention to Steve. "That'll work. Tell me about the Apartado photo?" The photo of Apartado had a circle around what appeared to be a large estate on the outskirts of the town with the name "Luis Delgado" scribbled above the circle.

"Luis Delgado is the head of the Malagua cartel. His residence is circled in the photo."

"How would I know whether he's there or not?"

"He drives luxury cars. You might not be able to identify them in the photo, but there are several in his driveway. He was probably at home when the photo was taken."

"And Dmitri could spot the estate from the air?"

"Show him the photo. I'm sure he could."

"Do you mind waiting a second?" Laura glanced over. "Can you find this place from the air?" She showed Dmitri the photo.

"Where is it?"

"A small town in Northwest Colombia named Apartado."

"It shouldn't be a problem."

"Dmitri says he thinks he can do it," she said into the phone to Steve. "What's the jungle photo?"

"It's the region south of Yavisa called the Darien Gap. If you look closely, you can see a small clearing. I circled it. The white patch in the clearing is a tent. That's where we think the Malagua cartel processes cocaine."

"How do you know it's a tent?"

"Structures look different. You see that gray line by the clearing? It zig-zags back and forth in the photo."

"Yes."

"That's the river they'll use to bring the drugs into Yavisa."

"Anything else I need to know?"

"To give you a little background, apparently this op began as a drugs for arms exchange with the weapons going to the contras. Apparently, Pritchard ran out of money, so now there's cash involved. If you interdict a shipment, it's hard to know what you're going to find."

"Where does the cartel launder its money?"

"Noriega allows them to use The National Bank of Panama."

"That's what I thought. Anything else?"

"Pratt assigned two pilots and six men to Pritchard. They travel so you could find them on Pritchard's next mission. You wouldn't know any of them, except maybe Bret Wexler."

"I don't remember him."

138

"There's no reason you would. How about Greg Smith?"

"That name sounds familiar."

"Remember the kid at the front desk."

"Bates sent the kid to Pritchard?"

"Yeah, he did."

"That's not right. He's a rookie."

"I found the name of the second pilot, by the way. Hank Miller."

"Thanks, Steve. I owe you one."

"Laura?"

"Yes?"

"I worry about you. Be safe down there."

"I will. Talk to you later."

Chapter Thirty-Two

DMITRI FLEW THE Falcon 50 into Okaloosa Regional Airport, near Fort Walton Beach, mid-afternoon where he, Laura and Ben Postl met with Pierre and Sharp at a coffee shop in the terminal.

"Young arrived at Destin this morning as scheduled," Pierre said. "They walked around a large transport plane sitting on the apron."

"How many men came with him?" Laura asked.

"Eight, including Young. I took photos of them." He passed photos across the table. "When they finished inspecting the plane, they rented a couple of cars and left."

"Did you follow them?"

"No. Young's guards were looking at everyone as they walked through the airport. Sharp and I dropped coverage and concentrated on the plane."

"That was smart. Is it the same plane that landed in the Bahamas?"

"I think so. Here's a photo." Laura glanced at the photo and then pushed it across to Dmitri.

"What do you think?"

"The tail number isn't readable, but it's the same kind of plane," Dmitri said.

Laura showed Dmitri the photo of the landing strip in Yavisa again. "Are you're sure that plane can land at this airstrip?"

"It's certainly long enough to accommodate a C-123. It'd have to be dry, though. That's a dirt landing strip."

"My intel indicates that's where they're going."

"I'll have to check Yavisa on a map, but flying to Southern Panama, they'd have to layover twice. Those are long legs for a C-123. Unless they've modified the plane with extra fuel tanks, that plane only has a range of about a thousand miles. I'm guessing they'll layover in Merida in the Yucatan and again in Panama City."

"How long would their layovers be?"

"That plane is difficult to fly, so they'll probably stay overnight. If that's the case, they'll fly out of Panama City on the morning of the third day." Dmitri looked at Pierre. "Do they have mechanics working on the plane yet?"

"No," Pierre replied. "It's just sitting on the apron."

Dmitri turned back to Laura. "Unless that plane's already prepped, they won't take off tomorrow. They'll be flying over open water on the first leg to Merida, so they'll pull the plane into a hanger and have mechanics give it a thorough service check. It'll take a day."

"So, you think they can take off on Saturday?" she asked.

"Probably. They can load cargo Saturday morning and be on their way," Dmitri said. "If they have to break it down for a repair, though, it'll take an extra day."

"Just so I understand what you're saying, if they leave Destin on Saturday, they'll layover Saturday night in Merida, layover again in Panama City on Sunday night and fly to the airstrip on Monday?"

"That's about as fast as you can get there in a C-123."

The waitress interrupted them. "Excuse me, Ma'am. The gray-haired British gentleman in the corner," she said motioning to one corner table, "wanted me to give you this." She laid a piece of blue chalk on the table. Laura broke out in a big smile.

"Thank you." She stole a glance at the man who had his head buried in a newspaper. He looked at Laura for a moment and smiled. "Franz," she said to no one in particular.

"Who's he?" Sharp asked.

"Franz is my back-up. Young's guards will never expect him."

"What's the blue chalk for?"

"Franz isn't English, he's East German. I used blue chalk to signal the East Germans when I was stationed in Paris."

"You're expecting trouble?" Sharp asked.

"Wouldn't you? You saw Young's guards." Sharp saw the determined look Laura gave him and decided to remain silent.

"Continue the surveillance and call the DST phone drop when they take off," she said. "You have the number?"

"Yes," Sharp replied.

"After they leave, you and Pierre hop a commercial flight to Panama City. Check in a downtown hotel and let us know where you are."

"What about Merida?" Pierre asked.

"Trust me, Young's guards are pros. They'll recognize you if they see you in Merida. We know where they're headed and we know their timetable, so let's loosen the coverage."

"When are you leaving for Panama?"

"Tomorrow. Remember the special ops guys we used in Lebanon?"

Pierre broke out in a huge grin. "I love those guys."

"I'm going to contact them when we get down there."

"They're in the Canal Zone?"

"Lucky, isn't it."

"Those guys are fantastic."

"Well, their participation isn't a sure thing yet. The commander in the Zone must approve the mission, but we'll see."

"It'd just be a hell of a lot easier if we had those guys with us."

"I agree."

"Are you flying back to the Bahamas tonight?"

"I have to. We've got supplies and weapons to load."

"I guess we'll see you in Panama then?" Pierre asked as a final confirmation.

"Count on it," Laura said.

"We'll contact you through the phone drop as events change at Destin."

Chapter Thirty-Three

THE SECRETARY PICKED up the blinking phone in a tiny obscure office inside the Pentagon. "Asymmetrical Special Projects, Colonel Pritchard's office."

"Bret Wexler calling for Colonel Pritchard."

"One moment, please."

A few seconds later, Pritchard picked up the line in his adjoining office. "Wex, how are things going?"

"We're in Destin now, Sir, waiting to check in the hotel."

"Any sign of trouble?"

"No, Sir."

"What about surveillance?"

"None we can see, Sir."

"What's your security situation?"

"I've got two men watching the plane, two at the storage facility and one shadowing the pilots."

"Good. Where are your lay-overs?"

"Merida and Panama City."

"I'm glad you're using Panama City. Santa Domingo was a clusterfuck. When are you due at the airstrip?"

"Monday at noon if everything goes as scheduled."

"I want you to go down there early, Wex."

"Me? To the airstrip? Can I ask why, Sir?"

"Just to make sure everything's secure. If you see anything unusual, call me."

"If you don't mind me asking, what am I supposed to be looking for?"

"Anything unusual. Keep an eye out for an American woman named Laura Messier."

"Laura Messier? THE Laura Messier?"

"What's the problem?"

"She's a legend at Langley, Colonel, a dangerous person to mess with. You should have told me she was involved."

"She's not. If she shows up, your job is to keep her from GETTING involved."

"How am I supposed to do that? She travels with a team, Colonel. And, if you don't mind me saying, she's got some pretty bad-assed people working for her."

"If she shows up, kill her. Is that plain enough for you?"

"Kill Laura Messier? You're joking, right?"

"How hard can it be? She won't know you're coming."

"Colonel, the KGB's been trying to kill her for years. Every agent they've sent has ended up dead."

"All I'm saying is if you have an opportunity, take it. They'll be something extra in your pay if you can."

"I'll see what I can do," Wexler said half-heartedly.

"I'm arranging for extra security on Monday," Pritchard mentioned. "You won't be alone down there."

"Extra security is always wise. I guess I'll call you from Yavisa then?"

"Yes, and tell Derek to contact me before he takes off."

"Will do."

Pritchard disconnected the line and immediately dialed a number in Tallahassee, Florida.

"Yes?" the husky female voice asked.

"I have an arrival time for you."

"Go ahead."

"Monday at noon."

"I'll let our associates know."

"What's the security situation?" Pritchard asked.

"The Miami operation may have been compromised. I've asked FARC to send more men."

"Will they?"

"I'm not sure they can. Can you ask the Panamanians?"

"I'll demand it. It's time they earned their cut of the profit."

"Call me again Monday after the transaction is complete."

Pritchard hung up. We can't screw this one up, not two shipments in a row. I need overwhelming force down there. He dialed the Panamanian Defense Forces Central Headquarters in Panama City. "This is U.S. Marine Colonel Kevin Pritchard calling from the Pentagon for Lieutenant General Costa."

"One moment, please," the pleasant female operator said in heavily accented English. "Go ahead, please, the General is on the line."

"Good afternoon, General," Pritchard said.

"Colonel, why are you calling on an open line?" Costa said, aggravated that Prichard was calling the office.

"I apologize, General. I'm operating on a short time frame. We need extra protection for the next shipment."

"You're required to provide your own security."

"I realize that, but conditions on the ground have changed."

"Why is that my problem?"

"I'm taking precautions to prevent problems."

"There's an easy solution, Colonel. Postpone the shipment."

"At this late date, that's impossible."

"Then ask your partners to provide extra security."

"I've done that, but I need you to send a platoon down there. It's in everyone's interest the exchange is secure."

There was silence on the phone for an uncomfortably long time. "No, Colonel," the General finally said, "your shipments aren't in my interest. They're in yours. And, just for the record,

I'm not sending a platoon anywhere. The President sends a squad from his office. That should be enough."

"General, this is a special circumstance." Again, there was another pause.

"Colonel, the answer is no. This conversation is over. Never call my office again on an open line!" Costa shouted before slamming the phone down. The man is an idiot, he thought leaning back in his chair. He's not delivering weapons, he's transporting cash. And, without proper security, too. There's an opportunity here.

Chapter Thirty-Four

BEN POSTL WAS late to Dulles that afternoon which put Laura behind schedule. Arriving at the Bahamian compound at dusk, the group immediately went into a working meeting over dinner in the dining room at the main house. Besides Laura and Jean, seated at the table were Rick Williams, Jack Mason, Ben Postl, Dmitri Polzin, Pete Franklin and Leon Bernard, captain of the guard unit at the compound.

"Let's review our preparations, shall we?" Jean asked. "Rick, regarding supplies, how are we doing?"

"Everything we need to sustain us two days in the field is packed and ready to load."

"I assume you're bringing your toys?"

Rick grinned. "You mean the RPGs? Of course! I had a luggage maker build cases for 'em."

Laura's ears became more attuned to the conversation at the mention of the weapons. "What are you talking about?"

Rick and Jean smiled broadly. "Didn't we tell you?" Rick asked. "We've got two RPGs."

"Where in the world did you get RPGs?"

"Rocket propelled grenade launchers to be precise for those who are unfamiliar with battlefield weapons," Rick said glancing at Postl. "As to who got their hands on them, well, you've got

Sharp to thank for that. He found them lying on the ground during the battle in Lebanon. He threw them in the evac helicopter."

"I never saw them."

"That's because you rode in the other helicopter. Jesus, I'll never forget watching you that day. You were magnificent."

"She probably doesn't want this known," Jean said, "but President Reagan awarded her the Distinguished Service Cross for that mission."

Rick whistled. "No shit? I had no idea."

"I'm afraid General Carey got a bit excited writing his report to the President," Laura said with humility.

"No one could have done what you did that day," Rick said with respect in his voice. "I couldn't believe it when I saw you climb out of the helicopter at Ramat David. I never expected to see you again."

There was a moment of silence as Laura, caught by surprise at the shift in subject matter, began to get embarrassed. Her face turned red and she quickly returned to the issue at hand. "How did you find RPG shells?"

"That's an interesting story. You remember Colonel Belkin?"

"Of course, the Russian defector."

"I tracked him down in Virginia. I figured he'd still have Russian contacts and he did. Belkin introduced me to an arms dealer who ended up selling us 32 shells. We'll take twelve with us. We've used a few for testing, by the way."

"Rick's been scaring the shit out of the wildlife," Jack Mason added.

"Not the dogs, though," Rick said, referring to the four Doberman Pinchers that patrolled the grounds. "They follow me down to the beach when I test 'em. They bark up a storm when I fire those things."

"When you raise dogs around live fire," Leon mentioned, "they become immune to the sound. Those dogs are a potent fighting force."

"It's kind of weird you named them for Santa's reindeer," Rick said, laughing at Laura.

"Yeah, Dasher, Dancer, Prancer and Vixen seemed great when they were puppies," Laura replied. "Now, not so much."

"Each one is easily worth two fighting men," Leon said. Leon was charged with taking care of the animals and probably spent more time with them than anyone else. "They're like ghosts. They move silently around the perimeter at night. Anyone who attacks us here is in for a nasty surprise."

Jean glanced at his watch. "Let's move on, shall we? We've got an early start in the morning. Mademoiselle, I think I understand my role in the mission. Ben," he said to Postl, "if I can get you inside the bank, do you feel confident you can break into the bank's system."

"From a terminal inside the bank, the only hurdle is a password."

"I'll insist they provide one," Jean replied.

"I shouldn't have a problem then."

"Excellent." Jean looked at Dmitri. "Let's review the transportation. Dmitri, talk to us about the helicopter."

"There are six Russian helicopters at a clandestine airbase in Chitre, about 150 miles northwest of Panama City. They're operated by the Panamanians under the supervision of a Soviet advisor."

"The question is, will they allow you to use one?"

Dmitri smiled a cynical expression. "Those machines are on loan from the Soviet government. Pete and I will wear Soviet captain's uniforms and have a Defense Ministry requisition in hand. The commander is required to allow it under the agreement with the Soviets."

"What if he decides to call Moscow for instructions?" Rick asked.

"You're forgetting it will be nighttime in Moscow."

"That's right, I didn't think of that."

"They'll find it difficult to contact anyone."

"What kind of capability does the helicopter have?" Jean asked.

"The Mi8-T has a range slightly less than 400 miles, which will be plenty to get from Chitre to Yavisa. We'll refuel at the airstrip and have adequate reserves for our actions in theater."

"What about armaments?" Jean asked.

"Good question," Dmitri continued. "The Mi-8T has six racks for missiles. It uses S-5 rockets and we'll insist it come fully loaded. Beyond that, it contains a heavy machine gun in the cockpit."

"Excellent. Let's move on," Jean said.

"Could I make one additional point?" Dmitri asked.

"Of course."

"The Mi-8T doubles as a personnel carrier. There'll be plenty of room to fly everyone out afterwards as long as we can re-fuel."

Jean raised an eyebrow. "That's a good point. We need to avoid hitting the fuel tanks if we want to get out of there."

Jean looked at Laura. "Here's an issue we haven't discussed. What happens if we're denied the use of special ops troops? Are we still capable of performing the mission?"

"Jean, you weren't with us in Lebanon to see the effectiveness of the Israeli helicopters," Laura replied. "We were outnumbered 20 to 1 and we still won. It was simply due to air support."

"Besides yourself, you'll have Rick, Pierre and Sharp. You'll be facing the men Young brings plus an unknown number of men from the cartel. There is the possibility you'll be overwhelmed, especially if they can down the helicopter."

"The helicopter has plating on the bottom and sides to repel small arms fire," Dmitri said. "And with the 12 mm machine gun firing at the enemy from above, I believe we'll dominate the battlefield."

"Remember, Jean, we'll also have the RPGs," Rick added. "We'll have an overwhelming advantage in arms."

"The Mademoiselle feels confident of victory with such small numbers?"

"The confidence I feel is in my colleagues, Jean, not in our numbers. Rick, Pierre and Sharp are among the best fighters I've ever seen," Laura replied. "And, if we receive help from Major Jordan's men, you should know that I've never been associated with a more professional group."

Jack Mason decided he needed to mention the obvious. "Look, if we need to increase our numbers, that's an easy fix. We could send more men from the compound. Hell, even I could go."

Both Laura and Jean shook their heads. "Jack, I appreciate the thought," Laura said, "but we must keep our defenses strong at the compound. With you in command and Leon leading our remaining ten guards, we have a potent fighting force here. If we can't defend our home, we could lose everything."

"Yeah, you're right," Jack replied. "They've already attacked the office. They could possibly attack again."

Jean paused and looked around the table. "Have we addressed all the remaining issues?" After he saw a tacit agreement around the table, he answered his own question. "Excellent." He glanced at Dmitri. "What time is our departure tomorrow?"

"Nine hundred hours."

"Rick, you'll have our supplies loaded?"

"Yes, Sir. We'll start loading at 7:00 a.m. and be finished before departure."

"Have a restful evening, everyone, and we'll meet across the road in the morning."

As was Laura's tradition before a mission, she spent the evening alone in a small hut Rick had built along the path between the main house and the beach. A quiet refuge away from the busy atmosphere of the compound, it was a perfect place to focus her mind on the mission ahead. She walked down to the beach for a time to watch Vixen, the Doberman who was her constant companion, plunge into the thick undergrowth off the beach, only to dash down the beach to splash in the water as it lapped the sand at low tide. It was chilly that evening and with only a thin sliver of a waning moon visible, the stars shone brilliantly.

Of most concern was the potential to come into conflict with CIA personnel, other Americans like herself. While Laura had always chaffed under the restrictions the agency put on her as an employee, she'd always believed the policies of the United States were just and fair. How could the Americans be so wrong this time? How could my former colleagues transport drugs in good conscience? It's against everything we were trained to uphold. Can I kill Americans? I can't think about that right now.

She finally returned to the hut in the early morning hours, falling asleep with the conviction that the mission was consistent with her values. However, whether Laura could actually kill her countrymen was a question unresolved.

Chapter Thirty-Five

LIEUTENANT GENERAL COSTA leaned back in his chair and thought about the right man for the job he had in mind. It must be someone out of the chain of command here in the capital, willing to do a job without asking too many questions. Perhaps an officer with a blemished record, eager for redemption. Who was that Captain who got himself in trouble a few months ago defending people in the slums from Noriega's thugs? The newspaper publicized the story and the man became a hero to the working poor. He's perfect. Young, naïve and expendable. Costa picked up the phone and dialed his Chief of Staff, Major Gomez, whose office was in the same building.

"Gomez, this is Costa."

"Yes, Sir?"

"Do you remember the name of that Captain who got himself in trouble a few months ago down in the favela? The one who stopped Noriega's thugs from beating people in the street."

"Ramos."

"Yes, Ramos, that's the name. Whatever happened to him?"

"The police wanted him prosecuted so we assigned him to Colon to get him out of the city."

"He's still there?"

"As far as I know."

"What are his political sentiments?"

"The incident made him appear to oppose the President. I'm not sure that's true."

"How old is he?" Costa asked.

Gomez thought for a moment before answering. "Late 20s, I'm guessing. Maybe 30. You want me to pull his file?"

"No, I don't need a background check. Just tell me what you know about him."

"I talked to him before we transferred him out. He's a talented young officer who, unfortunately, made a mistake."

"What do you mean?"

"In the incident last summer, he exceeded his authority."

"Was he right?"

"In his actions? Probably. The President's not going to get public support beating up women."

"I see," Costa replied. "Will he follow orders?"

"I think he'll do anything to gain favor here in the capital." There was silence on the line for the briefest of time as Costa reconsidered his decision.

"I want you to send Ramos' commander an order. I'd like the Captain to report to me tomorrow."

"I'll do it right away."

"Is Sergeant Garcia in town?"

"Yes, Sir. He's on leave from Nicaragua."

"I'd like him to attend the meeting as well."

"I'll make sure he's there."

"And order a platoon here in the city to prepare for a trip to Yavisa on Monday morning. I want them fully armed."

"You'll follow up with written orders?"

"No. Everything we do on this will be verbal commands only. No paperwork."

"Of course, Sir."

Chapter Thirty-Six

Friday, January 6, 1989
MISSION DAY ONE

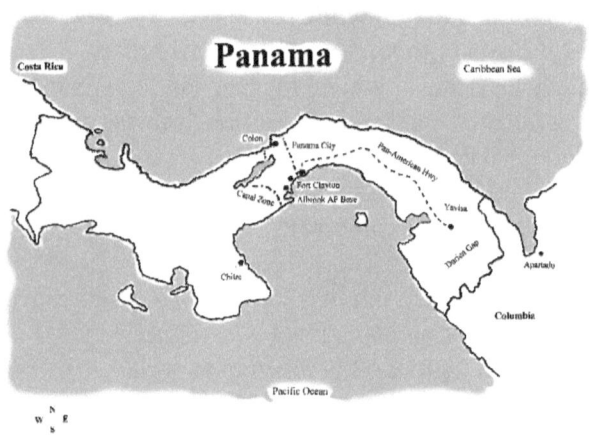

THE DASSAULT FALCON 50 jet rose from the Bahama airstrip shortly after 9:00 a.m. the next morning bound for Albrook Air Force Station, situated on the Pacific side of the canal, north of Panama City. The plane carried its usual flight crew of Dmitri, Pete and Svetlana, plus Laura and Rick who'd travel on to Yavisa, along with Jean and Ben who would infiltrate the First National Bank of Panama. Pierre and Sharp were still in Destin watching the transport aircraft but would join them in Panama City over the weekend.

Landing at Albrook after a three-hour flight, the group was directed to a hotel between the airport and Fort Clayton, a place where family and friends of those stationed at the Zone stayed during visits. After checking into the hotel, Laura confirmed her meeting with General Carson that afternoon at 15:00 hours and headed to the Fort.

Chapter Thirty-Seven

THE HEADQUARTERS BUILDING at Fort Clayton was a long three-story structure with a bright red roof and a row of palm trees along the front that separated the building from a large parade ground. The structure was part of several buildings grouped together in a quadrangle. Laura found the General's office easily where she discovered Major James Jordan sitting in the outer waiting area in his service uniform. He immediately rose to meet her.

"Ma'am, it's a pleasure to see you again." His face broke out into a broad smile and he held out his hand, but instead, Laura gave him a robust hug.

"Jim, it's wonderful to see you," she whispered in his ear. "You look well."

"You look as beautiful as ever," he said softly as his strong arms embraced her. Laura smelled the cologne he wore, realizing she was physically attracted to him. She quickly pushed the thought away. Now's not the time, she thought.

"I came looking for you at Bragg."

"They shipped us out shortly after the Lebanon mission. We were informed that we'd be part of a large build-up of forces here," he said with a shrug, "but so far, there isn't much for us to do besides guard duty."

Laura smiled a knowing expression as though she held a secret. "I have something for you if I can get General Carson to approve it."

"Apparently, the General has already heard about it. I assume that's why I'm here. I'm anxious to hear the proposal. We're bored stiff."

The duty officer interrupted the conversation. "Excuse me, the General will see you now. Please follow me."

Major General Richard Carson was a large, barrel chested man in his fifties with a flat-top haircut. Neat and trim, he looked like a relic from World War II. His large hands swallowed Laura's when they shook. "Ms. Messier, it's a pleasure. Major," he said glancing at Jordan.

"Sir," Jordan replied standing at attention.

"At ease, Major."

Carson looked back at Laura. "Please sit, both of you." He motioned to chairs in front of his desk. Carson's impersonal tone of voice gave Laura the impression he had better things to do than meet a civilian. "General Hitchens mentioned you had a letter of introduction for me?"

"Yes, Sir." Laura dug the letter out of her purse. Carson sat behind his desk, donned reading glasses and studied the letter. He looked up. "You have the necessary order and requisition forms?"

"Yes, Sir," she said, handing the paperwork across the desk.

The General unconsciously picked up a pen and held it while studying the forms. He looked at her over the rim of his glasses. "Do you have the CIA authorization with you?" he asked.

"Yes, Sir," she said, handing the letter to him. Again, he read the letter, dwelling on every word of the two paragraphs.

"Am I to understand this mission is to disrupt the production and transportation of drugs into the United States from Panama?"

"Yes, Sir."

The General laid the paperwork on the desk, took off his glasses and tossed them on the papers. He leaned forward and put his forearms on the desk, clasping his hands together. "Explain why this is within the purview of the Army, Ms. Messier. It seems to me this is a job for the DEA."

"With all respect to the agents of the DEA, they're not equipped to handle the troops President Noriega sends to guard the drug shipments."

The General responded harshly. "Ms. Messier, we're not here to start a war. Our mission is protecting the Canal Zone. Explain how this is directly connected with that?"

"It isn't," Laura replied.

Carson seemed surprised by the admission. He hesitated for a moment, not knowing how to respond. He turned his attention to Major Jordan. "Major, I asked you here today after a phone conversation with General Hitchens at Bragg. You and Ms. Messier have worked together before?"

"Yes, Sir, in Lebanon."

"The rescue of American hostages?"

"Yes, Sir."

"You rescued one of ours during that mission, didn't you?"

"Yes, Sir."

"Have you been briefed on this?" Carson asked pointing to the paperwork.

"Not yet, Sir."

"You would accept a mission without a briefing?"

"From her? Absolutely, Sir."

The General seemed perplexed at Jordan's answer. "Why would you do that, Major?"

"I trust Ms. Messier's judgment. Permission to speak freely, Sir?"

Carson nodded. "Go ahead, Major."

"Ms. Messier is the finest special ops expert I know, in or out of this man's Army. We could learn a lot from her tactics."

"I know about her reputation, Major," Carson said as though it was unimportant. "However, if I'm reading this right," he said nodding at the paperwork, "you could find yourself in direct conflict with the Panamanian military." Carson turned to Laura. "Ms. Messier, if Noriega chose to retaliate against us here in the Canal Zone, it would be difficult to repel an attack."

"Sir, I believe Noriega's likely to view this as a turf war among cartels."

Carson shook his head. "That's speculation. What I can say is General Hitchens' order is subject to my approval. And for me to approve the mission outlined here, I need something more than the Director of the CIA's authority. He doesn't command the United States Army."

Laura was ready for this line of argument. She dug a business card out of her purse and handed it to the General. "With all due respect, Sir, the President of the United States would be happy to endorse the mission. Here's the direct line to his Chief of Staff." Laura wasn't sure she'd receive an endorsement should he call, but she felt the leverage was needed.

Carson studied the card in the same fashion he'd studied the forms. He put his hand on top of the phone as though he'd place a call, then pulled it away. He laid the card aside. "Do you have a Presidential Finding for this mission?"

"No, Sir, I do not."

"Why not?"

"The action falls under previous DOD directives."

Carson stared at Laura, considering her comment. "What you're proposing is highly irregular and presents an unnecessary danger to our troops here in the Zone."

Laura thought Carson was about to deny the request. She wondered how far she could push him. "Sir, we will do everything possible to limit the risk of conflict."

"I see," Carson said, sounding unconvinced. He unconsciously tapped a pen on his desk, reviewing the paperwork, page by page, for an uncomfortably long time. He looked up. "You're requesting four men besides Major Jordan?"

"Yes, Sir. The names are listed on the requisition."

The General turned to Jordan. "Are these men available to you, Major?"

"Yes, Sir."

"Why these particular men, Ms. Messier?"

"I worked with them in Lebanon, Sir."

The General put down his pen, folded his hands in front of him and looked straight at Laura. "I'm aware of your reputation, Ms. Messier. General Hitchens speaks well of you." He motioned toward the White House Chief of Staff's business card. "Apparently, you have the support of the White House and the Pentagon. Despite my misgivings, your mission is approved." He suddenly picked up his pen and signed the requisition and order. "I'll send this to General Hitchens this afternoon. I presume he'll countersign it, or he wouldn't have sent you." He looked at the clock. "It's getting late in the day. I'm not sure whether I'll have the form back from Bragg this afternoon or in the morning. Major, I'd like you to return to my office at 10:00 hundred hours tomorrow to pick up the signed order. In the meantime, have the secretary copy the requisition and begin gathering the men and supplies listed." The General looked back and forth between them. "That will be all for today."

"Thank you, Sir," Laura and Jim said nearly simultaneously. Jordan stood, saluted and they left.

After waiting for the secretary to duplicate the requisition, Laura and Jim Jordan left together. "He's not so friendly," Laura said walking down the hallway. "I had the feeling he was going to deny the mission."

"The General's doing a great job down here considering the political situation," Jim said. "He's under a lot of pressure with the build-up of forces. The scuttlebutt is the Pentagon is planning something, but no one really knows what." They parted company at the front door. "I'm on my way to fill this," he said holding up the requisition. "See you tomorrow."

"You bet," Laura replied.

Chapter Thirty-Eight

CAPTAIN JORGE RAMOS walked down the hall toward Lieutenant General Costa's office regretting that he'd ever stopped Noriega's thugs from persecuting the poor people of the Panama City slums. Noriega's Dignity Battalion, as they were called, operated apart from the Panamanian military. Working directly for Noriega, they were responsible for breaking up street protests, intimidating the public and assassinating the President's political opponents.

After graduating from the Universidad de Panama with a degree in economics, Jorge Ramos resorted to military service to support his family and ailing parents. The Panamanian Defense Forces, known by the acronym PDF, were excited at the prospect of enlisting an educated man and recommended Ramos for the Officer Training School. Upon completion of the sixteen-week course, he was awarded the rank of Lieutenant and assigned to military headquarters in Panama City where he served five years before being promoted to Captain.

Ramos paused in the hallway outside the General's office for a moment to calm himself. He was convinced the subject of the meeting concerned his actions in the slums. Perhaps, I'm to be demoted, he thought. Or worse. They could dismiss me from the service. What would I do then? Ramos waited a few seconds outside Costa's office, straightening his uniform coat and adjusting his hat. He was stalling, trying to muster the courage to face whatever punishment the army had decided to dole out. He knocked and entered.

"Good morning, Sir," Ramos said as he saluted. "I'm Captain Jorge Ramos. My orders were to report here?"

General Costa looked up from his paperwork and studied him for a moment. He pointed to a chair along the wall. "At ease, Captain. Pull that chair in front of the desk and sit down." Costa waited until Ramos was seated before beginning. "I'd like to offer you a temporary command. It's a special unit I've created here at headquarters. Would you be interested in such an assignment?"

"Yes, Sir," a stunned and excited Ramos replied. Finally, my wait is over.

"I have a mission pending for the unit. The mission is top secret. That means you can't speak of it. You can't tell your wife. You can't celebrate with your friends. Do you have a problem with that?"

"No, Sir," Ramos said enthusiastically. This is the chance I've been waiting for.

"I'm giving you an experienced second in command to help you." Costa punched the intercom button. "Send the Master Sergeant in."

A grizzled Sergeant who looked to be in his late fifties entered and saluted. The General returned the salute. "Ramos, this is Master Sergeant Garcia." Ramos stood and saluted.

"Sit down, Captain," Costa said in annoyance. "This is a meeting, not one of your parade drills." Ramos quickly took a seat. Costa motioned toward the Sergeant who'd already taken the liberty of sitting. "The Sergeant has experience fighting in Nicaragua. He's just the man you need."

"Yes, Sir," Ramos replied, squirming in his chair. What's this about?

"Are you familiar with Yavisa?"

"Of course, Sir," Ramos replied. "I go fishing down there every year with my father-in-law."

"How about the airstrip there?"

"I've seen it from the highway, Sir."

"On Monday morning, you and Sergeant Garcia will lead an armed platoon to Yavisa and secure the airstrip. Your mission will be to stop an illegal sale of drugs between the CIA and FARC rebels."

"The CIA?" Ramos asked nervously. Costa nodded.

"The Americans are operating illegally outside the Canal Zone, Captain," Costa said. "They're flying into Yavisa on Monday to commit a crime. I want you to arrest the Americans and seize the money." Costa gestured toward Garcia. "This is where Sergeant Garcia's experience will help."

"The CIA will bring a small number of guards to protect the money," Garcia added. "Once they see an armed platoon, I expect them to surrender. But we must be ready to show force if they resist."

"What about the FARC rebels?" Ramos asked. Costa nodded to Garcia.

"Would you like to answer the question, Sergeant?"

"When the rebels arrive, we will inform them that the transaction is cancelled. We will order them to leave the area."

"What happens if they don't?"

"FARC will leave peacefully as long as we allow them to keep their drugs," Costa replied. I'm not so sure about that, Ramos thought. On fishing trips, the locals have warned us of vigilante groups who rob fishermen. Costa, seeing the doubt in Ramos' face, continued. "FARC has many buyers, Captain. They can easily arrange other transactions."

"I'm sure you're correct, Sir," Ramos replied, not willing to offer an objection to someone offering him a job.

"There's one aspect I haven't told you about yet," Costa said. "The President will send a squad of men from his Dignity

Battalion to collect a fee. They expect to receive ten percent of the cash. You will give them their fee and ask them to leave."

"What if they demand more money?" Ramos asked.

"Excellent question," Costa nodded. "You'll tell them you're securing the money on my orders. They won't argue with a platoon of rifles at your back."

"You'd like me to bring the money and the Americans back here?"

"Yes, right here to military headquarters. You should be back in the city by the end of the day."

"You make it sound easy," Ramos responded.

"It will be if you're the first to arrive on Monday. Again, secure the airstrip, allow the plane to land, confiscate the cash and make your arrests. When FARC arrives, tell them the transaction is cancelled and allow them to leave. Following that, you'll return to military headquarters with the money and the Americans."

Garcia looked at Ramos. "Do you think we can accomplish that, Captain?"

"Yes, of course."

"On Monday morning at 06:00 hundred hours," Costa said, "you'll have a fully armed platoon waiting for you in the courtyard behind the building. Forty men, two personnel carriers and a Jeep for you and the Sergeant. You'll arrive at Yavisa in due course where you will carry out your orders. If you need assistance between now and Monday, my aide in the outer office will help you. Good luck, gentlemen."

After Ramos and Garcia left his office, Costa flashed a big smile. *Someone's about to become very rich next week. If not, Ramos would not have done his job properly.*

Chapter Thirty-Nine

Saturday, January 7, 1989
MISSION DAY TWO

JEAN BROUSSARD AND the two pilots, Dmitri and Pete, left the hotel early to drive along the coast to Chitre, a small town 200 miles northwest of Panama City. The two-lane road was slow with farmers pulling onto the roadway for the obligatory Saturday trip to town. Occasionally, they'd catch a glimpse of the ocean when the road came near the coast. Otherwise, the trip was uneventful, just one cattle farm after another. They arrived at the outskirts of Chitre around noon, five hours after leaving Albrook.

Jean, who made the trip posing as an interpreter, wore a camouflage patterned Panamanian Defense Forces uniform while Dmitri and Pete wore solid green Soviet Air Force captain's shirts and khaki pants. Jean parked along what appeared to be the main downtown street and asked numerous townspeople where to find helicopters, but they simply shrugged and went about their business. Jean finally decided to stop at a police station for directions.

The police sergeant looked up from his desk and said, "May I help you?"

"I hope so," Jean said politely in Spanish. "I'm taking my friends," motioning to Dmitri and Pete, "to the helicopter base here in town, but we can't find it." Jean made a circle with his hand to denote propellers. The sergeant hesitated, not quite understanding Jean.

"Helicopters?" the sergeant asked.

"Yes, do you know where they are?"

The sergeant looked puzzled. "You mean the whirly-birds?"

"Yes, of course, the whirly-birds," Jean said with a smile.

"Go north on Route 2 about 15 kilometers."

They climbed back in the car, found Route 2 and traveled what seemed to be 15 kilometers without seeing anything that resembled a military installation. "What do we do?" asked Dmitri.

"Let's go back to Highway 50 and ask someone for directions," Jean said, turning around and going back the way they'd come. He stopped at the intersection, got out of the car and waved at several vehicles before someone pulled off the road to help. "Are you lost, soldier?" the farmer asked from an old rusted out red pick-up truck.

"I'm looking for a helicopter base around here. Would you happen to know where it is?"

"You mean the whirly-birds?"

"Yes, the whirly-birds," Jean replied.

"Goddam things frighten the livestock. They rile up the cattle to the point where they can't gain weight. Those whirly-birds belong down in the capital."

"You're quite right," Jean responded diplomatically. "I'll tell the President to remove them. But first, I need to find them. Where are they?"

The farmer jerked his thumb behind him. "Go back that way about two kilometers until you see a dirt road with a gate and no sign." The farmer sped off, muttering something unintelligible. Jean turned the car around and drove again until he found the small dirt road with a gate fastened to a post with wire. There was just enough room to pull off the highway in front of the gate.

"Is this it?" Jean asked Dmitri. "It looks like a farm driveway."

"Let's try it," Dmitri replied. He hopped out and opened the gate.

They traveled two more kilometers on a bumpy, pothole filled road until they found the helicopter pad tucked into the middle of a clearing surrounded by dense foliage. Sitting on a large flat graveled area, four large Russian helicopters were sitting evenly apart in a row. To their left sat a one-story barracks building and, on the right, a fuel tank, a parked fuel truck and a barn. The barn door was open, and two jeeps were parked inside. There seemed to be no one around.

"Gentlemen," Dmitri said pointing at the helos, "those are Russian Mi8-Ts, the best helicopters in the world. Come on, Pete. Let's check them out."

Jean walked over to the barracks building and knocked on the door. There was no answer, so he tried the door and found it locked. He yelled and pounded on the door again to no avail. Wiping the dust off a window, Jean couldn't see anything inside the darkened space. He entered the barn and found it vacant as well, except for two Jeeps covered in gravel dust. He walked to the fuel tank and found it padlocked. He tried a door on the fuel truck and found it locked as well. Jean walked back to Dmitri, who'd opened the side door to the first helicopter and found what he was looking for.

"Jean, you find anyone around?" Dmitri asked.

"I can't find a soul anywhere."

"This one's armed, Jean," Dmitri said, pointing to the nearest copter. "I count 24 missiles and several boxes of ammo for the forward gun." He looked at Pete. "Pete, would you climb in the cockpit and check to see if the machine gun is threaded?" While Pete looked in the cockpit, Dmitri opened the engine compartment, did a quick inspection and then closed it up. "If this starts, we're not sticking around for someone to stop us. Hey Pete," he shouted, sticking his head inside the cockpit door. "What'd you find?"

"Dmitri, the gun is threaded. We're ready to go."

"What's the reading on the fuel gauge?"

"Full."

"We'll be flying over water most of the way, Pete. See if you can find lifejackets." He turned to Jean. "We should get the hell out of here right now."

"Don't you need a key to start it?"

"There aren't any locks."

"Why not? This is an expensive piece of hardware."

"How many helicopter pilots do you know?" Jean thought for a second.

"Only you."

"That's why they're not locked. Not many people fly these things." Jean nodded.

"I see. By the way, after you take off," he said pointing around the area, "do that farmer a favor and blow up this place."

Dmitri smiled. "With pleasure. It'll give us a chance to test the missiles. Come on, Pete, let's get on our way."

Jean walked back to the car and watched Dmitri and Pete start the engine. The propellers slowly began to turn and soon gravel dust kicked into the air with enough volume to obscure Jean's view. The next thing Jean saw was the helicopter lift off the pad. He watched it rise, then bank in a circle before Jean returned to the car and headed back down the road. As he drove back to the main highway, he heard a huge explosion and looked in his rear-view mirror as the pad erupted in fire and smoke. Dmitri fired two missiles into the parked helicopters on the pad. Flames from burning fuel belched thick, black smoke. Another swing around and missiles hit the barracks building and the barn. As Jean turned back onto the highway, he saw the helicopter head south toward the ocean. We've got air support, he thought.

Chapter Forty

BEFORE LAURA LEFT the hotel Saturday morning, she checked messages on the DST phone drop. Pierre called to report the cargo plane in Destin had taken off early that morning as they'd predicted it would, but only five of six guards had flown out on the plane. Laura wasn't sure what that meant, but she didn't have time to assess it. Pierre made reservations for Sharp and himself on a flight to Panama City later that morning. They'd be arriving at Torrijos International Airport in Panama City later in the afternoon.

Laura found Major James Jordan sitting in the General's outer office when she arrived at Fort Clayton Headquarters promptly at 10:00 a.m. "Good morning, Ms. Messier."

"You can call me Laura, you know," she replied.

"On base, Ma'am, you're Ms. Messier," he said with a hint of a smile. "Especially around this office. I took the liberty of picking up the official order early this morning. The supplies are pulled and loaded into the jeeps. When are we pulling out?"

"Tomorrow morning. 8:00 a.m. sound okay?"

"08:00 it is, Ma'am."

"Great. Where are we meeting?"

"At the motor pool. When you walk out of Headquarters, take the road to the left of the building and you'll find us. We'll be out front with the jeeps."

"See you then," she said.

After Rick picked up Pierre and Sharp from Torrijos airport and Jean had returned from Chitre, the group gathered over dinner in one of the small meeting rooms offered by the hotel. During dinner, Jean related his story of finding the helicopter base and Laura described her meeting with General Carson. "We found the sixth man, the one who didn't fly out on the cargo plane," Pierre said.

"He was on the commercial flight with us out of Fort Walton," Sharp added. "Pierre and I were sitting in First Class and he passed right by us on his way back to the cheap seats. I just about shit my pants when I saw him."

"Did he recognize you?" Laura asked.

"Not that we could tell," Sharp replied. "He just kept moving down the aisle."

"Did you see him in the terminal when you arrived?"

"We got off the plane before he did, so he was behind us going through customs. We were afraid to look."

"That was the proper way to handle it," Jean said. "We know he's here and we know he'll turn up in Yavisa."

"He's a scout," Laura said. "He'll show up early to check out the airstrip. When will we hear from Dmitri, Jean?"

Jean looked at his watch. "He should have arrived by now. If you'll excuse me, I'll check the phone drop." Jean used the phone on the wall to place the call.

Laura continued the conversation. "Ben, how are you feeling about the bank job on Monday?"

"If I can get a password, we won't have a problem. One question, though. What if we're caught?"

Laura realized Ben was nervous. "If you follow Jean's lead, you won't be. Jean's a master of deception and you'll learn a lot watching him work. I know I have. I don't think he's ever been caught at anything. Besides which, I've heard the banking system down here is a mess." Ben didn't seem convinced, so Laura continued. "But let's imagine for a minute that everything possible goes wrong." Laura shrugged. "If you get caught, we come and get you. It's as simple as that. Do you have the bank account number in Zurich?"

"Jean has it."

"Then there aren't any worries. Walk in, act confident, and wire transfer whatever you can find. Then get the hell out of there."

Jean returned to the table with a smile. "Pilots have all the luck, don't they? Dmitri and Pete landed in Yavisa where, apparently, their Russian uniforms are popular with the locals. The fuel truck filled their helicopter, they rented a room at the hotel and they're sampling the local cuisine as we speak."

Laura looked at Ben and shrugged. "See, I told you. No worries."

"What time are we pulling out in the morning?" Rick asked.

"08:00 hours. We'll have to swing by Albrook to retrieve our weapons from the plane and then we're on our way."

"Now, if you'll excuse me, ladies and gents," Rick replied, "I'm going back to my room to watch movies."

Sharp rose from the table as well. "I'm hitting the bar for a nightcap."

"I'll come, too," Pierre said.

Laura and Jean looked at each other. "I guess we're adjourned," Laura said with a smile.

Chapter Forty-One

Sunday, January 8, 1989
MISSION DAY THREE

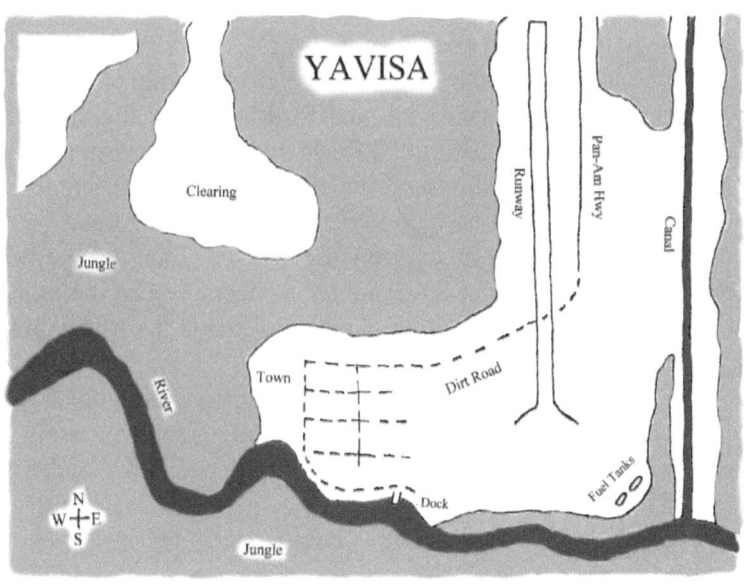

DMITRI AND PETE left the airstrip at first light to fly over the bay into Colombia to find the headquarters of the Malagua cartel. After an hour's flight across the bay, they flew up and down the coast until Dmitri handed Pete a pair of binoculars. They used headsets to communicate with each other since the engine and rotors made too much noise to talk over. "Here, take a look," Dmitri said. "Does that look like the estate in the photo?"

The helicopter made a wide turn around a large property just outside Apartado, Dmitri being careful to stay away from the house. Pete compared the sat photo from Steve Tilton with what he saw on the ground. "How do we know this is even Apartado?"

"It has to be," Dmitri replied. "We flew over Turbo a couple of minutes ago. Apartado is the next town south. I'm sure we're in the right place." Pete folded the photo and stuck it in a cargo netting pouch next to his seat.

"I hope so. I wouldn't want to blow up the wrong house in the wrong town."

"I'll swing around and do another pass."

"She said it was the largest place in Apartado?" Pete asked. He swung his binoculars back and forth studying the area before answering his own question. "I don't see anything larger than this one. I see several cars in the driveway. Whoever they are, they've got money. Why don't we go lower and get a closer look?"

Dmitri buzzed right overtop the house. Guards around the perimeter fired automatic weapons at them. The ammunition bounced off the helicopter shielding and made a distinct pinging sound.

"I think we've got the right house," Dmitri deadpanned.

"Damn!" Pete shouted. "They're a little sensitive about their privacy. We better pull up. They might get lucky and hit the rotors."

"Did you see what I saw?" Dmitri said, moving away from the gunfire.

"See what?"

"Kids out for an early morning swim in the pool," Dmitri said. "There are children down there."

Dmitri turned so the house appeared on Pete's side of the craft. He kept far enough away to discourage weapons fire. "I see them now," Pete said, staring below, "playing with a beach ball." He lowered the binoculars and looked at Dmitri. "We can't fire missiles at kids."

Dmitri gave Pete a grim assessment. "Laura's going to have to figure out another way. Let's get out of here."

An hour later, they landed back at the airstrip where Hondo, the man who looked after the fuel tanks, came running from a nearby shack that served as his home. "You want more fuel, Mr. Russian?" he asked. Since Dmitri had doubled the man's fee the first time, Hondo was eager to sell more.

"Yes, please." Dmitri handed Hondo a fistful of American dollars. "Is this enough for a couple of more fill-ups?"

"Yes, Sir." He handed Dmitri a spare key to the fuel truck. "Refuel whenever you like." He motioned toward the town. "Bar open if you like drink. Yellow building near river."

Dmitri scanned the buildings. "That one?" he pointed.

"Yes, Sir."

"They serve coffee?" Hondo smiled and nodded.

"My wife is owner."

"Thanks."

Dmitri and Pete walked across the dirt runway to the yellow building. "Have you seen Laura's group yet?" Pete asked.

"No, but they'll be here. Let's get coffee and hang out around the copter for a while. I'm sure they'll find us."

Chapter Forty-Two

BRET WEXLER LEFT Panama City in a rental car early Sunday morning headed for Yavisa. The hotel clerk had instructed him to head east on Route 1, the Carretera Panamericana. The highway ran along the coast through downtown and he found it easily. Once the highway turned south outside the city, Wexler figured he'd end up in Yavisa. It's the only main road south through the country, he thought. Traffic was light on Sundays and after a two and a half-hour trip, the paved road ended, and Wexler pulled into town. Making his way along the rutted dirt road, he found the only hotel in town, the same place Dmitri and Pete had stayed the previous evening. It was a small place, only six rooms for rent with a common bathroom. After paying in cash, Wexler asked to use the only phone in the hotel, the one at the desk. He laid more cash on the counter and dialed long distance.

"Colonel, it's Wexler," he said.

"Wex, good to hear from you," Pritchard replied. "Where are you?"

"I just arrived in Yavisa."

"See anything unusual?"

"Not yet, I just checked into what they call a hotel here."

"Deluxe accommodations, I'm sure."

"Yeah, it's a real shithole, just like the rest of the town."

"Call me again this evening after you look around. Keep an eye out for Messier."

"Will do."

Wexler hung up. Geez, what's his fixation with Laura Messier? He turned to the clerk behind the counter. "Have you seen an American woman around town? She's about this tall," he held his hand at eye level, "with long brown hair."

"No, Señor. You only American we see. Russians, yes, American woman, no."

"Russians?"

The man made a circular motion with his hand above his head. "Whirly-bird."

Wexler had no idea what he meant. "Are they still here?" The man shook his head.

"No, leave this morning." The man imitated a helicopter sound and moved his hand in a circle above his head again.

Wexler finally understood the man meant helicopters. What would a Russian helicopter be doing in Yavisa? "Ah, yes, whirly-bird," he replied, imitating the circular motion with his hand. The man nodded. "One more question, do you know of a restaurant nearby?"

"Food," he said with a nod, "next building." Wexler gave the man a patient smile. Communicating with these people is going to be a challenge.

"Thanks." Wexler headed out the door in search of breakfast.

Chapter Forty-Three

THE SMELL OF coffee hit Wexler as soon as he entered the restaurant. He'd failed to eat before he left Panama City. The waitress led him to a table, poured him a cup of coffee without being asked and handed him a handwritten menu in Spanish. He guessed panqueques meant pancakes. The locals stared at him briefly and decided he wasn't a threat. They returned to their casual conversation. Restaurants are the same all over the world, aren't they? Regulars sit and talk among themselves. Town gossip is the most popular subject and Wexler figured the waitress must hear it all. "Ma'am," Wexler said as she refilled his coffee cup, "have you seen any Americans in town?"

"Tu solamente gringo," she said in the disinterested tone of voice that wait staff use. What the hell does that mean? Wexler wondered. Maybe she means just me.

"What about Russians?"

"El Rusos? She asked. Wexler nodded.

"Dos soldados." Dos means two. Two soldiers. That confirms what the hotel clerk said. After consuming generous portions of pancakes, shredded potatoes and coffee, Wexler begrudgingly decided it was time to acquaint himself with the town. He paid his bill in cash and sauntered up and down the two main streets, stopping to peek in shop windows and nodding to residents. Children are running everywhere, people are smiling, relaxed.

Normal stuff for a small town. Nothing suspicious here. I'd better check the airstrip. Wexler headed toward a large open area on the east side of town where he found the dirt runway running north to south, parallel to the town. What do you know, they're here. He stopped to watch two men wearing military uniforms work on a large helicopter at the far end of the runway near the fuel tanks. He saw the large red star painted on the side. Russians. Maybe they'll talk. He headed in their direction.

"Don't look now," Pete said, sticking his head out of the side window of the cockpit, "but a man's approaching. He looks American."

"Let me do the talking," Dmitri replied, closing a bay door. "My English is bad enough as it is, but I can make it worse."

"You wearing your sidearm?"

"Always," Dmitri replied.

"Unbutton it."

Dmitri reached down and unsnapped the flap over top of the weapon.

"Everything checks out here," Pete said walking down the stairs after closing the cockpit window. "We're ready to fly."

They purposely didn't look in Wexler's direction until he stood next to them. "Hello there," Wexler said in a cheery tone of voice.

Dmitri used his thickest Russian accent. "No ride today." He waved his arm toward the dock. You take boat."

"That's a nice helicopter you've got there."

"Junk!" Dmitri kicked the bottom. "We almost crash."

"Those are pretty big missiles you've got there," Wexler said looking at the long, cylindrical objects attached to hangers off each side of the fuselage.

"Maybe blow up now. Boom!"

"Do you mind me asking why you're here?" Wexler asked as delicately as possible. Dmitri shook his head.

"No ride today."

"No, I don't want a ride. I just wondered why you're here."

"Fuel," Dmitri said shrugging, pointing to the fuel tanks as though it was obvious.

"Oh, I see. You're not staying long?"

"No fishing today. You take boat." Dmitri pointed in the general direction of the town dock.

"Have you seen an American woman in town?"

"American woman?" Dmitri mimicked the figure of a woman with his hands. "Ooo-la-la! Sexy American woman?" Dmitri smiled and shook his head. "No woman." Dmitri and Pete climbed in the copter while Wexler stood watching. Dmitri opened the cockpit window and stuck his head out.

"We leave. Watch head," he said pointing up toward the blades.

"Nice talking with you," Wexler said looking up at Dmitri.

Dmitri slammed the window shut and started the engines. He leaned over to Pete. "We better get out of here. That asshole's asking too many questions." Wexler ducked his head and sprinted away to a safe distance to watch the helicopter take off and head north following the Pan-American Highway.

"See that clearing west of us?" Pete said, pointing out the window after lift-off. "The military vehicles. I'll bet that's Laura." Dmitri glanced over.

"Let's fly north for a few minutes while that asshole watches, then swing out over the ocean and come in from the west. We'll land right beside them."

"Roger that," Pete replied.

Chapter Forty-Four

THREE UNMARKED JEEPS left Panama City Sunday morning, traveling the Pan-American Highway as it arcs its way around the Gulf of Panama. Loaded with weapons and supplies, the occupants wore combat fatigues that contained no insignia to identify them. They kept the soft tops closed to obscure the view of weapons and passengers. Major James Jordan's team included snipers Adam Wright and Nick Marshall, explosives expert Carl Thomas and field medic, Jerry Stock. All were on the team that rescued hostages in Lebanon. Laura's team included Rick, Pierre, and Sharp along with herself.

During the three-hour trip, the entourage passed the numerous farms that produced Panama's cash crops of bananas, sugar cane and corn. Laura watched farmers begin their workday in the fields, another day of toil for those who tended crops and livestock.

Laura, visualizing the mission in her mind, was deep in thought when Jordan leaned over to speak. "Laura?" Not receiving a response, he was more forceful the next time. "Laura!" She finally heard him and looked over.

"Sorry, Jim, I wasn't paying attention."

"Are you okay?"

"I'm fine."

"Do you have sat photos I can look at?" I only brought a map."

"Oh, yes, sorry," she said, scrambling to pull the photos she'd received from Steve Tilton out of her bag. "Here, take a look."

Jordan studied the airstrip photo. "This is the airstrip we're attacking?"

"Yes."

"It's a tight space. Three sides are blocked by the jungle, the town, and the river. The only exit's the highway to the north. We sure could use air support."

"We have it."

"Air support?" Jordan asked, not quite believing what he heard. "You didn't tell me."

"I omitted it because I wasn't quite sure how to explain it to the General. We're using a Russian helicopter."

"Russian?" Jordan asked, raising his voice in skepticism. "A Russian copter?"

Laura was amused by the reaction. She gave Jordan a reassuring smile. "Some say it's better than anything the Americans have. It's loaded with arms and big enough to carry a squad of troops."

"Do you mind me asking how you acquired it?"

"There's a small Russian base in northern Panama they use to support the Sandinistas." Laura hesitated, thinking of an appropriate explanation. "Let's just say we borrowed one of their copters."

Jordan laughed as though he didn't believe it. "And you didn't tell this to Carson?"

Laura gave him a coy wink. "I'll tell him when we get back."

"Who's your pilot?"

"My private jet pilot. He's familiar with Russian copters."

"He's rated to fly them? And I suppose you're going to tell me he just walked into a Russian base and flew one of their copters away?"

"Well," Laura said, with a slight grin, "as a matter of fact, he is and that's exactly what he did."

"The Russians didn't mind him taking one?"

"He's a former Russian military pilot, Jim. He walked in their base wearing his old uniform, he took a copter and blew up the base up on his way out," she said with a smile. "I hardly think they're in a position to complain, a couple of hundred miles from an American air base."

"How did he avoid our radar? Albrook can see anything in the air."

"I can't answer that. I have no idea."

"I don't mean to question your judgement, you understand, it's just difficult to believe."

Laura gave him a look of amusement. "That's how we accomplish our missions, Jim, by doing things no one expects." She glanced at the sat photos. "You've got a feel for tactics. What do you think?" Jordan studied the photo of the town.

"Well, FARC rebels will deliver the cargo."

"I'd heard that."

"They'll come out of the jungle on the river. And they'll come in force, maybe platoon strength, 40 men or so. They'll also come late. They'll want everyone present before they show themselves."

"Will they scout the airstrip before they arrive?"

"You bet they will," Jordan said, shooting her a warning look. "We've studied their tactics. They'll send one boat in with a scout team and hold the rest upstream until they get an all clear."

"We should put a set of eyes upstream," Laura said.

"Absolutely. Let's put a couple of men at the apex of this hairpin," Jordan said pointing to the map.

"I want to remind you; Noriega will send one squad of men to monitor the shipment."

"I read that in the mission description. How do you know he'll only send one squad?"

"I don't."

"How many men on the plane?"

"Five, maybe six guards."

"So, we've got a platoon of FARC, and roughly two additional squads. That's about 60 men, give or take." Jordan whistled to express his concern. "We're badly outnumbered. What's your plan?"

"We hide in the jungle and watch the plane arrive. We wait until the drugs are loaded, then the helicopter attacks the plane. Hopefully, the plane and the drugs are destroyed." Jordan thought about Laura's scenario.

"And if not?" Laura grimaced.

"In that case, we'll have some work to do." Jordan imagined what that might entail.

"Surprise should work in our favor. How do we hide a helicopter?"

"I don't think we have to hide it," Laura replied, as though it was evident. "I'm sure the airstrip gets plenty of traffic."

"Well, we're going to have to move it off the airstrip beforehand. And wherever we move it, the plane's gonna see it on approach."

"I'm sure they will, but pilots are accustomed to seeing parked aircraft. I don't think it's a problem."

Jordan nodded. "Let's hope so." Jordan pointed to the photo. "See this clearing to the west?" he asked.

"Yes."

"We should camp there. It can't be seen from the road or the town." Jordan drew an imaginary line with his index finger. "It looks like we can get there by pulling off the highway right before the town. With any luck, no one will know we're there."

"It's as good a place as any," Laura replied. Jordan thought about the strategy.

"You know, you could have just sent a helicopter down here to blow the plane." Laura grimaced.

"You mentioned it a minute ago. If the copter's not successful, we need boots on the ground to follow up."

"Well, I'm not going to argue the point. I'll just say the helicopter is the key to our success. You're sure it's at the airstrip?"

"We received a confirmation call last night."

Chapter Forty-Five

LAURA'S ENTOURAGE PULLED off the highway before Yavisa. "According to the photo," Jordan said, "if we head west across this grassy area, we'll be able to swing around to the south along a line of vegetation and find the clearing."

"It's impossible to tell how far it is from the photo," Laura replied.

"It shouldn't be far. Yavisa's a couple of miles ahead. The clearing's due west of the town."

"Let's go for it."

The Jeeps headed off the highway and drove over terrain much rougher than it appeared from the photo. The tall grass hid drainage ditches, pools of standing water infested with mosquitos, large ant hills, and rocks. They traveled west until they were met by a solid wall of jungle, vegetation so thick it was impossible to penetrate. They turned south along the vegetation line and followed the grassy area until they were surrounded by jungle on three sides.

"Stop," Jordan said to Nick Marshall, his driver. "This must be the clearing in the photo. The river would be that way," he said, motioning to the south. "Through that strip of jungle to the east should be the airstrip and the town."

The group began climbing out of the Jeeps to look around. Jordan turned to Nick. "Nick, can you take someone and cut your way straight east through the jungle. See if you can find the airstrip. The rest of us will start setting up the camp."

"Yes, Sir." He walked to a Jeep where Jerry Stock, the medic, was unloading supplies. "The Major wants us to find the airfield through that jungle over there. Bring your med kit in case I get bit by a big-assed snake."

Stock pulled a machete out of the back of his Jeep. "It's not the snakes you need to worry about, Nick. It's the scorpions. Here, you'll need this," he said handing a machete to Nick. "It doubles as my scalpel."

"That's not funny," Nick said.

"Oh yeah it is," Jerry said smiling. "You just fail to see the humor in it."

They headed off into the vegetation, thick with broad leaf ferns taller than men, trees with vines hanging to the ground and underbrush as high as a man's waist, so thick that the ground underneath couldn't be seen. A few yards into the vegetation and it was as though the jungle had swallowed them. Nick sliced his way one step after another, one hack after another, stopping after about ten yards.

"Shit, this is hard work."

"Here, we'll take turns," Jerry replied, reaching for the machete.

Nick allowed Jerry to move in front. "Not exactly the saber they give you at West Point," Nick said with a grin.

Swinging the machete several times for each step forward, their line of sight shrunk to the few inches in front of their face. They were completely in shadow; the trees and vines hanging above blocked the sunlight. Even the sky disappeared underneath the jungle canopy. Whatever wildlife existed in that thin strip of jungle had either vanished or decided to remain silent. The men took turns hacking their way through, vines and leafy stalks dropping to the ground after each slice, the men stomping them as they inched their way through.

"Stay away from anything that has spikes or thorns on it," Jerry advised. "I read a book last night. They're all poisonous."

Nick checked his compass periodically to make sure they headed east. "I can't see shit," he said. "It's easy to see why no one goes in the jungle." It took a half-hour to travel the couple of hundred yards to where the jungle appeared to thin. "Stop," Nick said. "I think we're here." They moved to a spot where they could see through the remaining vegetation. "Hand me the field glasses." Jerry pried the glasses from his belt and handed them over. Nick stepped on fern branches, bending them to the ground and moved forward a couple of steps. "This is it. A helicopter just took off and headed north."

"Let me have a look," Jerry said, reaching for the glasses. He followed the path of the helicopter as it headed north. "We can see the entire field from here. Come on, let's go back. Leave the ferns in place so it won't look like there's a path."

"Fine by me. I'm sick of the jungle." They took turns widening their path on the return trip, popping out of the jungle right where they started about ten minutes later.

Meanwhile, Jordan had ordered the Jeeps driven back and forth to flatten the grass. They were parked in a large triangle to establish a perimeter. Inside the triangle, he'd asked the men to set tents in another triangle to provide an inner ring. Nick and Jerry walked inside the camp and found Jordan staking out a tent. "Sir, we came out at the center of the runway," Nick said. He pointed toward the path they'd cut. "We can see everything."

"You boys look a little winded," Jordan said with a smile.

"You need a bulldozer to get through that crap," Nick replied.

Jordan stood and looked up and down the line of vegetation. "We need two more paths, one to the edge of town and a third to the river. The path to the town should be just south of the one we cut. The river should be straight south," he said, pointing to a spot farther away. "Adam, you and Carl do one and get Sharp and Pierre to do the other."

"With pleasure, Sir."

Adam and Carl had a similar experience hacking through the jungle to the town, but they emerged again having created a second path through the vegetation. "All done, Sir," Adam said. "Piece of cake, really. I don't know what those guys were complaining about."

"I heard that," Nick said, walking past carrying a load of supplies.

By the time Sharp and Pierre returned from cutting a third path, the makeshift campsite was complete. "I think we've done what we can to bivouac. Let's gather everyone together." He brought the group together in the middle. "We won't begin surveillance until morning, but let's set a defensive perimeter tonight in case we're discovered. No fires this evening; MRE's for dinner. Use flashlights inside the tents and glow sticks outside. Four-hour shifts on the perimeter. Sharp, you and Pierre have the first watch. Let's get to it."

Sharp and Pierre walked away to don vests, night vision goggles, sidearms and automatic weapons. "Geez, you'd think we were back in the fucking Army," Sharp said, walking out of camp. "First, we do landscaping and now guard duty." He pointed in the opposite direction. "I'll take that side."

"Go right up to the edge of the clearing on each side," Pierre replied. "At least we won't be standing out in the open when we're shot."

"You need an attitude adjustment, Pierre," Sharp replied with a chuckle. "Take a look around. We're in the beautiful jungles of Panama."

"That's what I'm talking about."

"Oh yeah, it's not so great, is it."

"Nope."

Chapter Forty-Six

DMITRI MADE A wide circle before approaching the clearing from the west, skimming the treetops hoping the sound of the helicopter blades would be muffled. He gently set the craft down in the clearing next to the camp. Laura and Jordan ran over as Dmitri and Pete climbed out.

"Dmitri! Pete! Am I glad to see you," Laura said, embracing both of them.

"No worries," Dmitri said with a smile. He spread his hands out wide. "As you can see, we've got air support."

"Nice to meet you," Jordan said, shaking hands with both pilots after Laura introduced them. Jordan nodded toward the copter. "That's a nice machine. I like those missiles you've got."

"Soviet S-5s," Dmitri said, nodding, "a very reliable weapon. If we're the only thing in the sky, it's a huge advantage." He looked at Laura. "By the way, before we left town, there was a man asking about you. An American. Seemed to be in his thirties. He didn't identify you by name, but I'm sure he was looking for you."

"He's a scout for the American drug runners. Did he suspect anything?"

Dmitri glanced at Pete then back at Laura. "Not as far as we could tell."

"Dmitri did his best 'I can't speak English' routine," Pete said with a smile. "It was a short conversation."

"How'd the mission go in Apartado?"

Dmitri frowned and looked embarrassed. "We had a problem." He kicked at the ground when he spoke. "We found the house all right, but there were kids playing in the swimming pool." He looked up at Laura. "We didn't blow the house, Laura. We're not going to kill kids."

Laura hugged him. "It's okay. You're a good man, Dmitri."

"I hope you're not angry."

"Not at all," she said with a smile. "We'll do it another way. Do you think you could find the place at night?"

"If I had night vision goggles, I'm sure of it."

Laura looked at Jordan. "Could you spare a pair for my friend here?"

"Sure," he replied. "Do you mind telling me what this is about?"

She hesitated before answering. "I didn't tell you because it's not part of your mission, Jim. It's across the border in Colombia."

"I see." Jordan thought for a moment. "Explain it to me."

"I'm going to kill the leader of the Malagua cartel tonight."

Again, Jordan hesitated, thinking about his orders. "You're right; operating in Columbia would exceed our orders. I doubt the General would approve it, but I do have the authority to act as conditions change. If we know where the cartel leader is, let's go get him. I'll deal with the General when we get back. I need a minute to ask the men, though. This is strictly voluntary."

"Of course," she replied.

Jordan called his men together. "Fellas, I'm going on a mission tonight that, technically, violates our orders." He looked each one in the eye. "I want to know whether any of you would be willing to come with me. If you're not comfortable with it, stay and guard the camp. Dmitri here," he said, gesturing toward the copter, "is going to fly us inside Colombia tonight. The target is the leader of the drug cartel. We need some back-up."

Jordan watched the instantaneous reaction. Nick Marshall decided to speak for the group. "We're coming, Sir. All of us."

Jordan smiled. "Thanks, guys." The men walked back to Laura. "We're in," Jordan said. "All of us."

"That's great news," Laura replied. "Let's do some planning."

"There's something you should know, Laura, as you plan this," Dmitri mentioned. "There are guards patrolling the grounds. They took shots at the helicopter as we passed over."

"How many?"

Dmitri looked at Pete. "How many would you say, Pete?"

"Three or four we could see. Well-armed, too."

"What do you think?" Laura asked Jordan.

"We take six and leave three to guard the camp," Jordan replied. "It's not enough for either job, but we'll make it work." Jordan looked at his group. "Nick, Adam? You two come with me." He looked at Laura. "That's three from our group. We need three from yours." Laura looked at her group.

"Rick, if you'll stay here to guard the camp, I'll take Sharp and Pierre." Rick nodded.

"That's fine. I would like to point out, though, that helicopter noise is going to be a problem. You could alert the target on your approach."

Laura glanced at Dmitri. "Can we do anything to muffle the noise?" Dmitri nodded toward the helicopter.

"This one has noise suppression features absent on most battle copters. It's perfect for special ops. The rotors are staggered, and the tips have been modified. It's about as quiet as you can get. If we land, say, a half-mile away, I don't think they'll hear anything."

"What do you think?" Laura asked Rick.

"Fine by me."

Laura and Jordan proceeded to work out a plan. Dmitri and Pete described the configuration of the house in much greater detail than the photo and Jordan explained how to coordinate the attack. As darkness began to fall and the glow sticks reflected an eerie green shade of light around the camp, everyone came together around a plan to attack the house.

"We should get some rest," Jordan said after the group had coalesced around the plan. "Dmitri, when are we pulling out?"

"It'll take about an hour flight time, so if we leave here at midnight, we'll have enough time to do the mission and get back before dawn."

"Spread the word then. We leave at zero hundred hours."

Chapter Forty-Seven

AFTER BRET WEXLER watched the helicopter leave the airstrip, he walked back to the hotel and placed another call.

"Hello Wex," Pritchard said. "What have you got?"

"Sir, no one in Yavisa has seen Messier."

"Any sign of trouble at the airstrip?"

"The only thing unusual was a Russian helicopter that stopped for fuel. Two uniformed Russians were on board. They left after refueling and headed northbound toward Panama City."

"You don't know where they came from?"

"My guess is Colombia or maybe Ecuador."

"I'm not sure how the Russians could have helicopters in Panama without us knowing about it. I'll give General Carson a call at Fort Clayton. This is something he should know about. I appreciate the tip, Wex."

"Other than that, there's nothing to report."

"Let me know how things go tomorrow."

"Will do, Colonel."

Pritchard hung up and immediately asked his secretary to contact Fort Clayton. When she had Carson's office on the line, she connected Pritchard.

"Major General Carson's office, Lieutenant Hinch, speaking," the Duty Officer said.

"This is Colonel Kevin Pritchard, Pentagon Office for Special Projects calling for General Carson."

"I'm sorry, Sir. The General has left for the day. Can I have him return your call tomorrow?"

"It's important that I speak with him first thing in the morning. He can reach me through the Pentagon switchboard, Colonel Kevin Pritchard, Special Projects."

"Yes, Sir. I've got it. I'll let him know."

Pritchard slammed the phone down. Damn, he said under his breath. Security problems, Messier's missing and now Russian helicopters? What else can go wrong? Another failed mission and we're shut down permanently. I can't let this fail; I'm going down there myself. Pritchard found a commercial flight later that evening from Dulles to Miami, continuing to Panama City. He booked a first-class ticket and hustled to the airport.

Chapter Forty-Eight

Monday, January 9, 1989
MISSION DAY FOUR

THE HELICOPTER PLUNGED eastward into total darkness after midnight. The moon was just a sliver in the sky, a waxing moon that provided no light, but allowed the stars to twinkle brightly. Still, that wasn't enough light to see much on the ground. Looking out a window, Laura thought she saw a light or two from an isolated village near the coast, but it could have been a fishing vessel. She wasn't sure. Laura thought she remembered the bay being called Brazo Leon Rio Atrato.

The darkness made it impossible to tell where the jungle ended and the bay began, but once over the Colombian coast, Laura saw lights to the north on the horizon. That must be Turbo, she thought, the largest town in the area. Inside the helicopter, dim red bulbs lit the interior. She watched as the men prepared themselves for a drop, putting black grease paint on their faces, checking their gear and loading weapons.

When Pete looked back and gave them a warning that they were getting close, the men put night vision goggles over their foreheads. These Special Ops troops had done this scores of times, even Sharp and Pierre knew what they were doing. But for Laura, it was new. She watched and copied their routine.

Laura saw lights from the small village of Apartado as the helicopter made a wide arc around the town from the north to the eastern side. She knew they were close to their drop zone. Pete climbed back into the cargo area.

"Okay, we're coming up on the estate. You won't have any trouble seeing it, they've got security lights everywhere. We're dropping you off about a half-mile straight east and we won't land. Dmitri will hover near the ground. You'll have to jump and roll. Once you're on the ground, we'll land nearby and check coms."

Laura felt the copter descend, then hover a few feet off the ground. "Ready?" Pete shouted. He flung the bay door open and the cool, humid air hit Laura's face with a blast. "Jump!" Pete yelled. One by one, the attackers jumped while Dmitri slowly moved forward to keep the jumpers clear of each other. Once the team was on the ground, the helicopter rose and banked away farther east. Jordan moved from man to man to inquire whether they were injured in the jump.

"Messier, you okay?" He asked as he passed her.

"I'm fine."

"Check your gear. You got everything?"

Laura felt her belt and pockets. "Yes."

Jordan moved on down the line to check the next jumper. Laura heard a distinct command, "Squad to me!" It was Jordan's voice and the group moved in his direction. "Time check. Coming up on 01:22." He waited a few seconds, "Mark! Everyone, tap your breastplate." Laura heard everyone rap on the steel plate sown into their vests. "Goggles down. We'll move single file. I've got point; Sharp you take the rear. We don't move until we hear Dmitri on coms."

A minute later, she heard Dmitri's voice through the com set. "Bird to ground. You read me?"

"Loud and clear, bird." That was Jordan's voice in response.

"Proceed. Bird out."

Jordan moved forward. "Fall in line, team. Can everyone hear me on coms?"

"Yes, Sir," each man said in response.

"Move out." Jordan, Nick, Pierre, Laura, Adam and Sharp moved forward silently, single file, each one an arm's length behind the other. Occasionally, Jordan would hold his right hand up in a fist and the squad would freeze in place. Then, he'd begin walking again. The terrain wasn't jungle as it was across the bay in Panama. It was tilled fields separated by rows of trees and brush that served as wind breaks. The group walked along those rows to avoid open areas. They moved efficiently and silently. It wasn't long until the group could see the estate's security lights shining in the distance. "Coming up on target," Laura heard Jordan say in the coms. After another hundred yards or so, the house became visible through the trees. Jordan held his hand up. "Let's hold here. Count the guards, watch their rotation.

Chapter Forty-Nine

THE DELGADO HOUSE was a ranch style set along an asphalt paved road about a fifteen-minute drive from Apartado. The house faced westward and a three-car garage extended to the left, off the north side. A graveled circle drive made a semi-circle from the road to the house and back to the road. The ground sloped away from the back of the house, steep enough for a basement walkout that led to a swimming pool held in place by a retaining wall. The large lawn area was well manicured and surrounded by native trees and brush some distance away.

Over the next fifteen minutes, the attackers counted guards outside the house. Laura noticed Jordan's men weren't using night vision goggles due to the security lights. "I count six outside, Major," Sharp said to Jordan. "They walk the property three times in pairs. It takes four minutes to complete the trip." Sharp knows what he's doing, she thought. "They use that sliding door off the patio to enter and exit the house."

"Everyone hear that?" Jordan asked. "Six guards walking in pairs. Expect more inside. Messier, to me," Jordan said over the coms. Laura made her way to the front. Jordan looked at the house through field glasses while he spoke in hushed tones. He pushed the miniature microphone away from his face and whispered. "The configuration is just how the pilots described it. See that retaining wall?" He asked. Laura found her binoculars and studied the house as Jordan spoke. "It separates the pool from the lawn behind it. That sliding glass door on the pool patio could be our entry point."

"They cut away the brush to give them a perimeter," Laura said. "There's no cover."

"It's a kill zone. Adam and Sharp should be able to shoot from cover right here. We need Nick and Pierre on the other side of the house. And we've got to cut power."

"As soon as the lights are cut, they'll know something's wrong."

"Maybe not," Jordan replied. "The power grid's unreliable down here. It could be an everyday thing for them."

"What about a back-up generator?"

"If I were them, I'd have one. They're usually placed where the power goes in the house. See that extension to the house along the left?"

"Yes," Laura replied.

"That's the garage. I'll bet that's where the power goes in. See the streetlight across the road?"

"I see it."

"There's a power pole on this side. The electric line runs from that streetlight to the pole on this side and then to the garage on our left. Pierre, to me," Jordan said in the coms. Pierre made his way to the front.

"Did you bring those wire cutters?"

"Yes, Sir."

"You take Nick and make your way to our left around the house. Stay in cover. Stop when you see where the power goes in the house. Let me know when you get there. Sharp, you and Adam get in a firing position on either side of me. Make sure you use suppressors. No noise, people." Laura watched both men take their positions inside the brush line and thread suppressors onto their rifle barrels.

Pierre and Nick moved silently through the brush line to a point where they had a visual of the electric line attached to the house right below the roof line. "We've got eyes on the penetration into the house, Major," Pierre said. "There's an air conditioner and a generator right next to the meter."

"Copy that," Jordan replied. "Pierre, approach the house on my mark. Nick, cover him." Jordan waited until the guards were farthest away from the garage. "Go!"

Pierre made a dash to the house and knelt between the air conditioner and the generator, using them as cover. "Ready to cut, Major."

"Cut power now." Pierre took the insulated cutters out of his belt and cut the line from the meter to the house. The line showered Pierre with sparks where he made the cut and the lights around the house immediately went dark. Jordan heard guards shouting. "What are they saying, Messier?"

"They want guards to walk around the house and start the generator."

"Okay, shooters, fire at will."

Sharp and Adam each dropped a man on the back side of the house. Sharp shot an additional guard as he exited the patio door. A second guard behind him saw the man drop and withdrew back into the house. Adam shot him through the glass. There was silence until Nick shot one guard walking around the front corner. The guard that followed retreated.

"Major, I took out a guard," Nick said, "but his partner ran back around the front."

"Okay, people. They know we're here. Nick, make your way to the front of the house," Jordan said. "Find that guard if you can."

"Roger that."

"Pierre, make your way around to the pool area. Use the retaining wall as cover. Hold when you get there."

"Roger."

Two guards appeared near the pool area, running around the house from the far side. Sharp and Adam immediately shot them in the chest. Both fell.

Another man appeared inside the sliding glass door. Sharp took him with one shot. Again, there was silence.

"Nick here. In position behind a car in the driveway. I can't find that guard."

"Roger," Jordan said.

Pierre crept around the house and crawled half the length of the retaining wall to approximately the middle. "In position, Major."

"We see you, Pierre." Jordan turned to Laura. "You ready to approach the retaining wall?"

"Yes."

"On my mark. Adam, Sharp, cover us. Go!"

Laura and Jordan sprinted the thirty yards to the retaining wall and dove behind it alongside Pierre. No shots were fired. "Sharp, what's happening around the pool and patio?"

Sharp looked through his scope. "Nothing, Major. No movement."

"The guards are waiting to ambush us. Sharp, you and Adam put a few rounds through the walls on either side of that patio door."

Sharp and Adam each put several 7.62 automatic rifle rounds through the wall. A body fell in front of the door. "Major, one fell inside the door," Sharp said. "You're right, they know we're here."

Jordan looked to Laura and Pierre on either side of him. "We're going to jump the wall. Move around the swimming pool to the door. Pierre and Messier take the left side, I'll take the right. On my mark. Sharp, Adam, you still with me?"

"Yes, Sir," both said simultaneously.

"We're moving to the door. Go!"

All three hopped the retaining wall and sprinted around the swimming pool to the door. A shot rang out from inside the door. It was immediately followed by a hail of gunfire from Sharp and Adam. Another guard fell into the doorway

.

Chapter Fifty

ALONG THE FRONT of the house, the double front doors opened, and two men sprinted toward a car parked in the circle drive. Nick, hiding behind the car near the garage, shot them both before they could enter the car. To Nick's right, one of the three garage doors opened slightly, and shots rang out from below the door toward Nick's position behind the car. He peppered the opening with automatic fire and the shooting stopped.

Jordan heard the firing on the front side of the house. "Nick, report!"

"Eliminated two adult males. There's one active shooter in the garage."

"Roger. Sharp, Adam, advance to the retaining wall on my mark. Go!"

Sharp and Adam sprinted from cover to the retaining wall and set a firing position behind it. "We're right behind you, Major."

"The glass is broken in that door. I'm going to throw a flash-bang inside," Jordan said. He took one from his belt, pulled the fuse and lobbed it inside. A flash-bang is a device that creates a shock wave upon detonation and its flash of light is blinding. It's meant to stun, not kill. After the flash and the explosion, guards inside shot wildly in every direction. "Answer that fire, Sharp." Jordan, Pierre and Laura lay prone on the patio deck while Sharp and Adam pummeled the entire wall with gunfire that passed through the wall and into the room. The rest of the glass in the patio door collapsed, leaving the doorway completely open.

"I'm throwing another, then we're entering," Jordan said to Pierre and Laura. "I'll go to the right, you two go to the left. Stay low and make sure you don't trip over bodies on the way in." Jordan slipped another flash-bang from his belt, pulled the fuse and pitched it into the room. The explosion left smoke billowing out of the door. "The room may have caught fire. Enter on my mark. Go!"

The three rushed though the opening into the room. Weapons up, they crouched near the floor on either side of the door. Two men inside fired wildly from behind an overturned table. Laura and Jordan each shot an entire clip through the table and the men slumped over. The firing stopped.

Both Laura and Jordan stopped briefly to reload. Laura used her P226 pistols with suppressors attached while Jordan used his M16A2 automatic rifle. Pierre, with his Beretta M9, covered Laura and Jordan while they reloaded.

Shots were fired through the ceiling above them ricocheting off the tile floor. Jordan, Laura and Pierre all moved to the walls to avoid the gunfire. Each one pointed their weapons to the ceiling and returned the fire. "We've got to make it up those stairs while we've got the initiative," Laura said pointing to a stairway on the far side of the room.

"I'm out of flash-bangs," Jordan said. "The only thing I've got left is grenades. They'll tear the shit out of the house."

"Do it," Laura replied.

Jordan made his way around the walls to the stairs. He pointed his weapon around the corner and up the stairs. After emptying a clip, he pulled the fuse on the grenade and climbed a couple of stairs before throwing it to the upper floor. He ran back down. "Cover yourselves," he shouted right before a huge explosion sent debris flying everywhere. Drywall came down from the ceiling and dust billowed everywhere. "Nick, what can you see from the front?" Jordan asked into the com.

"An explosion in the front room. The front doors have been blown off their hinges. The picture window's blown, too."

"You see any movement inside?"

"No."

Jordan talked to Laura and Pierre. "Let's move upstairs on my mark. Go!"

The three climbed the stairs, stepping over debris in the stairway. The front room was vacant, a mass of torn up furniture, glass and collapsed building material. They found no bodies. Jordan pointed to the right. "Laura, Pierre, you go down the hallway on my right. The bedrooms should be there. I'll go left and search the kitchen, dining room and garage. On my mark. Go!"

Two men, apparently having hidden in a downstairs bathroom, escaped outside through the patio door. Sharp and Adam dropped them immediately. "Two more killed downstairs, Major," Sharp said. "We're entering the house to make sure you're not flanked."

"Roger," Jordan said.

Sharp and Adam sprinted to what was left of the patio doors and stepped inside. "You go right," Sharp said. "I'll go left. Search everything."

As the downstairs search began, Jordan, Laura and Pierre split up. Jordan entered the kitchen and found nothing. He reached for a doorknob to a pantry, turned it and kicked the door open, stepping aside immediately. Shots fired from inside. Jordan pointed his sidearm, also a Beretta M9, into the space and fired several rounds blindly, then moved into the doorway. An adult male was on the floor, still alive, but wounded. Jordan shot him in the head, then took a moment to replace his magazine.

He checked the dining room, found it empty, and proceeded to the door leading to the garage. He held for a moment and listened to an auto being started. "Nick, a car in the garage is coming right at you."

"Roger that, Major."

The car squealed its tires and backed right through the closed garage door, which broke free from its track and landed on top of the car as it backed out. The car turned to the right, the garage door fell off to the side and Nick began firing at the back glass. As the car turned to drive away, Jordan moved into the garage, ran to the opening and began firing at the vehicle as well. Despite their best efforts, Jordan and Nick watched it turn onto the road and drive away. "We better finish up before they bring back reinforcements," Nick said.

"Damn straight about that," Jordan replied.

Creeping down the hallway toward the bedrooms, Pierre kicked open a door and found a vacant bathroom. He motioned Laura forward. She overlapped him and opened the bedroom door on the opposite side of the hall. She stepped into the room holding both P226's in front of her. She found four children and two women huddled together in the corner. "Anyone else in here?" she asked in Spanish.

One of the women shook her head no. "What about in there?" Laura asked, pointing to a closet.

"No," the woman said. Laura shot twice through the door and then opened it to make sure. It was vacant.

"Where are they?"

The woman pointed to the next bedroom down the hall.

"Stay here and don't move."

The woman nodded her head. Laura left the room and spoke to Pierre. "Women and children in there. Make sure the woman doesn't flank us with a weapon."

"I've got your back," Pierre replied.

The next room was on Pierre's side. He motioned for Laura to open the door. She entered to find a man in the process of climbing out a bedroom window on the front side of the house.

She hit the man with a shot, and he tumbled the rest of the way, wounded. "Nick," Laura said, "you've got one coming at you. He climbed out a window."

"I've got him," Nick said as he took aim and fired. The man went down.

Jordan walked out of the garage and joined Nick in the driveway. "Watch for men escaping out the windows," Nick said.

"The bedrooms on that end of the house are being searched now," Jordan said pointing to the last few windows on the left side of the house. "Watch that road. Stop anything coming our direction."

"Yes, Sir."

Jordan spoke into the com. "Messier, Pierre. I'm coming in the front."

"Roger," Pierre said.

As Jordan entered the front door opening, he heard shots from below. "Sharp, report."

"We're good here, Major. We found a man hiding in a closet. He's neutralized. The downstairs is clear."

"We're searching the upstairs bedrooms now," Jordan said. "Go back outside and split up. You come around front to help Nick and tell Adam to go back to the retaining wall to cover us. We're about ready to pull out."

"Roger that, Major. We've been here too long."

Chapter Fifty-One

PIERRE MOVED DOWN the hallway and opened another bedroom on his side and found a woman with two children huddled in a corner, whimpering. "Laura," he said, "come and talk to the woman and kids here. I'll cover you."

Pierre retreated into the hallway while Laura squeezed past him and entered the room. "Anyone else in here?" she asked in Spanish.

The woman shook her head.

"What about in there?" Laura asked, pointing to a closet door.

Again, the woman shook her head. Laura fired two shots into the door, then opened it. It was vacant.

"Stay here and don't move," she said.

The woman nodded. Laura left the room. "Make sure she stays put," she said to Pierre. "I'm going in the last bedroom." She pointed her P226 toward the last door on the other side of the hallway. "I have a feeling it's the master."

Laura approached the door slowly and silently. She stood aside the door and took the hilt of one of her P226s and knocked. A burst of gunfire came through the door. She counted seven shots, then the firing stopped.

"Stop firing," she said in Spanish. "You're surrounded. You can't escape."

The gunfire resumed, again she counted seven shots. One of the shots pinged off the doorknob and it released itself. The door swung open a crack.

"If that's the way you want it, that's the way we'll do it." She took a flash-bang from her belt, kicked the door open and pitched it inside. Both she and Pierre turned away before the explosion. Afterward, Laura ran into the room with her pistols held in front of her. She found a woman covered in dust, curled up in the corner. "Do you have a weapon?" The woman shook her head. "Show me your hands." The woman held up her hands. "Where is he?"

She motioned toward the master bathroom.

"Anyone inside here?" Laura asked, motioning toward the closet door.

"No," the woman said.

As she did before, Laura shot through the closet door, then opened it and found no one inside. She turned her attention to the bathroom door, keeping well out of the line of fire. "Drop your weapon and come out," she said loudly.

Gunfire erupted through the door and wall. Again, she counted seven shots. "Go ahead and reload," she said. "I'll wait." There was a pause. "If you come out, you live. Stay in there and you die. Your choice." There was another pause. "I'm tired of waiting. I can throw a grenade in there and tear you into a thousand pieces. Do you want to live or die?"

There was another pause. Laura walked over to the woman, took her by the arm and forced her to her feet. "Talk to him. Tell him to give up and both of you will live." The woman looked too frightened to speak. Laura drug her over to the bathroom and shook her. "Talk to him!" she shouted.

"Luis," she said softly. Silence.

"Again, louder," Laura said, shaking her by the arm.

"Luis, come out. They'll let us live." More silence, then finally, the bathroom door opened a bit.

"Listen to me carefully," Laura said, standing well away from the door. "Do exactly as I say. Throw your weapon out first, then come out with your hands on top of your head. Do it now or I'll kill your woman."

Pierre stood outside in the hallway to provide back-up.

The bathroom door opened, and a .357 Magnum was thrown onto the bedroom carpet. "Come out slowly with your hands on your head. No sudden movements." The short man who appeared in the doorway wore pajamas. He was balding on top, had small slits for eyes and was overweight. He looked to be in his late fifties.

Laura motioned with her gun. "Kick the gun farther away." The man pushed it with his foot. "Farther," Laura shouted. The man took a step and pushed it harder.

Laura gave the man a hard, cold smile. She looked down at the gun, then looked back at the man. "That's a very nice gun. What is it? A Smith and Wesson?"

The man stayed silent.

"That gun's worth a lot of money, but I guess you've got a lot of money."

Again, the man stayed silent.

"Okay, I'm tired of this," Laura said. She pointed her P226 at the man's chest.

"Wait," he said.

Laura raised the barrel of her weapon.

"I'll pay you," he said.

"I already owe you 30 million."

The man gave her a quizzical look. "You're the woman from the Bahamas?"

"Yes."

"You owe me nothing. Forget about it."

"What about Sanchez?"

"I'll talk to her. She won't bother you again."

213

Laura looked at the woman with a sardonic grin. "Did you hear that? He's going to talk to Sanchez for me."

"He will," the woman said with an urgency in her voice. "You owe us nothing!"

"You're part of this, too?" Laura asked the woman.

Her eyes dropped to the floor. She said nothing.

Laura turned back to the man. "I'm not here for money, Luis. I'm here for justice. Lady Liberty sends her regards."

The man glanced at the gun on the floor wondering whether he could grab it quickly. Laura read his thoughts and before he could make a move, Laura shot him at nearly point-blank range in the forehead. The back half of his head exploded, and bone, hair and brains flew against the wall. He slumped to the floor as the woman shrieked and ran toward the closet. Laura pointed the gun in her other hand and shot her in the back of the head. "Shut the fuck up," Laura said, walking to stand over her body. "He killed entire villages and you did nothing."

Laura turned to face Pierre standing in the doorway. "We're done here," she said coldly.

This was the first time Pierre had witnessed Laura Messier, the assassin, the one whose reputation was made by killing the world's worst criminals. He turned away, sickened by the killing of the woman. He walked back down the hallway where he met Jordan entering the house from the front. "It's over," Pierre said quietly, walking past Jordan and out the front door.

Jordan looked at Laura who followed Pierre. "Anyone left alive back there?" he asked, nodding down the hallway.

"Only women and children."

"Let's get the hell out of here." Jordan spoke in the coms, "Attention everyone. We're pulling out. Meet at the retaining wall on the double. Adam, cover us."

Chapter Fifty-Two

THE SOMBER MOOD on the return trip from Colombia was heightened by the lateness of the hour and the red glow from the interior lights of the helicopter. The group was exhausted after close quarter fighting at the Delgado home. They'd come through the ordeal without casualties, but each person knew they'd been lucky.

The drone of the engines and noise from the rotors made casual conversation difficult, but Pierre looked especially troubled. Jordan, a natural leader, understood that an esprit de corps was necessary to maintain the performance of the unit he commanded. Sitting next to Pierre, Jordan leaned closer. "Something on your mind, Pierre?"

"Major, killing the woman back there was unnecessary," Pierre replied pointedly, appalled by what he'd witnessed.

"You're referring to the wife of the drug lord?"

"Yes," Pierre replied, casting a downward gaze as though he blamed himself.

"She cut the head off a snake, Pierre."

"I didn't sign up to kill women," Pierre said emphatically, raising his head to look Jordan in the eyes.

Jordan thought for a moment about how to respond. "Let me ask you something. You don't think the wife was complicit in the acts of her husband?"

"I'm sure she was, but still …" Pierre's voice trailed off.

"She would have become the cartel leader."

"It was the cold-blooded nature of the killing that bothered me. Laura had no mercy."

"I'm not going to argue the ethics of it, Pierre. We had to be quick. We didn't have the government's permission to enter the country.

"But it was the way she did it," Pierre continued. "She used the woman as bait to lure the man out of the bathroom. Then she shot them both. It was murder." Jordan thought carefully about how to justify the killing.

"Pierre, those people were guilty of grave crimes. If the Columbian government had wanted to prosecute them, they'd have already done so. At the end of the day, we eliminated the head of an international crime syndicate and personally, I'm not going to lose any sleep over it." As an afterthought, Jordan motioned toward Laura and smiled. "She does have a mean streak in her, though, doesn't she?" Pierre nodded.

"You've got that right."

"You didn't see what she did that day in Lebanon," Jordan said. "You were injured when we pulled out. She stayed behind to cover the copter. Just her against a hundred militia. I've never seen anything like it." Jordan smiled. "That woman's got some sort of death wish."

"Well, I don't," Pierre replied.

"Look, was there too much risk tonight? No question. We got lucky."

"Let's hope it continues so we don't get ourselves killed."

Chapter Fifty-Three

AS MONDAY MORNING broke, Rick Williams came off his overnight watch while Jordan and his squad sat on fold-up stools and opened ready to eat meal kits. "Morning, Jordan," he said, propping his rifle against one of the empty stools. "Another tasty meal courtesy of the government?"

Jordan tossed Rick a meal kit. "Uncle Sam saved one for you."

"We ought to pack up the camp before the plane arrives."

"Here, pull up a chair." Jordan motioned to a stool. "Let's pack everything into the Jeeps and pull them into the vegetation where they're hidden. Dmitri should prep that copter before the plane arrives, too. I'd like to think we can get out of trouble faster than we got into it."

Rick poured a cup of coffee from a pot sitting on a small propane canister heater. "Anyone got some bug spray?"

"It doesn't do much," Adam said, handing a can of insect repellent to Rick, "but it's better than nothing. We've already lathered up this morning."

A little smile broke out on Rick's face. "I wondered what that smell was."

"Military deodorant," Adam replied with a grin.

"Have you brought the pickets in?" Jordan asked.

Rick looked around. "Yeah, everyone's back in camp except Jerry. He's watching the airstrip. Where's Laura?"

Jordan nodded toward the helicopter. "She slept in the copter."

Rick chuckled. "At least it kept the bugs out," he said, slathering on insect repellent.

No sooner than he'd said that, the sliding door to the copter opened and Laura, Dmitri and Pete climbed out and walked over. "We smelled coffee," Pete said.

Jordan nodded toward the pot sitting on top of a small propane stove. "There's plenty there if you can find a cup."

"You made coffee and didn't tell me?" Laura asked with a mischievous grin.

"It might be a little strong for you. It doubles as disinfectant." Jordan looked at Adam. "Can you find the lady a cup?"

"Yes, Sir," Adam replied with a fawned air of seriousness. "Follow me, Miss Laura." He walked over to one of the Jeeps and rummaged through a box until several collapsible metal cups were found. "Here ya go," he said, handing her a dirty cup. "I'd wash that out if I were you. Who knows what's been inside that thing." Laura, Dmitri and Pete each grabbed a cup.

"How'd it go last night?" Rick asked Jordan while Laura was out of earshot.

"It was a real hornet's nest in that house. But we got it done."

"Superwoman do all right?"

"She seems to take a peculiar delight in killing people at point blank range."

"You know, the Russians have a code name for her. They call her 'Shewolf'."

"I've heard that before. Believe me, the name fits. Pierre was with her when she killed the cartel boss and his wife last night. He said it was ugly."

"I'm sure it was," Rick said with a shrug. "We've all seen her handiwork. It's something you must get used to. I'm sure she killed that guy in Lebanon the same way. I was interrogated by that asshole, by the way."

"What's odd to me is, otherwise, she seems to be a completely normal person."

"What's the quote from that old-time radio show? 'Who knows what evil lurks in the hearts of men?'"

Both men chuckled. "Yeah, I've heard the phrase," Jordan replied.

"No one sees how much she grieves after missions, though. She goes off in that little hut of hers back home and won't talk to anyone."

"It does take its toll on you after a while."

"Yes, it does," Rick said nodding his head.

Laura walked back from the Jeep. "What's so funny?" Jordan shrugged.

"We were just talking."

"Where's the disinfectant?"

"Here," Jordan said, extending the coffee pot to pour her a cup. "Did you wash that out first?"

"I poured water over it."

"Well, you got the dead bugs out of it." Jordan glanced at Rick. "Can you quietly gather everyone together?"

Rick went in search of Sharp and Pierre while Jordan continued to talk to Laura. "How are you feeling this morning? Did you get enough rest?"

"The copter was a bit stuffy and Pete snores a lot, but I got some sleep. I'm ready to go."

"With any luck, by mid-afternoon, we'll be out of here."

"Not a moment too soon for my taste," Laura said. "Have you seen the size of the bugs down here?"

Jordan gave her a knowing smile. "Every morning in my quarters, I squish some giant thing running across the floor."

The entire group, one by one, gathered in the center of the camp to receive the morning brief. "Everyone here?" Jordan looked around and answered his own question. "Okay, Laura, you want to do announcements?" Jordan asked with a smile.

"You've got the floor, Senor. Go right ahead."

"Jerry's up the path watching the airfield. He'll report in as needed. We need everyone on coms all day, people. Stay frosty. When this thing goes down, it's gonna be real quick."

"If anyone needs a com set, they're in the back of the Jeeps," Rick said.

"Make sure we stay real quiet today. Do not compromise your position. We'll wait until later this morning to surveil the river, but that could be a fighting position so whoever we send down there, dig in. I know it's going to be warm today, but I want to gear up right now. Take as many extra cartridges as you can carry. We're going to be outnumbered so stay on your com sets and be ready to move at a moment's notice. Dmitri," Jordan said looking his direction, "is that copter ready to go?"

"We're ready to fly."

"All right. Let's get the camp packed up while we wait for Jerry to report in."

Chapter Fifty-Four

COLONEL KEVIN PRITCHARD passed through the front gate at Fort Clayton at 07:30 on Monday morning. He showed a military ID, his name was recorded in the visitor's logbook, and he was instructed where to find General Carson's office. Wearing his brown Marine service uniform, Pritchard arrived at the General's office shortly after.

"I'm Colonel Pritchard from the Pentagon," he announced to Lieutenant Hinch, as though the rank of Colonel would impress the aide. "I'd like speak with General Carson."

The Lieutenant checked the General's daily schedule. "I'm sorry, Sir, but I don't see you on his schedule for today. Did you make an appointment?"

"No. I called yesterday."

"If you'd like to take a seat, when the General comes in, I'll let him know you're here."

General Richard Carson, governor of the Canal Zone, parked his car behind the Headquarters building a few minutes later and entered his office through a side door, as was his usual custom. He walked out into the waiting area and stared at Pritchard before addressing his adjutant.

"Good morning, Lieutenant. Could I have a copy of today's schedule?"

"Yes, Sir," he said, handing the schedule over.

"Who's that?" Carson asked, referring to Pritchard.

"A Colonel Pritchard from Washington wants to see you. He left a message yesterday."

Hinch handed Carson a stack of pink message slips. Carson went into his office, sat behind his desk and riffled through the messages until he found Pritchard's message requesting a return call immediately. He picked up the phone. "Lieutenant? Who the hell's Colonel Pritchard?"

"I'm not sure, Sir."

"All right, send him in."

Hinch looked at Pritchard and smiled. "The General will see you now."

Pritchard gave the General a quick salute when he entered. "General, I'm Colonel Kevin Pritchard, U.S. Marine Corp from the Pentagon Special Projects Office." Pritchard began to sit down.

Carson gave Pritchard a suspicious look. "Don't bother sitting, Colonel. This is going to be real quick." He looked at the date on the phone message. "Apparently, you called from D.C. yesterday. What's important enough for you to travel 2,000 miles overnight?"

"Did you know you've got Russian helicopters operating in Panama?"

The General began to get angry. He sarcastically paraphrased the question. "Did I know the Russians are operating helicopters in Panama?" He gave Pritchard an angry expression. "Colonel, every time a flea lands on a horse's ass down here, I know about it."

"So, you're aware of it?"

The General raised his voice. "Isn't that what I just said? If that's all you came down for, you're wasting my goddam time. Get your ass on a plane and go back to D.C."

The meeting wasn't beginning the way Pritchard envisioned. "Sir, I have an op running in Panama today and I want to make sure my men are safe."

The General's anger increased. "You're running an op down here today? Is this a military op?"

Pritchard thought about how to answer. *If I say it's a CIA op, he'll tell me I don't have jurisdiction.* "Yes, Sir."

"And you cleared this op with my office beforehand?"

"No, Sir, I did not."

"Who's your superior officer, soldier?"

"That would be General Carey at the Joint Chiefs."

"I mean your direct superior, Colonel." Pritchard hesitated before answering.

"I'm unattached at the moment, Sir."

"And you bypassed my office? Who the hell do you think you are? Where's your paperwork?"

"I'm sorry, Sir, there's no paperwork. The op's classified."

"It's classified he says," Carson said, mimicking Pritchard. "This is the goddam Army, Colonel. Everything has paperwork attached to it, classified or not. And nothing, I repeat nothing, happens down here without my approval. I must sign your paperwork before you're allowed to take a shit in Panama. Have General Carey give me a call when you get back to D.C."

"Yes, Sir."

Carson glared at Pritchard. "Well? What are you waiting for? You're dismissed."

"Sir, if I could just make one additional point?"

Carson slammed his hand on top of his desk. "There will be no missions of any kind in Panama without my expressed permission," he shouted. "And you don't have it. Do you understand?"

"Yes, Sir, but if you'd allow me …"

Carson interrupted him. "Lieutenant Hinch?" He yelled. "In here on the double!"

Hinch stuck his head in the door. "Yes, Sir?"

Carson lowered his voice to a normal conversational level, but with a menacing tone. "The Colonel's leaving the country immediately. Would you call the MPs and have them escort him to Albrook? Tell them to put the Colonel on the next transport back to the States."

"Yes, Sir." Hinch looked at Pritchard. "Would you step this way, Colonel?"

Pritchard, red faced and embarrassed, walked out with Hinch.

"Welcome to Monday mornings around here, Colonel," Hinch said with a slight smile. "Do I really need to call the MPs?"

"No, I can find my own way to Albrook."

"I apologize for the General's mood this morning. Have a pleasant day."

Pritchard, fresh from his humiliation at the hands of Carson, drove out the front gate and stopped at a fuel station nearby. I'll be damned if I let that man destroy this. He asked the clerk the best way to get to Yavisa. The clerk unfolded a map and drew a line through town. "This is the fastest way through the city. Once you get south of town, it's a straight shot on the highway."

"How long will it take to get there?"

The clerk looked at his watch. "This time of day? About three hours if you hustle. You should be there around eleven."

Chapter Fifty-Five

CAPTAIN RAMOS' PLATOON drove their vehicles onto the airstrip at 8:30 a.m., Monday morning, and stopped in the middle of the dirt runway. Ramos and Sergeant Garcia climbed out to survey the area. "Keep the trucks running, Sergeant," Ramos said. "We'll move them in a minute."

"Yes, Sir."

"Tell the men to unload and assemble next to the trucks." Ramos looked over the airfield with an eye toward positioning his troops. To the south, the river ran east-west along the south edge of town. A line of vegetation ran along the western side of the runway. A shallow canal was parallel to the strip to the east. To the north, the paved surface of the Pan-American Highway turned into a dirt road that led into Yavisa. It's easily defendable, Ramos thought.

"Sergeant?" Ramos asked when Garcia returned from helping the men unload. "I expect the plane will follow the highway south and land right over those trees to the north."

"That sounds right," Garcia replied.

Ramos motioned the length of the strip with his arm. "And then it will taxi the length of the runway and park at the far end near those fuel tanks."

"I think that's likely, Sir."

"How would you set our defenses in case we're attacked?" Garcia took a moment to look over the surroundings.

"As we discussed with the General, if we stop the transaction and allow FARC to leave with the drugs, they won't fight us. I don't think Noriega's men are interested in fighting, either."

"I was thinking of someone else," Ramos suggested.

"What are you talking about?"

"An ambush," Ramos replied as though it was obvious. "My father and I have been warned about bandits when we fish down here."

"It'd take a large group to take us on, Sir." Garcia suggested.

"It's a lot of money, Sergeant. If we know about this deal, maybe vigilante groups do, too." Garcia considered the thought and took a second look around the area.

"If we were ambushed, Sir, we'd be attacked from behind. We'd see an attack coming anywhere else."

"You mean the river?" Ramos asked.

Garcia nodded. "Attackers would come up behind us in boats. You see that grove of trees behind the fuel tanks? That's where the canal meets the river. They'd probably come at us through those trees."

"What about the town?"

"Bandits could hide in the town," he said pointing toward the buildings, "but they'd still have to attack us over open ground. I doubt it could be done."

"I agree. Let's get our troops in position. I'd like to establish a command post down by those fuel tanks. Put the Jeep and one of the trucks down there. We'll keep most of our troops there, too."

"Yes, Sir."

"However," Ramos continued, "let's close the town right now. No one gets in or out without us knowing about it. Send the other truck and a squad back up the highway and set a roadblock a quarter mile north of the town. Tell them to pull the truck across the road and set the machine gun in the truck bed pointing at traffic."

"Yes, Sir."

Ramos pointed up and down the airstrip. "Put men lining each side of the runway. Spread them out over the entire length. We want to make sure we see trouble from any direction. Do we have enough radios for everyone?"

"Yes, Sir. Do you intend to have the men stand there all day?"

"As long as it takes, Sergeant." Ramos looked up in the sky. "It looks like it's going to be a hot one. Make sure they conserve water. We didn't bring extra." It took a half-hour to position the troops, but by 9:00 a.m., the trucks had been moved, the troop disposition completed, and a command post established near the fuel tanks. "Everyone's in position, Captain," Garcia reported. Ramos looked at their command position.

"We've got one more task, Sergeant," Ramos said. "Establish a perimeter around the command post. Put a line of men facing the town and a second line guarding our rear."

"Yes, Sir." As the Sergeant walked away, Ramos had one additional thought.

"Sergeant? We've got a long wait today. Make sure everyone stays alert."

Chapter Fifty-Six

"MAJOR, THIS IS Jerry. Come in."

Rick heard Jerry Stock over his com set. "Jerry, Rick here. The Major isn't available. What's up?"

"We've got an entire platoon at the airstrip. It looks like they intend on locking down the town."

"A platoon of what?"

"They look like Panamanian regulars."

"How are they armed?"

"Small arms only."

"Stay right where you are. I'll be back on the line in a minute."

Rick walked back to the group where Jordan was giving instructions. "Major, there's been a development. A platoon just rolled out on the airstrip."

"What color are the uniforms?" Jordan asked.

Rick spoke into the com set. "The Major wants to know the color of the uniforms?"

"Green," Jerry said.

Rick repeated the color to Jordan. "Those are Panamanian Defense Forces," Jordan said. "Noriega's guard wears black."

"What do you want me to tell Jerry?"

"We're coming up the path to take a look."

Rick spoke into the coms. "Jerry, the Major's on his way."

"Roger that. Jerry out."

Four Days in Panama

Chapter Fifty-Seven

JORDAN LOOKED AT Laura. "Come on, let's take a look." He stared at the helicopter. "Rick, in case we have to make a quick retreat, make sure Dmitri's got that helicopter ready."

Rick sent Dmitri and Pete back to the copter to run a pre-flight check. He called Pierre and Sharp over. "An entire platoon just showed up at the airstrip."

"Fucking great," Sharp said in disgust.

"I need both of you to set a perimeter on the double. Get in the vegetation between us and the airstrip. Stay alive on those coms."

Laura and Jordan headed up the path. Halfway up, Jordan grabbed Laura by the arm. "Hold on. I don't want him getting spooked." Jordan gave Jerry a warning on the coms. "We're coming up behind you."

"Roger," he whispered. "Stay low. I've got hostiles 50 yards from my position."

Laura and Jordan bent down behind the thin row of plants at the end of the path. "Here," Jerry said, handing the field glasses to Jordan. "Take a look." Jordan handed them to Laura since he'd brought his own. They pushed the broadleaf stems aside to get a clear view of the airstrip.

"What do you think?" Jordan asked Laura.

"Looks like they're going to be here a while. They've established a command post by those fuel tanks."

"They're not Noriega's troops, that's for sure. See that tall officer?"

"The dark haired one?"

"Yeah. He's their commander. The shorter man's a Sergeant. I can make out his insignia."

"Putting a command post close to the fuel tanks is a mistake," Laura suggested.

"No shit. Blow the fuel tanks and they've lost their command."

"They had two personnel carriers," Jerry added, "but one of them headed back up the road with a squad of troops."

"They're blocking the highway into town," replied Jordan.

"Could they be flanking us?" Jerry asked.

"I don't think so. It doesn't look like they know we're here." He turned around to face Laura and Jerry. "If this platoon is protecting the drug deal, they'll let the black shirts pass and we'll see them arrive. This could be some sort of renegade unit. We'll find out soon enough."

"The black shirts? Is that what you call Noriega's goons?" Laura asked.

"Technically, they're called the Dignity Battalion, but, yes, they're known by their black uniforms."

"Well, whatever they're called, we may have to deal with them," Laura said, in a matter-of-fact tone of voice.

Jordan was amused. "You mean kill them, don't you?"

Laura tried to avoid looking frustrated at his attitude. "Do you know any other way they get dead?"

"I think you're in full bitch mode now."

Laura looked at Jordan with a slight smile. "Only until this is over."

"Let me know when you're a normal person again, will you?"

"Roger that, Major."

Jordan backed away and turned to Jerry. "If those troops move this way, don't engage. Retreat back to camp. Otherwise, stay low and give us updates. You need someone up here with you?"

"I'd appreciate that, Major."

Laura and Jordan talked as they crept back down the path toward the camp. "If those troops search the jungle, we're in trouble."

"You're right. We can't fight a platoon hand to hand."

"Maybe they won't. They could be guarding the airfield. So, maybe we're okay. Let's continue on."

"I agree," Laura said.

"When Dmitri blows that plane, attention will be focused on the explosion," Jordan said. "They'll be disorganized. That will give us time to evac. However, if they charge into the jungle, we've got to be prepared to fight and retreat all the way back to the copter."

"It'll be like Lebanon."

"Yes," Jordan said, grimly, "it will."

"I counted six on this side of the airstrip, spread out in a line," she replied. "The same on the other side, plus they've got men guarding their command post."

"And men blocking the road. That disposition of troops is a weakness. As long as we're not flanked, I think we'll be okay."

Once they'd arrived back at the camp, Jordan sought out Carl Thomas. "Carl, take that 50 cal up the path and set it up to rake the airstrip. Once the plane is blown, we may have to fight the troops they've positioned around the airfield."

"Yes, Sir." He picked up the gun lying on a tarp beside one of the Jeeps and propped it against the vehicle while he opened a box of ammunition. Hanging strings of ammunition around his neck, Carl lifted the gun over his shoulder and began walking up the path toward Jerry Stock's position.

Laura walked over to Rick. "Who's on the picket line?"

Rick pointed to his left. "Sharp and Pierre are between us and the airstrip."

"Pull them in."

Rick spoke into his com set. "Sharp, Pierre. Report back to camp on the double." He turned to Laura. "They'll be here in a minute.

Laura looked for the sat photo in the Jeep and found it underneath a box of ammo. "Rick, look at this with me," she said, spreading it out on the hood. "See where the river makes this hairpin turn?"

Rick looked at the photo then lifted his head to get a visual orientation of the surrounding jungle. He pointed due south. "It should be straight south of here about where we cut that path."

"I want Pierre and Sharp down there. Tell them to find that hairpin and set a position right at the apex. We need a visual down both sides of the turn."

"Send an RPG with them."

Sharp walked up during the conversation and smiled when he heard Rick suggest they take an RPG. "You mean I finally get a chance to play with the toys?"

Rick chuckled at the comment. "Yeah, well don't get too excited. I didn't bring that many shells." Sharp glanced in the direction of the river.

"Just so you know, we're going to make noise trying to find that hairpin. We couldn't see it from the path." He looked at Pierre who'd arrived back at camp. "That's your job."

Pierre hadn't heard the entire conversation. "What's my job?"

"We're going to the river. Take that machete with you," Sharp said pointing to the large knife lying nearby on a tarp, "in case we need to cut through the jungle."

"Why don't you do the damn cutting?" Pierre asked sarcastically.

"Because I've got to carry the fucking gun," Sharp said, pointing toward the back of the Jeep where the RPG was stored. "That thing weighs 50 pounds."

Pierre gave him a look of amusement. "But you have to carry the shells, too. I'd rather use the machete."

Sharp, who had forgotten about the shells, expressed his frustration. "Fuck you, Pierre."

Rick interrupted. "Would you guys stop with the arguments? Get your asses on the move."

"Yes, Sir," Sharp said. Rick watched them walk off still arguing about the division of labor. Idiots, he thought.

Chapter Fifty-Eight

BRET WEXLER, HAVING been awake in the middle of the night, slept late on Monday morning. Although the day promised to be warmer than usual, he decided to wear a blazer to hide his shoulder holster and handgun. In case he was asked to help unload cargo, he donned jeans and sneakers. His sunglasses gave him a typical CIA appearance, the tough guy American look, not that he cared. Today, he wasn't trying to hide his identity.

After paying the hotel bill, Wexler stowed his bag in the trunk of his car and headed toward the restaurant next door. He glanced at his watch. *It's going to be a long day. This may be the only chance I have to eat.*

After enjoying a terrific plate of food and especially strong coffee, Wexler began to feel guilty he hadn't checked the airstrip yet. He ordered another cup to go and headed back to the hotel. *I'll ditch the car. What the hell, I'll never be here again.* He gulped a swig of coffee before opening the trunk. *Damn that shit is good.* Wexler pulled his bag out, slung it over his shoulder and headed toward the airstrip on foot. He smiled seeing Panamanian soldiers on the airfield. *Wow, this is great! Pritchard really came through this time.*

Seeing the American walk toward them, two Panamanian soldiers aimed their rifles at him. "Detener!" one of them shouted in Spanish meaning stop. Wexler raised his hands awkwardly to avoid spilling his coffee. "Hey, take it easy. I'm a friendly."

Neither soldier spoke English. One kept his rifle pointed at Wexler's gut while the other moved close to search him. Finding the pistol in Wexler's shoulder holster, he was disarmed, and the soldiers began screaming while pointing at the pistol. Wexler figured it was about the gun. "I'm here for the delivery. I'm CIA." He nodded toward his gun held by one of the soldiers. "That's my standard issue weapon."

Everyone in the Panamanian Defense Forces recognized the letters, 'CIA.' so they pushed Wexler toward the command post at the end of the runway and called Ramos on their radio. It was a brief conversation which, again, Wexler didn't understand except the phrase, 'CIA.' He cooperated and made no protest at the occasional shove in his back as they walked him across the runway to the command post. "Does your commander speak English," Wexler asked, turning around as they walked. That resulted in a strong shove that nearly knocked him over. They shouted something he couldn't understand so he continued with the hope that the commander could understand him.

"It looks like we've caught our first fish," Ramos commented to Sergeant Garcia while watching Wexler cross the runway under guard.

"He looks like CIA to me," Garcia replied.

Ramos laughed. "How would you know that?"

"An American this far south on the same day as a drug delivery?" He answered his own question. "He's CIA all right."

"We'll see," Ramos replied.

The soldiers marched up to Ramos and handed Wexler's pistol over. Ramos admired the gun before looking up at Wexler. "It's a Beretta, isn't it?" Ramos asked in English.

"Yes, Sir," Wexler replied. "If you'd allow me to explain …"

Ramos held up his hand and interrupted. "We'll get to that in a moment. I accept the gift." He pushed the gun into his waistband. "Who are you?"

Wexler was only too eager to clear up the misunderstanding. "My name's Bret Wexler. I'm here for …"

Again, Ramos interrupted him. "I only asked your name. Do you have identification?"

"Yes, Sir." Wexler began to reach into the breast pocket of his blazer. Sergeant Garcia reacted immediately, reaching over and twisting Wexler's arm down to his side.

"Keep your hands where we can see them," Garcia said sternly. He withdrew Wexler's billfold and handed it to the Captain.

Ramos thumbed through the billfold nonchalantly. "You must be here for a fishing trip in the Darien," he commented.

Wexler hesitated for a moment. He wants me to avoid any mention of the drugs. I'll play along. "Yes, I'm here for the fishing."

Ramos smiled at the statement. "I knew it!" He glanced at Sergeant Garcia. "Didn't I tell you he looks like a fisherman?" Garcia remained silent. "However, I'm troubled by something. I don't see a fishing license," he said pointing to the billfold. "Do you have one?"

Wexler struggled to come up with a response. "I thought I could pick one up in town," he blurted out.

"They're not sold here in Yavisa. If you'd done your research, you'd have known that." Ramos gave Wexler a hard, cold stare. "Fishing without a license is a petty crime here in Panama." Ramos held up the gun. "However, carrying a gun without a permit is a more serious crime." He waited for a reply, but Wexler was incredulous. Beads of sweat appeared on his forehead. What the hell is going on here, he thought.

"I'm afraid we're going to have to arrest you," Ramos said with a sly grin. He looked at Garcia. "Sergeant, in the back of the Jeep, you'll find plastic zip ties. Tie his hands together behind his back and set him down next to the Jeep."

Wexler raised his voice in protest. "Wait a minute! I'm CIA. I'm here to help with the transfer," he complained as Garcia bound his hands. "You're supposed to know I'm here."

Ramos held his hand up. "Stop talking!" He motioned to Garcia. "If he utters one more sound, beat him until he's quiet. Post one of the men to guard him."

"Yes, Sir."

Jerry Stock observed the incident through field glasses from his vantage point inside the vegetation line and reported it to Major Jordan.

Chapter Fifty-Nine

COLONEL PRITCHARD SPED down the Pan-American Highway, passing every truck and automobile in his path, hoping to get to Yavisa before eleven. He encountered light traffic traveling southbound and slowed outside Yavisa at the sight of the roadblock outside the town. Ramos' squad had already turned away several vehicles during the morning hours and had perfected their routine. As they watched Pritchard's car approach, Corporal Jiminez motioned for the tarp to be pulled back so the driver could see the heavy caliber machine gun pointed at the car. Pulling up to the roadblock, Pritchard stopped, put the car in park and left the engine idling. Four of Jiminez's soldiers approached the car, two on each side, with automatic weapons pointed at the driver. Pritchard rolled down his window as the soldiers approached.

"I'm Colonel Pritchard, United States Marine Corp. I need entry into the town."

The soldier shook his head. "The town is closed," he said in Spanish. "You'll have to turn around and go back."

Pritchard had a working knowledge of Spanish and understood. However, he kept speaking English. "I have a mission at the airstrip this morning. Let me speak with your commanding officer."

The soldier motioned for Corporal Jiminez to approach the car. "Can I help you?" Jiminez asked in English. He leaned in the window.

"I'm Colonel Pritchard of the United States Marines. I'm here on official business. I demand to be allowed into the town."

"I'm sorry, Sir, but no one is allowed in until later in the day. You'll have to turn back."

"I don't think you understand, soldier. I'm here for the same purpose you are. Get your commander on the radio."

"One moment, please." Jiminez walked back to the truck and called Captain Ramos on the radio. "Captain, we've got an American military officer at the roadblock. He insists we let him pass, says he's here for the same reason we are."

"Disarm him and escort him to the command post."

Jiminez put the radio down and walked back to the car. "Pull the car off the road and step out, please."

"What's the goddam problem, soldier?"

Jiminez remained calm, but insistent. "Pull the car off the road and step out!"

"I don't take orders from a Corporal," Pritchard said angrily.

Jiminez turned to his man in the truck bed behind the machine gun. "Spray a few rounds, Miguel," he yelled.

Miguel smiled because it was the first action he'd seen that morning. He pulled off the safety and ripped off ten rounds into the air above Pritchard's car. Jiminez looked back in the window and talked with more insistence. "I'll ask one more time, Sir."

Pritchard backed off the roadway, shut off the car and stepped out, slamming the door in anger. "I'm a full bird Colonel, Corporal. You need to show some respect to a superior officer."

"Unless you have an authorization to travel outside the Canal Zone, you have no authority here. Do you have such a document?"

"Call General Costa," Pritchard replied instantly.

Jiminez asked his men to surround Pritchard. "We're going to disarm you, Sir. Do not offer any resistance. Please put your hands in the air." Jiminez's men searched Pritchard and removed the sidearm from his holster. "I apologize, Sir. We're operating under the General's direct orders."

Jiminez turned to his men. "Walk this American out to the airstrip and turn him over to the Captain." Two men motioned Pritchard forward and gave him a shove as they began the long walk out to the airstrip. Pritchard took offense at the shove and turned around to push back. Jiminez intervened and readied his weapon to fire. "I have the authority to kill you, Sir."

"Do you know the ramification of killing an American Colonel, young man?" Pritchard answered his own question. "It could start a war."

Jiminez smiled, revealing that one of his front teeth was missing. "But you'll still be dead, Sir." Jiminez looked at his men. "Turn him over to Captain Ramos and then report back here. If he causes any trouble, kill him."

Chapter Sixty

RAMOS AND GARCIA watched with amusement as the American colonel slowly walked the length of the airstrip. "Another fisherman?" Garcia asked.

"Without a license, no doubt," Ramos chuckled.

The guards accompanying Pritchard gave him one last shove before he faced Ramos. "And you are?" Ramos asked.

"Colonel Kevin Pritchard, United States Marine Corp. By whose authority do you disarm an American Colonel?"

Ramos shrugged. "By whose authority are you here, Colonel?"

"Call General Costa. He knows I'm here."

"You don't have a written order to be outside the Canal Zone?"

"No, I don't, and I'll tell you why. I'm on a classified joint mission between the Pentagon and President Noriega."

"No documents?"

"Didn't you hear me? It's a secret mission."

"I have no way to verify your story, Colonel. Since you're outside your jurisdiction without proper authority, I'm temporarily placing you under arrest."

"I'll have you court martialed over this," Pritchard glared at Ramos' insignia, "whoever you are."

"It's Captain Ramos, PDF." Ramos shrugged and looked at Sergeant Garcia. "I thought he was here for the fishing." They both laughed before Ramos grew serious. "Secure him and sit him down with the other one."

"With pleasure, Sir."

Garcia bound Pritchard's hands behind him and led him to the Jeep where he threw him to the ground beside Wexler. Garcia warned the guard. "Watch these men closely," he said. "Don't allow them to stand."

Wexler leaned over and whispered to Pritchard. "What the hell is going on, Colonel?"

"I don't know. I talked to General Costa before I left. These are his troops. There's a breakdown in communication somewhere."

"What do we do?"

"I guess we'll have to wait. Do you have anything in your pocket to cut the plastic with?"

"I've got a pocketknife, but I can't reach my pocket.

"Turn your back toward me when the guard isn't looking. I'll try to get it. By the way, did you ever track down Messier?"

"She's not here."

"Well, that's one problem solved," Pritchard said. "Let's see about these restraints."

Fortunately for them, the guard was inattentive while Pritchard and Wexler set about to free themselves.

Chapter Sixty-One

ROBERTO BENEVIDES WAS a third-generation Columbian landowner who maintained a mid-size farming operation in the Magdalena District of Northwest Colombia. At slightly over 800 acres, Roberto's farm occupied a middle ground between large corporate growers and small individually owned farms. He cultivated the oil palm tree from which palm oil was produced, an important export for the country. By all accounts, Roberto was a model citizen who maintained friendly relations with everyone in the district.

Benevides ignored the fight between the Columbian government and the Revolutionary Armed Forces of Columbia, or FARC, as they were called. However, government officials in the capital of Bogota suspected him of being a FARC sympathizer since many of his farm workers were part-time members of the local FARC militia. When hundreds of government troops rolled up to Benevides' front door unannounced and accused him of being associated with FARC, he and his family barely escaped with their lives. Government troops killed his workers and shoved paperwork in his hand that gave them the authority to seize his entire farming operation. Benevides and his family ran for their lives. It was this experience that resulted in Roberto Benevides becoming the commander of the 58th Front of FARC.

The 58th was the wealthiest of the FARC chapters around the country due to their association with drug cartels. The 58th's territory, running along the northern coast, was the prime spot from which to move cargo to Mexico and the United States.

Cartel leaders were never more pleased than when Benevides took command of the local militia. He had the respect of the local population. Which local officials could be bribed, which port was safest, and which small airstrip could handle increased traffic, Benevides knew it all. The idea of using Yavisa as a shipping point was his after the Colombian military began patrolling the coastline and ports. Acquiring a dual engine Huey helicopter and the means to maintain it, Benevides discreetly contacted the Panamanian government with the idea of shipping out of Panama. President Noriega gave his personal assurance the drug shipments would be protected.

The 58th created a staging point deep inside the jungles of Panama from which to ship downriver to Yavisa. The new, alternate route through Panama seemed to work well. The local population appreciated the payoffs, Noriega's troops arrived on time to protect the cargo and the entire operation went smoothly. So, when Benevides suggested using the route to the Malagua cartel leader, Luis Delgado, he readily agreed.

Benevides and his men spent a week ferrying men, supplies and drugs to the staging point to ready themselves for a delivery on Monday, January 9, 1989. By the time the Delgado estate was attacked in the early morning hours on Monday, they'd already arrived at the staging point. As far as Benevides knew, the transfer was on schedule and without problems.

Benevides was happy to see morning break on Monday deep in the Darien jungle. Sleeping in a mosquito netted tent overnight and eating cold food wasn't his choice of amenities. He couldn't wait to get back to the comfort of his rented home in Apartado. He spoke to his second in command as they inspected the boats tied to the bank. "Samuel," he said pointing to the boats, "I want the boats loaded early. Spread the cargo out over three of them," he said, pointing to the boats, "and we'll use the fourth as a

245

command boat. Put six men in each cargo boat and we'll put the rest in the command boat."

"What about arms?" Samuel, the second in command asked.

"I want every man armed, Sam. I'm not expecting trouble, but you never know."

"We'll be overloading the boats, Sir."

David shrugged. "There's nothing we can do about it." David looked around the sky. "We need the men for security. Oh, one more item."

"Yes, Sir?"

"Have the helicopter ready to go when we get back."

Samuel smiled. "Yes, Sir."

Benevides nodded. "I want to get out of here. Three days is a long time in the jungle."

"What time are we pulling out for Yavisa?"

Benevides looked at his watch. "Let's be ready to leave at eleven."

"That'll make us late, won't it?"

Benevides nodded. "I want everyone waiting on us." He gave Samuel a stern look. "No surprises, Sam. I want to see who we're dealing with."

Chapter Sixty-Two

JEAN BROUSSARD, DRESSED in an expensive business suit and looking every bit like a bank examiner, stood in a Panama City hotel lobby waiting impatiently for Ben Postl. He began pacing, glancing at his watch every couple of minutes. When Ben stepped off the elevator fifteen minutes late wearing jeans and sneakers, Jean's facial expression showed his displeasure. Ben defended himself before Jean ever spoke.

"What? You don't like the way I look? It's all I have. I didn't bring anything else."

"You're late," Jean said glancing at his watch. "And those clothes?" Jean rolled his eyes. "Heaven help us, Ben. You're supposed to be a bank examiner. You've been in a bank before. You know what employees wear. At least look the part," Jean said, trying to maintain a civil tone.

"How did I know you wanted me to wear a suit? No one told me." Ben was inexperienced at field operations and Jean knew he wouldn't get Ben's best effort through anger. He relaxed and smiled.

"No matter, we'll deal with it. Before we hit the bank downtown, we must find a department store and see what can be found in your size off the rack. Follow me."

Jean found a taxi waiting in front of the hotel and asked to be taken to the main branch of the National Bank of Panama. Once there, Jean and Ben walked to a nearby sidewalk café to discuss their plan over coffee.

"The credentials you created are quite nice," Jean commented between sips of espresso. "You're a talented forger." He pulled a slip of paper from his breast pocket and slid it across the small table. "Here are the numbers you need to make a wire transfer to Credit Suisse in Zurich. How long will it take to initiate the transfer?" Ben studied the numbers.

"Once I put an order into the bank's system, it's automatic. The money will be transferred the same day."

"Can they stop it?"

"It'd be hard. They won't know I hacked their system for a while. Once they discover it, if they discover it, then they'll have to trace the accounts I changed."

"Doesn't someone monitor their system?"

"Sure, but I'll have a password. In other words, the system will believe I'm a legitimate user. By the time they figure it out, we'll be back in the States."

"Could the bank unwind the transaction?"

"What do you mean?"

"Request the money be returned." Ben thought about that for a minute.

"I don't know much about international banking law, but I do know Swiss banks are secretive. I doubt Credit Suisse would cooperate without a great deal of evidence." Jean smiled.

"Which they won't have." Both of them chuckled.

"You're turning me into a criminal," Ben said.

"You're already a forger, Ben."

"I object to that." Ben laughed. "Forging is a legitimate business."

"Touché! Follow me. Let's get you dressed before we hit the bank."

After dress slacks, shoes and a sports jacket were purchased at a local department store, Ben retreated to a dressing room where he changed clothes. He stuffed the old clothing into his backpack. Jean watched with amusement as Ben exited the dressing room struggling to zip the backpack. "Now you look the part. Are you ready?" Ben nodded. "Off we go then."

The two walked the few blocks between the store and bank. Upon arriving at the bank, Jean used his impeccable language skill to sound like a native Panamanian. He requested a bank manager and the two waited in the lobby until a short, overweight and busy floor manager made his way over.

"Can I help you?"

"Yes, I hope so. I'm Enrique Matize," Jean replied, "and I've been instructed by the Ministry to inspect certain accounts maintained here at the bank. Here's my Presidential Order." He handed the manager a business card and the Noriega letter.

The manager appeared indecisive, staring at the letter as though a mistake would cost him his job. He looked back and forth between Jean, Ben, and the letter several times before finding the courage to decide. "I see," he finally said. "Would you follow me, please?"

They were led upstairs where they were asked to wait in an outer office for a Vice President. Jean watched the manager show the letter to the VP at his desk through the open doorway. The bank manager and VP had an animated conversation, looking at the letter and business card several times until the VP walked out and approached Jean with the letter in hand. Ben decided to hang back, afraid of being forced to speak. Without language skills, Ben was helpless.

"Mr. Matize, is it?" The Vice President asked Jean.

"Yes, Sir. I apologize for the unannounced visit, but orders are orders," Jean said with a wry smile and a shrug. Jean looked at the man's name tag on the lapel of his suitcoat, Felix Lopez.

"This is irregular, Mr.," he looked at the business card to remind him of the name, "Matize. We send monthly statements over to the Ministry. I'm not sure we can provide them with more information."

"That's not the response the President will want to hear. His secret police can be here within minutes and force you to comply," Jean said as a warning.

The VP understood the threat. "What exactly do they want to see?"

"The President wishes an independent examination of accounts related to his office."

"He doesn't trust the bank statements we send him?"

Jean leaned closer to the VP and lowered his voice. "If I might offer a piece of advice, Mr. Lopez, it would be best to give the President what he wants. He's an unusual client, as I'm sure you know."

Lopez studied the letter again. "Would you mind waiting for another minute? I've got to inform the bank chairman of this inquiry."

"Of course."

The VP went back into his office and shut the door. Meanwhile, Ben had discretely walked to an empty workstation to inspect the terminal sitting on the desktop. "Jean?"

"Please, Ben, call me Enrique."

"I think there's a password taped to this monitor. Take a look."

Jean walked over and watched Ben point to a small note taped below the screen. It read NBP5555. "That's got to be a password."

Jean glanced at the VP's door to make sure it was closed. "Look around and find an empty office somewhere and see if that password gets you in the system. If it does, log yourself in and do your work." He glanced at his watch. "You've got about five minutes before they call the police. When you're finished, change your clothes in a restroom and make your way out of the bank.

Don't wait for me." Jean glanced at the closed door again. "Now go before that Vice President returns." Ben nodded and left.

After another wait, Lopez finally came out of his office. "Mr. Matize, I'm sorry for the delay. Would you mind showing me your identification?"

Jean pulled out a billfold and handed Lopez a national identification card and a driver's license Ben had forged before they'd left the States. "Thank you, Mr. Matize," Lopez said. "I'm sure you can understand that we must protect the security of our bank records. I'll be back shortly."

"I understand, Mr. Lopez. Take all the time you need," Jean replied. Lopez took Jean's documents back into his office and closed the door.

Chapter Sixty-Three

MY JOB IS done, Jean thought. I've gotten Ben in the building and he has a password. I should get out while I can. He quietly left the office, looked up and down the hallway and found an exit sign above a door at one end of the hall. Through that door, he found a stairwell back to the main floor. He briskly walked across the lobby where a security guard standing inside the front doors nodded to him. "Have a pleasant day, Sir."

Jean gave him a confident smile. "You as well," he said before exiting the bank. Once on the street, he walked to the intersection at the end of the block and spotted a large hotel a block away. He got into a taxi at the hotel entrance. "Where to?" The driver asked.

"The Sheraton hotel at Albrook Air Force Base." The driver punched his meter and pulled out onto the street where Jean watched bank security guards running down the sidewalk. Jean bent down in the seat as they passed.

A couple of minutes earlier, Felix Lopez had opened his office door expecting to find Enrique Matize. What the hell, he thought. Lopez picked up the phone in the outer office and dialed Security.

"Security, can I help you?" The male voice said.

"This is Vice President Lopez calling from upstairs. There's a man in the building, sixties, short, thin, gray hair, wearing a black suit. He says his name is Enrique Matize. Find and detain him. Inform the guards at all exit points."

"Yes, Sir." Within a minute, a description of Jean was distributed to all guards working in the building and a search began. The lobby guard at the front doors recognized the description of the man who'd left not a moment before. He and a second guard bolted out the front door and began searching the sidewalk for Jean. Lopez hung up and then dialed the local police to help with the search.

Chapter Sixty-Four

BEN MIGRATED TO the third floor where he found an empty office with a terminal. He locked the door, sat down and found that the password worked. Once inside the system, he searched for accounts under the Delgado name and found three. Two personal accounts under the names Luis Delgado and Anita Delgado, plus an additional business account under the name Delgado Investments, LTD. Each of the individual Delgado accounts had balances exceeding twenty million U.S. dollars, but Delgado Investments, LTD, was the big one. It contained a whopping 176 million dollars. He stared at the screen for a few seconds contemplating the enormity of the money.

Ben heard footsteps walking by in the hallway, so he quickly figured out how to initiate wire transfers and executed them electronically, leaving only nominal sums in each account. He logged off the system, turned off the monitor and thoroughly wiped down everything he'd touched to remove fingerprints. He quickly changed into his street clothes and pushed a baseball cap over his eyes. Stuffing the suit into his backpack, he left the office, then used the elevator to appear like any other customer.

Once he arrived in the lobby, he sauntered unhurriedly to the front door and left. He quickened his pace outside the bank, stopping in an alley to toss the suit into a dumpster and then flagged down a taxi to return to the hotel. Fortunately, the taxi driver spoke English. He smiled once the taxi was on its way.

He'd just performed his first bank robbery and gotten away cleanly.

Jean arrived at the hotel first, grabbed a cup of coffee in a Styrofoam cup and sat in the lobby nervously waiting for Ben. When Ben walked in the door and spotted Jean a few minutes later, he walked over with a big grin on his face. "Well?" Jean asked.

"Over two-hundred million dollars, Jean. All safely sent out of the country to Credit Suisse in Zurich. We did it!"

Jean began laughing and once Ben joined in, neither man could stop. After their moment of celebration, Jean realized they needed to check out to remove all traces of their whereabouts. "Let's check out and head to the air base. We can sleep on the plane if we have to, but we won't be completely safe until we're on the base. Did you leave anything in the room?"

"No, I have everything with me," Ben replied.

"We should check out immediately."

The men paid their bills and hopped in a taxi where Jean began picking at his right hand.

"These things are exceedingly difficult to remove," he said out loud.

"What are you doing?" Ben asked.

"I'm removing fingerprints I glued over mine that will provide the police with a lead. That assumes, of course, that the police down here are competent enough to dust Lopez's office for prints."

"Perhaps they won't."

"It would be better if they did. It draws their attention away from us."

"Are they real prints?" Ben asked as Jean rolled the window down slightly and released the small, clear plastic pieces into the air.

"Most assuredly so. They were taken from one Marcel DuMont, a legendary French safecracker and jewel thief."

"He knows you're using them?"

Ben saw a wry smile develop on Jean's face. "If he were alive, I'm sure he would. He exists only in legend now, working his way across the globe, increasing his fame with each print the authorities find. He's been on Interpol's top ten list for years."

"And he's dead?"

"Of course," Jean said with a nod. "He died in his sleep several years ago. His daughter and I quietly buried him in an unmarked grave outside Pao, a small town in Southern France. Not before I was able to get a good set of prints, though."

The taxi dropped them off at the main terminal building at Albrook. Once inside, Jean turned and gave Ben a pat on the back. "Now, we're safe. Are you hungry?"

"Starving. Let me buy you lunch. I think I can afford it."

"You're going to buy me lunch? I love this turn of events," Jean said with a laugh. He glanced at his watch. "I accept, young man. It'll take my mind off the Mademoiselle. Derek Young's plane should be arriving in Yavisa soon."

Chapter Sixty-Five

TWO PANAMANIAN JEEPS slowed as they approached the roadblock set by Ramos' troops outside Yavisa. The eight black shirts dispatched by Noriega's office were led by Lieutenant Hernandez, a veteran of illicit drug transactions. Corporal Jiminez approached the Jeeps after motioning to his men to lift the tarp revealing the machine gun in the truck bed. "Good morning, Lieutenant. Can I help you?" Jiminez asked politely.

"We're here to monitor the shipment," Hernandez said.

"Please wait while I inform the Captain." Jiminez walked back to the truck to call Captain Ramos.

The Lieutenant asked his driver, "Are PDF regulars supposed to be here?"

"I didn't hear anything about it."

Jiminez talked briefly on the radio before returning to the Jeep. "Captain Ramos would like you to report to the far end of the airstrip by the fuel tanks. Wait a moment and we'll move the truck for you."

Hernandez shook his head. "No need for that, Corporal, we'll drive around it." The two Jeeps drove onto the shoulder, steered around the truck and headed toward the airstrip.

Captain Ramos watched the two Jeeps kick up dust as they drove straight toward him down the middle of the dirt runway. "What would you wager they had no idea we'd be here?" He asked Sergeant Garcia.

"I'm sure they didn't. What would you wager Noriega's men are a problem?"

A confident Ramos chuckled. "We have three times their numbers, Sergeant. I'm sure they'll be real polite."

Garcia looked around the airstrip and grimaced. "Three times their numbers," he said nodding toward the approaching vehicles, "What if more of them are coming?"

Ramos gave the Sergeant a questioning look. "Do you know something I don't?"

"A lot of people know what's going on here …"

Garcia stopped mid-sentence when the Jeeps pulled up and the ranking officer climbed out. He saluted Ramos. "Lieutenant Hernandez from the President's Office."

"Captain Ramos, under General Costa's command," he said returning the salute.

Hernandez looked around at the placement of Ramos' men. He did the mental math and knew they were outnumbered. "We weren't told you'd be here," he said diplomatically.

"We were sent by a direct order from General Costa to stop the transaction. There will be no deal today."

Hernandez stood there, not quite believing what he'd heard. "With all due respect, Captain, you don't want to follow those orders."

"You didn't hear me properly, Lieutenant," Ramos said brusquely. "I'm here to stop the transaction. Turn around and go back to Panama City. General Costa will send the President his fee for today."

"I heard you, Captain. I want you to think about what you're saying for a minute."

"I have," a confident Ramos said.

Hernandez gave Sergeant Garcia a warning look. "Sergeant, you know what's happening here. Talk to your Captain."

Garcia leaned closer to Ramos. "Let's hear what the man has to say, Captain."

Ramos nodded to avoid a confrontation. "All right, Lieutenant, go ahead."

"Stop the transaction if those are your orders. Tell FARC to take their shipment back to Columbia. Tell them …" Hernandez hesitated thinking of how to phrase it, "…the transaction is postponed for security reasons. Tell them whatever you like. They'll go away and sell their product to someone else."

"I follow you so far, Lieutenant," Ramos said. "If you have a point to make, please make it. I'm busy right now."

"In a few minutes, the Americans are going to land a plane here," he said, nodding toward the airstrip behind him, "with millions of dollars in cash. They won't have much security guarding the money."

"What are you suggesting, Lieutenant?" Hernandez shrugged as though it was obvious.

"We steal the money."

Ramos shook his head. "I have orders to confiscate the money, Lieutenant," he said firmly.

"Well, I didn't mean we steal all of it," Hernandez said with a sly smile. "We give President Noriega enough to satisfy him, you do the same with General Costa and we take the rest for ourselves."

"I could have you arrested for that statement, Lieutenant."

Garcia whispered to Ramos. "Could I talk with you privately for a minute?" Garcia pulled Ramos away by the arm. They walked far enough to conceal their conversation. "Captain, I urge you to consider the idea."

"And why would I do that?"

"Because you don't want a mutiny on your hands." Garcia pointed to the troops distributed around the airfield. "The Lieutenant will talk among our men and turn them against you. They'll take control of the platoon, kill you and throw your body in the river."

"They'd kill me over money?" Ramos asked, with astonishment.

"What do you think?" Garcia said with a smile. "Do I have to spell it out for you? The short answer is yes, they'd kill you over money."

Ramos was unsure of what to do. He walked back to Hernandez. "Have you done this before, Lieutenant?"

Hernandez shook his head. "The money's never been delivered here before."

"How did you handle it in the past?"

"The Trade Minister handled the money."

Ramos vaguely remembered the name. "Valera?"

"That's right."

Ever cautious, Ramos continued his questions. "What's changed this time?"

"I don't know," Hernandez said, shrugging his shoulders, "and I don't care. All I know is the money's coming here and we're in charge."

"What happens when some of the money turns up missing?" A still skeptical Ramos asked.

"The President doesn't know how much money there is and neither does the General. I doubt the American government knows. It's CIA slush fund money. If some of the money disappears, CIA will cover it up. Nobody keeps records."

That doesn't sound right, Ramos thought. "No records?"

"With all due respect, Captain, records incriminate people," the Lieutenant replied.

Ramos remained unconvinced. The Lieutenant seemed to have an answer for everything. "What about the Americans on the plane? They're not going to stand aside and allow us to take their money."

"That's easy," a smiling Hernandez said, making a motion of slitting their throats. "We kill them."

As though killing people is easy to do, Ramos thought. "Lieutenant, if you kill Americans, the commander in the Canal Zone will want answers. This whole scheme of yours will fall apart and we'll be tried for murder."

"The Canal Zone commander doesn't know they're here. The plane's coming from Florida."

"Well, someone knows they're here, Lieutenant. We arrested two Americans this morning, one of them is an American Colonel who said he'd talked with General Costa. Officers don't disappear without questions being asked."

"Where are they?" Hernandez asked looking around.

Ramos nodded toward his Jeep. "They're sitting behind that Jeep."

"Have you questioned them?"

"Of course."

"Do you mind if I try?" Ramos shouted at his guards to bring the men forward. Pritchard and Wexler were lifted and pushed forward.

The guard handed Ramos a pocketknife lying on the ground beneath the Colonel. "I found this, Sir."

Ramos waved the knife in front of Pritchard. "This is a stupid idea, Colonel. If there are any more stunts like this, I'll have you shot."

"You wouldn't dare," Pritchard replied in anger.

Ramos pulled Wexler's Beretta from his belt and held the barrel against Pritchard's forehead. "You're not in command here."

This guy's batshit crazy, Pritchard thought. "Captain, I'm a protected prisoner under the terms of the Geneva Conventions, Article 3. Go read your fucking manual."

Ramos suddenly punched Pritchard in his gut. Pritchard wasn't expecting the blow and bent forward, his breath knocked out of his him. "You're in my country dealing drugs, Colonel. I'm quite sure that isn't covered in the manual." He motioned

261

toward Hernandez. "This is Lieutenant Hernandez from the President's office. He'd like you to ask you a few questions."

Pritchard struggled to stand up straight, still recovering from the blow.

"Who are you?" Hernandez asked.

"Colonel Kevin Pritchard, United States Marine Corp," he replied, his voice strained from the lack of air in his lungs.

"What are you doing here, Colonel?"

"I'm in charge of our side of the drug deal. I command the men and it's my plane."

"We weren't told the American military was involved."

"It's our cash."

Hernandez was puzzled by the answer. "I thought this was CIA cash."

"It's a joint mission with the CIA."

"I see." Hernandez looked at Wexler. "And you? Who are you?"

"Bret Wexler. I work for the Colonel. I came down yesterday to scout the town."

Hernandez found that interesting. "And what did you find?"

Wexler looked at Pritchard wondering if he should talk. Hernandez motioned with his hand. "Out with it! What did you see?"

Pritchard kept glaring at the Panamanian officers and offered no help. "The only thing unusual were two Russians who stopped for fuel in a military helicopter."

Hernandez suddenly stared at Ramos. "Russians?" They both asked simultaneously. They were alarmed by the revelation.

"How did you know they were Russians?" Ramos asked.

"I recognized the red star on their helicopter, and they wore Russian uniforms," Wexler said. "They had thick Russian accents."

"Which way did they head when they left?" Hernandez asked.

"North."

Hernandez leaned toward Ramos and lowered his voice. "I think this is okay. The President allows Russians in the country to balance the Americans. But they're supposed to stay in the north. Maybe it's just a coincidence."

"Maybe not," Sergeant Garcia suggested, overhearing the conversation.

"What do you mean, Sergeant?" Ramos asked.

Garcia shrugged as though it was obvious. "It's a lot of money. Maybe we're not the only ones who know about it."

Hernandez glanced at Ramos. "Let's talk privately."

Chapter Sixty-Six

THE TWO MEN walked out of earshot a few yards away. "We don't need to worry about the Russians," Hernandez said. "They don't have enough men in the country to cause a problem for us."

Ramos considered the explanation. "How do you know this?"

"I work in the President's office."

"You're saying we don't need to worry about Russians?"

Hernandez was exasperated by Ramos' inexperience. "Isn't that what I just said?"

"Lieutenant, I'm just confirming it. None of us want to end up in prison or dead."

"I suggest you release the Americans and give them back their sidearms."

"Why would I do that?"

Hernandez laughed out loud. "Because the plane will make a pass over the field before it lands. If the pilot sees his commanding officer being held captive, he's going to fly away, and we won't get our money." Do I have to explain every detail to this man? Hernandez asked himself. "Look, here's the way this works," Hernandez continued. "Apologize to those two and tell them it was a misunderstanding. Make them believe we're on their side. The plane will land, we'll kill the Americans and we'll have our money."

In the back of his mind, Ramos had been thinking about the money. *It's enough money to secure my family's future. I could move out of the country and get away from this mess.* "Lieutenant, I have one more question. Let's suppose everything works as you claim. How do we divide the money?"

Hernandez smiled. He was finally getting through to Ramos. "I've watched them unload money in Colon, Captain. There's more than you can possibly carry. You'll see. I don't think we'll have a problem."

Ramos had run out of questions. He decided to stop stalling. "Okay. Let's do it." He held out his hand and they shook on the deal.

The two walked back to Sergeant Garcia and the Americans. "Colonel, I'd like to apologize for the misunderstanding this morning," Ramos said. "I'm going to release you. You're free to go." He looked at Garcia. "Cut them loose."

Garcia shrugged his shoulders as though he wondered why they'd taken so long to make a simple decision. He cut the bonds and both men rubbed their wrists to get the circulation going again. "Here's your sidearm back," Ramos said to Wexler, pulling the pistol out of his waistband. "Colonel, we'll retrieve yours immediately. I apologize for any inconvenience we caused you."

Pritchard grinned. "No offense taken, Captain. I'm glad you realized your mistake. Let's move on. Do you have a radio that uses aircraft frequencies? I'd like to contact my pilot."

"I'm sorry, Sir. Our radios can't handle that."

"No problem," Pritchard said. "If you don't mind, I'm going to make myself visible to my pilot, so he knows it's safe to land."

"Of course, Colonel."

Pritchard slapped Wexler on the back. "Come on, Wex, we're back in business. Let's stand out there," he pointed toward the runway, "and direct air traffic."

Wexler had closely observed the Panamanians talk among themselves and wondered what had been decided. "Colonel, I don't trust these guys," he said quietly as he and Pritchard walked onto the runway. "This could be a set-up."

Pritchard slapped Wexler on the back as they walked out onto the runway. "Relax Wex. Do you know what Noriega would do to these men if they disobeyed orders? He'd shoot them on sight."

Pritchard's assurance did nothing to satisfy Wexler's suspicion. However, he was free of his bonds, he wasn't being threatened at the moment, and he had his sidearm back. "If you say so," he said glancing at Pritchard. "You're the boss."

"Atta boy, Wex. Let's go make this happen."

Chapter Sixty-Seven

WATCHING THE PANAMANIANS from the edge of the jungle, Jerry Stock radioed Jordan. "Major, something's going on up here you should see."

"We'll be right there." Jordan and Laura headed up the path again. "What's going on, Jerry?" Jordan whispered, crouching behind Stock.

"Move up beside me and take a look yourself." Both Laura and Jordan squeezed themselves between the large ferns, careful not to disturb them. "First, this CIA type walks out on the runway and the Panamanians arrest him," Jerry said. "Then, this Marine Colonel shows up and they arrest him, too. After that, the black shirts show up and they release the Americans. Now, they all look like they're waiting for the plane. What the hell is going on, Major?"

"I'm not sure," Jordan said. "Laura, what do you think?"

"I know exactly what's going on."

Jordan stared at her. "Would you mind telling me?"

"I'll explain it back at camp."

Jordan turned to Jerry. "Keep watching while we sort through this. I'll get back to you."

Laura and Jordan walked back to camp. "I believe that Colonel is Kevin Pritchard from the Pentagon," Laura began. "He runs an illegal drug op under the table."

"He must have the approval of someone in authority, Laura, or he wouldn't be here."

"No, he's doing it on his own. I'll bet General Carson has no idea Pritchard's here." Jordan tried to sort through the possibilities in his mind.

"It's hard to believe a Colonel in the United States Marines would be involved with drugs."

"He is, Jim, and I'll tell you something else. The guys on the plane? They're all CIA. It's corruption pure and simple."

"So, you lied in the mission documents about your purpose here?" Laura looked Jordan squarely in the eyes.

"Not about stopping a drug shipment. Pritchard and the CIA are importing drugs into the U.S. I've researched this for weeks, Jim. It's true." Laura could see Jordan struggle with the new information.

"The question I have is why?"

"To buy arms for the Contras." Jordan shook his head.

"Congress banned that."

"You're right, but Pritchard's doing it anyway."

"Who else knows about it?"

"There are a few in government who do, but they let it go on."

"How did you get involved?"

Laura told Jordan the entire story, from the flight landing in the Bahamas, to the attempted assassination, to discovering the next shipment. "I must stop this, Jim. Otherwise, they'll kill me."

"Okay, I understand. I believe you. But I'm going to say something I want you to understand. Pritchard's an American officer. He's subject to military justice. And CIA employees must follow U.S. law. I'm honor bound to capture them, Laura. I won't kill them unless it's in defense of my own life."

"I understand."

"We're in agreement then?" Jordan asked. "We capture the Americans?"

"I agree. That's what we'll do." Jordan nodded.

"Having said that," Jordan continued, "we have to change our plan because of the PDF troops. If they attack us, we could be pushed back to the copter in a matter of minutes. We need a second firing position to hold them off."

Laura thought for a minute. "Okay, how does this sound? I'll take Adam with me and we'll climb on the roof of one of the buildings in town where we can get a view of the airstrip. You keep Nick, Carl and Jerry with you at the edge of the runway. That way, we've got them in a crossfire."

"I follow you so far, but what if FARC flanks us?" Jordan asked.

"Let's send Rick to the river with Pierre and Sharp. We can stop FARC right at the hairpin."

"That works. We'll have a decent defensive position, and we can attack if we choose to."

Back at the camp, Laura and Jordan brought the rest of their men together and explained the evolving situation. Adam rummaged around the back of one of the Jeeps and brought a sniper rifle to Laura. "From a rooftop, I don't think you can hit diddly-squat with those handguns. Take this," he said handing the rifle over.

"This is a Haskins rifle," Laura said, surprised. "When did you start using these?"

"We got them right before we came down. They're as accurate as anything I've ever used. Put these in your pocket," he said handing her three extra clips.

Laura slid them into a deep front pocket. "Are you ready to roll?"

"Yes, Ma'am. If we go down that middle path," Adam pointed, "we should come out just yards from the town. We'll have to cross an open stretch, but once we're in the town, we should be able to find cover."

"You want to take point?"

Adam smiled. "Yes, Ma'am. You read my mind."

Laura and Adam hustled down the path but hesitated before stepping out into the open. "You might want to take off that patch," Laura suggested, nodding toward the USA flag attached to Adam's sleeve with Velcro.

He pulled it off and smiled sheepishly. "I forgot about that." He stuffed it in his pocket, looked in every direction and saw no one. "I think we're clear. Let's walk slowly like we're in no hurry."

"Okay, but I'm pulling my handgun just in case." She slung the rifle over her shoulder and withdrew one of her pistols. She held it at her side. They walked into town and found the streets vacant. "People are hiding," Laura observed. "They know something's going on."

The entire town was just two parallel streets with connecting alleyways, so it didn't take long to find a suitable shooting position. "How about this one?" she asked, pointing to a one-story brick building with a flat roof.

"That should work," Adam answered. A dumpster behind the building gave them access to the roof. Once on the roof, they found a perfect line of sight to the end of the runway where the Panamanians had parked their Jeeps and the truck.

Meanwhile, Rick gathered the second RPG and the bag of shells, then headed toward Pierre's position at the river.

Jordan walked over to Dmitri and Pete who were in the final stages of prepping the copter. "Are you guys ready to go?"

"Yep. Give us the go ahead and we'll be airborne."

Jordan turned and found that Carl and Nick had already prepared themselves. "We're moving up to Jerry's position on the double."

"Yes, Sir," Nick said.

"Once we get there, let's spread ourselves about ten yards apart."

"I'm bringing a few grenades just in case," Carl said.

"Good," Jordan replied. "This thing could turn into a shit sandwich real quick."

Chapter Sixty-Eight

THE LUMBERING FAIRCHILD C-123 transport plane crept south over the Gulf to stay in international airspace. Using the rear ramp, two plastic wrapped pallets had been loaded and strapped to the floor inside the cargo bay. Totaling eighty million dollars in small bills, the pallets were heavy enough that a forklift was needed to load them. Young decided to bring the forklift along since he wasn't quite sure how they'd unload the pallets at the airstrip. Five guards sat in jump seats along the interior sides of the cargo bay that included a lavatory and a small refrigerator stocked with sandwiches and soft drinks. It was an uncomfortable ride, but well worth the inconvenience since each of them would be paid handsomely. That would be in addition to the money each man slipped off the pallets and stuffed into his pocket. Derek Young laughed when one of the men entered the cockpit and handed him a thick stack of hundreds pulled from one of the pallets. "Thought you could use this, Skip," the man said.

"You got that right. Totally non-taxable, too," Young replied, chuckling.

At the correct latitude, Young executed a slow 90° turn to the right and headed toward the coast. Shortly after passing the Panamanian coast, he spotted Yavisa on the horizon. Descending to 500 feet as they passed over the airstrip, Young asked his co-pilot, Hank Miller, to inspect the condition of the runway. "It looks smooth and dry, Derek. I don't think we'll have a problem. I see a lot of military down there."

"PDF regulars and a few of Noriega's men," Young said. "I think that's Pritchard and Wexler waving at us."

"Pritchard's there?"

"Pretty sure that's him."

"Good," Miller said with emphasis. "That prick will never pick up the phone in D.C." They both laughed.

As they headed out over the Pacific, Young alerted his passengers on the intercom. "Heads up, boys and girls. We just flew over Yavisa. We'll be swinging out over the ocean to make a 270 into the airfield. Go ahead and strap yourselves in. We'll be on the ground in fifteen minutes."

Miller continued. "Did you see the copter sitting west of the runway?"

"I did," Young replied. "That's pretty common down here. VIPs rent those for fishing trips. It was probably moved aside to clear the apron for us."

"Sorry, I guess I'm a little nervous."

"No problem. It's not every day we haul around eighty million."

Young began a slow three-quarter turn over the Pacific Ocean to line up his approach into Yavisa.

Chapter Sixty-Nine

CAPTAIN RAMOS HAD an idea watching Pritchard waving madly at the plane as it passed overhead. He leaned toward Sergeant Garcia who stood next to him. "Sergeant, get on the radio and order the men at the roadblock back here on the double. Tell them to park the truck here," he said pointing to the end of the runway near the fuel tanks. "The Americans won't argue with both 50 calibers pointed at them."

The Sergeant smiled. "Yes, Sir."

"Sergeant?" Ramos asked.

Garcia had begun to walk away but turned back for a second.

"Do it quietly."

Sergeant Garcia was back within a minute. "The truck won't start up at the highway. They'll have to come back on foot."

"We need them back before the plane lands, Sergeant. Tell them to double-time it."

"They'll have to leave the 50 cal," Garcia advised.

"Fine. We've got one here. Just get the men back."

"Yes, Sir."

Chapter Seventy

AFTER A DISCUSSION at the FARC camp with two spies who slipped a boat out of Yavisa, David Benevides asked Samuel, his second in command, to call the men together. "Here's the situation, men," he began. "We've got a platoon of PDF regulars waiting for us at the airstrip. I'm not sure why they're there."

"Does it mean trouble?" Samuel asked.

"Maybe," Benevides answered, wondering the same himself.

Another of Benevides men, Santos, shouted a question. "Are they going to hijack the shipment?"

A third man voiced a third opinion. "They've been sent to arrest us."

Benevides chuckled. "There aren't enough of them to do either one," he replied to the third man, raising his gun. "We're armed. Here's my best guess. Noriega's worried about security so he's using regular army."

His men looked at Samuel who spoke for them. "How can we be sure?"

"We can't."

"What do we do?"

Benevides grimaced. "Let's hold the cargo boats at the hairpin turn before the town. We'll take the command boat in and find out what's going on. If there's any trouble, we'll let you know by radio," he said pointing to the cargo boats. "You can turn the boats around and return to camp." Benevides watched the men nod their heads in agreement. "Make sure your weapons are loaded with the safeties off on the way in. Keep your eyes open. We're not looking for trouble, but we need to be prepared for it." He turned to Samuel. "Is the cargo loaded?"

"Yes, Sir," Samuel replied.

"Then let's be on our way."

Chapter Seventy-One

DEREK YOUNG USED the Pan-American Highway to line up his approach into Yavisa and skimmed the treetops before gently setting down on the dirt runway. The landing was smoother than he anticipated, and he needed only a portion of its length to slow, so he taxied the rest of the distance to the apron and turned around to put the rear of the craft facing the fuel tanks. He lowered the rear ramp before shutting down the engines. Five guards exited down the ramp all dressed identically, jeans, pull-over shirts, leather jackets and sunglasses. They looked like they'd just walked off a movie set, tough guys ready for action. Each carried an Israeli made Uzi submachine gun of the 32-mag variety, and all carried extra magazines clipped to their belts. They were followed by Derek Young and Hank Miller, both dressed in flowered print shirts and jeans.

Colonel Pritchard and Bret Wexler eagerly walked forward to greet Young. "I see you made it, Derek," Pritchard said, grabbing Young's hand.

"Hey, you know me," Young said, smiling. "Always on time for a party. You know my co-pilot, Hank Miller."

"Greetings, Colonel," Miller acknowledged.

Pritchard gave Miller a nod, then continued. "You boys have any problems getting down here?"

"Piece of cake, no problems at all. Where do you want the cargo?"

Pritchard looked around and settled on a spot halfway between the plane and the fuel tanks. "Set it out in the open," he said motioning with his hand, "between the plane and those tanks. You need help?"

Young laughed. "Nah, I brought a damn forklift with me. The money's shrink wrapped on pallets."

"Okay. I'll let you guys get to work then."

"Any sign of our South American friends?"

"No, but I called Costa before I left. He assured me they'll be here."

"Roger that, Colonel." Young turned and addressed his men. "Did you boys hear the Colonel? Put the pallets over there," he said, motioning to the same spot Pritchard had identified.

As Young's men began to work, Pritchard grabbed Young by the arm and nodded toward Captain Ramos. "Come on, I'll introduce you to the locals."

Chapter Seventy-Two

AS PRITCHARD'S MEN churned the starter on the forklift, Ramos and Lieutenant Hernandez nodded to their men. The Panamanians casually began forming a half circle around Pritchard and his men. It appeared as though the Panamanians wanted to see what eighty million dollars in cash looked like and why not? The movement could have been viewed as an encirclement; however, Pritchard hadn't commanded troops in the field in years. What could go wrong? He had an agreement with high officials in the Panamanian government.

By the time the pallets had been offloaded, a platoon of PDF regulars and black shirts surrounded the Americans. Seeing this, Pritchard's men suddenly became nervous. They moved their hands to their weapons and swung their heads side to side looking for sudden movements. There were none. Ramos' and Hernandez's men looked completely relaxed, talking among themselves without even a glance at Pritchard's men.

Pritchard, oblivious to potential danger, walked toward Ramos. "We're ready to take delivery, Captain," he said, impatient that FARC was nowhere to be found. "Where the fuck are the FARC rebels? Are these guys going to show?"

"I imagine they will, Colonel." He glanced at his watch. "I've been told they're usually late."

"Late?" Pritchard repeated the word sarcastically. He turned to Wexler and spoke underneath his breath. "Do you see how frustrating it is working with these people?"

Wexler took a quick look at Ramos before answering, worried that the Captain may have overheard Pritchard. "I think we're okay, Colonel. Everything seems to be in order."

Ramos nodded to Sergeant Garcia who stood next to the truck. The Panamanians began to back away while Garcia pulled back the tarp to reveal the 50-caliber machine gun. The gunner swung the weapon back and forth at Pritchard's men. "I'm sorry, Colonel," Ramos said. "This is necessary to maintain security."

Before Pritchard's men had time to react, the machine gun opened fire. Machine gun fire tore through everything, money, men, the plane behind. Small bits of paper money shredded and flew into the air. The sound of the gunfire echoed off the buildings in the town and then there was silence.

Chapter Seventy-Three

"SHIT!" LAURA SAID loudly into the mic. "Did you see that?"

"Hold!" Jordan said into the radio. "Nobody move!"

Jordan's men leveled their rifles at the Panamanians, fingers on the triggers. They could have easily killed what they aimed at, but not an entire platoon in one volley. Jordan relied on the military discipline of his troops.

"Don't tell me that, Major," Nick said into the mic. "They're killing Americans."

"Fuck you, Major," Carl Thomas hissed. "They murdered Americans."

"The Major repeated his command. "I said hold! You'll have revenge today."

"Nobody wants to hear that, Major," Jerry Stock said.

Jordan repeated himself slowly with anger in his voice. "We! Hold!"

Rick could hear the firing from the river position. "What just happened?" He said into his mic.

"The Panamanians just killed Pritchard's men, Rick," Laura replied. "Keep the channel open."

Chapter Seventy-Four

"WHAT THE FUCK?" Pritchard shouted. He crouched and began a quick movement of his head, instinctively looking for an escape. Young and Miller, standing next to Pritchard, reached for their weapons, but seeing the guns in Ramos' platoon pointed at them, they froze.

"Don't!" Ramos shouted to Pritchard and the two pilots. "Don't do it! If you point those weapons, you'll be killed." Pritchard and his men stopped. "Take your hands off your weapons!"

After the briefest second of analysis, Young and Miller realized they could not fight their way out of the trap. They slowly released the grip on their pistol handles and the weapons dropped to their feet.

Ramos withdrew his pistol and pointed it at Pritchard. He spoke to Lieutenant Hernandez without looking, keeping his eyes on Pritchard. "Lieutenant? Take your men and make sure those men are dead." Hernandez and his men walked among the carnage and checked each body. Ramos cautioned Pritchard. "I'm warning you, Colonel. Remain still."

Hernandez and his men shot those still alive in the head except for one man, Greg Smith, who'd sheltered behind a pallet and was completely unhurt. Hernandez jerked him up by the collar. "What do you want me to do with this one?" He asked Ramos.

"Bring him here and put him with the others." Hernandez hauled him up by the collar, disarmed him and pushed him forward. Ramos waved his pistol at the four remaining Americans, Pritchard, the pilots Young and Miller, along with the young agent Greg Smith. "The rest of you are an insurance policy. You'll stay alive if you cooperate. Get on your knees with your hands on top of your head. Sergeant? Take those plastic ties in the Jeep and tie their hands together behind their back. When you're done, sit them on the ground behind the vehicles. Shoot them if they try to escape."

"Yes, Sir," Garcia enthusiastically replied.

Chapter Seventy-Five

DAVID BENEVIDES LOOKED alarmed. "Was that gunfire I just heard?" He asked Samuel over the din of the motorboat engine.

"Did one of the boats backfire?" Samuel asked.

"It sounded like machine gun fire. Stop at the hairpin ahead. Tell the cargo boats to pull to the bank and tie up in those overhanging trees."

Samuel relayed the orders on his radio and the three cargo boats headed for the bank. Benevides slowed his boat to an idle and watched while the boats tied themselves to trees that leaned over the bank. "We're secure back here," an unidentified voice barked over Samuel's radio.

Benevides turned to the men in his command boat. "Keep your guns up and eyes open. We may be walking into a trap. Sam, take us in slowly." Samuel inched the boat around the hairpin while every man on board had eyes and guns pointed at one bank or the other. "See anything?"

"No," Samuel replied. "Nothing."

"Keep alert the rest of the way in."

Chapter Seventy-Six

"DAMN, THAT WAS close," Rick whispered to Pierre after Benevides' boat passed within a few feet of their position.

"It's as though they knew we were here," Sharp leaned over and whispered. "They're good."

"Yes, they are," Pierre replied. "They're jungle fighters."

Rick talked quietly into the radio. "Laura, Rick here. The FARC command boat just passed us. I can take them out if you like, but I've got to know right now."

"Hold your fire until we figure out what's going on. Where are the drug boats?" Laura replied.

"Tied to the bank a few yards upstream."

"Have you got a shot?"

"We can hit them from here."

"Major, are you hearing this?"

"Yes."

"What do you think?" Laura asked.

"Stand down. We don't want the Panamanians killing the rest of the Americans."

"Rick," Laura said, "let the command boat pass. Continue to hold."

"Roger," Rick replied.

Jordan spoke in hushed tones to Jerry Stock, right beside him. "One FARC boat on the way in. Pass it down. Hold your fire." Each man in the line whispered to the next.

Chapter Seventy-Seven

THE NEGOTIATION BETWEEN the two Panamanians was brief. "One pallet for you and one for me," Hernandez suggested.

"Agreed," Ramos replied. "Let's get the money out of sight right now before FARC arrives."

"You've got more men, so you take the undamaged pallet," he said to Ramos. Hernandez turned to his men. "Unwrap the damaged pallet and hand carry the money to the Jeeps. Put it wherever it fits. Stick it in your pockets if you have to. Go!" Hernandez' men ripped open the pallet, backed their vehicles near the money and began packing stacks of banded money in their Jeeps.

"Sergeant?" Ramos asked. "Have the men break down that other pallet and load the money onto the truck. On the double!" Once that job was complete, Ramos walked over to the truck. "Distribute some of the cash to the men, Sergeant."

"How much for each?"

"We don't have time to count it. What denominations are we dealing with?"

"Hundreds and twenties, Sir."

"Give each man enough to fill his front pockets."

Garcia shouted to his soldiers. "Line up, men." He motioned with his arm. "Right here at the back of the truck." The men formed a single file behind the truck while Garcia instructed the gunner, Miguel, to pass out money. "Give every man a stack about this thick." Garcia spread his thumb and index finger. He watched the distribution for a couple of minutes and then stepped in. "Miguel don't try to count it," he admonished. "We don't have time for that. Here, I'll help." Garcia climbed in the truck bed to help. "Keep the line moving, men," Garcia shouted. "We've got to get out of here pronto."

Chapter Seventy-Eight

"THEY'RE ALL TOGETHER in a group, Jim," Laura said into the mic. "We'll never have a better chance."

"What about the Americans?" Jordan asked. "We can't risk their lives with an attack."

"We're playing into their strategy by holding, Jim."

"We can't shoot from here. What are they doing around the truck?"

"They're passing out cash to their men."

"No wonder they shot Pritchard's men," Jordan said. "They're witnesses."

"We cannot allow them to dictate the engagement. Adam and I have a line of sight to the entire scene. Can you see anything at all?"

"We can see the black shirts and their Jeeps. The plane blocks everything else. Where are the Americans?"

"They moved them behind the PDF Jeep."

"Rick? Have you got a clear shot at the drug boats?" Laura asked.

"Affirmative. They've tied up to the bank waiting."

"Jim let's go now. If we have to deal with FARC, Adam and I have a line of sight to the dock."

"How in the hell are we going to rescue the Americans?"

"We'll have to figure that out later."

She's right, Jordan thought.   What the hell are we here for? "Laura, I agree. Let's go."

Laura spoke to Dmitri in the mic. "Dmitri, can you hear us?"

"Roger that," Dmitri replied.

"Get the copter in the air and blow the plane."

"Rick?" she asked."

"Right here, Laura."

"As soon as the copter's in the air, sink the cargo boats."

"Roger that."

"Jim?" she asked. "Let's begin firing before the copter blows the plane. Our view may be blocked by the smoke afterwards."

"Roger that." Jordan spoke to Carl Thomas. "Carl, get on that 50 cal."

"Yes, Sir," he replied. He moved behind the gun.

"Can everyone hear me?" Laura asked.

The entire group responded in the affirmative.

"On my mark, we go together." She paused for the briefest of seconds. "Go!" she shouted.

Chapter Seventy-Nine

SAMUEL TIED UP the speedboat to one of the pillars of the dock. Benevides turned to his men.

"Gather together off the dock," he said pointing to where the dock joined the concrete sidewalk. "We'll walk up to the airstrip as a group. Sam, you stay with the boat and keep the engine idling."

The helicopter caused their heads to jerk upward to find the source of the noise. They stood briefly watching Dmitri's helicopter rise above the treetops. And then the crackle of gunfire began. Conditioned to the Columbian military's pursuit of FARC members, Benevides reacted immediately.

"Back in the boat, men," he shouted. "Now!" He gesticulated wildly with his arms. "Hurry! Get back in the boat." The men climbed over each other trying to get on the boat all at once. The boat became unsteady, rocking back and forth. "Sam," Benevides roared as he hopped on the boat, "untie us. Full throttle back upriver."

The boat churned the water white as it backed over its own wake and made a three-quarter turn heading into the middle of the stream. The men weren't secured yet and some nearly fell out. "Keep your heads down and weapons up, men. Sam, get on that radio and warn the cargo boats. We'll meet back at camp."

Chapter Eighty

STARING AT THE sight of the helicopter, every man in Ramos' platoon made themselves a target for Adam, one of Fort Bragg's best Special Forces sharpshooters. At 400 yards, it was a tough shot for Laura, but this is what Adam trained for. The sound of gunfire from Laura and Adam echoed off the buildings as men around the truck began dropping one by one.

Adam was quick and deadly accurate. He'd hit a half-dozen in the chest before Laura squeezed off her first shot. He didn't bother to double tap them as there were too many targets left. The wounded men writhed on the ground calling for help as Adam quickly lined up other targets. Those left alive were confused, not immediately understanding what was happening.

Jordan's men loosed a volley at Hernandez as the black shirts panicked. Caught out in the open, they hid behind their Jeeps and were pinned down while Jordan and his men made Swiss cheese out of the vehicles. The windshields and headlights shattered; the tires flattened while round after round pinged off hard metal surfaces. Every time one of Hernandez's men peeked above or around a Jeep, one of Jordan's men put a shot right where the man had looked. Hernandez wondered whether the Jeeps would start. "Jiminez," he shouted to his second in command, "stay low and climb into the front seat of one of the Jeeps and see if you can get it started."

Jiminez began to wriggle himself between the front seats along the floorboard of the lead vehicle. He pushed the clutch in with one hand and turned the starter with the other. The Jeep cranked, then started. Jiminez reached up and moved the shifter to neutral, then slid back out of the Jeep.

Hernandez shouted to the men behind the other Jeep to try the same maneuver and it worked. Both Jeeps were running.

Laura aimed and fired at the truck bed where Miguel and Sergeant Garcia were standing with money in their hands. Miguel went down immediately, but Laura's shot at Garcia buzzed by his head and glanced off one of the metal supports holding the canvas. Sparks scattered in the vicinity of Garcia's head. He ducked instinctively, then raised up and shouted to his men. "Take cover! We're under attack." He jumped off the truck and ran toward the Jeep they'd used as a command post. Laura just missed him again as he ran. She shot a third time and Garcia went down near the Jeep. Laura hesitated out of fear of hitting the Americans huddled behind.

Ramos dove to the ground and lay flat out in the open with several men. He began to formulate a response and organize his troops. "The fire is coming from the tops of those buildings," he said pointing toward the town. "Use the truck as cover." They rose together and made a run for the truck. Adam picked off three as they ran. Laura directed her fire there also, downing two additional men.

Once behind the truck, Ramos counted his men around him as Laura and Adam kept pounding his position. "You two," he pointed. "Climb in the truck bed and fire at those building tops. Keep the tarp closed so they can't see you." He pointed to others. "You! Sling your rifles over the hood of the truck and return fire." He motioned to several more. "Crawl underneath the truck," he said pointing. "Position yourselves to fire beneath it. Use the wheels as shelter." He looked at his remaining men. "The rest of you? See Sergeant Garcia? Move behind those Jeeps."

Ramos' men, now understanding what was happening, began to follow orders. Men closest to the plane ran up the ramp and hid inside the plane. Some were slow and were shot by Laura and Adam, but most made it safely.

Hernandez had an idea of how to escape. "Men, let's use one Jeep to block the fire while we get in the other and drive to the canal. We'll swim the canal. We should be safe on the other side."

"What about the money?" one of his men asked.

"Take whatever you've put in your pockets and leave the rest."

The group that had run inside the plane decided to return fire. One of the men went to the cockpit to fire at the buildings out of the cockpit window. Two more jumped off the ramp and ducked under the plane to fire from behind the landing gear.

Ramos sprinted from the truck to the Jeep in front of the fuel tanks. Pritchard shouted to Ramos. "Cut us loose, Captain. We can fight."

Ramos crawled to Pritchard and jerked him by his uniform shirt. He laid his pistol on Pritchard's forehead. "You shut your mouth. You did this!"

Pritchard tried to protest, but Ramos cocked his weapon. "One more word and you're a dead man."

Ramos turned to his men. "Direct your fire toward the building tops. Go! Go! Go!" His men found places to shoot from and began putting fire on Laura and Adam's position.

Chapter Eighty-One

"LAURA, WE'RE TAKING too much fire. It's time to move."

"Let's go," she replied. They crawled across the roof face down, jumped back onto the dumpster and then onto the ground. "What now?" Adam asked.

"Hang on a minute," Laura replied, hearing Rick's voice on the com set.

"Laura, these cargo boats are turning around. It's now or never."

"Sink them," she replied.

"Yes, Ma'am," he said with relief. He turned to Pierre and Sharp. "You ready?"

"Do you even have to ask?" Sharp responded.

"Okay, boys, open fire."

Rick and Sharp shot their RPGs simultaneously and they scorched a path across the river and slammed into the first two boats. The explosion caught the gas tanks on fire and the eruption hurled boat fragments into the air. Men and boats disappeared in thick, black smoke. The blast swept up the third boat in the wake, but it was largely unscathed and sped away out of the smoke and headed upriver.

"Fuck!" Rick shouted at seeing the fleeing boat. "Pierre, load me up again." Pierre slipped another shell into the cylinder and slapped Rick on the shoulder.

"Go!" he shouted. Rick shot, but the distance was greater, and his shell missed the moving target hitting the far bank, exploding on contact with a tree. "Too high, Rick," Sharp said.

Pierre reloaded Sharp's weapon. "Go," he shouted.

Sharp aimed lower and the shell slammed into the back end of the boat hitting the motor. The explosion disintegrated the boat. Once the smoke drifted away, only fragments remained floating on the water. No men were visible.

"We're done," Rick said. "Let's get back on the double." He contacted Laura by com set. "Laura, boats sunk. We're on our way back."

"Meet Adam and me at the edge of town by the path," Laura replied.

"Roger that."

Chapter Eighty-Two

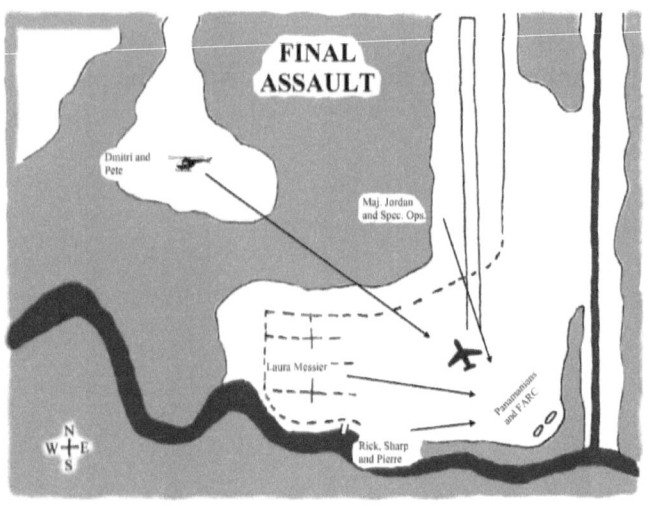

BENEVIDES AND HIS men heard the boat explosions traveling back toward the hairpin. "They've attacked our boats," he shouted. His men watched the cloud of smoke extend into the sky above the trees. "Sam, get them on the radio."

Samuel tried several times to contact the cargo boats ahead. "They're not answering," he said looking at Benevides.

As Benevides' boat approached the hairpin, he shouted to Sam. "Slow down. This could be a trap." He pointed at the bank. "As we go around this turn, men, fire along the banks. Both sides." His men emptied their clips at the vegetation as Samuel maneuvered around the turn. The effort was wasted as Rick, Pierre and Sharp had already abandoned their position and were on their way to meet up with Laura and Adam. Benevides could see the floating wreckage of his boats ahead of him. Fuel was still burning on top of the water and the floating wreckage was smoldering, smoke billowing upward in plumes. "Look for survivors," he commanded as Samuel slowed the boat to weave in and around the wreckage.

Miraculously, four men were found alive clinging to pieces of wood and fiberglass, stunned by the impact of the explosions. "Help pull them in," Benevides shouted, leaning over the side. Samuel steered the boat close so Benevides' men could haul them into the already crowded boat.

They were laid prone wherever room could be found and the medic, a former military doctor, checked each of them for injuries. Benevides climbed forward to look. "How are they, doc?"

"First and second degree burns mainly," the doc replied. "A couple of them are concussed, but they're conscious and moving around."

Benevides stood among his men and addressed them. "Listen up, everyone. We've got a decision to make." He hesitated until all eyes looked up at their commander. "Someone is attacking the Panamanians. I'm not sure who, but one thing I'm damn sure of. The Delgado's are going to hold us responsible for the loss of the shipment." Benevides looked each man in the eyes to make sure they understood. "We need to go back and get enough money to pay for the shipment. I know it's there because I saw the plane sitting on the runway."

"And fight a helicopter?" Samuel asked.

"And RPGs, too, Sam," Benevides added. He pointed at the wreckage of the cargo boats. "This is the work of rocket propelled grenades."

"Let's go back to the Delgado's and explain what happened." Samuel asked. "We can't fight RPGs and helicopters."

Benevides frowned. "Sam, the Delgado's are not going to accept the loss of a shipment. We're responsible."

"What'll they do if we don't have their money?"

"They'll kill our families. I don't think we've got a choice. We've got to go back."

"How do we fight helicopters and RPGs?" Samuel asked.

Chapter Eighty-Three

DMITRI HOVERED OVER the clearing briefly to arm the missiles. "You have the machine gun threaded?" he asked Pete.

"Yep, ready to fire," Pete replied.

"See that Jeep headed toward the canal? I'll give you one chance to hit it before I turn toward the plane. Once I've turned, I'm going straight in, firing two missiles then veering to the right to avoid the explosion. I'll head over the town and then make a swing back to make a pass over the airfield." Dmitri paused to flip switches in the cockpit. "You ready?"

"Let's do it," Pete replied.

Dmitri forged ahead toward the fleeing Jeep. The machine gun erupted as Pete tried to control the gun. He missed. "Sorry Pete. I'm turning now." Dmitri turned sharply and headed toward the plane. He fired two missiles at his target and then turned abruptly and flew over the rooftop Laura and Adam had just vacated.

Dmitri could hardly miss from close range and the missiles slammed into the fuselage. The explosion was immediate and twofold. The first blast tore into the fuselage and broke the main body of the plane in half. The plane's fuel tanks erupted a couple of seconds later. The fuselage virtually disappeared, blown into pieces that flew in every direction. The wings dropped to the ground and burned from the fuel that ignited them. The tail section collapsed onto what was left of the ramp. Chunks of metal were hurled all over the airstrip as though they'd been shot from a cannon. All of Ramos' men near the plane were instantly killed.

The flames and smoke blocked the view of everyone fighting on the field. Ramos was surrounded by dense black smoke that drifted over his position. He could do nothing, except shelter in place. Jordan's line of men at the airfield's edge hesitated out of the fear of shooting blindly. They were blocked from any view of their targets.

Hernandez's men at the canal stopped, turned briefly to glance at the explosion, and then panicked, jumping pell-mell into the canal and wading across chest deep water holding their rifles above their heads. Only after climbing the far bank did they turn to watch the scene.

Chapter Eighty-Four

LAURA AND ADAM made their way back behind the town to meet Pierre, Rick and Sharp. The sound of the plane explosion echoed off the buildings and carried miles in each direction. They turned to watch the debris cloud rise high in the air. "Damn," was Adam's only comment.

"With fuel aboard, there's probably not much of it left," Laura said. They watched Dmitri fly the copter right above their heads. She looked at the line of jungle. "Is that where we came out?"

Adam nodded. "Yes. We ought to be seeing Rick and his bunch any second." No sooner than he'd said that, Rick emerged through the brush.

He swung his head back and forth and then spoke into the radio. "Laura, we're at the end of the path. Where are you?"

"We've got a visual on you. We're hidden behind the yellow building you see on your right."

"Are we safe to cross?"

"Go now. We've got you covered."

"Roger," Rick replied.

Rick disappeared for a moment, then he, followed by Pierre and Sharp, burst into the open and sprinted toward the building. They carried the RPGs with them, so they were slow, but made it safely across. Laura and Adam emerged into view and they met at the back of the building. "Glad to see you guys," Laura said. "How'd it go at the river?"

301

"The boats are destroyed," Rick answered, "but we didn't stick around to watch. We didn't get their command boat."

"Where is it?" Adam asked.

"Somewhere between the town and the hairpin, twelve men on board."

"We'd better prepare to meet them, wherever they are," Laura said.

"They're gonna be pissed as hell we sunk their boats," Sharp added.

"Damn straight about that," Rick added. He looked at Laura. "What's the plan?"

Chapter Eighty-Five

"JORDAN WANTS TO rescue the Americans," Laura said flatly.

"The guys who flew in on the plane?" Rick asked.

Laura nodded. "Yep."

"Fuck that," Sharp said. "They got themselves in trouble. They can get themselves out."

"I agree," Rick said. "What are we going to do with them?"

"We'll have to carry them back in the copter with us," Laura replied, "and turn them over to the MPs. What do you think, Pierre?"

"Let's get out of here. We've got no casualties. Why risk it?"

Laura looked at Adam. "What do you say?"

Adam grimaced, not wanting to provoke a confrontation. "I'm under the Major's command. His opinion is my opinion."

"All right," Laura replied, "let's confirm it with him."

Laura spoke into the com set. "Jordan, can you hear me?"

"Loud and clear. What's your status?"

"Adam and I have linked up with Rick's group," Laura replied. "We're at the back edge of the town. What about you?"

"We're still at the vegetation line looking out over the airstrip."

"We're done here, Jim," Laura said. "The drugs are destroyed, the plane's on fire and we've got an exit. Dmitri can pick us up back at the clearing and we're out of here."

"What about the hostages, Laura?"

Laura hesitated a moment before deciding. "Sorry, guys," she said suddenly, "we can't afford an argument in the middle of battle." She looked at Sharp and Pierre. "We're going in after them." She spoke into the com set. "Jim, you still with me?"

"Yes, Ma'am."

"Let's go get them."

"Good news," Jordan replied emphatically. Adam spoke up.

"Laura, I ought to join up with the Major." Laura talked to Jordan through the coms.

"I'm sending Adam back to you to even our numbers."

"That would be best. We're going to advance to the plane and use it as cover. Dmitri, can you hear me?"

"Yes, Sir," Dmitri replied through his com set.

"Can you keep the Panamanians pinned down while we advance?"

"We'll keep them occupied."

"Roger that," Jordan replied.

"The rest of us will go through town and take the dock," Laura said. "Once we're all in position, we'll make one push forward."

"We'll advance to the plane and hold until you're at the dock. Contact me when you're there," Jordan said.

"Will do." Dmitri turned to Pete. "They're on the move. Have you figured out how to aim that gun yet?"

Pete scratched his head. "I think so."

Dmitri nodded. "All right. Let's get to work."

Chapter Eighty-Six

"WE'RE READY TO take the dock," Laura said.

"What if we have to fight our way through town?" Rick asked.

"Well, that's what we do then," Laura said with a shrug. "Let's divide into two teams, walk down both sides of the street until we get there."

The town was three blocks in length and two blocks wide. The group found the streets vacant, the townspeople hiding in their homes. They moved quickly; Laura and Rick took one side of the street, Rick and Sharp on the other. They walked the length of the town, from doorway to doorway, building by building, careful to cover each other's advance. The dock area was easy to capture. It was vacant. They sheltered themselves between overturned boats pulled up on the bank. Dmitri made low passes overhead, occasionally firing short bursts from the machine gun to keep the Panamanians in place. After Laura's group established a position between the boats, Laura contacted Jordan again. "Jim, we've taken the dock area. No resistance."

"Can you see the Panamanians?" Jordan asked.

"No. They've taken a position behind their vehicles."

"What about the Americans?"

"Negative."

"We've advanced to the plane."

Jordan and his men peered around the burned-out wreckage toward the Panamanian position. Nothing moved, neither men nor vehicles.

"I don't see anything. Are they still there?" Nick asked.

"They have to be," Jordan replied. "They've got nowhere to go. They're pinned against the river."

Chapter Eighty-Seven

BENEVIDES' BOAT SAT low in the water as it made its way back to the dock where Samuel began to pull in. Benevides saw the burning plane. "No, Sam, not here. Go past the dock." Sam turned back into the middle of the river and bypassed the dock. Fortunately, they'd passed the dock before Laura's group had arrived.

"How far are we going?" Samuel asked.

"See those trees ahead on the left? Where the canal empties into the river? Pull in there. If we use the trees as cover, we'll come up behind the Panamanians."

"Won't they fire on us?" Samuel asked.

"They know we're coming, Sam. Believe me, they'll welcome reinforcements."

Dmitri passed overhead and Pete tried to strike at Benevides' boat but missed. "That's okay, Pete," Dmitri said. "We'll circle around and make another pass. You'll get another shot."

By the time the copter had swung around, though, Benevides had run his boat onto the bank behind the Panamanians. They'd slipped under the trees and weren't visible from the air. "Everyone out, men. Let's go get our money." Benevides turned to their medic. "Doc, stay here with the injured. And, for goodness sake, stay under these trees."

"Yes, Sir."

A FARC contingent of eleven men crept forward, hidden among the trees. "Straight through these woods, men," Benevides said, pointing ahead. "Stay low."

Once through the woods, FARC found themselves behind the fuel tanks.

"Panamanians!" Benevides shouted.

Ramos, sheltering behind a vehicle, was surprised to find he'd been outflanked and thought an attack from behind had begun. "Quick, men. Fire behind us!"

"Stop!" Benevides shouted. "Don't fire! We're FARC!"

Ramos raised his hand. "Hold your fire," he shouted to his men. He partially stood to view the wooded area. "We've got weapons pointed at you," he shouted at the FARC contingent. "Show yourselves."

Benevides stepped into the open and spread his arms wide. "We've got eleven men here. How can we help?"

Ramos looked around the sky and saw nothing. "Come," he said motioning with his arm. "Hurry. That helicopter's around here somewhere."

Benevides' men dashed around the fuel tanks and crossed the open area quickly. Ramos rose to meet them. "Captain Jorge Ramos, Panamanian Defense Forces," he said as an introduction.

"Commander David Benevides, 58th Front." Benevides quickly looked around at the Panamanian position. "It looks like you're in trouble."

That brought a smile to Ramos' face. "You could say that."

"How many men do you have?"

"Fifteen. Seven here and eight behind the truck."

"We've got eleven." Benevides pointed to the hostages. "Who are these people?"

"Americans. They flew in on the plane."

"They're prisoners?"

"Yes. We're stealing their money."

"You mean our money?" Benevides corrected him. Ramos grimaced.

"I don't want to fight you for it. You can have part of it."

"Fair enough." That must be why the PDF's here, Benevides thought. Who are the attackers, though? Is this the PDF and black shirts fighting each other? "What are you going to do with the hostages?"

"We'll have to kill them," Ramos said.

"Why aren't you using them as shields?"

Ramos looked puzzled. "What do you mean?" Benevides pointed to the sky.

"That's a Russian helicopter. If the attackers are Russian, they'll want to capture the Americans alive." He pointed to Pritchard. "He's an American officer, isn't he?"

Ramos nodded. "A U.S. Marine Colonel."

"He'd be a nice catch for the KGB. Tie the hostages to the vehicles and they won't shoot at us."

"We can try it," Ramos said with a shrug. He directed the men to bring the Americans forward. They were forced to stand, then lashed to the Jeep and the truck.

Once that had been accomplished, Benevides watched for a moment. "See! They're not shooting the prisoners."

"You're right," Ramos replied.

"Have you checked your rear perimeter?"

"The attack seems to be coming from two places, the town and that line of trees on the other side of the airfield," Ramos said pointing towards the airstrip.

"Let's make sure we're not flanked." Benevides turned to Samuel. "Sam, pick two men and send them behind us to the canal. Send two others to the river. Let's get eyes on our back side."

"Yes, Sir."

Benevides turned back to Ramos. "We were expecting the black shirts."

"They were here, but they fled when the shooting began."

"If you don't mind me asking, why are you here?" Benevides asked. Ramos hesitated, thinking of a way to nuance his answer.

"We were sent from Panama City to provide extra security," he blurted out.

That's a lie, Benevides thought. The PDF has never provided security. Benevides pointed to the burned-out plane. "The helicopter blew up the plane?"

"Yes."

"The Americans wouldn't blow up their own plane. We're being attacked by Russians. I'm sure of it."

"That makes sense. Russians were seen in town yesterday. I can't understand how they found out about the drug deal." Benevides chuckled.

"You'd be surprised at the intel capabilities of the Russians."

"What if we tried to negotiate? We could give them the Colonel."

Benevides shook his head. "They'll want the money, too, and unfortunately, we can't give it to them. They sunk our cargo boats. We must pay the cartel for the loss."

Both Ramos' and Benevides' men saw the helicopter approach over the treetops. Everyone dropped to the ground, except Benevides who stood up straight, smiled and waved at the copter as it buzzed their position without firing.

"Relax, Captain," Benevides said looking down at Ramos with a smirk. "They're not going to shoot. They're afraid of hitting the Americans."

Benevides helped Ramos to his feet. "You appear to be right," Ramos muttered brushing himself off.

"I know I'm right. We have a stand-off. They're not going to shoot, and we can't get out of here. Do you have a plan?"

"Not yet."

"If we can hold them off until dark, we can evacuate using our boat," Benevides said, pointing behind him. "It'll take several trips, but it can be done."

"Evacuate to where?" Ramos asked.

"El Real, southeast of here. You can contact your headquarters from there."

"Why would you help us?"

"As I said, we must take enough money to satisfy the cartel."

"There's plenty of money in that truck over there," Ramos said nodding toward the truck. "Millions of U.S. dollars. The problem is getting it. The attackers have been shooting right into the truck bed."

"We need to move the truck next to the Jeep to establish a defensive position. We can get your machine gun working and get access to the money."

"What about the dead and wounded?"

"I have a medic behind us at the boat. I'll send for him."

"Thank you, Commander," Ramos said.

"One more question, how are you fixed for food and water?"

"We have nothing."

"We don't, either." Benevides looked up at the sun. "We have about five hours of light left. It'll be a long afternoon. What about weapons and ammunition?"

"We have plenty of small arms and ammunition."

"Where's your spare ammunition?"

"In the truck."

"Let's get that truck moved over and get ourselves organized," Benevides said more as a command than a comment.

Chapter Eighty-Eight

"LAURA, I FOUND the FARC rebels," Jordan said into the com set.

"Where?" she asked.

"I'm looking at them now through field glasses. They've linked up with the Panamanians and they're digging in. That FARC commander knows what he's doing."

"Explain."

"My view is partially blocked, but it looks like the FARC commander is setting up a defensive position. He's using the Americans as human shields. I think they're going to try to hold us off until dark."

"We can't let that happen. They'll escape and kill the hostages before they leave," Laura said.

"I agree, but whatever we do endangers them."

"Dmitri, come in," Laura said.

"We hear you," Dmitri said into the com set.

"What are you seeing?"

"Pretty much the same as you. We can't risk firing. We could hit the hostages or those fuel tanks. If those fuel tanks go, everyone dies."

"We're at a stalemate," Laura said. "Jim, could we take a boat and come up behind them?"

"I don't think that'll work. I watched the FARC commander reinforce their rear flank. Whatever direction we approach, we'll have to fight our way in."

"Jim, hang on a minute. I've got an idea."

Laura turned to Rick. "Anyone speak Spanish?"

"I do," Sharp said.

"How well?"

"Well enough. We learned it in Foreign Service."

Laura smiled and shook her head. "You studied Spanish and they sent you to the Middle East?"

"Yeah. Go figure," Sharp said with a laugh. "Messed up, isn't it?"

She turned to Rick. "Can you and Pierre hold the dock without us?"

Rick shrugged. "Sure."

"And block the river?"

"Laura, no one's going upriver. We've got these." Rick held up one of the RPGs.

"That's what I need to hear. Jim, you still there?"

"I hear you," Jordan said.

"If I could infiltrate their position on the pretext of delivering food and water, I might get inside."

"FARC's too smart for that, Laura. They're not going to allow you in."

"A woman carrying food isn't a threat."

"Laura, forget it. They're not going to fall for the Trojan horse trick," Jordan said flatly.

"Do you have a better idea?"

Jordan hesitated, thinking about how the subterfuge would play out in real terms. "We can't protect you inside their perimeter."

"I only need to survive a few seconds because you're going to advance as soon as the shooting starts."

"We'd have to take out that 50 cal before we can advance," Jordan replied. "It's pointed right at us."

Laura turned to Rick. "Can you sneak along the riverbank and attack the truck? That 50 cal's got to be disabled."

"We can try, Laura. We'll use the weeds along the riverbank as cover."

"Does that work for you, Jim?"

"If Rick can disable the 50 cal, we can be inside their perimeter in less than a minute."

"That's our plan," Laura said. "It'll take me a few minutes to get ready. Dmitri, can you hear us?"

"Yes," Dmitri replied.

"Once this starts, can you provide back-up for us?"

"We'll do our best."

Laura turned to Sharp. "I need you to help make this food delivery convincing. Are you in?"

Sharp swatted the back of his neck. "It beats sitting here by the fucking river getting eaten by mosquitos. Fucking bastards are huge."

That brought a smile from Laura. "I take that as a yes. Let's go."

Chapter Eighty-Nine

LAURA AND SHARP carefully made their way back to the town without being seen. "We passed a clothing shop before," Laura said once they'd entered the town. "I'm going there. You go find the restaurant we passed next to the hotel. Order sandwiches and bottles of water." Laura dug into her pocket and produced a rubber banded roll of hundred-dollar bills. "Take a few of these." She peeled off several.

"You want a receipt?" Sharp asked cynically.

"Get the hell out of here, Sharp," she said. "I'll come up to the restaurant when I'm done."

"Okee-dokey."

Laura found the clothing shop and tried the front door. It was locked. She peeked in the front window and saw no one inside. The lights were off. She pounded on the door, waited and then walked around the building and tried to open the back door. It was locked as well. She rapped loudly and heard a woman's voice speak through the door. "We're closed!"

Laura spoke in her best Central American Spanish dialect. "Can you help me, please? It's an emergency. I need a few articles of clothing. I promise I won't hurt you."

Laura saw the woman draw the window curtain back. Laura smiled and waved. She heard the door unlock. The door opened just a bit. "You should not be on the street."

"Please, would you help me?" Laura gave the woman an innocent smile.

The woman opened the door, looked up and down the alley and then motioned with her hand. "Quickly. Come inside." An older woman in her sixties locked the door and led her through the back of the building. "Follow me." The front of the shop had a small display in the front window, two mannequins dressed in traditional Central American dresses. "What do you need?" she asked.

"Something like that," Laura replied pointing toward the display.

The woman motioned to clothing stacked on shelves along the wall. "You can look through these. I have shoes also."

Laura picked out a colorful skirt and pullover blouse that looked to fit her. "I have a fitting room in back," the woman said. "Come with me. We passed it on the way in."

Laura found the clothes fit her reasonably well, so she wore them back to the front of the shop. "You said you had shoes also?"

"What size?"

"Six."

The woman rummaged around a cabinet and pulled out two pair. "This is all I have."

Laura tried them on and chose the best fitting pair. "Would you have a seam ripper I could use?"

The woman walked behind a long counter at the back of the front room and reached in a drawer. "If you alter the clothing, you must pay."

Laura reached into the pocket of the pants she'd worn and peeled off two one-hundred-dollar bills. She handed them to the woman. "This is too much," the woman said.

"The rest is a gift," Laura said with a smile. "Thank you for your help." She took the seam ripper and cut a long slit in the skirt, then cut a smaller one down the front of the blouse.

"You look like a whore," the woman said, disgusted by the look.

"A girl can make money," Laura replied, "when soldiers are here."

The woman hesitated and stared at Laura right in her eyes. "I don't know you. You're not from here."

"The soldiers brought me."

The woman seemed to accept the answer. She picked up a brush off the counter. "Here, let me fix your hair."

"Would you?"

The woman nodded. "Sit down on the stool."

Laura sat while the woman brushed and pinned back her hair. "Look in the mirror," she suggested.

"I like it. Thank you."

"Here is a nice perfume you can use." The woman handed her a sample vial of fragrance.

"You're very kind to me. Thank you."

The woman gave her a matronly smile. "I was young once, too, dear." She patted Laura on the shoulder. "You go now and be safe."

Chapter Ninety

LAURA CARRIED HER handguns, holsters and the clothing she'd worn earlier up the street toward the restaurant. She couldn't remember the last time she'd worn a skirt. The light cotton clothing fell loose around her body and she felt a freedom of movement she hadn't felt since she left the Bahamas. I feel almost normal, she thought.

She found Sharp sitting at the restaurant counter munching on a burrito. He turned his head upon hearing the bell attached above the front door. He motioned her inside. "You should try one of these," he said holding up the half-eaten burrito. "They're fantastic. Eggs, ham and green peppers."

Laura rolled her eyes. "Enjoying yourself?" she asked cynically.

Sharp pointed to a waitress wrapping sandwiches. "Ham and cheese sandwiches coming up." He continued to consume the burrito as though he'd just taken his lunch hour from an office job. "They're going to throw in a few of these, too," he said referring to the burrito.

"We need something to carry it," Laura said ignoring the air of detachment that Sharp exhibited.

Sharp pointed outside. "Already taken care of," he said through a mouthful of food. "I found a wheelbarrow in an alley. It's sitting out front."

"A wheelbarrow? Seriously?" she asked.

"I thought a wheelbarrow would make you look authentic. Very sexy, by the way." Sharp glanced at Laura's cleavage which exposed a great deal of her breasts.

"You're an idiot, Sharp!"

Sharp shrugged his shoulders and laughed. "What do you expect? I'm not going to notice?"

"It's a costume, Sharp. A costume!" Laura said raising her voice in frustration.

"I know," Sharp said, smiling, "and I'm loving it."

An overworked and disinterested waitress began stacking bags of food on the counter. "Drinks are in the cold case along the wall."

"How much do we owe you?" Laura asked.

"The bill has been paid," the older woman said looking at Sharp.

Sharp stood and picked up the bags. "You get the drinks. I'll come back and help."

Together, Laura and Sharp piled the food and drinks into a rusty wheelbarrow sitting in front of the shop. Laura's furtive glances up and down the street elicited a comment from Sharp.

"Relax," Sharp said. "No one's around. I checked. You've heard the phrase, 'to die for?'"

Her quizzical look betrayed her confusion. "What are you talking about?"

"Have you heard the phrase, 'to die for?' These," Sharp said holding up a burrito, are worth dying for."

Laura rolled her eyes. "Oh, God," she replied, frustrated by Sharp's laissez-faire attitude. She lifted her skirt, took her holsters and strapped them tightly around her waist. Sharp watched with interest. "Don't get too excited, Sharp, it's business." She lowered her skirt. "Can you tell I'm armed?" She asked pulling the blouse down over the skirt.

"Do you want the truth?"

Laura gave Sharp a look of anger. "One more sex comment and I'm shooting you."

Sharp raised his hands. "Hey, I'm being serious now. Men's eyes are going straight to your cleavage. No one's going to notice."

"Take these," she said handing Sharp the metal plates she'd taken from her uniform. "Just in case you're shot at, shove these extra plates in your clothing."

"Shot at? What are you asking me to do?" Sharp asked, pushing the metal plating inside his clothing.

"When I walk the food across the airstrip, I want you to try to stop me."

"I don't understand," Sharp replied.

"Run after me, yelling in Spanish for me to stop."

"Run after you?"

"Yeah, rough me up a little. Point your rifle at me. The commotion ought to rouse their interest."

Sharp finally understood what Laura had in mind. "You mean like a scene from a play?"

"Exactly."

"I can do that. After our little acting job, though, I'm going back to join Rick."

"Get back ASAP. Once I start shooting, I'll only have a few seconds before they kill me."

"Are you sure you want to do this?"

Laura frowned and shook her head. "If it was up to me, we'd already be flying back to Panama City." Laura saw a thick wad of paper protruding from Sharp's breast pocket. "Is that another burrito?"

"Yeah, it's gonna be a long ride back tonight. You want one?"

"No. Are you ready to go?"

Sharp shrugged. "I'm ready. Let's go."

Chapter Ninety-One

"CAPTAIN RAMOS," THE private shouted, running toward the command post Benevides had established near the fuel tanks.

Ramos watched the man approach. "What's so important you'd leave your post, Private?"

"Come quickly, Sir," the man said motioning for Ramos to follow. "There's something you need to see."

Ramos and Benevides gave each other a concerned look. "Let's go," Benevides suggested.

They followed the man to his post behind the Jeeps. The private pointed across the airfield between the Americans tied to the vehicles. "Take your field glasses and look. There's a girl pushing a wheelbarrow out on the airfield. A soldier's trying to stop her."

Both Ramos and Benevides stared at the woman. "She came from the town?" Ramos asked.

"Yes, Sir," the private replied.

"What the hell is going on?" Ramos asked Benevides. "Did you see that? He pushed her to the ground. Damn, he's pointed his rifle at her."

"He's going to kill her," Benevides said. "Private? Fire at that man."

The crack of the private's rifle echoed off the buildings in the town. The shots missed their target, but they stopped the soldier from shooting. He focused on Ramos and Benevides standing behind the Jeeps. He turned and fled back toward the town. The woman rose, brushed the dust from her clothing and resumed pushing the wheelbarrow onto the runway.

"If she keeps going, the soldiers behind the plane will get her," Benevides added.

"She already knows about those soldiers," Ramos said, staring through the glasses. "Look. See? She's angling away from the plane. What's in the wheelbarrow?"

Benevides strained to see the contents. "I can't make it out."

"Is she trying to approach us?"

"It looks that way."

Ramos saw the glint of the sun off the bottles of water. "I think she's us bringing water."

The soldiers behind the plane began to fire on the woman. Ramos looked up and down his perimeter line. "Protect that woman!" He shouted. "Lay volleys on those men. Force them to keep their heads down." Ramos' men began to pummel the plane with rifle fire. They didn't hit anyone, but the tactic had its desired effect. The firing toward the woman ended.

As word spread among the troops that a woman approached with water, many ran to the Jeeps and shouted words of encouragement. "Don't worry, we'll protect you," shouted one man. "Keep coming," said another. Men stood and waved her forward.

Benevides smiled at Ramos. "You see what happens when you have the support of the civilian population?" He answered his own question. "If that town," he said pointing, "turns against the attackers, we'll survive this." He beamed at the unexpected development.

Ramos, who had earlier been despondent over their predicament, saw the white bags in the wheelbarrow. "I think she's got food with her," he exclaimed loudly. The men erupted in a cheer and the shouts of encouragement became louder.

Derek Young, tied next to Pritchard, watched the girl also. "Well, this is interesting."

"A young woman from the town trying to play hero," Pritchard said with cynicism in his voice.

"Have you ever seen a professional soldier miss like that?" Young asked. "It's what, 75, 80 yards from the plane to the woman."

"Poorly trained Russian infantry," Pritchard said with disgust. "It's no wonder they've lost Afghanistan."

As the woman kept inching closer, Ramos had an idea. "Let's send men out to help her." He turned to his men. "Do we have any volunteers?" Several men spoke up. Ramos picked two men. "You," he pointed at one man, "push the wheelbarrow for her and you," speaking to another, "guard her."

The men readied themselves to sprint onto the airfield and expose themselves. "Ready?" Ramos asked. One man nodded, the other said, "Yes, Sir."

"Go," Ramos shouted. The men sprinted into the open towards the woman, still about a hundred yards from the defensive perimeter.

Chapter Ninety-Two

JORDAN SHOUTED AT his men. "Fire close enough to worry them, but don't kill 'em. Make this believable." Jordan's men, all excellent marksmen, nipped at the heels of the men, some shots coming only inches away, but never striking them. "Keep firing at Messier, too."

Messier looked up and saw Jordan's head rise above some of the plane's wreckage. Jordan chuckled into the com set. "I don't think she likes it. Keep it up. Rick, can you hear me?"

"Loud and clear, Major."

"Advance parallel with her along the river. It looks like you've got cover among the weeds on the bank."

"Yes, Sir. That'll put us just yards away from their truck."

"Do it. That 50 cal must be disabled before we can advance."

"What about Sharp. He's not back yet."

"He'll find you."

"On our way, Major." Rick turned to Pierre. "Saddle up, buddy. It's time we earned our money. Let's go kick the shit out of some drug runners."

"Copy that," Pierre replied.

Rick and Pierre moved away from the cover of the dock area into the weeds along the riverbank. "Damn, this is shitty cover," Rick said as they made their way into the waist high brush along the bank.

"The cover's fine, Rick," Pierre answered, following Rick into the thicket. "You're too damn tall. Don't worry about it. Everyone's watching Laura."

"We need the short guy to run point for us."

Pierre smiled. "Sharp'll find us. Either that or he's in town getting lunch."

"Yeah, well he better hide from Laura once this is over. Slapping her around like that? She's gonna be pissed off."

"Don't make me laugh," Pierre replied. "We're close enough they can hear us."

"Let's hold here." Rick raised his hand. "There's at least one of those bastards in the truck. When we go, I'll take care of him while you run around the other side and attack the camp."

"Roger that." Rick and Pierre held up just a stone's throw away from the truck.

Chapter Ninety-Three

RAMOS COMMANDED HIS men to increase fire onto the attackers to protect his soldiers dashing toward the young woman. The volleys went back and forth, the Panamanians never quite able to hit anything.

Ramos' men reached the woman, one man grabbing the handles of the wheelbarrow while the other took her by the arm to help her walk. They quickly made their way to the Panamanian defense line.

Jordan glanced a shot off the wheelbarrow itself, causing sparks to fly in the face of the Panamanian man who pushed it. "Damn, those guys can shoot," the Panamanian said to no one. The men quickened their pace toward the Panamanian line, running the last few yards until they squeezed between the vehicles parked end to end and were safely inside.

Jordan spoke into the com set. "She's in."

Chapter Ninety-Four

GREG SMITH, THE quick-witted CIA agent who dove behind the pallet of money, was the first to recognize her. This was Smith's first mission. He'd come to the agency right out of college and had manned the visitor's counter in the lobby at Langley for a year before leadership trusted him with an actual assignment. Messier had spoken with Smith when she visited Steve Tilton. He whispered to Derek Young, tied next to him, "That's Laura Messier. We're going to get out of this."

"Is that the fucking woman from the Bahamas?"

"I don't know about the Bahamas, but I'm sure that's Messier."

"What the fuck is she gonna do?" Young asked rhetorically. "There are thirty men behind us. She's gonna get us all killed."

"They're going to kill us anyway," Smith said. "Maybe she can do something."

Young chuckled. "Those men will carve that little girl up in seconds." Young leaned over and raised his voice. "Colonel!"

Pritchard looked in his direction. "This agent here," Young said motioning with his head toward Smith, "says that woman is Laura Messier."

"That's Laura Messier?" Pritchard asked in disbelief.

"That's what he says," Young replied with a shrug of his shoulders.

"I've got to warn the Captain. She's going to get everyone killed." Pritchard turned around as far as his bounds would allow and shouted loudly "Captain! Captain Ramos!"

Hank Miller, lashed on the other side of Pritchard, kicked him. "Shut up! Are you out of your fuckin' mind?"

Pritchard turned to Miller. "I've got to warn him before it's too late." He resumed shouting. "Captain Ramos! Captain! I need to speak with you!"

Miller kicked Pritchard so hard that the Colonel momentarily lost his balance and went to his knees. "Shut the fuck up. She's our only chance. They're going to kill every one of us when they leave."

"You don't have a clue, you idiot. I can negotiate our release. It's the money that saves us, not Messier." He resumed shouting.

Chapter Ninety-Five

THE ARRIVAL OF the attractive, young woman brought cheers from the Panamanians and FARC members. As soon as she passed the Jeeps into their protected area, men raised their rifles in celebration, yelling, crowding around her, clamoring for water and food. Neither Ramos nor Benevides could hold them back. Men guarding the perimeter abandoned their posts, afraid of being left out and there was little either Benevides or Ramos could do to keep their troops organized. Nearly the entire contingent of troops gathered around the woman and her wheelbarrow clamoring for water and food.

No matter how loudly Pritchard yelled, he couldn't be heard over the shouts of the soldiers.

Benevides stood behind, nervous that his troops had abandoned their posts. "Get back!" He shouted. "Back to your posts. We'll bring water to you." He couldn't be heard over the celebration, either.

Ramos walked over smiling and stood by Benevides. "Let them have their water, Commander. The men are thirsty." He nodded toward the woman in the middle of the mass of men. "She's a brave woman."

Benevides didn't share the mood of his men. "Don't you think it strange she wasn't shot bringing that wheelbarrow across?" Benevides asked.

Ramos shrugged, still smiling. "Moving targets are hard to hit, Commander" he replied. "And our return fire protected her."

Benevides looked across the airstrip for a moment. "You told me they were shooting from the buildings over there earlier, right?"

"Yes. What's your point?"

"That's nearly four-hundred meters away and they were hitting men in the forehead. And you think they can't hit a woman pushing a wheelbarrow 50 meters away? Perhaps she's one of them."

"What are you talking about?" Ramos asked in disbelief.

"She's one of the attackers."

"Impossible," Ramos said, dismissing Benevides' suggestion. "It would be suicide to send one person into the camp, especially a woman."

"Perhaps they knew we'd let a woman in. Pull her out of the celebration, Captain. I want to talk to her."

Ramos scoffed at the suggestion. "We have plenty of time for that later, Commander," Ramos replied. "She can do no damage. She's surrounded by soldiers."

The men cheered and slapped each other's backs as the water and food was passed among them. Men scattered in twos and threes to sit under trees while they consumed their food. Several pointed their weapons in the air and fired celebratory shots, something that was accepted behavior among Panamanian troops. Those innocent shots, however, were interpreted differently by Rick Williams.

Chapter Ninety-Six

SHARP ARRIVED BEHIND Rick and Pierre just before shots were fired inside the perimeter. Rick turned around. "What took you so long?"

Still out of breath from sprinting, he said, "Sorry. The restaurant's all the way at the other end of town."

"Here's the plan," Rick said pointing to the truck just a few yards away. "As soon as the shooting starts, I'm going straight for the truck. You and Pierre go around it and attack the camp. After I neutralize the machine gun, I'll join you. Watch for Jordan's men charging into camp."

"Got it," Sharp replied.

"How was the food?"

"I highly recommend the burritos."

Pierre glanced at Rick. "See! Didn't I tell you? While we're sweating our asses off in the weeds, Sharp's having lunch."

"Fuck you, Frenchie," Sharp retorted.

Then they heard shots from inside the camp.

"That didn't take long," Rick said. "Let's go!"

Chapter Ninety-Seven

WHILE THE CELEBRATION continued inside the camp, Rick, Pierre and Sharp charged, handguns in hand, rifles strapped to their backs. They arrived at the truck within seconds. Rick lifted the canvas cover along the side of the truck and saw Miguel sitting behind the 50 cal enjoying a sandwich. Miguel turned toward Rick and froze. Rick double-shot him in the chest. Miguel slumped over the 50 cal, Rick climbed in and kicked him to the side. He quickly pushed the 50 cal out the back of the truck, stood and waved to Jordan, hoping he'd see the signal.

Jordan, watching through field glasses, spoke to his men into the com set. "The 50 cal's down. Go! Go! Go!" He shouted. Jordan and his men charged across the open ground between the plane and the Panamanian defense line.

Pierre and Sharp stood behind the truck and leveled their handguns at the throng of men gathered around the wheelbarrow. They began firing and Panamanians began dropping immediately. "There she is!" Sharp yelled as Laura became visible inside the circle of men around her.

Benevides recognized the different sound of the American handguns. What the hell is that? He thought scanning the camp. Those aren't our weapons. "Where's that fire coming from?" He shouted. Then Sharp and Pierre came into view advancing around the truck. "We're under attack!" He yelled. "We're under attack! Find cover!" He pulled the handgun from his belt and ran toward the center of the camp. His men, slow to react, looked confused as one by one, men around them began falling to the ground.

One Panamanian with a sandwich in one hand and water in the other, tripped on the body of the man lying behind him. He looked up, astonished at seeing strangers in the camp. Pierre pointed his weapon and the man fell dead after a shot to the head.

Pritchard watched, mouth wide open, as Americans charged across the tarmac. He recognized the uniform. "Captain Ramos!" He screamed. Ramos was frantically looking around, trying to understand what was happening. Pritchard became animated, pulling at the plastic ties that bound his wrist to the rear-view mirror of the Jeep. "Captain, you're under attack!" he shouted.

Ramos pulled his handgun and tried to pick a target, the scene being so chaotic. His men were running back and forth, firing wildly. Ramos aimed his handgun at Sharp, but accidently shot his own man when he ran in front of Sharp. Ramos watched his men continue to fall as Rick jumped off the truck and advanced along with Sharp and Pierre. They stopped only to reload. Benevides pushed Ramos as he ran past him. "We're under attack, Ramos. Take cover!" Ramos dropped to the ground and rolled underneath one of the Jeeps.

It took Sharp, Pierre and Rick only a couple of seconds to reload before firing again. Their fire was continuous and none of them had taken any return fire yet. The ground between the Jeeps and the fuel tanks became littered with bodies.

Laura was pushed to the ground by a Panamanian who sought to protect her. As she fell, she pushed at him with her feet, forcing him to roll off her. She withdrew a pistol from underneath her skirt and shot him in the chest as he rose to his knees. He clutched his wound and fell. She rolled to avoid him, rose to her knees and fired at targets around her, often at point blank range.

As Jordan and his men closed the distance, two Panamanian men guarding the perimeter at the Jeeps shot at the charging Americans, but completely missed, worried about being shot from behind. Men quickly realized they were overwhelmed and ran pell-mell, trying to find cover. It only served to put them into the line of fire of Laura, Rick, Sharp and Pierre. Jordan and his men ignored the American hostages and burst through the perimeter, rifles firing at anything that moved.

Benevides recognized his men had failed to organize a counterattack. "To the boat!" he shouted. "Retreat! Retreat! Get to the boat!" It was a useless command as his remaining men were already heading in that direction. Once a few of the men ran toward the boat, the rest of them did, pushing each other as they frantically made their way around the fuel tanks toward the river. Rick's group advanced into the open area and met Jordan to form a line. They stood firing at the retreating Panamanians and FARC members, shooting them in the back as they fled.

Laura rose to her feet and intercepted Benevides, who'd crept around the fringe of the camp on his way to the woods. "Stop!" She shouted, stepping into his path with her P226 pointed directly at him. He attacked her. Deftly moving to her left to avoid his charge, she pushed him to the ground. Benivides pulled at her clothing as he fell causing her to lose her balance, but she managed to stay upright and stand above him. He grabbed her foot and twisted. She spun in that direction to negate the twist and went to her knees, falling on top of him. She punched his face with her fist, but he absorbed the punch and pushed her off.

Jordan stepped in and stood over Benevides. "Halt, Commander!" Benevides looked up at Jordan and realized there was no point in fighting any further. "Drop your sidearm," Jordan said calmly, "and don't move." Benevides let loose of his weapon, which Laura picked up as she rose.

The firing inside the camp suddenly came to an end as the remaining Panamanians and FARC members disappeared into the woods. Jordan nodded toward the wooded area and motioned to Rick. "Rick, pursue those men."

Chapter Ninety-Eight

PIERRE, SHARP AND Rick ran to the fuel tanks and peered around into the woods to make sure the Panamanians weren't mounting a counterattack. "I don't see anyone, Rick," Sharp whispered. "Let's move."

Rick motioned them forward. "Go slow, boys." Using trees as cover, they moved into the woods, overlapping each other as they advanced looking for straggling soldiers. They found the woods empty. As they moved closer to the river, they heard the boat engine start.

"They're getting away," Sharp shouted.

"Let the fuckers leave," Rick replied. "Let's clear the woods. I don't want anyone up my backside. Look for snipers." The three continued a slow advance to the river. One man appeared from behind a tree and pointed a rifle at Rick, but Pierre saw him first and shot him before he could fire. Rick walked over, stood above him and shot him again, this time in the head. "Thanks, buddy" he said looking at Pierre.

"That's what I do every day, Rick. Save your ass."

"Yeah, I know," Rick said, cynically. "That's your job."

They continued forward until they arrived at the river where they found several wounded men sitting on the bank being tended to by the FARC medic. The boat had already left. Rick could see the wake still churning. "Don't touch your weapons. Let's see your hands!" Rick shouted to the injured men. The doctor stopped, turned and raised his hands.

"Sharp? You know Spanish. Talk to the doc while Pierre and I search these men for weapons. Pierre? Throw their weapons in the river. Shoot anyone who resists." Sharp addressed the medic in Spanish.

"Step away, doc. Let our men through." The doctor moved aside, saying nothing.

Sharp held his weapon over the men while Rick and Pierre walked among them, tossing their weapons into the water. The wounded men offered no resistance, even though they outnumbered Rick's group. Pierre walked back to Rick. "I count eight, plus the doctor."

Rick pointed to the medic's bag. "Search that bag, too." Rick turned to the medic. "You speak English?" The medic shook his head. "Sharp, ask him if they're coming back for the wounded."

Sharp relayed the question. Rick heard them talk for a moment and then Sharp turned to Rick. "He says the boat is dropping survivors off at a town upriver called El Real. They'll come back for the wounded."

"Ask him how long," Rick said.

Again, Sharp questioned the doctor.

"He says they'll be back in an hour."

"Ask him if he's got a radio."

Sharp turned to the doctor and relayed the message. The doctor reached for a radio near his bag. "Slow, doc," Sharp said in English. "Move slowly." The medic didn't understand the words but figured out their meaning. He slowly grabbed the radio and held it up for Sharp to see.

"Tell him we'll allow the boat in to pick up casualties," Rick said. "One man brings the boat back. Only one. Make sure he knows that. If they bring more, we'll sink the boat and kill everyone. Have him get on the radio and relay that."

Sharp repeated the instructions to the medic, who used the radio to contact the boat on its way to El Real. Rick heard the exchange on the radio. "What are they saying, Sharp?" Rick asked.

"Just like you said, one man and the boat."

"Pierre, you stay here and stand guard. Shoot anyone who moves. If you need help, use the coms." Rick turned to Sharp. "Come on Sharp, let's go."

They returned to the camp where Jordan and his men were checking the dead and wounded for weapons. "Major, the river's secure," Rick said. "We left Pierre guarding their doctor and eight wounded. We stripped them of weapons."

"What do we do with them?"

"FARC is bringing their boat back to pick them up. I agreed to allow the evac."

"Fine," Jordan replied. "Dmitri?" Jordan asked into the com set.

"I read you, Major."

"What's your status?"

"We're trailing the FARC boat upstream. It looks like they're aiming for a small town along the river. You want us to take them out?"

"No, let them unload. Be advised the boat is coming back to pick up their wounded. Only the pilot onboard. If they bring back troops, sink it. Otherwise, continue to monitor and report in as needed."

"Roger that, Major."

Jordan turned to Rick. "Rick, you and Sharp search the perimeter."

"Come on Sharp," Rick said. "You heard the man."

Captain Ramos was discovered during the search and pulled from his hiding place under the Jeep. "Bring him here and sit him down beside the FARC commander," Jordan said. Nick stripped him of his handgun and pushed him down beside Benevides in the middle of the camp. "No talking, gentlemen," Jordan directed the two. "We'll interview you in a minute."

The dead were pulled together in a pile while the wounded were gathered. "Jerry?" Jordan asked his medic. "Take a look at their wounded and do what you can."

"Yes, Sir," Jerry said, unpacking his medic kit.

Jordan looked around his own men. "Anyone hurt?"

The men either said no or shook their heads. "What about you, Laura? Are you okay?"

"I'm fine, Jim," Laura said, standing above Benevides.

"Carl, would you shut that Colonel up. Tell him I'll get to him in a minute. I'm tired of hearing that man scream."

"Yes, Sir." Carl Thomas walked in between the vehicles to address the Colonel. "The Major requests your cooperation, Sir."

"Cut me loose, soldier," an angry Prichard said.

"The Major asks for your patience, Colonel, while we wrap up the battlefield."

"You didn't hear what I said, soldier," Pritchard said in his command voice. "I'm the ranking officer here. Cut me loose or I'll have you court martialed when we return to the Zone."

Carl Thomas slammed the butt of his rifle into Pritchard's ribs, causing him to double over in pain. "With respect, Colonel. The Major will address your issues in a moment. Please be quiet."

Pritchard looked up at Carl with hatred but said nothing more. "Thank you, Sir," Carl said politely.

Carl walked back into the camp with a smile on his face. "That's the only time I'll ever be able to strike a full bird Colonel and get away with it.

Jordan chuckled. "That asshole deserves it. Nick, get this one on his feet," Jordan said pointing to Benevides. Adam and Nick lifted Benevides to his feet then stood back with rifles pointed. "Who are you?" Jordan asked.

"I'm David Benevides, Commander of the 58th Front, the Revolutionary Armed Forces of Columbia. I demand to know by what authority you attacked my soldiers today."

"You killed Americans, Commander."

"We killed no Americans. He did," Benevides said nodding toward Ramos. "I demand to be turned over to the Panamanian government."

"Your demands are fully noted, Commander. Nick, sit him down." Jordan motioned to Adam. "Stand the other one up."

Jordan waited for Adam to help Ramos to his feet. "Identify yourself."

"Captain Jorge Ramos, Panamanian Defense Forces."

"Are you the commanding officer?"

"I'm acting under a direct order from General Costa."

Jordan was familiar with the Panamanian general. "I guess that means yes. What were your orders here today?"

"To stop a drug transaction."

"Was killing Americans part of that order?"

"No. That was a mistake. We were supposed to arrest the Americans. I apologize."

Jordan considered the answer for a moment. "You were in charge, Captain, and in every army I know, the commander's held responsible." He turned to Adam. "Help this man off his feet."

"Yes, Sir," Adam replied.

"Laura, I need a word."

"Of course," she replied.

Laura and Jordan walked a small distance away where they could talk privately. "What do you think?" Jordan asked.

"Maybe FARC didn't do the shooting, but they didn't release the Americans, either. I blame both of them."

Jordan nodded his head. "Yeah, that's how I see it, too. We've got a full load going back. Nine of us, the four Americans, we don't have room for these two."

"I'm not letting them walk, Jim," Laura said firmly.

"You're the overall commander, Laura. It's your decision."

"I'll handle it."

"Yes, Ma'am," Jordan replied. "Before you do, let's question the Colonel."

They walked back to the group. "Carl, untie the Colonel and bring him over."

Chapter Ninety-Nine

PRITCHARD, STILL HURTING from Carl's rifle butt to his ribs, threw insults. "You'll be in the brig before this day is done, soldier."

"I've been there before, Colonel. Come with me."

He grabbed Pritchard by the arm. Pritchard jerked it away. "Unhand me soldier. How dare you touch a Marine Colonel?"

"Sorry, Sir. Just following orders. Step this way, please."

Pritchard strode into the camp as though he commanded the unit. He walked up to Jordan. "Identify yourself, Major," he said using his command voice.

"Major James Jordan, First Special Forces Command, Fort Bragg, North Carolina."

"You're a Green Beret?"

"Yes, Sir. And you are?"

"Colonel Kevin Pritchard, United States Marines assigned to the Pentagon. Who ordered you here?"

"General Carson, with the approval of General Hitchens at Bragg."

"I'm taking command of your unit, Major." Pritchard reached out and pulled Nick's sidearm from his belt. "You don't mind if I borrow this for a minute, do you, soldier?" Nick wasn't quick enough to stop it.

Pritchard leveled the gun straight at Laura's chest. Before he could squeeze off a round, though, Pritchard's head exploded in blood, the sound of the shot coming a moment later. Pritchard slumped to the ground, dead instantly.

"Everyone down!" Jordan shouted. Everyone dropped to the ground, except Laura, who looked in the direction of the vegetation line at the far end of the airstrip runway. She looked down at Rick, sprawled in the dirt beside her. "Rick, stand up for goodness sake," she said calmly. She reached down. "Here, let me help you up."

An alarmed Jordan continued to shout. "Where'd that shot come from? Find that shooter!"

"Belay that order," Laura said calmly to the group. "Stand up, everyone." She waited a moment. "Come on, you fellows are dirty enough as it is. Stand up."

The men slowly climbed to their feet. "There's no danger," Laura followed. "He won't fire again." She turned to Rick and pointed. "How far would you say it is to that wooded area at the far end of the airstrip?"

"At the other end of the field?"

"Yes."

"A thousand yards, maybe more," Rick estimated. "Anyone have a range finder?"

"I do," Carl said. He unpacked it from a pouch.

"What's the distance to that far tree line?" Rick asked.

Carl calibrated the instrument and pointed it at the vegetation line. "One-thousand, one-hundred yards. That's where the shot came from?"

"It could only come from there judging from when the sound arrived," Laura replied.

Jordan stood and looked around the area. "Well, it couldn't have come from the town, it's too close." He looked across the airstrip. "Or the vegetation line we came from. The plane wreckage blocks a shot from there. I think you're right, Laura." Jordan looked up at the tree line again. "That's one hell of a shot."

"If it came from there, it's the best shot I've ever witnessed," Nick commented.

"No shit," Rick added. "I thought I was good, but that guy's on another level."

"One shot, too," Sharp said. "Who the hell could do that?"

"Why'd he target the Colonel?" Jordan asked.

Laura smiled. "Because the Colonel was about to kill me. That shot came from my back-up."

"Your back-up?" A surprised Jordan asked.

"I was shadowed here. I knew he'd be good, but I didn't think he'd be that good."

"How do you know it was him?"

"Is he firing at anyone else?" Laura asked.

Jordan looked at Adam and Nick. "Go find that guy."

"No!" Laura said curtly. "You'll never find him. And if you got close, you'd be dead before you ever saw him."

"You know the guy?" Jordan asked Laura.

"Well, I've never met him. He was assigned to guard me. He goes by the name of Franz. He's an East German."

"An East German?" an incredulous Jordan asked.

Laura shrugged. "As I said, I don't know the man. I just know of him."

"He worked under your orders?"

"No, a friend sent him to protect me. Pritchard wasn't killed by us, the Panamanians or FARC. None of us can be blamed for it."

"I need more proof than that to show General Carson." Jordan inspected Pritchard's body. "The bullet went clean through his head." He looked behind where Pritchard stood. "The truck was directly behind him. Nick, you and Carl walk back to the truck and see if you can find the round."

"Yes, Sir."

"Rick, you, Sharp and Adam untie the rest of the prisoners and bring 'em here."

"Yes, Sir," Rick said. He motioned toward Sharp who'd been inspecting the overturned wheelbarrow.

"Hey, guys. There are sandwiches and water left," Sharp said.

"We'll take it with us," Rick replied. "It's going to be a long ride home."

The rest of the Americans were brought into the camp at gunpoint and ordered to sit in front of Laura and Jordan. "Secure their hands behind their backs," Jordan said to Adam.

Jordan addressed the men sitting in a row. "Gentlemen, we're taking you back to Fort Clayton where you'll be processed. General Carson will decide what's to be done with you. We're going to leave your hands tied behind you in case anyone gets any ideas. We're not exactly enemies, but we're not friends, either. Stay quiet and we'll be underway soon."

Laura walked behind the men and pulled Derek Young's head back by the hair. "Hello Derek." Young said nothing. Laura punched him in the face, breaking his nose. Blood began to dribble out his nostrils. "That's for landing on my property and waving an automatic rifle in my face." Jordan watched patiently while Laura proceeded to the next man. She pulled his hair, jerking his head back. "Who are you?"

The man stayed silent, so Laura pulled the P226 from her holster and laid the muzzle on his forehead. "One more chance. What's your name?"

"Hank Miller," he croaked, his voice strained from his neck pulled at an odd angle.

"You're a pilot, too, aren't you? I remember your face. You were there that night, right?"

The man stayed silent.

"I take your silence as a 'yes.'" Laura struck him in the face with the handle of her handgun. She missed his nose but landed a direct hit on his cheekbone. "That's for landing a drug plane on my property."

She walked to the next man and jerked his head back. "Greg Smith?"

"Yes, Ms. Messier."

"What the hell are you doing mixed up with this bunch?"

"This was my first assignment, Ma'am. I had no idea what it was. I just followed orders."

"Are you with me or them?" she asked.

"I'm with you," Smith said.

"Have you killed anyone today?"

"No, Ma'am."

Laura took her knife and cut his bonds. She looked up at Jordan. "This man's with me. He's not to be arrested."

"Whatever you say," Jordan replied.

Chapter One Hundred

"ARE WE READY to pull out?" Laura asked Jordan.

"Almost." He nodded toward Benevides. "What are you going to do with him?"

"We're gonna to have a little talk in the woods. Lift him up for me."

She waited while Jordan and Rick lifted him up. "Come on, Commander." Laura pushed him from behind with the barrel of her handgun.

Carl walked back from the truck with a round of ammunition discovered there. "Look at this, Major." Carl Thomas, an explosives expert, held a round in his hand. "It's not from anything we use. The Panamanians, either. This is different."

Jordan inspected the bullet. "Where'd you find it?"

"We found it embedded in the seat. It went clean through the windshield."

"What do you think it is?"

Carl shook his head. "A 7.62 round from a foreign source. Maybe Russian."

"Thanks," Jordan said. He slipped it in his pocket. "I'll have it analyzed back at base."

"What do you want us to do with the money," Nick said.

"What?"

"The money in the back of the truck. There's millions of dollars there."

"Burn it."

"Could I mention at this point that it's illegal to destroy American money?" Nick asked.

Jordan laughed. "Technically, you'll be burning the truck, Captain. We're not responsible for its contents."

"Yes, Sir." Nick and Carl turned to walk away.

"One more thing, Captain," Jordan said.

"Yes, Sir?" Nick replied.

"I didn't see the lumps in your front pockets. I will only say that a team shares everything in the field. Ammunition, rations, whatever it may be."

Nick saluted Jordan. "Yes, Sir, Major."

"Sharp?"

"Yes, Sir?"

"Bring the rest of those sandwiches over here."

"On the double."

Laura pushed Benevides into the trees and kicked him down. She stood over him as he rolled over and sat up, her P226 aimed at his head. He doesn't look frightened, she thought. He's calm. He doesn't really have the look of a soldier, either.

"What's your background, Commander?"

"I was a farmer," Benevides replied.

"What happened?"

"The Columbian Army took my farm and killed my workers."

Laura thought for a moment. "Why?"

"They accused me of hiring FARC members to work my fields."

"Did you?"

"Yes. Most of the community supports the rebels."

"Where are you from?"

"My family owned a farm in the Magdalena District for generations. It was passed to me by my father."

"And now you've become rich running drugs."

Benevides said nothing.

"Do you have family back home?"

"I sent them over the border into Venezuela."

"Do you know how many families you've destroyed in America?"

"That's not my responsibility," Benevides retorted immediately.

"Oh yes, it is. You've become rich working for drug cartels." Benevides shook his head.

"It's the only work available. The Columbians took my farm."

"That doesn't make it right."

"We're not interested in right and wrong. We're trying to survive."

Laura sighed. "Then it's unfortunate we met. I am interested in right and wrong. You're killing American children."

"You've never seen your homes destroyed; your families killed. Members of FARC are fighting back against injustice."

"If you fought the government, I'd have respect for you. You're just a drug runner."

"What we do feeds thousands of families."

"At the expense of American children."

"They're not my concern."

Laura smiled. "Well, they're mine. And Lady Liberty has come to seek her vengeance. This conversation is over."

She shot Benevides in the forehead. He died instantly.

Chapter One Hundred One

LAURA WALKED SLOWLY back to the camp. "What are you going to do with him?" Jordan asked, nodding toward Ramos.

"He's next."

"Okay. I'm calling the copter. Dmitri?" Jordan asked into the com set.

"Yes, Major, I read you."

"We're ready to be picked up. Land on the airfield close to the burned-out plane."

"Roger. We'll set down in a few minutes. Dmitri out."

Jordan looked around the camp. "Can everyone hear me," he yelled. Everyone stopped and looked at Jordan. "Wrap it up, people. We're pulling out as soon as the copter lands."

Laura walked toward Ramos. "Jim, help me get this man to his feet." Laura pushed Ramos in the back with her P226. "Into the woods, Captain. That way" she motioned. Ramos had heard the shot that killed Benevides. He began trembling. After they'd walked away from the others, Laura said, "Stop." She walked around in front of him. "Sit down." Ramos collapsed onto the ground. "You're a shitty soldier."

"I studied economics in college," Ramos stammered in English.

"You have a family?"

"Yes," he nodded, "a wife and two children."

Laura continued to stare until she noticed the bulges in Ramos' pocket. "Is that the profit for your day's work?" She asked, pointing her gun at his legs.

Ramos was suddenly ashamed. "I apologize for killing the Americans."

"Do you think an apology is adequate?"

Ramos hung his head. "No."

"You're right, but I'm tired of killing people who deserve to die. And you do deserve to die. But I'm going to let you go for the sake of your kids. Take off your boots."

Ramos was confused. "What?"

"You heard me," she said. Laura cut his bonds so Ramos could pull his boots off. "Now, stand up." Ramos complied. "Do you want to live to see your children again?"

"Yes."

"Run up the airstrip to the tree line." Laura pointed approximately where the shot had come from. "If you stop, I'll shoot you. When you approach the tree line, turn right and wade across the canal. From there, head north back to Panama City."

"Thank you," Ramos said with tears in his eyes.

"Now, listen closely. You will disappear when you return to the city. You will not return to the Army. Take the money you've stolen and care for your children. And if I ever see you or hear your name again, I'll kill you. Now go!" Laura shouted to Jordan as she walked back into view. "Let this man pass, Major." Ramos ran.

Chapter One Hundred Two

THE FLIGHT BACK to Albrook Air Force Base was delayed by one task left to be done. Dmitri followed the river upstream to the FARC camp where he fired one missile at the tent and another at the Huey helicopter that sat nearby. The explosions burned long after he'd headed back to the airstrip.

The ride back to the base was crowded and silent. There was no celebration, only relief. It had been a long day full of controversial decisions that left both Laura and Jim Jordan wondering whether they'd acted honorably.

The difficulty of landing a Soviet battle copter at the base was overcome after Jordan made an appropriate explanation over the radio. The sight of a Soviet aircraft sitting at an American air base surrounded by military police was unusual for those who witnessed it.

After a brief conversation between Jordan and the MPs, the drug running pilots were checked by medical staff and then thrown into the brig at Fort Clayton to await their fate. Laura could not protect Greg Smith who received the same treatment. Jordan and his men left to return to base while Laura's group convened at the hotel late that evening where they showered, changed clothes and shared their experiences over a meal and wine. The following morning, as they loaded their gear into Laura's jet, Major Jordan walked across the tarmac. "Laura!" He shouted over the hum of the jet engines at idle.

Laura waved and ran toward him. They embraced and for the first time, Jim Jordan kissed her. And, not surprisingly, she kissed him back. "Jim," she said, their faces just inches apart.

"I had to say goodbye," Jordan said quietly, stroking her hair.

"When do you get out of here?"

"Four months."

"Do you have leave coming up?"

"Two weeks next month."

Laura took a piece of paper from her purse and wrote down her contact information. "Here," she said handing it to him. "I'll be expecting a call."

Jordan smiled. "You'll get one. I'd like to get to know the real Laura Messier."

"It's Laura Grayson, although you won't find that name anywhere."

"It's a beginning," Jordan said.

She glanced at Svetlana waiting at the top of the stairs. "I've got to go."

"I know," Jordan said. They kissed once more before Laura walked up the stairs, lingering at the top to look back. She waved and Jordan blew her a kiss. Laura disappeared into the plane, Svetlana hoisted the door up and Dmitri slowly backed the plane onto the tarmac. As Laura sat in her seat, she buckled her seatbelt, leaned her head against the headrest and exhaled. It's over.

Chapter One Hundred Three

LAURA HAD ONE administrative task remaining before the mission was complete. She waited a month before making an appointment with Dan Jenkins in D.C. On the day of the appointment, she walked into the Hoover Federal Building with none of the concern she'd felt on the day of her last visit. More of a social call, she thought, not a real meeting. Dan came downstairs led her up to his office, closed the door and hugged her. "I'm glad you're safe," he said.

Laura laughed. "Safe from what?"

Dan gave her a wry smile as he sat behind his desk. "Safe from whatever you've been doing." He paused before continuing. "Have a seat. I've got an update for you." Laura recognized by his tone of voice that Dan considered the meeting to be business.

He shuffled files around his desk before he found the one he was looking for. Opening the file, he studied it for a moment before speaking. Just like he did with Sanchez at the prison, Laura thought. He's pausing for the effect. "First," he said looking up, "I'm sure you'll be pleased to learn that Derek Young was captured in Panama a month ago participating in another drug deal." Dan looked at Laura for a reaction. Finding none, he continued. "He and his co-pilot," Dan scanned the document for a name, "Miller, I believe his name is, were taken to the Canal Zone and turned over to the American military. General Carson, the Canal Zone commander, insisted they be prosecuted for drug running. They've been transferred back to the states where they're in custody."

"Whose custody?" Laura asked.

"Ours. The South Florida office."

"I'm glad to hear it," Laura said flatly. Dan closed the file and leaned back in his chair.

"I haven't seen a written transcript of the interviews yet, but according to a source, they claimed to be working for the CIA at the time."

"That's interesting," Laura said, still in a deadpan tone.

"Just so you know, the source told me your name came up during the interviews." Laura gave Dan a hint of a smile.

"It's nice to know I'm popular." Dan looked up at her and grimaced.

"You could have some liability here, Laura. You might consider hiring an attorney."

"I appreciate the advice." Dan paused, staring at her before continuing.

"Anyway, they're due to stand trial in Miami on drug charges in a few weeks. I know the prosecutor handling the case. They'll serve a lengthy sentence."

"They deserve it," Laura said.

"Off the record, were you in Panama when they were captured?"

"Wasn't it you who told me to never discuss a pending case?"

Dan gave her the look of a prosecutor who knows a subject is withholding information. He answered curtly. "Make sure you have an answer for the prosecutor if he asks."

"Are you suggesting I'm withholding information?" Laura asked. Dan stared at her, wondering whether to push her. He decided against it.

"No. We have learned, though, that several Americans were killed in the same incident." Laura nodded.

"I'd heard that," she said.

"So, you do know something about it!" Dan said pointedly. Laura shook her head.

"Not firsthand. I'm only giving you the scuttlebutt I've heard coming out of Langley."

"What do you know about a Marine Colonel working out of the Pentagon?" Dan opened the file again and scanned the document looking for a name. "A Colonel Kevin Pritchard."

"Dan," she said with the most innocent of faces, "is this an interrogation?" Dan looked up from the document again.

"No, it's not. However, if I were you," Laura interrupted him.

"I heard you the first time, Dan," she said raising her voice. "Hire an attorney." Dan grimaced. She's not making this easy.

"Pritchard was killed in the incident. I just thought you might have knowledge of it, that's all." Laura gave him a blank stare, as though she hadn't heard him. Dan looked for a reaction, and finding none, went on. "The incident's become something of an international dispute between Panama and the United States. The Panamanian government has filed an official protest with the State Department. Apparently, several Panamanian military personnel were found dead at the scene. I don't have an exact number."

"I'm sorry to hear that."

"They've blamed the United States for the deaths. Coincidentally, on the same day, a robbery occurred at the National Bank of Panama in Panama City. I'm not sure it's connected, but the timing is interesting." Dan waited for a response, but knew he'd get nothing from her. "You wouldn't like to tell me your whereabouts over the last month, would you?"

"My private life stays private, Dan."

Dan gave up. He closed the file. "You'll be happy to learn the White House has declared these incidents Top Secret. The records have been sealed. Lucky you, huh?" Laura sighed.

"Yeah, lucky me."

"The President told Noriega to go fuck himself, so it'll probably never be known what actually happened. Would you care to comment?"

"No, Dan, I wouldn't."

"Well, that's my update. What about you?"

"I stopped by to give you a donation for the federal drug rehab program. I'd like you to handle it for me." Dan looked confused.

"We don't handle donations here, Laura. Those programs fall under the DEA. Would you like me to call and find out where you can send it?"

"It's a fairly substantial amount of money, Dan. I'd appreciate your assistance." Laura leaned over Dan's desk and handed him a check drawn from a numbered account at Credit Suisse, Zurich, Switzerland.

Dan whistled and then looked up at her. He read from the check. "Two-hundred million dollars." He looked up. "That's a lot of money. Do you mind if I ask where it came from?" Laura smiled.

"You can ask, but even the FBI can't crack Swiss bank accounts, Dan." He held the check up toward the overhead lights to check the watermark.

"Would this have anything to do with the bank heist in Panama?"

Laura ignored Dan's question. "I'd like the funds spent on drug treatment only."

"That's it?" Dan asked with an astonished look. "That's your only comment?"

"That's my only comment," Laura said with a shrug. "I just thought the DEA would be more inclined to accept the check if I gave it to you."

Dan laughed. "Okay. I'll send the check over today."

Laura stood and reached over Dan's desk to shake his hand. "Thank you, Dan. I appreciate your time today."

"One more question, if I may?" Dan asked, rising from his chair.

"All right, one more and then I have to run."

"Have you ever heard of a French jewel thief named Marcel DuMont?"

"Nope, never heard of him," Laura replied.

Dan laughed again. "Okay, I give up. It's always a pleasure to see you." He took Laura's hand. "How long are you in town?"

"Just the day."

"Let me know when you're in town again. We'll have dinner."

"That sounds great."

Laura's last task was a call to Steve Tilton which she made from the lobby of the Hoover building. She called his direct line at Langley. "Steve?"

"Oh, hi Laura," Steve said. "I'm glad to hear from you. I heard things went well in Panama."

"I shouldn't comment on it."

"That's smart of you. No one's commenting. The White House has thrown a blanket over the entire mess."

"How are you?"

"I'm fine, Steve."

"Are you really fine of just saying that?"

"Actually, I'm doing well," she replied.

"I see you managed to keep the kid out of trouble."

"You mean Greg Smith?"

"Yes. Bates brought him back to put him on another assignment, but he resigned."

Laura chuckled. "Greg's working for me now."

"Good for him. He'll make more money and learn proper tradecraft. You should know that Bates fired Mike Pratt the other day. I thought you'd be pleased about that."

"I am. He was in way over his head."

Steve laughed. "I agree. So, why do I have the pleasure of talking with you?"

"I'd like to use the cabin in Ouray for a few days."

"Sure, no problem, except I sold it. I bought a condo over the mountain in Telluride. It's closer to the ski resorts. You're welcome to use it, if you like."

"I'd appreciate that."

"Why don't you swing by the building and I'll leave the address and the keys at the front desk. Are you planning some R and R?"

"I thought a bit of snow would be a nice change from Panama."

"Do I know him?"

Laura hesitated. "Know who?" Steve laughed.

"The man you're going with."

Laura was amused. *He knows me too well.* "No comment. I'll stop by today and pick up the keys. Thanks."

"You're welcome. You take care, Laura."

"And you as well." Laura walked out of FBI Headquarters with a smile on her face. *Well, if Jordan can't ski,* she thought, *I'm sure we'll find something to do.*

Thank you for reading my book. If you enjoyed it, won't you please take a moment to leave me a review at your favorite retailer?

Thanks!

Lawrence Scofield

Follow me on Twitter:
http://twitter.com/LScofieldAuthor
Friend me on Facebook:
https://facebook.com/LawrenceScofieldAuthor
Favorite me at Smashwords:
https://www.smashwords.com/profile/view/LawrenceEScofield

Sneak Peek

From "The Laura Messier Files" Series

Three Days in Tripoli

A Spy Thriller

By Lawrence Scofield

Prologue

Sunday, April 13th, 1986

Located beneath the White House, the Situation Room's contact with the outside world comes only through video, telephone and telex. The room's only access point is one heavily guarded elevator. On the particular morning in question, the video screens were turned off, the telephone and telex were silent and the insulated quiet of the environment served to amplify the conversation around the conference table.

Senior staff came into the building underground through the White House tunnels to avoid alerting the press. There was a certain tension in the air, the kind that could be expected given the gravity of a situation where military action was imminent. Secretary of State George Shultz, Chief of Staff Don Regan, National Security Advisor John Poindexter, Chairman of the Joint Chiefs Admiral William Crowe, Director of the Central Intelligence Agency William J. Casey, and National Security Agency Head General William Odom, all sat at the conference table talking quietly among themselves awaiting President Ronald Reagan. Secretary of Defense Caspar Weinberger, who would normally have been present, was traveling abroad that day. Vice-President George H. W. Bush would arrive late, having just returned from a trip to Saudi Arabia.

As President Reagan entered the room a few minutes late, he flashed his signature smile. "Good morning," he said, shaking his head. "Sorry I'm late, guys. Nancy and her damn questions." That caused a fair amount of amusement around the table, but the comment served a purpose, for Reagan wanted to put his colleagues at ease. Reagan carried himself with an air of

1

confidence which projected onto his staff. He had sound judgment and made clear and convincing decisions. Reagan was a big picture president and his people liked that about him.

"Okay, fellas, let's run Operation Eldorado Canyon from top to bottom," Reagan said as he lay a briefing book on the table. He sat at the head of the table, opened the folder and studied it while his subordinates waited for the President to speak. He raised his head and looked around the table. "Let's go around the room and ask everyone if we're ready. Mr. Secretary?" Reagan asked the Secretary of State George Shultz.

"Yes, Sir," Shultz responded. "Prime Minister Thatcher gave permission to use the bases in England last week. I would remind you, Mr. President, that we must notify our allies tomorrow morning. It would be wise to avoid informing the Soviets until shortly before the bombing commences."

"I agree," Reagan said. "It would be just like those bastards to inform Gaddafi in advance. What about Congress?"

"We're required to brief Congressional leaders, Mr. President, but if we want a surprise attack, we should brief them late tomorrow afternoon after the planes are in the air. White House meetings attract the press."

The President turned to his Chief of Staff, Don Regan. "What about the press on this, Don?"

"Mr. President, as you know, there's been speculation about an attack for weeks. The networks and wire services already have people in Tripoli. They'll begin reporting as soon as the attack begins. We should be prepared to have you address the nation shortly afterward."

The President nodded his head. "Get Larry Speakes to write something for me. Wait until late tomorrow to reserve time on the networks. We don't want rumors coming out of the Press Office."

"Yes, Sir," Regan answered.

Reagan looked at Joint Chiefs Chairman Admiral William Crowe. "Bill, how are we doing on the military side?"

"Mr. President," Crowe replied, "we're ready to go. NATO has scheduled a joint military exercise called 'Salty Nation' starting tomorrow in Britain. We'll use those maneuvers as cover for our aircraft. We should be able to take off without being noticed. France and Spain will deny overflight permission, but we've planned for that. We'll be flying around the continent and through the Strait."

"That'll be one hell of a long bombing run, won't it?" Reagan asked.

"The longest in history, Sir. We're confident we can execute it. The Air Force has practiced for it and our pilots are ready."

"Fine," Reagan said, nodding his head.

"What about the NSA, Bill?" Reagan asked William Odom.

"Mr. President, we've heard nothing in our phone intercepts that lead us to believe the Libyans know anything about our plans," Odom said. "At the present time, only the British have advance knowledge of the mission. Our concern is Gaddafi could receive a last-minute warning of the attack from aircraft flying through the Strait or carriers moving into position near Malta. Gaddafi will want a radar confirmation before he calls a full alert. If we're able to shut down Libyan long range radars, they'll be caught by surprise."

"It's my understanding we have someone from CIA in Libya this weekend working on that. Is that right, Bill?" Reagan asked CIA Director William Casey.

"Yes, Sir," Casey replied. "She's coming out of the country today."

"She?" Reagan asked. Reagan paused for a few seconds as though he didn't hear Casey properly. "You have a woman in there?" That raised eyebrows around the room.

Luckily, Casey had brought Messier's personnel file with him in case the subject came up. "This is Laura Messier, Mr. President, the agent we sent into Libya," Casey said as he slid the file across the table.

Reagan began thumbing through the pages. "She's pretty, Bill," Reagan said, looking at her pictures. "Isn't it dangerous to send a woman?"

"That was the point, Mr. President. Women are one of Gaddafi's weaknesses."

Reagan passed some of the pictures around the table for the others to see. SecState looked at Messier's modeling pictures. "This is her as a model, Bill?" Shultz asked.

"Yes," Casey said, hoping the entire subject would go away. "She was a runway model before she joined CIA."

"Wow," Shultz said. That raised the interest of others and parts of Messier's file were spread across the table.

"The others are more recent?" the President asked.

"Yes, Sir," Casey said. "In the first one, she's walking into the American Embassy in Paris. That was taken just a few months ago. Her cover job is an aide to the French Minister of Foreign Affairs in Paris."

"I remember this girl, Mr. President," Shultz said to Reagan. "Every time we have meetings with the French, she's in the room on the French side. She acts as a kind of personal aide to the Minister. I always thought she was a clerical employee."

Reagan smiled when he spoke to Casey. "You mean we have people on both sides of the table when we talk to the French?"

"Yes, Sir," Casey replied.

Reagan laughed, "Too bad we don't have someone in the Libyan government."

"We do, Mr. President," Casey said. Every person in the room stopped, looked up and stared at Casey.

There was a pause in the room before the President said, "Go on, Bill."

"Well, he's not American. He's a French double agent positioned inside the Libyan government. Messier will bring the radar and missile codes out of Libya today. We'll relay them to the double agent. He'll be the one who shuts down the radars."

4

"Well, I'll be damned," Reagan said with a smile. He sat back and slapped the table with his hand. "Gentlemen, this is how you win wars. Nice job, Bill."

"Thank you, Mr. President."

The Vice-President entered the room with appropriate apologizes. "Mr. President, I apologize for being late. I just got back. Barbara insisted I change my clothes before I came over," he said. That brought a few chuckles from the group.

"You're lucky, George. Nancy would have asked me to walk the damn dogs," Reagan said with a smile. Bush sat down next to the President.

Reagan directed his next question to Shultz. "How's the world going to react to this?" Shultz hesitated before he answered. "Mr. President," he finally said, "the Canadians, Australians, Israelis and British will support us. The rest of NATO will, too, although they'll appear neutral in the press. The Italians and the French are big trading partners with Libya, so they'll issue mild condemnations, but the French, as we heard from Bill Casey, are helping behind the scenes. The Chinese, Soviets and East Germans will offer strong criticism, but it's unlikely to go further than that. We don't believe they'll interfere."

"George?" the President asked the Vice President, "what about the Saudis?"

"Mr. President, I spoke with King Fahd yesterday. He feels Gaddafi's had a destabilizing effect on the Middle East. They'll support us even though they'll publicly condemn the raid."

"That's good news; thanks."

Reagan heard what he needed to hear. He made his decision. "Gentlemen, here's what we're going to do. If our agent gets out of Libya," Reagan hesitated. "What's her name again, Bill?" Reagan asked, looking at Bill Casey.

"Messier. Laura Messier."

"If Ms. Messier gets out with the codes, that's great, but whether she does or not, we're moving ahead with the attack.

Tomorrow morning, I'll call the allies to inform them of our plans. I'll brief Congress later in the day. What's the timetable from there, Bill?" Reagan asked Joint Chiefs Chairman William Crowe.

"Our bombers in Britain will leave around 6:00 p.m. tomorrow local time, twelve noon here," Crowe replied. "We'll fly around the continent and through the Strait of Gibraltar. That will put our forces in Libyan airspace about 2:00 a.m. local time, 8:00 p.m. here in Washington. They'll get in and out in fifteen minutes and return to base."

"Caspar should be back this afternoon," Reagan said to Crowe. "I want you fellas over at the Pentagon running the show. Keep me informed. Gentlemen," he said looking around the table, "let's keep this quiet. Everyone continue their normal routine today and tomorrow. Okay?"

"Yes, Sir," everyone answered nearly in unison.

"Bill?" the President asked William Casey.

"Yes Sir, Mr. President."

"Keep me updated about our agent. Call Don with any information, day or night."

"Yes, Sir," Casey replied.

"Gentlemen, we stand adjourned. Good luck and may God Bless the United States of America."